LIMITER

LIBRARY SYSTEM RESET

K.T. HANNA

Book Cover by Illustration by Marko Horvatin
Typography by Inorai
1st edition 2025

Eric
Both imp and human form
Thank you for being unapologetically you

PREVIOUSLY IN THE LIBRARY

After being isekaid into the Library of Everywhere, Quinn and Lynx (the Library manifestation) begin the arduous task of restoring the Library.

Milaro the grandfatherly king of the elves, and his grandchild Malakai become an integral part of the hunt for overdue books and help teach Quinn all about what it means to be the Librarian.

The Library is full steam ahead. With Misha, Tim, Tom, Cook, and Farrow, she has the golem contingency thriving. Her helpers Dottie, Jasper, Eric, Geneva, Finn, Narilin, and Aradie assist in managing the day-to-day organizing of staff, book returns, and borrows.

The books they retrieved from the wrecked Dabilian homeworld allow Quinn and her team to truly begin rebuilding the Library. Now that the filtration chamber is back online and ramping up the amount of filters that pump mana back out into the universe, the team has to focus on getting Ashiron (the tenth pillar), back up and running.

With Quinn's first synchronization out of the way, and her cosmicisodracus heritage revealed, her depths of power and the reason for her affinities means more focused training.

The holes in the memories of Lynx and the Library aren't filling in as quickly as they'd like. Different times require different approaches, and many aren't revealing anything like what they'd imagined.

Only the Culinary branch has opened so far, but two more are hot on its tails. The Librarya's enemies are tricky, often visiting Quinn in dreams she is almost certain are traps.

Kajaro and his allies, that include but aren't limited to the Library's cosmicisodracus brother Dravishk, don't want the Library to retrieve the books, or maintain power, or exist. They'll do everything they can to complete the sabotage they started.

After walking into a trap that leaves many of her allies either injured, dying, or dead, Quinn understands the stakes on a more intimate level and knows she'll have to train accordingly.

THREE BOOKS AWAY

A SUBTLE BLUE SHIFT OF LIGHT PERMEATED THE INFIRMARY.

Quinn stood at the window—she could have sworn that wasn't there before this whole fiasco—looking out at the vastness beyond. It reminded her of the windows in the restricted vault and how she could stare at the universe beyond for days.

Hundreds of thousands—if not millions—of stars glittered back at her, through an expanse of space she couldn't even perceive properly.

Looking out into the nothingness but stars, she held up her hand and willed her shielding into place.

Scales subtly shifted from under her skin to over it, encasing her in an ethereal blue and golden glow. She still didn't understand the mechanics of it. If it came through her skin, shouldn't it break through and leave blood everywhere?

But instead, it shifted into an invisible wall around her, leaving her to question if it had ever really appeared at all. And right now, she still had to concentrate to maintain it.

The last two weeks had taught her that sometimes magic was the only explanation, even if it was difficult to get her logic around that fact.

Quinn shrugged to undo the tension in her shoulders and

continued to focus on her shielding of scales. After a fortnight of relentless instruction and practice, she was finally able to manifest it and maintain her shielding through a fair amount of interference and combat. It wasn't second nature yet . . . but it was progress.

"Quinn?"

Malakai's croaking voice pulled her out of her reverie, and she let go of her hold on her scales, *tsk*ing in annoyance as she turned to look at the elf in the bed.

He still wasn't healed up, and she felt such waves of guilt for it. She'd do almost anything to make it better again.

Though turning back time didn't seem to be a viable option. She knew because she'd researched it.

Desperation gave her illogical ideas.

His face looked fine, like nothing was wrong, apart from the undertones beneath his skin. In some areas it almost seemed like a pale blue light shone through, making it thinner than it should have been. She studied him for a second before speaking. "You doing okay?"

"Mm." He sounded croakier. "What are you doing here?"

There was some worry in his voice, and Quinn just took his hand and gave it a light squeeze. "Thought I'd check in on my favorite elf."

Malakai laughed, but a second later it devolved into a horrible, racking cough. Quinn cringed as she watched him settle. She still woke up in a sweat every night, memories of that damned attack by Kajaro that was meant for her. One load of those vortex frisbees was possible to recover from, but two of them . . .

She remembered Milaro muttering something about Malakai's energy and mana pathways being all messed up. Guilt gnawed at her, vying with her desire for revenge.

"You don't have to look like a thundercloud," Malakai rasped out.

"And you're supposed to be resting and not worrying about me." She sighed out the words, knowing he'd take no notice of them at all.

"I'd be out of here if I could." He chuckled, even if it sounded like his chest was rattling, and then he stopped, sobering up. "You know Arnekai is here."

Quinn winced slightly. She understood why he refused to call her Mother. Arnekai always put her work and position first. So Quinn couldn't really blame him for it. Still, even though it was mostly her doing . . . Milaro's begrudging agreement meant Arnekai was here to treat her son.

Funnily enough, despite the history Malakai held against her, she'd dropped everything when they sent for her. Well, not immediately. It took her three days, but Quinn was under the impression that for Arnekai, that was paramount to leaving immediately.

"And since she got here, you've stopped looking like living death. So please, don't discount her too much." Quinn offered a smile, even if her mind was starting to work over ten thousand problems at once again. "At the very least, she's a competent Darígháhnish healer, right?"

"It's fine." Mal sighed and his eyes fluttered closed as if he was trying to fight it. "I'm so sleepy."

"Then sleep," Quinn said softly, watching as his breathing evened out, before returning her concentration to the view outside the newly expanded window.

You must practice holding your scales in place until it's second nature. The Library spoke into her head once Malakai's slumber was obvious.

Their connection had deepened yet again once the Library's power levels increased. They were only one away from optimal efficiency now. But there was still so much to do to get it there.

Yeah. Yeah. I know. Quinn closed her eyes, summoning her innate protection again with a single thought. She was proud of her improvement, even if a part of her seemed to think she should be further along. She moved out of Malakai's room and toward the hall, determined to check on the others.

Ikeshal still hadn't woken up. Hal went back to Halschius to prepare for Ikeshal's treatment. Something to do with acclimation of the injuries and lava. She didn't pry.

"You're moping around again," Eric said, startling Quinn out of her thoughts. His wings were still healing, and he couldn't hover as long as he used to yet, but the rest of him was fine. That appeared to be one of the perks of being nigh-indestructible.

"No. I'm thinking. You should try it sometime." She flashed him a grin, secretly grateful he'd pulled her out of those darker thoughts. Their ambush went so terribly wrong, they were lucky any of them returned home.

Her scales flared for a split second, as if recalling the entire incident gave her a power surge. And for a fraction there, her veins felt like they were on fire again. Quinn took a breath, forced herself to focus on the here and now and not be swept up by memories, overwhelm, and frustration . . . and resettled her entire power center.

"You're getting better at that," Eric noted, settling on the edge of Ikeshal's bed, which was the partition over from Malakai's.

Quinn nodded, unsure of how else to respond. The foundations of her innate abilities were difficult to grasp and keep a hold of, but she made progress every day. Her fingertips practically itched to be able to grab onto more power.

"That look in your eye, eh?" Eric laughed, and the sound peeled up into the high ceilings.

"What look?" Quinn said grumpily.

"Little taste of power, eh? Careful, Librarian, power can go to your head." Eric winked at her and flitted out of the room, listing slightly to the side of his injured wing.

Quinn rolled her eyes. "Me? Power hungry?" She wanted to play it off, but there was a part of her that yearned for enough power to deal with the problems that kept cropping up. To just wave a hand and say *begone.* That was only logical, right?

The imp's chuckles could be heard all the way to the front desk.

She sighed and turned around, glancing at Ikeshal's prone form. He was still pale, especially considering he was a satyr. But Hal was coming to get him, so he'd be okay too. He had to be. So engrossed was she in her thoughts that she failed to sense the light footsteps that approached her until Arnekai spoke.

"You're lingering in here. Shouldn't you be training?" Arnekai's tone was more subdued than when Quinn met her originally. It made sense though. Her son was severely injured and required some hefty healing, and she seemed entirely preoccupied by it, or at least by something.

"Yes, to both of those," Quinn said, smiling tightly. Lately, it hadn't felt like a smiling environment.

Arnekai's white hair didn't flow freely this time, instead, it was braided tightly falling most of the way down her back. It still contrasted with her almost navy skin in a starkly beautiful way, yet this time Quinn wasn't as intimidated by the almost seven-foot-tall Darigháhnish. Perhaps it had something to do with Quinn being on her home turf.

Mal's mother glanced at the Librarian, a slight frown on her face. "You know none of this was your fault, right?"

Quinn shrugged. She might technically know it, but she was also the one who had the dream. Surely, there were hints about the trap and she'd missed them. "Maybe. But I should be able to protect people."

Arnekai laughed. "Maybe. We all wish we could protect everyone, right? Don't be too hard on yourself. My son will be fine, he just needs a few more treatments, and some magic free time to regain his strength."

"I hope you're right," Quinn said.

"Of course I'm right. Go do your work. We have a healing session, and he'll probably welcome your company for a bit later. Don't . . ." Arnekai paused, glancing toward the cubicle curtain that concealed her son. "Don't wallow in a past you cannot change. Seek out the knowledge you need for the future instead. It'll make us all stronger."

And then she practically teleported to Malakai's bed, disappearing behind the partition.

Quinn watched the empty space for a few seconds, speechless. Determination stole over her and she found the spark of a new resolve. Stepping out of the infirmary, she decided to absorb more of what the Library could teach her as soon as possible. Drevicia was an extremely exacting task master, but at least Quinn had finally gotten her own core control down.

Mostly.

"Librarian!" Dottie stood directly in the way of exiting the infirmary.

Not that it bothered Quinn. She was genuinely fond of the talking bench. Superellex futora—the sapient furniture. She felt like she was in an animated movie on a regular basis. All she had to do now was find the bloody teapot. "What can I do for you, Miss Supervisory Assistant?"

Dottie's laughter rang through the hall, adding a levity the area sorely needed. "Oh, it's good to have you back in high spirits, Librarian." Dottie sounded genuinely happy.

"Well, I don't know if you'd call them high, but I'm definitely feeling better right now."

Dottie frowned, even though Quinn still wasn't sure how she could tell. Perhaps it was a sense, more of a telegraphing the aura than anything else. "You're positively glowing. Is that . . ." The bench trotted closer. "My dear! Your scales are showing."

Quinn felt the blush keenly. "Yeah, been practicing."

"But does she have wings yet?" Geneva's soft voice asked, and Quinn spun to see the Furionas fae. She hovered at eye level with Quinn, her tiny two-and-a-half-foot frame resplendently gold as usual. Her hair cascaded down her back and her gorgeous red outfit accentuated the whole fairy vibe she gave off.

"I don't have wings yet." While Quinn knew she'd eventually be able to shapeshift, she wasn't relishing the idea. For all intents and purposes, it was supposed to hurt like the dickens, and she didn't do pain well. Plus, what had Hal called her? An egg? She was technically still a baby.

"Soon enough. And then you won't even need a spell to fly." Geneva smiled gently, as if she was trying to lessen the blow. "We needed to talk to you, if you have a few minutes."

Quinn cast a furtive glance toward the Restricted Vault that was slowly getting out of reach for the day and sighed. The Library needed her to get stronger, but it also needed her to run the Library, to take care of it, considering how many functions it performed simultaneously. There were reasons the Library had a manifestation *and* a Librarian.

Sometimes, Quinn had to choose. As much as she might want to spend another three years simply powering up, she couldn't neglect the duties she had outside of the acquisition of power. "Sure. I have a few minutes."

"Excellent!" Dottie trotted in front of them, leading the way to Quinn's office. "You know, Lynx sent out another recruitment message. What after the debacle with the Aracnio twins, and then the whole trip you just took to get *Ririn's* book back? With the other two branches getting so close to opening, we're going to . . ."

Quinn stopped short. "Wait, back that up. What did you say?"

"Oh. It's just been so busy the last few weeks, and Geneva and I spent a large amount of time making sure we focused on book collections, like you gave us permission to do. We've been spread quite thin with all the assistants that require time off." There was distaste in that last phrase. Like the bench didn't understand why organic living organisms required personal days or recuperation time.

"Don't be like that, Dottie," Geneva chided gently as they began moving again. Her wings hummed in a soothing tone as she moved. "You know everyone has been working hard."

Dottie sighed and made a noise that sounded oddly like a tongue clucking, except Quinn had no idea how, considering the bench didn't have a tongue, or fingers . . . or any appendages apart from her legs. "Fine. Fine. I just wish we could all power through like I do; then we wouldn't need to be so rushed."

"I appreciate you doing it all." Quinn wanted to make sure they knew she really did value all they did. But at the same time, she'd asked a question no one had answered yet. "Can you please explain what you meant by the other two branches opening up soon?"

Dottie paused this time, right outside Quinn's office, and turned to point at the check-in desk that was some ways away. There were a few assistants there that Quinn didn't recognize.

"Has Lynx already interviewed new assistants?" Quinn asked, distracted for a moment and unsure why she felt a little sad about it.

"Nope. Lynx has *not* already interviewed new assistants," Lynx said, popping into view right next to her with a sound like a burst balloon.

Quinn started and shot him a glare, which he grinned off.

"These are the last batch. You haven't really been around as much as usual, so they appear to feel foreign to you." Lynx squinted as he examined Quinn. "You're pushing yourself too hard. Don't go getting a backlash headache.

"Right-o boss," Quinn partially ignored his warning. "So, can you tell me, since Dottie seems incapable of staying on track, what she means by two branches close to opening?"

Lynx blinked at her, his deep purple to the sclera eyes blinking like a lizards, while the runes in his hair swirled irritably. "You realize you can access the information through your personal console, right?"

"Well . . . yes." Quinn felt oddly small. While she did remember it, she just hadn't thought of it. There were so many segments she had her mind running that she'd forgotten to include the more mundane things.

Lynx sighed, a small grin tugging at his lips. "Here. Look."

The shared information popped up directly in front of her face and Quinn stood there, gaping like a fish out of water for several seconds. "Almost all of them?" she finally said as she turned and looked over at Dottie.

The bench preened a little, but all she said was "It was both of us," giving a little half bow in Geneva's direction.

Quinn looked over the numbers again. Combat was so close to opening, but it was the alchemical and medicinal branch that caught Quinn's eyes.

Three books. They were only three books away.

And she had an awful feeling she knew who had to go and retrieve those three damn books.

2

RUMBLINGS BENEATH

Quinn suppressed a groan as more information flickered across her vision.

Main Branch Tome Report

4,214 are still outstanding from the initial overdue amount. 13,828 books returned. No books in reproduction. 312 in repair status. 17 missing restricted books.

Horticulture: 575/720

Bardic Musical: 632/897

Crafting: 529/730

Alchemical/Medicinal: 381/384

Combat: 791/837

Academy: 645/785

Culinary Arts: 282/282 - Culinary Branch Open – 3,015 Books of 3,795 remaining, 780 culinary specialist books returned. Would you like a categorical breakdown?

Yes or No?

No. It was always going to be no. For now, anyway.

She didn't have the bandwidth to take in a whole heap of other information. Frankly, she was ever so slightly scared that opening the categorical breakdown would show her a gazillion other things the culinary branch needed. Since it wasn't needed to reopen branches, she wouldn't allocate time to it yet.

She pinched the bridge of her nose and counted to five. It wasn't that Dottie and Geneva had done anything wrong. On the contrary, they'd done everything right, she'd just not been expecting such fast results.

Or so much talking.

"This is impressive," she said finally, unable to think of another way to express it. Because it truly was a feat in and of itself. "How did you manage that?"

If Dottie had been able to, Quinn was fairly sure she would have blushed right then.

"I just had to organize the assistants and enlist several of my own friends to help gather the books. Since they weren't coming to us, we had to go and get them." Pride and certainty filled her voice. She was certainly excited about what she'd pulled off. But there was a hint of *un*certainty in her next words. "It's been almost three weeks since you said I could take care of it."

Quinn didn't want Dottie to feel like she'd done something wrong. "I appreciate you taking care of that while I got myself sorted. I'm taking it the last three have been difficult things to gather?"

"Yes," Dottie said, her tone certain once more.

"Actually," Geneva started, glancing at Dottie to check if she had the go ahead. "We're not entirely certain where the last three books for the alchemical and medicinal wings have gone."

"How do you mean?" Quinn asked. Losing books appeared to be becoming a habit. "Have they been abandoned by the families they were left to? Have they disappeared? Is the system not able to track them?"

"All of the above, really. We have locations for two of them, but the other, while the system knows it is still checked out, it cannot find a location." Geneva sounded so apologetic. "We'd really hoped to have this all sorted before you got back on your feet."

Quinn glanced over at the check-in desk where the assistants she largely didn't know were working furiously under the guidance of

Eric. He sat on the desk for once, instead of hovering in place. She really hoped he'd end up being fine. Hal promised he would.

"I'm okay, you know," she said to Dottie and Geneva without looking back at them. "My wounds healed pretty fast, and I got my energy and stamina back almost immediately. I just have to gain control now or else I'll burn myself and all of us to the ground. Not exactly the best sort of Librarian behavior, right?"

The silence was sort of uncomfortable in the wake of her words. Quinn sighed heavily this time. It felt like the weight of the universe pressed down on her shoulders. "Do we have any idea where I begin to find this book?"

Lynx cleared his throat in that annoying fake way he did. Considering he didn't technically have an actual throat. "You'll need all three of them. Two of the households are disbelievers of the Library's return and the third book is . . . going to be difficult to find."

Quinn suppressed a groan. As if that wasn't the story of her life since coming to the Library. Finding those pesky, difficult-to-retrieve books was her thing. Even if it was usually slightly sociopathic possessive people who decided they just didn't want to return the damned things. "Show me what you've got."

Dottie practically bounced into Quinn's office, and the Librarian followed her, smiling to herself.

Once inside, Aradie swooped in, intoning a low, soothing hoot as she swept over to the back of Quinn's massive office chair and perched on top of it. With Lynx in tow, Dottie and Geneva by her side, everything felt pretty good with her own little world.

Except for Malakai and the others who were badly damaged by Kajaro's vortex frisbees, not to mention the fact that they couldn't even put an end to Kajaro because the snake had nine lives . . . literally.

But if she tried to just push all of that to one side, squint a little bit, and tell herself lies, then things weren't too horrible.

Quinn turned around thoughtfully, taking in the space. Right now, the room wasn't filled to the brim with the conference table and seats. In fact, it had an additional comfortable couch in it. About to ask why it was there, her answer came in the form of Jasper launching herself from the door, across the room to lounge on it.

Quinn raised her eyebrow at the tall Alyenarvor. "You're looking mighty comfortable there."

"Aren't I?" Jasper grinned, her anime-like eyes sparkling. "And you look like you're in one piece and not going to set me on fire today."

Quinn cringed. The whole fire thing had become somewhat problematic. Her temper flared, so did her fire affinities. All at once, regardless of how close she was to people or any other type of flammable material. "It's slowly getting better."

Thing was, it didn't have to be a temper. Any start emotion shift could spark a flame. Scared. Startled. Sudden worry. Panic. All of those triggered a shift in the volatile affinities that were her thirty-seven different fire affinities—as far as she'd counted anyway. It took time, too much time in her opinion, for her to understand how to react to things without setting herself and everyone else on fire. But she'd get there.

Her ability to compartmentalize her tasks and thoughts constantly hovered in the back of her mind as an excellent way to avoid setting herself and other people on fire. It just wasn't always a viable option.

For example, Jasper catapulting her way across the room by surprise would have probably ended in her being set on fire the previous week, but now Quinn could give her a wry smile and simply ignore the impulse.

For the most part.

"I hear you have a book you need to find." Jasper grinned toothily, wiggling her eyebrows.

"You hear that right?" Dottie said, her body puffing up with importance without changing in the slightest visually. One of these days, Quinn would learn to judge auras and how they altered perceptions around them.

Today wasn't that day.

Lynx rapped his hand on the desk where he stood close to the chair and Aradie. "There are three books we need. *The Hunter Guide to Field Dressings; The Jezishian Solution to Maladies of the Mana Pathways;*

A Beginner's Guide; and *The Mattiniman Balance Between Mana and Energy: Explained for the Beginner."*

"So they're all beginner books, then?" Quinn asked, curious.

"Mostly, yes. All introductory texts to their more advanced counterparts that'll be in the branch once we open it," Lynx explained.

"We hope?" Quinn added, her brows furrowed in thought.

"More accurate," Lynx said. "I have no idea what's in there or not supposed to be in there at this stage. But I'd imagine those books were unlikely checked out by anyone nefarious."

This time Jasper sighed. "Why did you have to say that?"

Lynx shrugged. "The Library is jinxed enough. I don't think that's going to change anytime soon."

Quinn motioned for Aradie to jump on her shoulder. But the owl shook her head looking pointedly at that specific shoulder. *It's really fine now. I can bear your weight.*

Aradie quite literally rolled her eyes in disbelief, and Quinn couldn't help a chuckle. *Fine, but it should be good tomorrow, right?*

Slowly, the owl nodded.

"All right, then. Where do I go for the first one?" Quinn asked mostly of herself as she scrolled through all the information they had on *The Hunter Guide to Field Dressings.*

Except Lynx refused to meet her eyes, in all likelihood hiding something from her—again.

"Not the time, Lynx," she said, marginally irritated. Miracles could happen, though; the fire didn't even threaten to leak into her veins. She chalked that up as a win.

This time Lynx sighed, quite theatrically. "You'll need to go to Narilin's home world."

"Can I visit Escadril while I'm there?" Quinn asked immediately. He'd been removed immediately into his home forest for ease of healing. She'd developed a soft spot for the large, oak-like Salosier. He was gruff, but strong and protective. And they wouldn't have come through the last battle without him. His injuries still woke her up at night. She wasn't sure how Salosier healed, but she wasn't sure if anything could replace the arm he lost to rot.

The smell of rotting vegetation from his wound felt like it was stuck in her nostrils.

"Probably. I'm not sure entirely how much distance is between his convalescence and the book."

"Who has the book?" Quinn asked.

"Narilin's rivals," Jasper called out with a certain hint of glee in her voice.

"Why is that so amusing?" Quinn didn't understand the context here.

"Because!" Jasper was practically cackling by now. "Narilin is the epitome of what the Salosier aspire to be. She's smart, well versed in so many different languages and scripts it's amazing. Her abilities with books? I've never seen anyone like it."

Quinn counted to five. For the second time in far too short order. "And why is this amusing?"

Jasper looked at her like she couldn't believe Quinn didn't understand the situation. "Their rival family is nowhere near the level needed to help restore the Library's actual tomes. It's just ludicrous that they're holding onto a book and incurring potential fines in the process."

"Not potential," Quinn said firmly. "It's overdue. They're getting a fine and I'm going to have Eric craft it. It'll put him in a better mood before Uncle Hal gets here."

"You're going to make his day," Lynx muttered. "He'll be insufferable."

"Well, then . . . I guess that's a lot of us lately." Quinn winked at him and turned to Dottie. "Point me to the right location and you and I can go fetch this book. Then we'll have an easy one, right?"

But Dottie was sort of dancing back on her feet, like she was backing away.

"What is it now?"

"I can't leave. It's part of my library pact." It felt like the bench was looking anywhere but at the Librarian.

Quinn blinked. Rapidly, trying to sort that piece of information out in her head. "Wait. You have a pact with the Library?"

"Of course I have a pact with the Library," Dottie repeated, as if it was common knowledge. "A superellex futora can't survive away from our world without a pact."

Another chunk of species specific information Quinn needed to look into. At this rate, when she had the time, she'd grab every single volume on every species she could find, and spend a few months devouring them. "Anything else I should know about that pact right now except for the fact that you can't leave the Library?"

"Nothing relevant," Dottie said without even a hint of hesitation, her usual mode back.

Quinn didn't push it any further. It wouldn't get them anywhere anyway. Instead, she focused on the information being shared with her. Feshpa-Alin region of space. Which was the adjacent region to the Tecopsis, the cousins of the Salosier.

It was difficult to picture just how vast the universe was when she could just open a door and step into another region of space as easily as breathing.

"Will we have any resistance?" she asked. "Like, other than the fact that they are withholding the book."

Geneva shook her head. "Shouldn't have any. This family probably just wants the Librarian's attention." She added the last somewhat dubiously.

Quinn's immediate reaction was to not give them that attention, but that was just her obstinacy speaking. She checked over the information on the region, relieved to see that she wouldn't require any special gear to breathe there. Except . . . she sighed as she noticed some fine print.

"You will need specific foods to combat the elevated alkaline in the atmosphere."

Quinn turned, her mouth open in shock. "Cook?"

She'd never seen them out of the kitchen in all the months since he'd first entered the small one they started with.

"One and the same, Librarian." Cook held out four small bags, each packed with a selection of dense squares Quinn couldn't identify.

"These are?"

"Make sure you take only the bags as labeled. Each species has different levels I need to combat against. These will keep you safe whenever you decide to go." Cook bowed once briefly.

"You should visit more often," Quinn said, smiling. She was glad to see them out of the kitchen, even if it felt a little odd.

Cook shook their head. "I am less comfortable out here. But should you need me . . . I would return." They whispered the last of that with a hint of actual emotion, of determination.

Quinn smiled. "Thank you."

She watched them go and was about to start gathering those coming with her when she stopped cold. No one looked even remotely like they were getting ready to leave. "Are we not going yet?"

"Ah. No," Lynx said, his eyes flickering as if he was scouring the data collections. "Not quite yet."

"And why not?" Quinn prompted.

"Because while you've been sequestered away learning how to control your awakening stuff, the power levels ticked over, and you have to visit the core." Lynx crossed his arms and stared her down.

"Oh," said Quinn. "Why didn't you just say so? Do I need to synchronize?" she asked, almost hopeful. Although considering the news she learned the last time . . . maybe she shouldn't be.

"Not yet. The system is still getting used to the new influx and our memories haven't all been recovered. But we do have one big problem to address."

"Ah." Quinn nodded as the pieces clicked into place. New influx of power meant they needed to activate more pillars. And it meant . . .

There was a rumbling beneath Quinn's feet, and she looked up at Lynx in confusion, even though she sort of, kind of, had an inkling. A guess she didn't want to be true.

"Yes. That would be Ashiron straining at its bindings."

"Well, hell."

3

UNDER NO ILLUSIONS

Quinn blinked at Lynx, her mind, for just a second, completely blank. It wasn't that she hadn't heard him; it was more than she didn't comprehend what he'd said. "Wait . . . come again?"

"Ashiron is straining at the bindings which keep it just outside our pocket dimension," Lynx said, as if everyone everywhere knew.

"And I've just not felt these tremors before?" she asked, raising an eyebrow.

Lynx stared at her for a second, his purple eyes flickering in and out of focus. "Ah. Sorry. The ah . . . vault"—he glanced around at the others in the room as if hoping they wouldn't catch on that he didn't mean the Restricted Vault—" . . . is restricted for a reason," he finished lamely and out loud.

But he spoke telepathically to her. *The Library's vault isn't actually a part of the space the Library structure exists in. It's more a part of the Library itself . . . distinct and separate. You wouldn't have felt it in there.*

Quinn digested that information. While she'd been aware Drevicia's vault space was unique and not exactly a part of the Library itself, she hadn't realized it was completely separated, either. She'd simply assumed they were still in the same pocket dimension and her mind didn't want to contemplate the existence of multiple pocket dimensions within or next to one another. Surely dimensional shifts had to have a scientific explanation, right?

"Why didn't anyone else mention the tremors?" she asked, looking at each of them pointedly.

Jasper pushed herself up from the couch, bouncing to her feet. She grinned. "That's simple. Because you've been working so hard to get your powers under control. Everyone knows you've been running on fumes since you got here. I don't think it's super urgent, right? The seal on the pillar thingy isn't about to break or anything."

There was a flicker that passed over Lynx's visage before he could take care of it. But Quinn caught it. "What aren't you telling me?" she asked, crossing her arms.

"First. I want you to know I'm not *not* telling you things to keep them from you, but instead to avoid misinformation that comes from not having all the information on a subject yet," Lynx said, quite eloquently. Then he sighed. "However . . . with this last tremor, it seems we probably need to go down and actually interact with the column itself."

"Could these tremors disrupt the seal?" Quinn asked.

Lynx shrugged. "Those are some of the memories I still haven't been able to access yet."

He sounded so exasperated with himself that Quinn felt a pang of pity. After all, she remembered the car accident that killed her caretakers now . . . and it had been such a blow to realize what she'd forgotten. She couldn't imagine how bad it would be to realize you had whole sections of your memories carved out by someone you'd trusted. "Can I help?"

"Probably not. But I appreciate the sentiment." Lynx grinned at her and then paused; his head cocked to one side.

The Library's voice came through to Quinn loud and clear, but obviously not to the others in the room.

Right now it would be best to visit the filtration chamber. We do need to open a sixth and seventh pillar anyway to assist with the renewed flows of mana and energy.

Sure, Quinn said, *but is it wise for us to get close to it?* She knew just how vast the underground filtration chamber was. Like football fields filled with the thick, blue magical source. At least this time the chaotic miasma shouldn't be present, or at least, not much of it. She wasn't entirely sure how it worked when there was more than one filter available to the cavern.

It's less wise of us to play a guessing game when Lynx and I are still in the process of regaining our memories.

Quinn guessed it was going to be more like a couple of months or so to regain all the data they'd lost. She'd really hoped the Library had been exaggerating when it told her Cadre was being generous with his time window of retrieval. "Okay. We should probably head down to the filtration chamber. Who do I need to bring with me?" she asked, turning to Lynx.

"Not me." Jasper spoke up. "Not after last time."

"You didn't even enter the filtration cavern. The runic circle is outside of it." Quinn studied Jasper's body language, noting how stiff she appeared. "Why, what's wrong?"

"Had a headache for days after that trip. The Alyenarvor are highly susceptible to mana waves and it sort of knocked me about a bit." Jasper grinned. "Probably not the best use of my time. I can, however, research the rest of this trip to go get this snazzy book you want to retrieve. We can go as soon as you're done with the other stuff."

Quinn nodded slowly. That made sense. They didn't need a lot of people to check the pillar out anyway. It also impressed on her the urgency with which she should know more about as many species as possible. Good thing her lifespan wasn't limited anymore . . . technically. "Dottie will help you. She and Geneva have done most of the work locating the previous books anyway."

Dottie preened, and there was a bounce in her step as she trotted up to Jasper. "Let's get going, shall we? We have a lot to do!"

Quinn noticed as they opened the door that Misha was standing a few feet in front of it, their back to them all. It was one of the few times she'd seen the supervisory golem out and about without having summoned them. Maybe things were getting less hectic for them the more of the Library they restored. She wished that would rub off on everything else about the Library.

Hell . . . she really wished they'd been able to take care of Kajaro and Hoodie and put this whole thing behind them once and for all. She could get used to checking in books, following upon fines, and absorbing all the information in the universe.

Not today, though.

Not yet.

Geneva cleared her throat. "If you don't mind, I'll take Eric's place. His wing isn't quite healed enough for the amount of hovering he'll have to do, and I wouldn't want him to be down in the chamber when Hal comes to fetch him and Ikeshal."

Quinn nodded. Geneva made sense, and since the Ishiposa isle incident where they'd totally caught the usurper King of the Esposian fae, cousins to the Furionas fae like Geneva was . . . well, her Library Assistant Supervisor had grown in strength. Not like she could now lift huge weights, but she was more determined, and far more outspoken. She'd gained a level of confidence Quinn was grateful for, even if it'd been under less than ideal circumstances.

"Okay, that sounds like a good idea. Will you leave Danio in charge if Eric has to go before we're done?" Danio, the centaur, had been with them since the first batch. He was probably the easiest other assistant to trust.

Geneva nodded and Quinn was relieved. The centaur seemed firm and quite solid. He didn't budge on any type of enforcement, least of all the fines Eric had set up. Between the two of them, Quinn wasn't sure who enjoyed metering out the fines the most. She still thought Eric might have the edge.

"Should I . . ." Geneva began and paused, like she was struggling to find the right words.

"Should you . . ." Quinn prompted.

"Tell Eric where we're going? He'll likely want to come along." Geneva sounded as if she didn't want to make the imp angry, and Quinn couldn't blame her. He'd been a little more irritable since his injury. Even if it was perfectly understandable.

Quinn mulled over the question. Telling Eric could go one of two ways. Great, because he wouldn't have to do any work. Or badly because he, despite all his grumblings, liked being in the thick of things.

Aradie hooted quite pointedly.

"Fine," Quinn said. "I'll tell him." She strode out of the office, with Geneva, Lynx, and Aradie in tow, and almost ran straight into Misha, who still hadn't moved. Quinn stepped back.

"Sorry, Librarian," Misha said, not sounding sorry at all. They were looking away, or more, around the Library like they'd lost something.

"Everything okay?"

"Quite," Misha said, sounding rather distant. That clang in their tone was back, as strong as it had been on day one.

Quinn frowned. "Did you need me for anything?"

Misha looked at her and blinked three times very slowly. "No. The pulse from below just put me off. I apologize Librarian." And Misha blinked out of sight.

For several seconds Quinn watched the vacated space before leaning over to Lynx and asking him very softly, "Does that pulse put out any waves of power you know of?" as they continued toward the check-in desk where Eric sat, dangling his tiny legs down.

Lynx shook his head. It made Quinn wonder why the pulse had bugged Misha, then.

Eric strummed his fingers on the countertop next to him, and looked decidedly bored. His eyes narrowed as they approached. "What brings you here?" he asked, gruff as ever.

Geneva glanced at Quinn before speaking. "We need to head down to Ashiron and I was going to go with the Librarian." She didn't add *instead of you* onto the end, but then again, she didn't need to.

"Oh," Eric said, looking down at his feet as they swung back and forth. There were several seconds of silence before he looked up.

Quinn had to suppress a gasp. She'd never seen him look so dejected before.

"Guess it makes sense, right? Can't very well be of any use down there. What with the wing and all," he grumbled, but forced a small smile. "Besides, this way I get sole control over all the fines for a few hours. Right?"

Quinn laughed. He might be down about the wing, and still struggling with the fact that his nigh-indestructible form had taken some hefty damage, but he'd be okay in the long run. "Yeah, If you want, I can create a position for you and call you Master of Fines." Eric's eyes lit up greedily, and Quinn rushed to amend her statement. "Master of Fines, subject to my approval so you don't go overboard."

"Aw, you got my hopes up there, Librarian. That's not fair." He gave her a wink and then laughed. "But it does make me feel a little better. I just wish you'd let me do the whole five-hundred-year-fine instead of letting them start when the Library first reopened."

"We have to be somewhat fair." Quinn chuckled despite herself. "Still, you'll be okay overseeing things up here, right? Dottie is busy nailing down some details with Jasper."

Eric nodded, his expression solemn for a moment.

Geneva piped up, "And Danio can help you. He's due on shift in a bit. That way, if Hal comes, you can still . . ."

But Eric cut her off. "I know. I can go without having to worry about things here too much. It's fine. I'll be fine, and everyone will be fined." Eric fell onto the top of the counter, rolling in laughter as his wings held themselves skillfully out the way of being squashed. "Haha. I kill me," he gulped out between laughs.

Quinn sighed, mostly happy. It seemed like Eric, at least, would be okay. That meant she only had to worry about Ikeshal, Escadril, and Malakai . . . and there was plenty to be worried about with them. She had her worry bucket full as it was. "I'm glad you're doing okay," she said to Eric, meaning it.

"Yeah, my wing just needs to be tweaked. Hal'll take care of me. Don't you worry, Librarian. I'll be back to hassling you before you know it." He winked at her, a definitively impish smile on his lips.

"Good. I'll hold you to that." Just one. One less person Quinn had to worry about for now.

Out of how many billions? Trillions? She wasn't sure about the quantity of the universe.

She shook her head, clearing out those thoughts.

Save the Library, save the universe—that should be where she kept her head.

"Should we prepare to head down?" Quinn asked, looking over at Lynx, who shook his head.

Then he paused and looked up. "Well, you and I don't have to, but Geneva will need to moderate her chaotic absorption rate through food or armor." He stopped again and chewed on the end of a pencil he suddenly had in his hand. "I think it'd be better with one other person. I'll go grab someone we can trust."

He blinked out of sight, and Quinn suppressed a soft groan. Still, that meant she was already ready to head down. The quicker they got this out of the way, the better. She was under no illusions that this was going to be a fast fix. "Let's go and get you supplied up," she said to Geneva.

Just another thing to check off her lists.

4

THOUSANDS OF PIECES

QUINN FROWNED AS MISHA TRIED SEVERAL APPARATUSES FOR GENEVA. They were tiny inserts to go in her elf like ears that projected a protective barrier around the Furionas fae. The idea, as far as Quinn understood it, was for a magical current to connect around her using those two inserts as a type of anchor point on each side of her body.

"Why didn't we use these last time we ventured down?" Quinn asked, feeling slightly put out. Not that it mattered now she was practically immune, anyway.

Misha paused and looked over. "We did not yet have the correct components to manufacture these devices. While magic might make things easier, most contraptions require ingredients. Creating something out of thin air pulls on all sorts of potentially disturbing variances."

Theory of magic. That's what Quinn needed. She made a note of it for herself to look at once she'd got through the next few days of tasks. Another thing added to the list, which was truly starting to get long.

Priority listing - Librarian: Quinn.

Prioritize:

Strength - progress halted - immediate attention required

Fine Definition - in progress 18%

Pillar Activation - in progress 5/10

Note: Pillar Ashiron is damaged and unreachable

Task Delegation - in progress 32%

Library Returns - Culinary complete, Alchemical/Medicinal close to completion. Please be advised, Library requires Branch activation priority.

Energy Amplification - 50% Level 3. Please visit training location.

Repair the filtration system - Ashiron - urgent.

Calibrate and find the corrupted and missing files - urgency level - critical

New assistants required - Urgency level - medium

Replenish building and operational supplies - Maintenance mode

Defensive applications: Intermediate Level 4

Offensive applications: Beginner Level 9

Mind magic applications: Intermediate Level 6

Quinn blinked at the list in front of her. It had changed slightly since the last time she'd bothered to pull it up. Her tasks had definitive levels now, something to actually judge her progress by. This helped her brain a lot.

She added Theory of Magic to the list and it took a few seconds, but it added itself to the bottom.

Theory of Magic - Novice Level 3

Quinn winced. Surely it didn't have to be so blunt about it. Then again, while the System was a huge part of the Library, it wasn't completely the Library if she'd understood everything correctly.

Even though understanding it was starting to incite headaches.

Having checked the list, she glanced back to where Misha assisted Geneva. The golem's movements were more staccato in nature than usual, making it seem like they were irritated.

Quinn frowned. Misha had been in a bad mood several times lately. Perhaps she'd been too dismissive of the fact that golems could have feelings too. She'd never really looked into golem physiology and exactly how they came to be. Yet another thing to add to her ever-growing lists. She refused to even glance at the other one she knew the system was keeping tabs on.

"You're still here?" Lynx said, suddenly standing beside her.

"No," Quinn deadpanned without even glancing at him. "We're not here. We're both figments of your imagination."

"Haha," Lynx said, but she could see out of the corner of her eye that he was actually grinning.

"You're back faster than I thought you'd be. Who'd you get?" She was still watching Geneva, because the Furionas was starting to get irritated. Geneva was a gem, and rarely got frazzled, but this had taken a lot longer than either of them anticipated.

"Me."

Quinn turned this time, a genuine smile on her face. Then she changed it to a smirk. "Thought you had like a sector to run or a grandson to help heal or something."

Milaro grinned back. "Both, actually. But we have this cool thing called magic, and it lets me do a lot of the work from a distance." He wiggled his fingers in the air. "Magic."

Quinn laughed. "You make it sound like it's special."

"Isn't it to you?" he asked, genuine curiosity shining through.

"No. You need to learn more about technologically based cultures, Mr. Elf King. We had something called the internet back home. And could do exactly what you're doing. You know . . . working from home." Quinn cocked her head to one side, thinking that over. *Working from home* wasn't quite the right term.

She paused and then tried again, as Milaro attempted to maintain a straight face, and was failing abysmally. "Well, it's more like you're working from your second home."

"Fascinating. You're telling me that people could work from their homes and be somewhere else at the same time with technology?"

He sounded so skeptical, Quinn wanted to rub his face in it. "Technically. It's amazing what video technology can do for in-person meetings."

"Video—like magical memory recreation, right?"

"So much better than that. One of these days, I'll get Malakai to adapt a hard-drive and a computer screen, and I'll show you amazing entertainment." She was proud her voice didn't crack when mentioning Malakai.

"I look forward to that day." Milaro was sincere.

She nodded, reached into her pocket, feeling the comforting weight of the cellphone Mal had adapted for her.

It didn't always work. It glitched a bit, but it enabled her to send messages back home by harnessing specific aspects of chaotic and pure mana. She didn't fully understand how it worked, but Malakai had been super excited about the accomplishment.

Pity she'd only gotten to try it out after he was injured.

She sighed as Geneva finally finished with Misha and flitted over.

"Be careful of the settings. Don't move about too much in case they fall out. I don't have the components to make an additional tiny pair." And with that, Misha pinged out of view.

"Is it just me," Milaro asked, "or was Misha in a bad mood today?"

Quinn shrugged. "They've been like that for a little while now. Perhaps they need a vacation. Wait . . . aren't golems people too? Shouldn't they have time off?"

Lynx looked at her incredulously. "They frequently get time off."

"Oh." Quinn realized she needed to pay more attention to the people who essentially worked for her, or for her and the Library as a general rule. She'd been far too caught up in everything so far. She had to be better about that. So much to improve upon, including herself.

"Let's head down then, shall we?" Milaro asked, taking the lead.

Quinn didn't mind. She'd been in charge of too much, too often. Plus, she didn't relish the walk down the stairs.

"Why can't you just teach me teleportation?" she grumbled as they made their way to the newly established elevator she'd had the Library insert when Jasper had to build her circle. She stopped short and laughed at herself. "We don't have to go down the stairs anymore, do we?"

Lynx shook his head, giving her a wary, side-eyed glance. "I was wondering what you were on about."

"I forgot we put this elevator in. Certainly makes it a lot easier."

Quinn couldn't shake the feeling of lightness that came over her. This wouldn't be nearly as arduous as she'd imagined. "Still, it'd be nice to be able to teleport."

"Sure," Milaro said as they stepped into the elevator and directed it to take them down. "I mean, if you'd like to be torn into thousands of pieces and flung into the mass of chaos all around the filtration chamber. Be my guest."

"What?" Quinn asked.

"Teleportation essentially rips you into millions of tiny pieces for a fraction of a split second and reconstitutes you in the exact place you want to go. It requires precise usage of your magic, both energy and mana, as well as mood maintenance, which needs to be perfectly contained and controlled for the duration. If you don't, your body will dissipate into nothingness. You must know the exact location well enough that you won't embed yourself half in and out of it . . ." He paused, giving her a very serious look.

"And?" Quinn asked, knowing there was something else coming.

Milaro grinned. "And chaotic energy can interfere with that process and scatter you to the winds. Teleporting so close to unstable magic is just asking to be spread all across the universe."

"Oh." Quinn took that all to heart. "But, like, worse in the filtration chamber?"

He considered her for a second. "Yes. The chaotic energies in that chamber are both embedded in the mana that gets cleansed, as well as the air around it. Areas can thicken with it, and cause sparks. Better not to interfere with genetic makeup being solidified."

"That's what the pillars filter, then?"

"Generally. Cleanses all the excess chaotic elements so they don't coalesce and cause damage when people utilize energy and mana. Then it ships all the clean stuff off via ley lines around the universe." Milaro shrugged. "Pretty simple, really."

Quinn didn't want to tell him how *not* simple that sounded, so she brought the subject back to before its tangent. "Are there different types of teleportation?"

"Yes, but none used by everyday people that would avoid that particular fate." Milaro flashed her a smirk just as the elevator settled and opened its doors. "Here we are. Safe. Sound. And still intact."

Quinn gulped. Perhaps teleportation would be something she learned after everything else. Right now, she could fly. That'd get her most places as fast as she wanted.

They stepped out into the basement . . . although this was such a subterranean area that Quinn didn't really think it could be called that. Off to the left of them was the path to the much smaller cavern she and Jasper had used in the location finding ritual. She wondered if it was a good idea to use it to find these new books for the other branches of the Library.

It didn't take long to get to the foot of the mana lake, and Quinn couldn't contain her surprise.

Where before it had been covered in a thick black sludge, only lending glimpses of bright blue through formed cracks? Where there had only been one lit-up, struggling little pillar, one completely dark one, and another riddled with warning lights and decayed filtration elements? Now there was a beautiful blue ocean ahead of all of them.

It stretched out for what seemed like forever, to the other side that Quinn could barely see now, because of the glaring light emanating off the bright blue mana.

Five of the filters were lit up, with blues and greens adorning them as they worked through the load of chaotic energy. The whole cavern seemed wondrous, massive, and simply breathtaking.

Mana filtered in, churned out the chaotic element, refined it down and transformed most of it. The excess that was too harsh then filtered off through different pipes as waste.

The newly minted mana, however, was dispersed through the filtration pillars and sent out, via ley lines into the universe beyond, just like Milaro said. Only now she could see it. She watched as those filters and their blue-green dazzle of lights mesmerized her and the others. She could sit there all day and just watch it happen.

Milaro cleared his throat. "Does it really look that different from the last time you were here?"

Quinn nodded. "Much. Even when I came down with Jasper, I

could only see a small portion of the lake. But this . . . it's not concealed by slime or sludge. It's quite beautiful."

"It is, isn't it?" Lynx asked, purely rhetorically. "This isn't even as nice as it gets. There are still several things that need to happen, five more pillars to activate, and then we'll be back up to operating on an optimum level for the entire universe."

"I get that you've explained, but how does a chamber this size filter for an entire universe?" Quinn knew it was magical, but at the same time, it made her highly skeptical. Four football fields were nothing in the grand scheme of things. The chamber was pretty much its own scheme of everything.

"The more filters we have enabled, the faster they separate out the chaotic elements. There are fields of it waiting to be filtered through here. And once it's fully operational again, everything will move properly. The chamber expands as needed but not necessarily in a way you'll perceive visually. We've begun filling the ley line nodes, and people are able, once again, to access the magic without hurting themselves or others."

Quinn frowned as she glanced back at the Ashiron pillar. Where before it had been completely dark, now it was surrounded by a strange black and red haze that permeated all around it, tainting even the mana near it.

"How the hell are we going to fix that?" she asked, feeling entirely too dubious about the whole thing.

Just as she spoke, it sort of burped, and a cloud of miasma escaped around it.

Quinn blinked.

"Well, we need to get over to it, so we'll take the larger skiff now that the chaos layer has been cleared and . . ." But that was as far as Lynx got.

He stumbled and for a few seconds went incorporeal, his hand passing through the ground before he hastily pulled it back.

"Lynx!" Quinn rushed to his side, but he held a hand up for her to keep her distance.

She did so reluctantly while he flickered through several color variations and a couple of forms that went by so fast she couldn't even tell what they were. Finally, after what seemed like an age. Lynx solidified and blinked up at Quinn.

Reaching out her hand, he took it wordlessly, bringing himself to stand next to her. He was still partially transparent, even if he was more solid now.

"That . . ." He flickered again and obviously had to spend some energy to keep himself from flickering out of vision.

"What was it?" Milaro asked, and there was even worry in his voice.

Lynx shook his head, as if he was still getting his bearings.

"Take your time," Quinn said, not meaning it in the slightest. She wanted to know, and she wanted to know now, but he didn't seem capable of it right then.

"That's just it. We really can't. I remember now." He sounded so very sad when he spoke, and Quinn didn't really want to know what made him sound like his heart was breaking.

"Did something trigger it?" she asked as gently as she could.

He nodded toward Ashiron. "Yeah. Something triggered it."

"What?" Geneva spoke up, her tone gentle. "What did you remember, Lynx?"

"Her. Korradine. What she was going to do . . . and what I had to do to prevent her."

A sudden pit opened up in Quinn's stomach. She got the feeling this was a lot worse than she'd anticipated.

Lynx took a shuddering breath. Even if he didn't need oxygen, it calmed him to mimic the action. "I didn't have a choice—I had to seal it so the Unusceros curse wouldn't kill us all."

"You mean she's *in* there?" Quinn couldn't keep the incredulity out of her voice.

"Well . . ." Lynx winced and flickered at the same time. "Her soul is . . . and it's set to curse mode."

5

———————

BEST EFFORTS

It took Quinn several seconds to digest what Lynx said. Apparently, it took Milaro and Geneva even longer.

"Wait." Quinn held up a hand and tried not to let Lynx's stricken expression get to her. "You're saying Korradine's corpse is locked inside that pillar?" No matter how she tried to imagine it, that was going to be one messy pillar to fix.

How long did the stench of decay even last?

Lynx shook his head. "No. It doesn't work like that. The Unusceros are an inherently magical species. Their very essence, what some would term a soul, has power both before and after death. Should they choose, they can create a boon, or a curse that activates shortly after their material demise, and before a soul would usually dissipate back into the ether, becoming a part of magic . . . it's usually quite poetic. Curses aren't a common occurrence."

The more Lynx spoke, the more distressed he became. Quinn wasn't entirely sure if the manifestation could cry, but he looked like he was about to. She reached out a hand, but he stepped away, shaking his head. "I can't right now. Just give me a moment to clear my head. The images . . . the memories, they're bombarding me right now, and it's difficult to separate myself from them."

She knew what that meant. He was so caught up in the visions of these memories that he might mistake one of them for someone in those recollections. Which, given the current volatile emotional state he found himself in, might be dangerous.

There was nothing from the Library either. All Quinn could sense was a hesitant hum in the back of her mind. Which meant the memories were likely triggering for both of them. While usually Quinn would be ecstatic they'd recovered something important, right now she was worried about the consequences of this particular memory.

Milaro moved closer to her as Geneva hovered with him and leaned down to speak softly. "Unusceros are notoriously scrupulous. This entire endeavor of Korradine's makes no sense as far as the species goes. But, there's no denying it happened. I'm unsure of how to proceed, Librarian." And his brow furrowed in consternation.

Quinn nodded. "Maybe . . . can we help him if we go into the memory with him and watch? Would that be sort of therapeutic for him to share what's obviously a traumatic event?"

Milaro opened his mouth to respond, but Lynx intervened between them. "Actually, that would help immensely. While I know most of what happened, the emotional response toward the memory from my viewpoint, the desperation I felt in that moment . . . it's clouding my judgment as well as my ability to analytically perceive the information. Perhaps having outsiders experience it will help?"

"We can observe if you'll give us permission, but I can't guarantee we'll manage to keep ourselves separated from your emotions. They're wild things, and from what you're saying, even you feel the unpredictability of it all." Milaro's tone was gentle. "Quinn's been learning about entering and experiencing memories ever since we tried to extract them from the owls."

Quinn cleared her throat. "Ever since Kajaro put a mind bomb in my head."

Milaro smiled. "That too."

Lynx nodded. "I understand. I give you my wholehearted permission. With the current tremors, we don't have the luxury of time for me to work through this myself."

Quinn nodded at the elf king, and they both placed a hand on Lynx. Even though he was a manifestation, he was currently in his solid form, and memory reviewing worked best with physical contact with the subject. "Here goes," she murmured.

Suddenly, she could see the chamber as it was when it had been fully functional.

The pillars rose up out of the mana lake, shining brightly. All ten of them with the filters gleaming blues, greens, and even white occasionally. It was like a beautifully lit-up set of Christmas decorations, if trees were made out of impossibly tall filtration pillars. The mana lake shone blue and bright, and Quinn could feel the power emanating off it in waves.

Korradine stood on the shoreline, facing Lynx.

She was still beautiful, ethereal, with her eight-foot-tall frame and wispy silver hair falling down her back, but her one eye blinked rapidly, and there was a sheen of sweat covering her body. "You can't stop this," she gasped out, shooting what Quinn somehow knew was another bolt of power in Lynx's way.

The manifestation dodged it, his anger palpable. "You're not cursing the Library."

Kor laughed. Threw back her head and full on, evil cackled. The sound echoed through the chamber, off the pillars, vibrating in a way that set Quinn's teeth on edge. "The curse is already activated. You can't stop this, and you can't run either. I won't let you!"

Lynx took several steps toward her, but she backed away, stepping both feet into the mana at the edge of the lake.

A blue glow suffused her, but instead of revitalizing, she visibly began to wither, as if the lake was sucking the life out of her. The cackle became hoarse, and finally she was gasping for breath.

The next moment, she lay on the sandy foreshore, looking up at a very angry Lynx. His purple eyes glowed maniacally. And the runes flowed down from his hair, circling his entire body. Quinn could practically hear the chant that should go along with their activation but knew he didn't utter a word out loud . It was mesmerizing to watch as a wind picked up from nowhere, whipping his hair around his head.

"You will not break the Library. I do not allow it!"

This time when Korradine attempted to laugh, it came out as a hoarse cough that wracked her ever diminishing frame. She was about Malakai's height now. She'd already lost a foot. "You don't allow it? I've been taking your memories for millennia now. You allow everything—you don't have a clue what all you've allowed."

Lynx started slightly, a vague look of concern passed over his face. As if he was trying to remember the gaps left by memories she'd taken. But that wasn't how it worked.

"Didn't you realize?" Korradine carried on, leveraging herself to her elbows, panting with the exertion. "You've allowed everything. You're the reason this was so easy."

Another wave of uncertainty passed through Lynx, and it was all Quinn could do not to get carried away with it. But he rallied. "No. You made choices for this to happen. That I trusted you is my fault. But that you betrayed that trust is yours."

A strange expression passed over Kor's features, twisting them briefly in sadness before the haughtiness and superiority complex took back over. "You have no idea what you're talking about. It doesn't matter anyway. You know you can't stop an Unusceros death curse."

"Actually," Lynx said, his eyes still swirling as if he was accessing every database in the history of databases, "technically, you're wrong."

"What?" Kor had shrunk a little more. She was barely taller than Quinn at this stage.

Lynx began reaching for something inside him, and Quinn could feel the massive swell of power that began. Korradine obviously could too. A look of panic entered her eyes, and she scrambled finally back up to her feet. By now her skin was practically translucent and she was still shrinking, sweating more profusely, and barely able to breathe.

It reminded Quinn of a scene from a movie she'd seen back on Earth—where one of the characters ended up dissolving into water . . .

"You can't . . ." She looked alarmed now, as if she'd never thought Lynx would take a stand against her. Then her jaw firmed, and she gathered power of her own, even if it was minuscule in comparison to Lynx's. "And you certainly can't if you have no idea what's happening."

This time a dark energy bolt—no, wait, that was a *mind bolt* she flung at him—barely missed his head. Lynx didn't even glance at her as she lobbed mind spear after spear at him. Each of them more frantic than the last. There was an edge around Lynx now, as if he was straining to contain the amount of power he'd pulled.

Finally, when Kor was smaller than an Ilgonomur, Lynx looked up, sheer sadness in his gaze countered by complete determination. His words were practically whispered when he spoke. "You will not doom this universe to live with chaotic magic. If I can't stop you, I'll halt the curse. No matter what I have to do."

"You don't have a Librarian to replace me." She cackled before her frame was racked by a severe cough. "Nothing you do will be . . ." But then she paused, coughed again, and her eyes grew wide.

Lynx laughed at her expression as the power he contained grew more and more. "You were saying?"

"You wouldn't do that . . ." But she no longer sounded confident.

"Maybe not if you'd given me another choice." He shrugged.

"But you'll drain so much of the power."

He glanced at her, all emotion out of his eyes now, the sadness pushed down deep to fuel the capacity for the power he was about to wield. After all, from all measurements, it had the ability to tear him apart if one tiny thing even went wrong. "But not all of it. And maybe I'll keep enough so we can limp along until someone turns up . . . but I refuse to allow you to rip the lives of trillions of people away just because you've got some vendetta." Even in those words, there was a hint of sadness.

But Korradine shook her head. "Don't you understand how better off we'll be? The Library was a mistake. You're a damned mistake. All of this. All of you!"

She was fading and as her size diminished, so too did the timbre of her voice. In the end, she started sounding like a chipmunk, but Quinn couldn't bring herself to laugh.

"Maybe," Lynx said, the melancholy achingly evident in his voice. "But at least we're able to live and share what we know with everyone." He began to move toward the ever-diminishing Librarian.

There was a jolt throughout the chamber, as her eyes began to grow dull. Quinn could only think it must have been when the Library began to uncouple from its caretaker. Korradine let out what might have been a scream of pain as her eyes began to dim.

Lynx knelt down, chanting under his breath. Quinn watched as the surrounding power began to coalesce and move toward Kor. It billowed around him, a sort of nimbus, floaty and yet final, scooping her up onto its main level. She was tiny now. Way smaller than Geneva and Eric, even. Her breath came in short gasps, and there was no recognition in any other part of her.

She wasn't dead yet, but it was close. Lynx sighed, and his eyes finally returned to their normal lizard like fully purple sclera. Quinn could see the pain this put him through, the anguish he felt. It emanated from him like a warning beacon.

He bent his head down, and then touched her forehead with one finger, closing the eye that now stared off into nothing at all. "Derest ye tirua," he muttered under his breath, and the translation ability failed to let Quinn know what it meant . . . but she could feel the sentiment behind it, anyway.

Power consolidated around them, and finally he rose up, nestling the rapidly fading body that grew brighter and brighter on the pillow of cloud. Maybe that was the soul, Quinn would ask him later.

And then, totally unexpectedly, he threw the cloud toward Ashiron. It catapulted toward the pillar at such speed, Quinn barely followed it with her eyes. When it hit, it didn't stick onto the outside, but instead melted right through the exterior. All the filters turned black and red, flashing warnings as if its life depended on it.

Meanwhile, Lynx chanted again in words Quinn and the translation module had difficulty with. Power began to flux around the pillar, bigger and bigger in a circle around it until finally a whoosh of energy gathered, pulsating around the pillar, drawing on massive amounts of energy from the others and the lake.

Blue swirls of magic inundated Ashiron as the ball of energy grew larger.

Until all at once, it snapped back in on itself, sending a shockwave out the entire length of the cavern, knocking Lynx into the far wall in the process.

Ashiron blinked out of commission, all of its lights suddenly dark and black.

One by one, the other pillars went offline, until only two of them remained, and the levels of the mana lake drained down several feet.

Light flickered in the cavern and Lynx lay prone on the ground.

But the Library remained standing . . . despite Korradine's best efforts.

6

NOT TO INVITE DISASTER

THE VISION FIZZLED OUT, AND THEY WERE STANDING BACK IN THE chamber of now. Quinn blinked as the bright light from the mana lake hurt her eyes when her vision returned.

Lynx sat on the floor, gazing out at the filtration lake with a saddened look of longing on his face. The mana waves rippled, lapping at the shore, while the activated pillars cast reflections, giving it a soft glow.

Quinn glanced at Milaro, almost nudging him before she remembered he wasn't his grandson and might not take kindly to it. He looked back and gave her an almost imperceptible shrug. It was a strange disconnect when someone who was thousands of years old also had no idea what to do.

Geneva hovered over Lynx, the concern on her face palpable. She flitted back and forth, staying close to him the whole time. Finally, she darted over to Quinn. "What was that? There were flashes, and Ashiron practically growled for several seconds."

That was enough for Lynx to stir, to pull himself out of his melancholy and straighten up. He morphed through lynx form and up into human just so he could avoid the difficulty of getting up. He was ancient. Maybe his fake bones hurt.

"It should hold. I don't believe there's anything to worry about." His voice sounded hollow, devoid of emotion, or perhaps just completely depleted of energy. "Maybe."

Quinn moved closer. "What happened after what we saw?"

She wasn't about to not worry. That pillar had been a thorn in their side almost since she got here. Well, since she found the book with the note, anyway. They needed whatever was in it to get out of it so they could operate at full capacity. At least once they had enough power.

Lynx slowly began turning to look at her. He nodded slowly. "I'm not sure what happened. I don't quite remember, but I do recall waking up in the Core chamber with everything having reverted to low-power mode."

"But the Library didn't shut itself down, did it now?" Milaro asked gently.

They were all cautious not to alarm or upset Lynx. He seemed like he was hanging by a thread. Quinn wished she understood how the Darigháhnish soothed the people around them. She thought Lynx could do with some soothing, even if she wasn't entirely sure it would work.

"No. No . . . it didn't do it by itself." Lynx paused and heaved a huge sigh. "I remember being worried we wouldn't find a Librarian. Frankly, I was certain of it. And right then we didn't have power to spare. We'd been looking for decades for a matching signature at that point. The council had met . . . we'd set out precautionary plans. It was a bit wild, to be honest."

Milaro chuckled, but it held no hint of mirth, more of memory and melancholy. "We did have several plans in place. Some of them even wilder than the one we resorted to."

Quinn knew she was that plan and wasn't entirely certain how to take it, but she was fairly sure it was complementary. "So . . . you set it up?"

"Yes. Once the Library hit a certain power level, it was going to go into quasi hibernation anyway. A form of self-preservation left over from cosmicisodracus heritage. That would allow us to conserve the power we needed, shut the doors, and give us enough time to figure out how to replace or find a Librarian, or failing that, figure out if there was some sort of recalibration we could do to keep the Library functional." Lynx turned around, spread his arms out, and smiled. "At least it stayed in one piece, right?"

"Good job." Quinn grinned at him, as she tried to parse all the information. "So the drain of power triggered the shutdown."

"Yeah. I—I'd always thought I just shut it down once she died, but now . . ." He just left the words hanging, and Milaro picked them back up.

"The shutdown triggered because in preventing the Library's destruction, you had to pull on so much power that it caused filters to shut off, and the whole operation to begin to shut down. It was a gamble that paid off, it at least brought you some time. You did save the Library, and it was able to filter just enough to have the universe survive until we found Quinn." Milaro paused. "You should be proud."

"Probably. But mostly right now, I'm tired. The memory is real, and I have no idea how I avoided the memory wipes she fired at me. Maybe it was determination, perhaps it was sheer willpower." Lynx laughed dryly at the thought.

Quinn knew there was a part of him reluctant to believe everything they'd seen played out. That a part of him had been hoping Korradine didn't betray him to such an extent. But she did, and now the bulk of his memories were returning there was no more denying that fact.

"So . . . she's in there?" Geneva asked hesitantly, gesturing toward the pillar.

Lynx shook his head. "That's not how it works. The Unusceros dissipate. They become one with the universe as they die. Their essence, or soul, would usually do the same unless they imbue it with power in their final days. Sometimes particularly powerful Unusceri have gifted power sources after their death or done other amazing things. However . . . they're also capable of the opposite. Not all of them could manage a curse, but Korradine. Well." He glanced over at the fluctuating shielding around Ashiron.

"She was always powerful," Milaro finished for him.

"Yeah. Super powerful. I should have known when she wanted to be the Librarian that something was wrong. No one has that much power and wants to serve others." Lynx sounded bitter. Not that Quinn could blame him.

Milaro preened a bit. "Hey, I take offence to that. I'm powerful."

Lynx raised an eyebrow. "But you run your sector, and you didn't try to become a Librarian."

"Point. But it's more what her attitude was, not powerful people in general." Milaro frowned. "Although . . . whatever. Let's move right along."

Quinn watched as his face flushed, and she smiled. "Anyway. What do we do now?"

Lynx turned to her, his eyes blinking rapidly. "We have to reseal it."

"I thought you said it wasn't dangerous."

He raised an eyebrow. "Not in this instant. But soon . . . so we have to reseal it."

"That sounds difficult."

"It is what it is," Lynx said. "It won't be easy and it'll only be a stopgap measure until we can figure out how to either seal it away permanently somewhere else, or we understand how to destroy it."

"Can't we just eject it?" Quinn asked, genuinely curious.

Lynx and Milaro looked horrified at the suggestion. They both stuttered as if trying to find the words to answer it until Milaro finally won out. "You can't punch a hole in a dimensionally bound subspace."

Quinn had no idea what that meant and waiting for some elaboration.

Lynx picked up the thread. "The pillars are intrinsically wound into the fabric of the Library, of this pocket dimension. To remove one . . ." He shrugged widely.

Despite herself and the lack of precise wording, Quinn shuddered. "Why is it reacting now of all times?"

"Power levels," Milaro added promptly. "When Lynx originally set up the failsafe, there were no fluctuations anymore because of how much it initially cost. Without a Librarian to activate all the Library's functions, the power levels receded. However, I'm guessing from the vision that when Korradine finally put her plan into place, when she finally knew she was going to die, she didn't expect Lynx to have built failsafes."

"Sort of," the manifestation said. "But not quite accurate. Basically, because it took a ridiculous amount of power for me to seal her away, the failsafe tripped. It should have taken a couple hundred years to get that low, but basically her attack meant we lost a few centuries' worth of power and had to shut down immediately."

"But in doing so, you literally saved the magic of the universe so . . . that's good, right?" Quinn asked.

"That is excellent," Geneva said. "I'm glad you saved us."

Lynx actually blushed. "Well, I didn't realize I'd be saving us in that way. But I'm glad it worked out . . . sort of."

Quinn sighed. "I'm guessing in order to seal that, we're going to need to go all the way out to the pillar, aren't we?"

Lynx nodded and glanced out toward where the skiffs were kept.

"Tell me," Milaro asked. "We can't teleport over because of the mana interference, but is there any reason we couldn't just fly over? After all, we all know how."

Lynx blinked at him and suddenly burst out laughing. "I don't know why I didn't even think of that."

Quinn laughed too, feeling ever so slightly better despite the fact that they had to fly out to the ominously glowing pillar. She felt lighter than she remembered as she lifted off, her scales shifting as she kept them in place, and she loved the sheen of blue and gold they projected, before settling.

What she didn't like was the looming pillar as it grew larger and larger the closer they got to it. The disturbing black nothingness where the operational lights should be was unsettling enough, but the miasma around the pillar, and the red overtones of the filters, just added to the gloom surrounding the whole section of Ashiron.

Quinn wasn't the best at hovering, unlike Lynx, Geneva, and Milaro. They had far better control over their flying spells or abilities. The base of the pillar as a landing area didn't fill her with confidence.

It, too, looked black, almost like the sludge that used to cover the lake before they repaired the failing pillar two or so months ago now.

It seemed so long ago, but in reality, she'd barely been at the Library for a blip in the grand scheme of things.

"I can't land there," she said. Not only did it look like chaotic magic sludge, but it also seemed slippery.

"Yes, you can," Milaro said, lowering himself to the deck of the pillar. Magic coalesced around him, sending the sludge running down the sides. As if a breeze had come and blown it all off.

Quinn stepped gingerly on the floor of the pillar, a frown on her face. "Was that chaotic sludge?"

Milaro shrugged as Geneva and Lynx landed. "Mostly. Something else too, leaking out of the pillar. Be careful. I'll try to keep an eye on it, but it feels sneaky."

That was when Quinn noticed it.

The pillar looked like it was bleeding. Oozing black and deep red sludge down from the gaps where the filters usually would be. It was held back by some sort of invisible barrier that no longer seemed to be working as intended.

Lynx paled. "That's not good. The seal is swelling as the curse reacts to the amount of power surrounding it."

"Oh, fantastic," Milaro said. "I like a good challenge."

The sarcasm that dripped from his words was almost as thick as the miasma surrounding the pillar.

"Good, because I have no idea what to do," Lynx admitted softly.

Milaro raised an eyebrow and leveled a stare at the manifestation. "You created the seal in the first place. You've regained your memories of the event, so how is it you don't know what you did?"

Lynx shrugged. "I have no idea. It came to me. It might have been . . ."

The Library's voice spoke to all of them, ringing in the air right above their heads. *I believe it was the both of us. Working in synchronization once we discovered what Korradine was truly doing. There were split seconds that made this possible, that saved the Library and universe from certain destruction. But we'll need to piece together precisely what we did.*

"Well, I know what I did in a general sense," Lynx said.

"Good start." Milaro crossed his arms and fixed a pointed look at the location the Library's voice had come from. "Get it together. We can't stay here forever. Literally. This pillar is unstable, and we need to reinforce it to give ourselves enough time to figure out how to save it."

He didn't have to mention that *not* saving the pillar would not only set the filtration system back, but interrupt the equilibrium of the entire pocket dimension. Quinn didn't even understand if replacing a pillar was possible.

"What did you do then?" Geneva prompted.

Lynx sighed and looked ever so slightly guilty. "I used a banishment ritual. That's why the pillar is slightly out of sync with us. Just a fraction. I took the soul curse, and I locked it inside the pillar, banishing it to a different dimensional timeless space."

For a few seconds, no one spoke. It sounded so fantastical to Quinn, and yet at the same time, eerily simplistic. "And then we further locked it down," she muttered.

Lynx simply nodded.

Milaro spoke solemnly. "It's just been floating in limbo. Essentially in stasis."

Lynx nodded, and Quinn could see how worried he was. His runes and eyes were practically tempestuous.

Geneva drew in a ragged breath. "And now it's feeding off this newly established power level. Is it close to breaking free?"

"Yes," Lynx said, his voice small.

Quinn had a lightbulb moment from one of her many, many books she'd absorbed. "Can't we reinforce the banishment and move the location?"

Milaro blinked at her. "Yes, but that'll require preparation, and we need a stopgap measure for right now. But . . ." he said slowly, a grin appearing on his face.

"But what?" Lynx asked, a hint of hope back in his voice.

"But I don't see why we can't just reinforce the shields within the pillar, even if the central section of it is technically frozen and shifted.

There's still the physical surface area. If we secure that, we buy a good chunk of time."

"I guess we have a plan." Lynx licked his lips nervously.

Quinn nodded. "I guess we have a plan."

She tried not to think about what could go wrong with the plan. After all, it was better not to invite disaster, right?

7

EXCELLENT MIMICRY

The pillar felt slimy.

Not in a physical way, but more of an aura-generating mystical one. It coated Quinn's senses every time she tried to reach out to it. Milaro tapped a finger lightly against her shoulder, and she looked up at him.

His pale hair was tied back in a pretty strict braid today, and his face held more seriousness than she'd ever seen. Granted, there were some hefty stakes involved.

"Breathe. Remember that anything you see or hear once I guide us inside to our goal is a warping of truth and reality." His words were even, measured, and softly spoken. "We've worked mind to mind before. We can do it again."

She nodded her head, glad of his reassurance.

"And I'll be here to help," Lynx said. But whatever else he'd been about to say, a visible shock jumped from the pillar to him, practically pushing him off the edge, and it was only Geneva's quick thinking shove back that saved him from falling into the one still chaotically sludged area of the lake.

"What was that?" Milaro asked, his eyes narrowing.

Quinn tried to pay attention, but to be honest, she was worried about what might have happened if he'd blinked himself back up. Wasn't that paramount to teleportation too? Could they have lost Lynx? She didn't think the Library would forgive her for that.

Lynx was analyzing the situation if his eyes were anything to go by, and they usually were. "Interference. I can't help you internally. I'll have to try to funnel power to you from out here. My creation of the dimensional shift means my presence within that confined space provokes dissonance."

Milaro nodded slowly. "Makes sense. Magical dissonance is a definite possibility when you're dealing with something this delicate and partially aware."

Quinn had no idea what magical dissonance was, but she knew what other books she was adding to her list. The list of things she needed to learn sooner rather than later grew by the minute. "I'm great with not knowing the intricacies, as long as you guide me, but since time is of the essence, we should move along."

Milaro colored slightly, nodding once before he closed his eyes, and a calm overcame them all.

It seeped into Quinn's being like a warm blanket on a rainy day.

"Are we ready?" he asked, giving her a kind and encouraging look as he asked the question.

"As I'll ever be."

"Good. Place your hands against the pillar." He saw Quinn's hesitation. Given that the pillar was covered in a decent amount of slime, it was understandable. "It will be fine. I've cleansed the area of any immediate negative effects. As long as we get this done in a timely manner, everything will be okay."

Quinn nodded and placed her palms against the pillar.

Immediately she was sucked into what felt like a whirlpool of hatred and regret, of violence and anger, messy and desperate. It only took a second for her mind to dismiss the sensations as mental manipulation designed to force her to capitulate to the underlying desire of freedom. Not for the first time, she thanked her lucky stars Milaro had given her as much mental fortitude training as he had.

Now she could see it for what it was. There within the massive, towering walls of the pillar was a round cage inside of which was a ball. It seethed, bounced around in its cage with tumultuous force, roiling and seething like a captured creature of the deep.

Quinn felt her whole body shudder with revulsion. The emotions reaching out to her leaked from this deeply dark sphere, through cracks of the cage in a desperate attempt to reach something, some-one, and cross over.

There was so much wrong with the outputted sensations, Quinn wanted to shower for ten hours and scrub herself down with a Brillo pad.

But she shook it off. She had to.

Centering herself, she followed Milaro's lead.

They skirted the edges of the pillar, rounding out the area with a level of mental and physically conjured padding to dampen the effects of the leaking barrier. Getting it in place first was paramount if they hoped to reinforce the seal around the curse without a potential acci-dent, causing everything to explode in a chain reaction.

The reinforcements were much like the protective blocks Milaro taught Quinn to use in her own mind. They clicked in together like the building blocks she'd had as a child, except she smoothed over where they joined, making the cracks disappear.

They moved, each around a side, slowly and deliberately, their own power supported from without by Geneva and Lynx funneling energy to keep the flow steady and the output even.

It took so much effort. By the time they reached the backside of the pillar, Quinn had not only lost track of time but also of where exactly she was standing. Even though a part of her knew Geneva and Lynx were keeping the ground clear so they had ease of movement, a portion of her worried that the instability would be an issue.

They worked tirelessly, creating smooth texture where the inner walls of the pillar had begun to crumble due to the onslaught of nega-tive energies emanating from the slight dimensional shift.

Finally, the protective sealant was back in place, and now, they could turn their attention to the prison itself.

Remarkable. Milaro's voice echoed through Quinn's thoughts, and she had to agree. How Lynx had managed to construct such an intricate and solid prison in the space of mere seconds was beyond her. She didn't understand the half of it.

But now there were cracks that needed reinforcing.

Follow my lead. I will need your strength and your power. When I tell you to use your elemental abilities, you must be prepared to act with pinpoint precision. I'll also need you to reinforce the shielding once we're done with your Draconic magic.

Quinn hesitated to agree when he said that, but he immediately sought to allay her fears.

I will guide you, but I don't have a Draconic line of innate magic. That's species specific. Do you understand?

She nodded and then realize he might not realize she'd done that. *Yes, I can do it.*

Quinn could feel his smile through their connection. Fine. She hadn't needed to speak at all.

Despite the prison appearing like a round ball, its surface was jagged and unpredictable. They felt around the surface and Quinn could feel Milaro frowning.

This should be smooth. He spoke into her mind.

Then . . . we need to make it smooth again? Smooth it over?

Yes, although it sounds much easier than I think it'll be.

We can do it, she said with a lot more confidence than she felt. Faking it until she made it all the way.

They dove into work.

Quinn could feel the lines of sweat forming on her forehead and the nape of her neck. Channeling so much power through such an intricate fine line was taking its toll. Her energy levels weren't depleting, though. They'd raised so much since everyone was injured.

She focused on finding the root of the jagged lines and filling them in like putty with clay. Smoothing them over and heating them with fire, as Milaro directed her to do, sort of melting them all together and reinforcing them with power and shielding of her own.

The arduous task began to take its toll on her, and she could feel her physical strength waning. Still, they powered through. With half of the prison smoothed and reinforced, the trapped soul, even located in the dimension just out of kilter with their own, began to squirm.

It thrashed and screamed, flashing all sorts of images their way. Most of them didn't make it but seemed to fall short, giving Quinn but a glimpse of what lay beyond, of what might be in store for them if this curse bomb were to go off. It was so much worse than anything she'd anticipated.

Visions of destruction, of chaotic energy eating at innocents, of waves of black sludge engulfing worlds and solar systems with frantic greed to take back the power it needed to thrive.

The frantic emanations shook the pillar and the platform all around them. As if from a dream, Quinn could feel a shower of something rain down over her head and knew even the ceiling of the cavern was being shaken enough to let dirt and debris loose.

A part of her hoped the Library could weather it.

She narrowed the focus of her concentration, determined to fix this, to fill it in and give them more leeway. They couldn't let this come to pass.

The closer they got to filling in all the cracks, the more the curse thrashed around, practically screaming to be let out.

It took all her willpower to maintain concentration. Part of what helped was the steady hand of Milaro guiding the whole process.

Closer and closer they moved to completion, containing all the anger and vitriol into that one space, plugging the leaks and leaving the prison smooth as brand new.

Finally, after going over it another three times, just to make sure, after smoothing, setting, and firing it up, the prison seal was complete. Even the wall containing it had been reinforced.

Quinn opened her eyes, blinking rapidly at the bright blue light all around them emanating from the mana lake, and stumbled immediately.

"Well done." Milaro caught her elbow and helped her right herself.

"That was . . ." Quinn searched for a word other than *scary*. "That was interesting."

Milaro laughed and Lynx landed next to them, an eyebrow raised in question.

"She said it was interesting," Geneva explained to the manifestation.

"Ah." Lynx cocked his head to one side, and a small smile spread over his face. "I do believe you have brought us some more time. Although the constant influx of newly reinforced cleansed mana will erode it fairly fast. Did you attune it to allow for fluctuating power levels into consideration?"

Quinn nodded, but then looked at Milaro for confirmation.

"We did," the elf king answered. "But it took a lot of energy and more mana than I like. Quinn might have some left, but mine is close to depleted. And it's still just a stopgap measure. We need to get back up top and take care of ourselves."

"How long do you think it'll last?" Geneva asked as they flew to the shore.

Milaro shrugged. "I'm not entirely sure. The power levels might be compensated for, but the variations of the system batters the whole prison around a bit. But it should be good long enough to allow us to figure out how to nullify it now we know what we're dealing with."

Back on the shore, Quinn looked toward the pillar. The black and red ominous glow had heavily diminished. She frowned. "Are you sure it's going to buy us enough time?"

"I can't be sure of anything, but it should buy us enough." Milaro began moving toward the exit as Aradie swooped into view.

She landed on Quinn's shoulder, hooting softly.

"Really?" Quinn asked, reaching up to scratch behind the owl's ears.

The look Aradie gave her was one of impatience. An *Of course I meant what I conveyed* sort of expression.

Quinn chuckled. "Jasper is in the ritual chamber getting ready to retrieve an exact location from the alchemical and medicinal books."

Geneva turned around. "It was a good idea to leave the circle there. Makes things a lot easier."

Quinn shrugged. "Back on my world, we have an app that can find almost anything. It finds phones, laptops, EarPods . . . if we had that for the Library, we wouldn't be in this mess."

"Sounds intriguing. Do you have anything more than vague descriptors to go on that we might make something similar?" Milaro asked, tempering the snark with a smile.

"No. I'm not techy enough for that. However . . . I'm sure Mal—" But she stopped short, not sure when Mal would be enough of himself to do much else. "Anyway. We can figure out adaptability of technology at a later date."

They came up to the room slowly. The thrum through the entire chamber was so much more peaceful now they'd re-confined the damned curse. It reminded Quinn of the soothing hum underlying the Library the first time she encountered it. As if it was an actual part of her being.

Quinn poked her head around the archway that led into the chamber. It was precisely as they'd left it. Jasper leaned over several of the runes carved into the floor, examining them and adjusting edges. She didn't even look up when they entered, lost in thought, concentrating.

Milaro cleared his throat when it became obvious that Jasper wasn't about to notice them and Lynx was currently connecting to the Core and completely out of it. "Jasper. Do you need help?"

Jasper started and turned to face them all, her usual excitable energy rippling across the room. "Yes! This is perfect. I need the names of the books and the last known locations. We should be able to determine where they are quickly."

"We know where the *Hunter Guide* is. We don't need to find that one. Just the other two," Lynx said, coming out of his trance. Something about him caught Quinn's eye. He was definitely doing a lot better than he had been. His subtle purple glow was back.

"Excellent." Jasper wiggled her fingers in an excellent mimicry of Milaro. "Got that map ready, Lynx?"

The Library manifestation nodded.

Jasper's eyes were practically on fire. They twinkled so brightly. "Let's get started, shall we?"

8

FIRST SIGN OF DISCOMFORT

Quinn poured over her map in her office, determined to understand exactly how maps of the damn universe worked. Try though she might, even months in now, it was still difficult to grasp the sheer magnitude and scope of an entire universe.

She maneuvered the projection made my by her console as she walked around her desk, trying to pinpoint just how close the book with Narilin's rivals was to the location where Escadril was recovering. It didn't appear to be too far away, but then again, walking through a door to anywhere in the universe sort of tended to skew one's perspective on distances.

Aradie nudged her head with a wing and cooed.

Quinn shook her head. "No. I have no idea why I'm trying to figure this out when it just is what it is. All I can say is I hate not knowing."

Aradie made a sound suspiciously like a chuckle. It earned her a pointed glare from Quinn. "If you don't want to help, you can go back over on your perch."

Images flashed in front of Quinn's eyes. Of forests filled with trees so tall she couldn't glimpse the top of them. Houses in and around trees, not cut into them, but a part of the entire wooded life around them. All filled in together, making it a simple natural habitat bustling with life.

"You could have shown me that in the first place you know," Quinn grumbled at the bird. Still, it was helpful. It gave her an idea of the area they'd be going to, even if it didn't tell her anything about the Salosier and their familial interactions. She didn't want to go in blind.

Aradie hooted this time, with a little chirp at the end that sounded oddly like an exclamation mark.

"I know, I know . . . just Narilin never really seems to like me much. And I don't have the energy right now to expend on trying to make her." Quinn was feeling decidedly grumpy. It was probably time for a nice sugar donut. That sounded like it'd hit the spot perfectly and help take away all the stress she was feeling. For five minutes, anyway. But that short amount of time would at least be filled with bliss.

Another short sound from Aradie and Quinn shooed her off her shoulder. "Go get her if you think she wants to help."

Aradie shot out of the room leaving but an image in Quinn's mind in her wake. One of Narilin and Escadril when the book doctor was so much younger. There was an air of vulnerability surrounding her, as Escadril sat going through books with her. Wonder in both their eyes at the knowledge in front of them, the materials. A sensation of deep understanding and love for what they did best exuded from them.

Quinn decided that Aradie was right and Narilin was the best person to take her after all. She turned her attention back to the maps overlaid on one another.

The Jezishian Solution to Maladies of the Mana Pathways: A Beginner's Guide, and *The Mattiniman Balance Between Mana and Energy: Explained for the Beginner* were sitting oddly close to the locations of the other two-dimensional books they had yet to retrieve. Both *The Parsneauvian Theory of Spatial Dimension Manipulation* and *The Crown and Fall of Pocket Dimensions Due to Spatial Interference* were maybe, from what Quinn could tell, a quadrant away from each of the others.

It might not mean something, but it could mean everything.

Maybe.

She sighed and let herself shuffle around to sit in her oversized chair. With Aradie missing from the top of it, the whole room felt rather lonely.

Not that she had to wait long. Aradie entered the room shortly thereafter, hooting softly with a triumphant ring to it. Sometimes Quinn wished the owl would just talk to her like she had on several occasions before. But it seemed Aradie was selective of when to use human speech since she could mostly communicate effectively through vocalizations, emotion, and images.

"She'll be along soon," Quinn muttered and pushed herself up from the desk. "You know. I think I have enough time to go and get myself a donut."

Without waiting for Aradie to respond, Quinn took off for the Culinary branch, hoping Cook simply had some donuts waiting for her. After all, they'd become a definite favorite of pretty much everyone in the Library. Cook tended to keep them on hand these days.

She walked through the crowded dining hall, making a note to herself to expand it, and finally entered the glorious culinary branch. Frankly, the scents and tastes became evident as soon as she passed through the gorgeously carved archway, making her mouth water and her hunger rise up a notch.

"Ah. Librarian," Cook said without looking up. "I hope this day finds you well."

Quinn had a definite soft spot for Cook. There were so many aspects of life in the Library made easier by their presence. The homesickness constantly curbed because of small culinary delights that reminded her of good times and the past in a way that didn't make her miss so many things.

"This day finds me quite well. Thank you." She found herself swinging to the formal when she was around Cook.

"Excellent. I take it you are hungry?"

Quinn nodded emphatically. "I'm actually almost starving."

Cook paused what they were doing and looked her up and down.

Quinn could have sworn they raised an eyebrow, even though their golem features didn't always allow for such adjustments. "I do not believe that you are starving, but I seem to recall you have not yet eaten today. If the Library activity from earlier is any sign, I am betting you used up more energy than you should have, given the fact you have not yet eaten." They gave her a disapproving look.

Quinn had the grace to feel slightly embarrassed. It wasn't the first time they'd had the conversation about balancing energy intake and output. "Sorry."

"No need. I will begin to make sure breakfast is brought to you wherever you are at the same time every day." Cook didn't sound put out, but instead like a grandparent figure.

For just a second Quinn was reminded of Milaro, and she smiled. "Thank you," she said, hoping her response came across as genuine.

"Of course. Must keep you healthy and strong. We need you." For a second there, Cook was more serious than Quinn had ever seen them.

They turned around and picked up a bag, holding it out to her.

Quinn took it, opening it to look inside. Nestled in the folds were two donuts separated from what looked like a quiche. It smelled heavenly. "Thank you, but how did you know I was coming?"

Cook actually chuckled. "Aradie informed me as soon as you left the office. Now you should get back because I believe you have a visitor."

"Thanks again," Quinn said, reaching forward to give Cook's arm a quick squeeze.

"Anytime," Cook said as she dashed off.

One of these days Quinn would find the time to sit down with Cook and chat, or help, or even learn to cook herself. The culinary branch fascinated her. It filled her with hope as she bit into one of the donuts and let a content nostalgia wash over her.

She imagined getting the books for the medicinal and alchemical branch and opening it too. So much more life came to the Library whenever they opened a branch. Or at least, she assumed it would work the same way once they opened another.

She dashed into her office, just ahead of Narilin, who she could see approaching it, and overtook her before she could reach the door. Quinn plopped the food on her desk and turned to greet her visitor, hoping that Narilin was in as good a mood as she'd been the last time they'd encountered one another.

"Librarian," Narilin said with a bow of her head. A smiled played on her lips showing genuine contentment at being where she was. At least, that's how Quinn interpreted it.

"Thanks for coming," Quinn said, motioning for her to take a seat across from her.

"Aradie said you needed to see me. Might I ask what this is about?" Narilin seemed mildly curious but also slightly cautious.

"Ah. Yes. I'll be traveling to the Feshpa-Alin region to visit with some people I'm quite sure you're acquainted with." Upon mention of her home region of space, Narilin stiffened somewhat. Quinn kept her eye on the Salosier, but continued. "They have a book we need for the alchemical and medicinal branch that they refuse to give back due to some sort of feud with your family? The feud isn't something for me to involve myself with unless it brings harm to the Library. That being said, I need that book. I was wondering if you might have some insight for me into the situation and how I could best approach them."

Narilin paused. It wasn't a frozen pause, but a thoughtful one where Quinn could tell she gave the request serious thought before answering.

"It is difficult for me to elaborate on, Librarian." It had to be the first time Quinn ever heard Narilin hesitate fully in what she was saying. She waited for the book doctor to continue.

"Our families have always been rivals. It is common amongst the Salosier. We push each other to greater heights and use rivalry to develop our current skills and discover new ones. The Jenishu clan . . . my own family line have always had a proclivity for book repair. Our abilities have been able to save magical tomes for millennia. It is what we do. It has always been what we are known for."

She paused for another moment. Narilin still seemed hesitant to speak, as if she didn't want to air dirty family secrets to anyone. Quinn understood the sentiment and gave her the time she needed.

"The Balisor clan has always been specifically good with the binding of books, with coaxing of out of all aspects of hardiness when it comes to maintaining histories and cycling through years of notations." Narilin paused again, but this time continued faster. "The thing is, a few generations ago, one of the Balisor married into the Jenishu clan. This resulted in the Jenishu clan taking on some of those specific skills and now we have surpassed where we were. Our own line is second to none in any aspect of book binding, maintenance, care . . . our affinity with the trees even exacerbates the connection we have to the books we care for."

She turned fully to Quinn, an eagerness radiating in her features. "As you know the Library is not the only library, but it is the pinnacle. It is where we regulate the magic of the universe. Being a Librarian or Assistant Librarian or even the book doctor, as you call me, is the highest my people aspire to. This is the accumulation of everything we have ever worked for, coming together in a harmony I never realized we could achieve."

"And this is why the Balisor people are holding onto the alchemy book?" Quinn asked. She suppressed the groan she wanted to let out. There was no logic to the whole fiasco, so she didn't understand them wanting to withhold a book in order to perhaps get the Librarian's attention? That didn't even make sense when she was available at the Library most of the time.

"I could not imagine there would be another reason. While this does not ingratiate them to the Library I cannot imagine another reason. I would assume they wish to regain some sort of status from the past? But if they wanted to talk to you, they could have just requested an audience."

For such a trivial thing to delay them opening a branch? Still, at least this one looked like it would be easier to solve than the others. As long as whatever they wanted to say wasn't somehow connected to the Sólem.

"I would gladly accompany you if you feel that will help, Librarian," Narilin said, serious again.

"I'd appreciate that," Quinn said and meant it.

Narilin gave a rare smile, small though it was, and stood up. "When do we expect to depart?"

Quinn paused for a second. "I'm not sure yet. Maybe tomorrow." She did feel bone weary. A good night's sleep would help.

"Very well. I will make sure to instruct Jane for my absence and be ready." With a brief incline of her head, Narilin practically floated out of the room.

Quinn watched her go, a thoughtful frown on her face, trying to figure out just how uncomfortable it'd be to travel with Narilin without Malakai as a buffer.

Images flashed in front of her eyes, causing her to stumble, as Aradie showed her a new visitor approaching. Another suppressed groan later, Quinn righted herself just in time for the brief knock against the doorframe.

"Arnekai," Quinn said as politely as she could. "What brings you here?"

The Darigháhnish leader gave a half-smile before entering. She wrung her hands together; the first sign of discomfort Quinn had ever seen her exhibit. Then she turned to face Quinn, determination in her gaze. "I need you to help me heal my son."

9

ONE STEP AT A TIME

Quinn blinked at Arnekai, unsure she'd heard her correctly. "What do you mean, you want me to help heal your son? I'm not a healer. Well, I mean, I can heal a little bit, but I haven't spent enough time with that affinity yet to be excellent at any of the techniques I know. There's been so many other aspects I've had to learn urgently . . ." She trailed off when she realized she was rambling.

Arnekai shook her head. "I *am* aware. But my son puts weight on what you say and how you act. His worry for you is impeding his recovery, and frankly, if I could just knock the stubborn child out and take him back home, he'd heal all that much faster." Her tone was curt, irritated.

"You know he'd fight you every step of the way once he wakes up." Quinn decided blunt was the best way to go.

Arnekai looked at her, like she didn't know what to say, and then burst out laughing. "You do know my son well. Better than I do, it appears." She sighed and walked in, plopping herself down on the couch. Her long arms reached out to either side across the back of the couch as she crossed one leg and eyed Quinn up and down without even an attempt to hide the examination. "I need your help and am not good at asking for it. I wasn't raised that way, and frankly, I didn't intend to raise my son the way I did. It may not seem like it, but I've always only wanted what's best for him."

Quinn took it all in, mulling it over, and realized she was right. She had done what was best for him. As far as the Librarian could figure out, Arnekai had left the rearing of her child to her husband, and after his death, to Milaro. She knew she wasn't the most nurturing, and that she was always busy. The realization softened Quinn's attitude to her ever so slightly. "Perhaps. But I'm not sure he understands it the way you intended it. Probably something you should rectify sooner rather than later?" she asked pointedly. Assumptions did cause so many misunderstandings, after all.

"Note taken." Arnekai let out a sigh and briefly closed her eyes. In that second, she seemed a little older than usual, perhaps almost ageless, and yet completely and utterly timeworn. As if the weight of the universe sat on her shoulders.

In a way, Quinn guessed, it kinda did. In a protecting an entire quadrant from the rampant approach of chaos sort of way, anyway.

The silence became awkward, and Quinn wasn't sure how to restart the conversation.

"Anyway!" Arnekai broke the ice first. "I need you to soothe my son. He's worried about you, and nothing I say belays that fact."

"Soothe him? Like . . . mind-magic wise? You want me to use magic on him?" Because Quinn couldn't think of any other way for her to help calm him. Malakai, as a general rule, didn't tend to listen to a word she said. Telling him to just calm down wasn't going to go over well anyway.

"No . . . not Milaro's tricks. Our racial traits."

Quinn blinked and rubbed her temples. "But I can't use that aura stuff . . . yet."

"You have our distilled essence as well. It should be no problem for you to suggest that my son relax a little more than he has been and to take the sting out of it when you do. He'll be far more susceptible to it coming from you." Arnekai crossed her arms, giving Quinn a pointed look.

First up, Quinn had no idea how Arnekai knew about the distilled essence, although she realized that Milaro probably didn't just kidnap a Darigháhnish and forcibly extract it from them . . . so it'd make sense for their leaders to be aware of the inclusion in the experiment. "I'm not trained in that yet. I'd be wary of using anything if I'm unsure about the results. I'm not going to hurt someone I care about because I blundered with something by rushing it."

She saw that Arnekai was about to object and held up a hand to forestall it. "But I can go and talk to him. He might even listen to me this time."

Arnekai's gaze narrowed and she pursed her lips as if contemplating what Quinn said in earnestness. "That might suffice, but you should have no trouble projecting a calming aura toward people. Soothe them, take away their worries. It makes everyone so much easier to deal with."

"By taking away their ability to have gut reactions? Or instinct checks? Nope." Quinn shook her head. "I'm not condoning that. I'd prefer to be kind, maybe a bit genuine even, and worry about the repercussions later."

"You don't take away their choices; you just help soothe their anxiety." Arnekai scoffed.

And it was in that moment Quinn could see the stark difference between the mother and son. Mal would never use his abilities in that way just to make his life easier for himself, or just to get his way. Perhaps it wasn't out of hand to stop him from worrying enough so he could heal. But she wouldn't feel right about doing something like that. It felt underhanded. "Why couldn't you just do it?"

Arnekai scowled. "He has his defenses auto set against me."

"So you tried?"

"I was talking to him, and it became obvious that . . ." She paused and sighed. "Yes. I did try to make him feel better. It'd just make everything so much easier."

"Did you ever think not everything is supposed to be easy?" Quinn asked softly. "Especially when it comes to people. You can't just push what ails them mentally aside for your own benefit." Not to mention the fact that this was probably one of the reasons that Milaro wasn't so fond of the Darigháhnish elves. After all, Nishpa and Milaro's mental healing was all about consent.

"Easy makes things move faster, and if they're faster, then I can get back to the things that I have to do. My responsibilities don't take a break just because I leave the sector." Arnekai let her head fall into her hands, the tight white braid down her back barely moving as she did.

Quinn wasn't sure what it would be like to be in Arnekai's shoes and hoped she never had to find out. Even though she didn't agree with the elf, didn't mean she couldn't find some sympathy. Especially when it was more directed toward Malakai than his mom. "Look. I'll go check on him. I'll talk to him. But I'm not about to talk him into leaving if he doesn't want to."

Arnekai nodded. "Thank you. It is appreciated, even though I think it'll do little good." She stood up, dusted her hands off on her pants for some reason and headed to the door. "I'll get back to the kitchen then. There are several Darigháhnish concoctions I can cook for him that should make him feel more comfortable in the interim."

Quinn watched the woman go, and Aradie flew to her shoulder, chittering in her ear. "I know, I know. Can't judge every book by its cover. Although maybe in this case . . ."

Aradie gently nipped at her ear.

"Not cool, bird," Quinn said, pulling away. She knew Aradie wasn't fond of being called a bird instead of an owl. In Quinn's mind, they were the same thing, but she could understand it.

With the owl still slightly disgruntled and sitting on her shoulder, Quinn made her way out of the office and toward the infirmary. She was certain Milaro was in there from the way his location pinged ever so subtly through her senses. Ikeshal was still there, so Hal hadn't been yet either . . . she wondered why it was taking him so long to prepare for the satyr and the imp. If she remembered, she'd ask him when he finally did arrive.

The infirmary sat on the other side of Farrow's apparently ever-expanding herb garden. Not for the first time Quinn wondered how the Library fit all that into itself. Not necessarily in a size way, but from the fact that Quinn was fairly certain it should have already pushed into the Library proper by now and it hadn't.

Still . . . its own dimensional pocket, right?

Apparently, it changed all the laws of physics.

The infirmary had evolved since Malakai was injured way back when they had to get the first book from Kajaro. It was no longer two little cubicles, but a series of rooms partitioned by removable walls. It was light and airy and gave a sense of peace with its pale blue walls and the plants Farrow had transported over to it.

Malakai actually sat up in bed, his black and white hair pulled back into a ponytail instead of his habitual braid, his eyes closed and face peaceful. Milaro stood next to him, administering magic of some sort. There were waves around the both of them, if Quinn squinted. Getting used to the whole magical sight thing was still a work in progress. She wondered if she'd ever hit a point where she knew most of what she needed to.

Right now, that seemed like a pipe dream.

Aradie hooted once, soft and calm, announcing their presence without startling the other two.

Malakai's eyes fluttered open, and he gave her a welcoming grin that echoed his grins from the past. He seemed to be doing better from a quick run over him with her senses.

"What brings you here? Did you want to come use me as a shield again? I am almost fixed up. Should be good to go in no time." He winked at her, like he was taking the bite out of his words, but it didn't work.

Quinn still experienced overwhelming guilt that he'd been hit by an attack meant for her, as well as the one for himself. She could practically feel the color drain out of her face as he spoke.

"Shit. Sorry," he said hurriedly. "I was just teasing. I didn't really think."

"It's okay," Quinn said, wishing it really was. He didn't need to be worrying himself about her current headspace on top of trying to heal. That wasn't his problem at all. Besides, she knew once he'd recovered better that she'd be able to give as good as she got. It was just going to take some time.

"You were here not too long ago? Why the long face? What's happened?"

He definitely sounded much stronger now. Finally, for the first time in weeks. Even if it was only because Arnekai was there, it was still a win in Quinn's book. "Just came in to see how you're going, that's all." She was unable to keep the relief from her voice.

His eyes narrowed, and he glanced up at his grandfather, who shrugged before turning away. "Arnekai went to see you, didn't she? Is she trying to convince you to let her take me back with her?"

Quinn shook her head. "I'm not about to intervene in anyone's life in that way when they're perfectly capable of making their own decisions. Don't worry, you get to stay here and worry and stress all on your own."

Malakai laughed quite heartily, and then winced as his body moved a bit too much. "Damn . . . don't make me laugh." The chuckling continued for a few more seconds before he finally sighed. "Look. I'm going to be fine. You do know that, right?"

"You're worried about *me*, though, and that can't be good for your recovery." She spoke softly, unsure whether she should bring it up at all. "I'm going to be finer than you. I mean, I have freaking dragon scales and you're just a Darigháhnish." She winked at him.

"True. That's pretty cool." He nodded at her arms.

Quinn smiled, still proud of her ability to coat herself in her new armor. Or, she guessed, existing armor that she'd only recently learned to harness consciously. There, that was a better description. It could cover her arms, legs, torso, even her feet and neck. It could extend over her face, but she was still having trouble figuring out how to allow room for her eyes, nose, and mouth.

That whole lack of oxygen thing? Bad for her health.

Still . . . being able to manipulate the scales somewhat gave her a level of safety she'd been lacking before.

"You realize I'm more worried about you than you are about me for a good reason, right?" Malakai said as Milaro basically tried to squeeze himself into the wall by the sink to disappear while he collected medications and measured doses, pretending he wasn't fully eavesdropping on every word they said.

"Well . . . I mean, I know you're worried about me, but I'm not sure why? I've been working at solidifying and enhancing the skills I do have before I move onto other affinities. I'm trying to be pragmatic about everything, and I'm not about to go and jump into danger on my own." She'd attempted to be mature about pursuing her abilities. Gaining power in the types she already possessed before moving onto others made complete logical sense in her mind.

"That's not what I mean." Malakai struggled to push himself up into more of a sitting position. "It's not that you can't handle or haven't handled it. That's not the point. The thing is Quinn, have you really sat down and examined how you feel about everything you've been through up until now?"

Quinn stared at him, trying to twine the words into something that made more sense in her mind. Only she then realized it made a lot of sense. Shoved into an extended universe, learning about magic, realizing she was a magical being with genetic code she'd never imagined, being chased by countless people who didn't want her to exist, and dealing with some of them one on one.

It hit her like a bit of a Mack truck.

She stumbled slightly and pulled a chair over to sit down as thoughts began to bombard her. When she'd thought they'd killed Kajaro initially, heck, even before that when she'd had to fight engorged bookworms, carrying it through to the Esposians and the demon tree . . .

"Oh," she said, breathing out. He was right, per usual, which was infuriating. She'd sort of just been going on and on without looking back. Soldiering through everything to just get them to a point where the Library was functional and working as intended.

Malakai didn't say anything but just followed with his gaze, his eyes full of an understanding Quinn now grasped all too well.

Milaro chose then to move. He didn't say anything, nor did he hide his movements, but was suddenly there with a comforting presence, and a steady hand against her shoulder. "Don't forget to breathe," he said, but not unkindly. His tone was filled with a level of compassion that almost brought tears to Quinn's eyes.

A lot had happened. A lot was going to happen.

All she had to do was take it one step at a time, right?

10

SO MANY QUESTIONS

Finding time just to herself since coming to the Library was a chore. A difficult one at that. After a brief chat with the two of them, Quinn headed upstairs toward the alchemical and medicinal beginners section, accompanied by Aradie of course, to do some research, and perhaps just be alone—or mostly alone—with her thoughts for a while.

You should research some of the basic mind healing methods specifically, Milaro had said. And when she asked him why, he responded so logically she almost felt embarrassed for asking. *To help you figure out how the new affinity you established slots into the already existing ones, and how you might best instruct others to pursue it.*

Which brought it all back to her that just over a month or so ago she'd managed to heal Eugea of that horrific dimension sucking tree curse, thus giving rise to the 1723rd affinity. She knew there'd be another few sprouting off it once it got established, too.

After all, that was how affinities worked. They had a main and overarching branch and simply needed to be broken down into different aspects. In this case, it would end up as healing, damaging, halting, and lending coping techniques or something. Maybe, if she was lucky, she could introduce an affinity called Kicking the Butt of Anyone Stupid Enough to Endanger Innocent People.

Quinn enjoyed the balconied second story where she could look over the banister to the Library below. It was often much quieter up here, since the seating areas weren't near the food. She glanced around, noting that only two other people were up here. Then she did a double take. She hadn't expected one of them to be Misha.

Walking over, she stood beside the supervisory golem, who was studying one of the shelves. "What's up, Misha?"

Misha turned, their eyes blinking rapidly as they processed who stood next to them. Or at least, that's what Quinn thought they were doing. "Librarian."

But that was all the answer Quinn got. She prodded again. "What are you doing up here?" She was genuinely curious, after all.

"Retrieving two books that have been requested. Only one of them does not appear to be here, even though the system says it is."

Quinn nodded slowly, not quite sure why they would be doing the work of the shelving golems. Surely, they could just have ordered the construction of others if the workload was too much. Still. "Did you see if Narilin has it? I know she has a heap of books still requiring rebinding, restitching, general repair. A lot of more recently returned ones are in desperate need of a little love and care."

Misha's mouth line frowned. "Perhaps that is it. Ah. Yes." They pulled away and bowed. "Please take care, Librarian. Remember. You must be careful, please. We can't afford to lose you."

And then the supervisory golem was gone leaving Quinn to gape at the empty space as she ran the whole conversation back through her mind. Misha wasn't usually that cryptic or uninvolved. It gave Quinn pause. She looked around the section Misha had been in, but there were only a few books on basic alchemy and some medicinal tonics.

Choosing not to delegate such a task seemed even stranger. "Librarian?"

Quinn spun around to see the other person in this specific division. He was rather cumbersome, always had been, which led her to think there had to be another way to get up to this level.

His smoothed down his hedgehog like spines and the sloth smile always gave her this measure of comfort and control. Carafax was, quite simply, enjoyable to be around. Even if the news he gave wasn't always welcome, he never spoke with such negativity that it could ruin your day.

"Carafax," she greeted him warmly and was rewarded by one of those sunny, lazy smiles he had. "What brings you here?"

He blinked slowly and then smiled again. "There were some books I wanted to check on. While helping Lynx and the Library lately, a few things have come to my attention, and so . . . I did think I might look into them."

"Is there anything I can help with?"

He frowned for a few seconds while giving it apparent deep thought. "Perhaps there is. Would you have time to speak with me right now?"

Quinn paused, but only for a second. She got the feeling he didn't just want to have a random chat. It might have almost been nighttime as per the Library clock, but Quinn could adjust her sleep schedule if this went too late. Not for the first time, though, she wished the Library was a part of a regular solar system so the passage of time didn't feel so magical. She liked it being based on moons and suns and tides and whatnot.

"What can I do for you?" she asked, taking a seat at the table where Carafax had dozens of books piled and notes made meticulously in one of his many journals.

"Ah. Yes," he said, a rare instance of momentary confusion coming over him as he rifled through different journals and finally pulled out one that was, not surprisingly, a deep purple. "You see . . . I've been finding some discrepancies in observations of the Library, and in the matching memories we've retrieved so far."

"How are those memory retrievals going?" Quinn asked, noting that he needed some time to pull himself back together. She waited while he gathered his thoughts, able to see how his mind worked in this flurry of information he had. It was like he had to flip through his own catalogues to find the references inside his brain. Carafax was one of the most fascinating creatures she'd ever encountered. She almost wished she could watch an entire group of Slothilis interact and react together.

"They have become, perhaps needlessly, complex," Carafax drawled out. He blinked as he continued to shuffle through notes and then moved surprisingly quickly to pull his chair up next to Quinn. Leaning forward, he pointed out several paragraphs, all in his tidy handwriting that almost looked like it was printed by a computer to Quinn.

Contradicting timelines of Korradine's presence in the Library.

Several encounters in different instances of the Library.

Example A: Memory of Korradine and Lynx's encounter in the former Librarian's study, while at the same time encountering several people at the check-in desk. Memory components require analyzing and mind healing is needed to delve in close to Lynx's memories and the Library's differing recorded events in order to establish which of these is the real occurrence and which the dupe.

Or perhaps if they are neither.

"Is this frequent?" Quinn asked, grasping that they basically had Korradine in two different places at once if the recollections were correct.

"It is not frequent enough that most people would notice it. However, it is a consistent occurrence enough that I have noticed it." He shrugged and smiled. "But this is something we can investigate in time. I simply wanted you to be aware of it."

Quinn frowned at the information, the documented incidents. There were, once she counted them up, only a dozen of them over what seemed like a couple of hundred years. "Are you always here?" she asked, only just realizing how much Carafax would have had to have been there for him to have these records in the first place. Like she knew he was technically the Library's chronicler, but she didn't think that meant he lived there permanently.

"I'm here much of the time, as is custom. However, I do not, as you are probably thinking, live here permanently. Technically." He gave her a slow wink, and a smile formed to go with it. "I am rather attached to the Library. As most of us are."

Quinn pondered that. She'd realized by now that many of the patrons enjoyed simply being in the Library's presence. There were people who came in day in and day out to be there. Just a handful, but they were there frequently. Others stayed and enjoyed the facilities for a few hours every week or two. But their presence was also felt.

One of the worst things Quinn had come across was this sense of longing for the academy to reopen. People who wanted knowledge, who sought it out, wanted to be taught but had nowhere the go that could provide it for them within their, "hey, I can open a magical door to anywhere in the universe for free" sort of budget.

Quinn got that more than most people would think.

Still . . .

"Did Korradine split herself up frequently, or is one of them really not her?" she finally asked. "I know we've had this suspicion before with Ardenil." Arnekai's aunt had come up before.

Carafax shrugged. "This is what we are trying to figure out now. It will come. In time."

In time . . . that was the component Quinn struggled with the most. It wasn't like they were in a huge rush anymore because they'd bought themselves some leeway by relieving Kajaro of another book and entombing him alive to figure out how he had so many lives to begin with.

Although, in hindsight, that sounded quite macabre and evil.

Quinn wanted to temper it with "but at least she hadn't killed anyone" . . . but in a way, she'd been responsible for deaths. And she knew that before all this was over, she'd be responsible for even more lives.

Those were sobering thoughts. Aradie nudged her head and hooted softly.

"You look like you still have not healed, Librarian." Carafax's tone soothed her, even if the subject matter rankled. After all, it wasn't like she wasn't trying to get a rest in.

"It's not that easy."

"It actually is. If you let it be. Put your foot down. Stop your brain whirring. Whatever it is you need to do to recenter yourself." He pointed at the scales on her arms flicking between blue and a deep purple, with some flashings of gold, before reverting to crystal clear for a moment. "That means you are unsettled. For your magic to be so resistant to peaceably ensconcing you in protection. For it to fluctuate to such an extent means your mind is at odds with your body and the purposes you have brought to the fore of your mind are at a cross ways. You should meditate and figure out the precise direction you are best headed in."

Quinn blinked. She'd heard him speak a lot by now, but his voice currently held such a soft and caring timbre, that it almost brought her to tears. "Thank you. I'll try."

Carafax chuckled as he began to gather all of his things together in a remarkably speedy manner. Once he was done, he spoke again. "I shall leave you to your own devices, but do not overthink things without understanding them or taking actions to rectify or solve the situation before you are ready. All that does is give you a headache."

He tapped his head as he turned and walked away.

Belatedly, Quinn called out, "Thank you." And he bobbed his head in acknowledgement before turning around a stack of books and disappearing from her sight.

Quinn slumped in her chair, quite certain he'd said something poignant, but also that she'd missed the entire point of most of what he said altogether. What she did get from it was that she needed to understand who and what *she* was better than she already did, and once she'd achieved that, then she needed to dig deeper into the mysteries of Korradine and why the hell she did what she did.

Not to mention how they were ever going to deal with the pillar bomb situation.

Leaning back, Quinn gazed up at the ceiling with its moving storyline, much like that of her bedroom. From this level it was much easier to see than down on the ground floor of the Library where the ceiling still seemed so distant.

Her thoughts, unless she consciously steered them away, always went back to the moment Malakai threw himself in front of her.

He'd saved her . . . at least that's what he'd thought, but Quinn was mostly convinced that her scales would have protected her even if she hadn't called them forth. They seemed to have a nasty habit of rescuing her and leaving her loved ones to die. She knew that thought was a little unfair.

She pushed herself to her feet with a soft groan as Aradie launched herself from her shoulder to the top of one of the bookcases. Sitting so much left her stiff, so she stretched before returning to the screen, this time remaining standing.

With the screen in front of her as she worked, Quinn tried to find the mind healing section. It wasn't difficult to locate, considering she had an owl to do it all for her. But there were about seventy books in the section, which she hadn't expected. She frowned, trying to figure out which ones would best work as a basis for her own affinity.

Mental Chaotic Fortitude Abolition

It wasn't exactly a friendly sounding affinity. But it had, in fact, done everything they needed it to do. Now, if she could only rewind and examine precisely what it was she had done, it would all be rosy. She flipped through the books she found, narrowing them all down to the three tomes she'd absorb tonight to help her clarify just how she'd gone about it in the first place. Perhaps it could help her break the steps down.

She piled them on the desk and began going through them. Better to get an understanding of the magic behind what she'd done before she absorbed the information fully. At least, that made sense to her.

The Gonnella Mind Over Maladies Dissertation; Theories of the Brain Core; Similarities Through One Hundred Species: A Comparison, and *Campbell's Guide on How to Eject Unwanted Visitors in Your Brain.*

She got so engrossed in the books that she lost track of time. In this space that was peaceful and lacking in all the hustle of the below level, it was easy to simply switch off and forget about anything outside of herself, the book in front of her, and the information contained within.

It was one of the more pleasant evenings she'd spent in the Library since arriving. The calm that came over her was welcome, and something she'd not witnessed for longer than she cared to admit.

Aradie hooted gently, as if she was trying not to startle Quinn.

"Mm-hm?" Quinn flipped another page. The absorbing of books came with a heady rush and sometimes blinding pain. Call her old-fashioned, but she still enjoyed sometimes just flipping through a book. Maybe she'd be able to go back home and get some ebooks downloaded onto her phone that Malakai had doctored. Reading for leisure and not saving the universe? Now that was something she missed.

Aradie hooted again, more insistently and Quinn looked up, focusing this time. "Oh, what? Uncle Hal is here?"

She pushed herself to her feet, grabbing the books, and dashed down the stairs. He'd saved her more than once and seemed to be the only person who unequivocally told her the truth or didn't mete out information. She needed to see him before he left.

There were so many questions.

11

SIGH OF RELIEF

Hal was about where Quinn thought he'd be. Just outside the infirmary.

She hadn't been expecting him to be deep in conversation with Milaro, but it made all sorts of sense. Reaching out, Quinn located Girilda, the healer who'd helped her when she was poisoned back in Halschius. She was in the infirmary with Ikeshal and Malakai. Quinn frowned and approached the two kings as they huddled in quiet conversation.

They had to have some sort of barrier around the sound, because she couldn't hear anything despite getting close to them. She frowned. Surely there was a way to hear them. She was the Librarian, after all. Maybe they didn't want her to.

Milaro spied her first. "Ah, Librarian. Are you finished?"

She studied him for a second before speaking. "I wasn't too busy to head over and check on Ikeshal's transport process. You could have sent for me." She did her best not to say the last in an accusatory tone, but she might have failed a bit.

Milaro half smiled. "You could also have set a perimeter check for it to alert you as soon as our guests arrived." He said it gently, but it was definitely an admonishment, considering it was something he'd taught her how to do relatively early on in her lessons.

Quinn winced. "Good point. Uncle Hal," she said, inclining her head. "Are you ready for Ikeshal and Eric, then?"

He nodded, his red eyes looking her over in that X-ray-like way he always managed. "Although I must confess, if you have time, there are several things I'd like to run over with you."

She cocked her head to one side, trying to read behind those words, but she couldn't find anything. "I have time, depending on how much of it you want."

"Excellent." He didn't make any attempt to move, but shifted weight onto his other leg, somewhat opening the small circle he and Milaro had formed.

Quinn felt a strange sensation brush her own shielding and knew immediately that it was whatever kept anyone from hearing what Milaro and Hal said. It engulfed her in a sort of cone of silence to only be shared between the three of them. For some reason, she felt oddly underqualified to be a part of this elite club, but at the same time, it was hugely flattering.

"How are things going with Adrito?" Quinn asked, blurting the words out before they'd fully formed in her head. Despite everything the Esposian leader had done, she didn't want him to die the same way Tenejo did back when they attempted to get answers out of him.

She didn't wish that sort of disintegration death on anyone.

Hal shook his head and there was a hint of sadness behind the action. "He's not doing any better. While we've had several cautious and talented mind readers attempt to extract anything useful from him, he seems to be stuck in a time-loop inside his mind that basically involves hunting you down."

Quinn shuddered.

"Don't worry, he can't find or reach you where he is, but he doesn't know that and so he keeps trying." Hal shifted his weight yet again, seemingly uncomfortable in either the response or his stance. She couldn't tell. "Anyway, we're unable to get his brain to focus on anything else, despite the fact that even a millimeter difference in where the arrow is could have killed him. Not to mention the fact that his body has begun to disintegrate due to the spell we still can't find the origins of. We can't stop it, and it isn't completely frozen, just moving at an infinitesimal rate. It's not a pretty situation."

"I didn't think it would be." Quinn couldn't help but feel responsible, considering how much she seemed to be a fixation for this being. But then again, she didn't make the choices he had that brought him to his current predicament. Not that she wished this slow torture on anyone. "What about . . ." She left it hanging. Every time she mentioned the serpensiril's name, she got this horrid overwhelming sense of anger that threatened to engulf her no matter what she did.

It started in the pit of her stomach and tried to devour her from the inside out, to turn her into an angry mass of vengeance. While occasionally it seemed like it might be nice to give into, that wasn't the person she ultimately wanted to become.

Meditation was her next step. While she didn't believe there was another mind bomb attempt planted in her mind, this deep seated and uncharacteristic hatred gave her cause for caution.

Hal still watched her, those wary eyes drinking in every single little thing she did. As if he watched her to make sure she, too, didn't tip over a precipice she couldn't return from. Then his gaze softened ever so slightly. If she hadn't recently spent as much time around him as she had, she probably wouldn't have noticed it. "He is manageable. Still being held in a stasis."

"What good is it to *keep* him in stasis?" she asked, genuinely curious, because leaving him in a state where he couldn't experience anything—let alone the fear and pain she thought he deserved—just didn't seem like a just punishment to her. While she knew she'd initially placed him in it, she'd really hoped they'd have some other sort of way to keep him frozen.

"He's stronger than we'd like, and so it's better to keep him in that state where we can examine his mind and figure out precisely where he belongs in our scheme of rehabilitation." Hal said the last with a wince on the word.

Quinn raised an eyebrow. "You can't be serious, can you? I mean . . . you can't think that rehabilitation is a viable choice for him?"

Hal actually laughed and Milaro rolled his eyes, answering instead of the satyr. "He's not, or at least that's not the aim. But keeping him in such a stasis allows for samples to be taken of his thoughts, his actions, and his current chaotic infection levels for us to see just what it is that makes him able to revive after death."

Quinn nodded this time, trying to devour every word.

"Don't worry, neither are in pain. We've taken care of that aspect."

She wasn't entirely sure she cared either way. Which was something she wasn't yet ready to examine in depth.

Kajaro, in her mind at least, was a being who made no sense. Powerful in his own right anyway, he'd latched onto these other people who had similar but not the exact same ideals. He'd almost destroyed himself trying to kill her and the others, but he'd get to come back.

What they needed to know was how he managed his resurrection. Essentially, she understood their motivation even if she wasn't entirely happy about it.

Basically, he was like an experiment in an ice cube. If he really had nine lives, they'd just have to figure how it worked so they could counter it.

"You know, Imps live for like ever, right?" Eric said from just behind her right shoulder.

Quinn, used to him enough by now that she'd felt the whisper of his presence as it crept up on her while she was lost in thought, didn't even start. She raised an eyebrow without fully turning to face him. "Well, at least I now know you're damageable." She cringed slightly. That didn't even sound like a word.

Eric shrugged and came down from his brief hover to stand on the ground. He seemed so pitifully small when she looked at him there. Usually, when he was practically floating everywhere, he seemed larger than life.

"Don't give me that look," he snapped. "I'll be good as new soon.

Frankly, it shouldn't even have hurt me. But I screwed up my shielding timing by trying to reach it out to Malakai."

His voice faded and for just a second, Eric seemed a bit lost.

"Sorry, but also"—Quinn smiled at him, glad she wasn't the only one feeling like a guilty wreck—"thank you for trying."

"Of course. Who am I supposed to trade insults with if Malakai leaves us? None of you hold a candle to him." While he sounded gruff, it was obvious the imp had been affected by Malakai's close call as well. Probably by the death of the other imps too. She was sure of it.

"Are you about ready to leave?" Hal interrupted them.

Eric shrugged and hovered up to meet Hal eye to eye. "As much as I'm ever ready. Girilda is in with Ikeshal now, right? She can give me a once over and see if I even need to come with you. I've mostly healed . . ."

But he didn't get any further, as Hal reached out and gave a light flick to one of his wings.

Eric screeched in pain and half fell, half spiraled to the ground. "That was unnecessary!" he half yelped out.

But Hal shook his head. "No, it wasn't. You need to take care of yourself and don't overdo it."

Quinn glanced into the infirmary in time to see the healer and Ikeshal working on an exercise she couldn't wrap her mind around. It looked uncomfortable, but he was a satyr and she had no idea how their physiology worked. Maybe they were bendier than their stature gave them credit for.

Girilda frowned and motioned for Hal to come in.

Quinn watched as he walked into the infirmary room, and then skittered over toward Malakai's area. Milaro followed her, touching her elbow briefly before she entered.

"You're not responsible, Quinn. You have this aura of guilt that follows you around. Don't let him think you feel guilty, okay? There was literally nothing you could have done. It was his choice to do what he did." Milaro's tone was gentle, but firm and Quinn nodded.

"I know that technically, but there's a part of me that just doesn't want to let go. I'm afraid if I do . . ." Quinn shook her head. She couldn't think about that. She couldn't explain that her imagination kept running so wild that she worried this part of her life might be a dream, and everyone actually died in the ambush.

Highly unlikely.

But there were so many movies with that sort of twist back on Earth, it was difficult to get the concept out of her head.

Milaro watched her, his brow ever so slightly furrowed with concern. "Is there something you're not telling me? Something I should know?"

She shrugged. "Not really. I just . . . it's one of those things where I'm letting my wild imagination take charge and go off on tangents. It'll be okay. I'll try not to telegraph my guilt. I promise."

Milaro sighed. "It's good that you realize that's what you were doing, but you also need to deal with everything that happened. You haven't talked to me . . . have you at least spoken to the Library?"

No, she hasn't. The Library sounded extremely disgruntled. Put out, even.

Quinn blushed. "I just haven't got around to it."

No, you've been absorbing all the books you can get your hand on and running yourself ragged to heal and try to take care of your friends. That isn't what I'd call dealing.

The Library had a point.

"I'll try to do better once we've got the next branch open." Quinn knew that was a huge caveat, but it was all she was willing to give right then.

She could sense the Library wasn't impressed with her offer, but it was all it'd get for now, so it was willing to accept it for the time being.

Milaro, however, was a bit more outspoken. "Look. I'm here, Malakai is here, Dottie, Geneva . . . there are so many people here for you. Just don't forget that. You don't have to shoulder the whole universe . . . you just have to fix the Library."

Quinn nodded and sensed Hal as he moved away from Ikeshal and approached them.

"Librarian." Hal inclined his head and focused on her for a second.

She felt a rush of heat wash over her, a calm spread as her own fire responded to his.

"There. That's better." He grinned at her. "You keep forgetting the very fundamental abilities I taught you. Focus. Practice your flow, and don't let it or anything overwhelm you. When you embrace fire as the true life source it can be, you'll find a lot of these worries of yours will disappear."

Quinn smiled at him while Milaro scoffed under his breath. "Always with the fire. Damn fire wielders."

"Quiet, Milaro, this is serious. Her magical flow is tempered by her fire. Everything she does is run through those avenues, and these moods she's having aren't going to subside until she learns proper control of the whole element." Uncle Hal turned back to Quinn. "I'd take you with us, but the bulk of my attention will be on Ikeshal and Eric's healing, as well as figuring out how the hell Kajaro summoned that power and manages to keep coming back from the dead."

He held up a hand to forestall her saying anything. "When that is solved, I'll return and we will take time to talk and work on more of your abilities. But I expect you to have practiced everything I've taught you until it's second nature, until you can do it in your sleep, until you can extend it to protect others. And I expect you to have spoken to Dre—the Library about everything going on in your head. Do you understand?"

Quinn nodded.

"Excellent." He clapped his hands and stood to attention. "In that case, I need you to do me a favor and assist with your minor healing as we move Ikeshal and get him ready for transport. To help him keep the pain at bay."

"Got it." She felt so much better with a task to perform. "I'll come back and see Malakai later."

Hal nodded and Milaro appeared to heave a sigh of relief. A part of her mind wondered just why they didn't want her to see him.

But the guilt still eating at her gave her enough of a reason not to ask.

12

SOUNDS SO SIMPLE

Quinn stood at the top of the spiral staircase, looking down toward the core room. She hadn't been there in what felt like an age, even though she knew it had only been a few weeks since they'd retrieved Lynx—after the sequencing for the Library and Lynx's memories was complete. She gazed down for several seconds, and Aradie hooted very softly in her ear.

"No, no," Quinn mumbled, "I'm going down, I'm just gathering my thoughts."

She didn't look at Aradie, but she was fairly sure the owl was giving her a side-eye, which she understood to a certain extent. After all, she'd never felt this level of trepidation before heading down to visit the core. Everything just seemed to be piling on top of one another now, so much so that she wasn't sure where to start. But she knew it'd help to head down there.

Quinn didn't feel like going to the Library's vault. The vastness of that space made her uneasy. This down here felt far more familiar, and right now that was what she needed. Quinn allowed herself to hover ever so slightly and wound down the stairs before reaching the ground and stepping foot onto the sponge-like surface.

This time, the lights all around them were beautiful, like leaves in the winter dipped in frost, blues and whites, the occasional shimmer of green poking through as if some of the leaves overhead carrying the information of the Library were actual evergreens and never stopped blooming. Quinn cocked her head to one side. That was a pretty good analogy, considering that knowledge never stopped growing and evergreens, as long as they didn't get that weird sickness, never stopped being green.

You're in an oddly contemplative mood today. The Library's voice filtered into her head as Quinn made her way across the vast chamber.

"I am," Quinn said out loud. This chamber was the first part of the Library she had seen. In a way, it felt like home.

Aradie still lent a slight weight to her shoulder, a comforting weight at that, something she'd grown used to and didn't want to let go of anytime soon, if ever.

Would you like to use the vault? the Library asked.

Quinn shook her head, glad that the Library wasn't dipping into her thoughts all the time anymore. Frankly, she still wondered whether it could breach her shields; after all, they were intricately connected now. Even so, she thought the mutual respect they'd garnered for each other probably meant that the Library at least wouldn't attempt it to cross that line.

"I don't really want to go into the vault. It's overwhelming," Quinn said. "I'd prefer to just, I don't know, kind of relax."

You find it overwhelming? the Library asked, curiosity hinted at in her voice.

"It's got such a vast an encompassing history that I'm not quite ready to digest." She trailed off, hoping she didn't seem ungrateful. "I need it in bite-sized pieces. Down here is a lot more peaceful."

She could almost hear the Library frown, which was absurd, because how could you hear somebody frown? Still, Quinn waited as she walked toward the central trunk, taking her time as she glimpsed the overhead intricate lines and twigs beneath, and between all of the leaves. The way it depicted a massive tree overhang always fascinated Quinn, considering it wasn't one.

Quinn, are you all right today? the Library asked, as if it didn't exactly know how to phrase the question, without coming across as either inconsiderate, unsympathetic, or downright blunt.

Quinn blinked and looked at the core tree. She cocked her head to one side, and then shook it ever so slightly. "I don't know. Something Milaro said to me has been sticking with me, about the guilt thing, about the aura thing, basically about how I just don't have the control I need to have over all of my abilities, which you'd think after four or so months I'd have, right?" The sarcasm might have made those words heavy.

You're being a little bit facetious, Quinn, the Library said. *But at the same time, you do have a reason to.*

"I know, right?" Quinn said. "Anyway, I wanted to come down here and just absorb some of what being the Librarian is. Every time I come down here, it's like a wave of calm suffuses me. Well, now that you're not blaring alarms anyway, and requiring books ASAP, and all that sort of stuff."

Yes, those were a few harried days, weren't they?

"I swear they seemed like a lot longer than days to me," Quinn said.

Aradie hooted.

Quinn laughed. "Yeah, except for that one world where time was longer and made it run out faster."

Aradie cooed, and the Library gasped ever so slightly.

Really, Aradie? You could have come and found us before you did. The Library sounded oddly irritated. *You didn't have to leave her in my clutches, as you say. Oh, you were tired.*

Quinn laughed, and the bird sort of patted her head with its wing. The more she thought about it, the more motherly the bird seemed to be about her. Protective, and whatnot. Quinn didn't mind.

Maybe you should sit, my dear Librarian.

And Quinn did. She nestled in next to the trunk, in that beautiful little dip that felt like a seat, just made for her, with the spongy floor all around her, and the twinkling lights above her. If she didn't know any better, she would think that she was nestled next to the trunk of a tree, overlooking the entire universe. Although, she guessed, in a way she sort of was.

"I think," Quinn said, "you need to teach me a little bit about me."

Yes, I probably do, the Library said.

And as Quinn watched, the air around her grew thicker, until it coalesced into a shadowy form in front of her, who promptly sat down on the floor, with its legs crossed, and tail whipped around behind it. And this time, Quinn swore she could make out slight horns on its forehead.

"You're very detailed today," Quinn said.

"I'm feeling particularly cosmicisodracusy today," the Library said. "Sometimes, it's easier to remember exactly who I am, and what I am, and what I was before this, if I take on a form similar to my original."

"Similar," Quinn said. "I don't think you had a humanoid form originally."

"No, you would be right. But as more and more species evolved in the universe, it was necessary to blend in a lot."

Quinn laughed.

"Why are you laughing?"

"I don't think Hal has ever tried to blend in a day in his life."

"You'd be surprised," the Library answered and then lowered its voice while leaning forward. "Eight feet. Eight feet is him blending in, Quinn."

"I'd believe that," she said, and suddenly felt more relaxed than she had in ages.

Despite everything going on around her, a calm suffused her. That even though things were kind of crap, they didn't have to stay that way for long. After all, wasn't her magic coming together? She glanced down at her scale-clad body, feeling that security melt around her in the way they protected her. In the way she could activate it with a mere thought these days.

But the guilt began to creep in again, and she couldn't help it. How could she be feeling more relaxed than she had in ages when she had multiple friends injured above her or back on their home worlds? Malakai, Ikeshal, Eric, and Escadril. There were people who'd been injured not precisely because of her, but instead because of what someone wanted to inflict on her, and therefore the Library.

"Don't think about it so hard," the Library said, echoing not only outside but also in Quinn's head.

Quinn could feel her own frustration boiling inside. "I know, I'm just ..."

"You're radiating powerful emotions. Guilt is going to eat at you if you don't start controlling it, if you don't start learning to understand it, and the circumstances around it, and realize that you have nothing to feel guilty for. The people who should feel guilty are those who attacked you, and us, and frankly, tried to destroy the universe and everything we've built to keep it stabilized." The Library's tone was hard.

"You're making perfect sense," Quinn said, "and I hear that perfect sense, but I ... I can't help but internalize the guilt anyway."

"I'd say stop it"—the Library sighed—"but I understand that isn't something always within our control, so instead, I'm going to ask you to also focus on the positives, to focus on the fact that you did stop him, and you put him in his place, and you're healing. The wave of replenishment you spread out to all of your allies in those instances helped save a lot of them. Your shielding helped protect them and gave them added regeneration. You mitigated a lot of the damage that could have otherwise been fatal."

"But it was fatal in some instances," Quinn said.

"Yes, but it wasn't fatal in all of those instances, Quinn, and to be fair, at least one of those instances was directly outside your radius of control. It wasn't even near you." The Library paused and its voice gentled. "I've seen the recollections."

Quinn took a few deep breaths. "True," she said.

The Library refused to let it go and continued. "Some of it has to do with the person who was hit. Let's take Eric as an example. Eric has a lot of his own power. He was able to mitigate the damage himself as well. Your shielding assisted him in that fact. However, the others weren't as lucky. Not all of them have the sort of constitution that enables them to take hits and keep on coming."

"I thought imps were impervious." Quinn could hear the sulkiness in her tone and hated it.

"Well, it doesn't always mean what it means."

"This is really no time to be cryptic," Quinn said.

"Imps are impervious to almost anything. But everything has a weakness, Quinn. You just have to find it." The Library let out a sigh that rippled through the entire cavern. Quinn could have sworn the leaves above her moved. After a second's silence, the Library continued. "Depending on its type, there are acids in this universe that can eat through anything and everything given enough potency and or even time."

Quinn sighed and leaned back against the tree trunk. This introspective analysis of her feelings and her emotions and above all her guilt was not why she'd initially come down to the core, but she was grateful for picking through her errant thoughts with logic. It was starting to prove to her that even though she might have been some of the cause as to why people were hurt, she was also the implement that managed to save most of them. That was something she could work on. That was something she could be proud of and strive for improvement with.

"No," Quinn said, "that works. I can . . . I can work with this. Thank you."

"Anytime. It's not exactly what I'm here for, but for you, I'm here for most things," the Library said. "I'll be busier the more power we gain, but I'm still here."

The shadowy figure leaned back a bit, casting its gaze up to the ceiling, watching the lights. There was barely a glimmer of yellow and red amongst the wide expanse that it covered. It was much more serene now the glimmers of orange and red didn't hail impending doom. Quinn watched until the Library spoke, and then she focused on the shadowy figure.

"A cosmicisodracus, Quinn, is all-encompassing. We are a part of this universe, the first breath of creation, and really, in most cases, except for my brother's, we are magnificent." The Library paused as if it was recollecting something. Quinn could almost feel its smile. "Anyway, what you need to understand is that you have the ability to expand to include all known affinities and any more that enter the universe. You can include new ones, discover old ones, discover surprises and hidden ones. We are now at 1,723, thanks to you. Once you research, I know it'll expand. Our magic automatically purifies and cleanses the chaotic element to protect ourselves from decay, from being . . . I guess regurgitated or reconstituted. We are capable of harnessing chaos for short periods of time, depending on what we're using it for."

Quinn snorted. "Short periods of time? You're, like, ancient and timeless. What's a short period of time for you?"

Quinn could practically sense the Library blink at her as if it hadn't exactly occurred to her that this was a possibility.

"Oh," the Library said, "that's a very good point. Um, I don't mean like short duration, like an hour or two, like you would."

"That's not exactly short either." Quinn laughed.

"Fine, Quinn, stick with me on this. Short, maybe a few years? A decade or so?" the Library offered.

Quinn decided to let it go, despite still finding it comical. "Is that why your brother is so intent on pursuing the chaotic element?"

"I don't know. We were there when chaos backlashed and began devouring itself and everything it had created. It was mayhem, Quinn. It was a disaster. It was horrific. You don't understand what it's like when something gets unmade. It isn't just . . . doesn't just disappear. It reverses itself. It's painful and grotesque and just horrible. It's like annihilation of a soul. Especially en masse. We established the Library specifically to avoid that. Chaos isn't something ordinary beings can control, not in the way that all these people seem to believe they can. These species don't have a sudden aptitude to wield chaos in a new and amazing way. What they have is a desperate hope that by wielding chaos they will somehow change their lot, gain more power, and they've been led to believe this because my brother has, I believe, fabricated the circumstances around my creation and well, the very beginning of the universe."

"So basically, we need to stop them and stop your brother."

"Putting it extremely simplistically, Quinn, yes, and not simplistically, we have to find out who he is working with, if anyone else is involved, and then we need to prove that my brother is lying."

"Oh," Quinn said, "why didn't you say so? That sounds so easy."

13

KNOWLEDGE AND MAGIC

The Library actually chuckled. It was a deep sound that sort of felt like a jolly rumbling in Quinn's belly when it resonated through her. But Quinn hadn't exactly been laughing. She was mostly serious.

"Why is that comical?" she asked. "He's dangerous."

"Yes, yes he is," the Library said, "but he's also just a dragon."

Quinn gaped for a second. She guessed in the view of a universal Library that had its own pocket dimension, referring to him as "just a dragon" was an actual thing. To Quinn, it seemed sort of ludicrous. But she was willing to let the Library have its little idiosyncrasies.

"Okay, let's just say that I'm buying into all of this 'Oh, he's just a dragon' thing that you're doing right now," she said. "Do you have a plan on how we're going to stop this weird cult-like behavior?"

This time the Library sighed again. "Not really. We just have to stop them from destroying me, right? I mean, don't get me wrong. I understand that we need to dig out all the collaborators of Sölem. We need to ensure that they're not trying to enslave or indoctrinate others. And we need to take into consideration if they have any valid points whatsoever to make the knowledge more available to more people."

"I really don't see how you'd do that," Quinn said. "There are . . . I don't even understand how you'd make it more available. Everybody who can access magic can access the Library."

"I know, Quinn, but maybe there's something we've overlooked." The Library sounded far too reasonable and willing to make changes. "Maybe there is something we can do better or more of."

Quinn absorbed what the Library was saying. Things could always be improved, right? "Okay, then. How about we simply make a list, check off, 'don't let them destroy the Library,' 'don't let them keep spreading lies that the Library is trying to hoard all the knowledge for itself,' and then we worry about making sure we're doing everything within our power to make this knowledge we have accessible?"

The Library paused for a few seconds and then the shadowy visage nodded. "That sounds okay for now."

Satisfied that the Library would at least think about doing things in that order, Quinn leaned back against the tree and stretched. "I'd like to know where we go from here."

"Oh," the Library said, "that's easy. You might have your scales under a modicum of control now, but you need more power. More intricate and advanced mind reinforcement techniques above everything. We can't afford for anything to get past your mental defenses. It could be disastrous."

Quinn balked at those words. She'd never really thought about that aspect before. Now it made so much more sense why Milaro was adamant about her training. She turned her attention back to the Library who was still talking.

"Milaro and I have discussed further training for you and the lengths we need to go to. But you'd do best to go over it with him."

The Library paused and gave Quinn a look over. Even without eyes it seemed to be boring into her.

"Cosmicisodracus heritage is also an important piece of your training. There are aspects of why and how your genetic makeup is important, but there are several instances of my memories I still haven't recovered, and I want to make sure I'm addressing everything at the same time with you and not leaving anything out. So we'll leave that for a later date."

"What about synchronization?" Quinn asked. "We've jumped up another power level. Shouldn't we be synchronizing again?"

"Yes," the Library said, "but again, our memories and data haven't completely returned. We're still garnering the effects from the sequencing we went through. Lynx and I need to mesh together first. We must ensure all the data is recompiled and the memories are intact. Until then, we can't make sure that the synchronization will go off without a hitch."

"Well, I mean, it didn't go off badly last time," Quinn said.

"Not according to you. According to me, it was less than ideal considering all the gaps that we had in everything. I don't . . ." The Library paused as if it was mulling over exactly how it should phrase what it was about to say. "I don't want to accidentally screw something up. While we managed to mostly avoid it last time, you and Milaro had several weeks of heightened tension because of the revelation of your heritage. I don't believe we have anything of that magnitude anymore, but before we synchronize this time, if there's anything I feel you should know, I'll tell you beforehand. In order to do that and know that I have a hundred percent covered my tracks, I need to regain all my memories first."

"Oh," Quinn said. "That makes perfect sense."

Aradie cooed as if in total agreement.

"There are, however," the Library said, "a few books that I believe will help you."

"Well, fire them at me," Quinn said.

"*Slifer's Guide to Extending Yourself for the Sake of Others.* This one is about shielding. Since it caused you consternation last time, I wanted to give you a reference guide about shielding for other people and not losing strength in your own shields. I feel like you spread them thin instead of retaining the strength your shield already has for yourself and metering out additional levels for everyone else."

Quinn mulled that over. "I think you're probably very right."

"I know I'm right," the Library said. "I also know when I'm wrong. And while I'm not as eager to admit being wrong, it only helps growth if I can do both."

Quinn raised an eyebrow. "You are being oddly wise today."

"I think I'll take that as an insult," the Library said. "I'd like to think I'm wise most days. Not all, just most."

"Okay," Quinn said. "I'll let that slide."

"Excellent. Next, *Not All Powers Are Equal.* I need you to read this. It's actually one from my vault and it is important that you understand the way the powers were distributed between the different dragons. Not all of our powers are equal and sadly, I have to admit that after me, my brother has some of the most powerful abilities."

"But didn't he basically give you your dimensional power?"

"Yes, in combination with my other siblings. I don't think a day has gone by where he hasn't regretted it."

Quinn wondered what Drevicia's expression would be like right now if she had a true face, because the Library sounded inordinately sad. She suddenly leaned forward earnestly. "It's okay, we're going to fix this. We're not going to let our little dimension be destroyed."

"I know," the Library said and paused a few seconds before speaking again. "Moving right along, let's get to the next book."

It sounded much like the Library just wanted to change the subject, and was trying its best not to dwell on impending doom. "Okay, this one was written by a dear friend. *Mystic's Conundrums of the Mind in Overpower.*"

Quinn raised an eyebrow. "That's a mouthful."

"Yes, it is a bit." It felt like the Library was smiling. "You need to understand that when your powers have built up substantially more than they have now, even though you're getting there, that your mind can almost play tricks on you. Power has its own way of seeding into you, of letting you know that it can do so much for you. Power wants you to take it. It's a . . . I guess a subset to chaos. So just . . . you need to be aware, and this book allows for that."

"Oh," Quinn said, "I wish I could send out a pulse and take in the entire Library all at once." Even with her rising energy levels, she knew that wasn't possible, healthy, or wise in any way, shape, or form. The reaction headache would probably kill her. "Anything else?" she asked, suspicious that there probably was.

"One more. This isn't exactly a book I would usually choose to give you at this juncture, but your energy levels are high enough to absorb it and, well, it's restricted. Very restricted."

"What do you mean, 'restricted, restricted'?" Quinn asked.

"As in, not on display for even normal people who gain access to the restricted section. It's a Librarian- and assistant-only book." The Library evaded an actual answer.

"Come on, spill," Quinn urged.

"*Quetzhal's Grand Scheme of Dimension Manipulation.*"

"What?" Quinn exclaimed. "That's not one of the forbidden ones?"

"No, it's not one of the *missing* forbidden ones. It's not one of the five that Hal entrusted to us because it's a juxtaposing point of view. I just feel that some of its elements might be useful to us when we're trying to, I don't know, prevent dimensional unraveling."

"Oh," Quinn said, "that's all, is it?"

"Yes." It was as if the Library had completely ignored Quinn's sarcasm.

Probably for the best. Quinn stretched against the trunk. "Will I need to go get these books?"

"No, they'll be sitting on your bed in your quarters waiting for you to absorb them. Be careful with *Not All Powers Are Equal,* please. I don't usually let them out of my vault." This time the Library stretched her arms right up into the air and the shadows began to dissipate. "I believe I'm tired," the Library said. "I think I'll delve into the memories I'm currently working on and see if there's anything I've missed."

"You should maybe rest up too," Quinn suggested.

"You know, I've occasionally thought of that. Granted, when the Library is running smoothly and not on the brink of being destroyed by misunderstanding cults, I can often take it very easy. It's almost like a bit of a fever dream nap. I like those. I want those days to return."

Quinn laughed and pushed her feet under her, standing in a fluid motion. She felt rejuvenated whenever she came down to visit the Core, whether it was from the conversation or the energy that pulsed through everything, connecting with her on a deeper level now that she was so aware of everything around her. "Then I'll head upstairs and absorb some books."

"Quinn," the Library said as Quinn began the trek out, "remember, it wasn't your fault."

She nodded. This time, she didn't autocorrect it in her brain because now she realized that even if some of it was, all she had to do was change actions in the future to make things better again. That's all.

Thankful for a little bit of downtime, Quinn made her way straight up to her room, making sure nobody really looked at her, using her aura sense to befuddle anyone who glanced in her direction. Not that she thought people regularly looked in that corner as she floated up the spiral staircase to her level. She knew the quarters upstairs could potentially have assistants coming in and out of them, but that didn't matter.

Once in her room, she noticed the books stacked on the edge of the desk, grabbed them, realizing they were a lot heavier than she'd anticipated, and fell onto the bed with them, spreading them everywhere. She lay there for several moments, simply staring up at her gorgeously carved and moving ceiling. It told stories in a way television didn't, but they never really stayed with her. People coming and getting books, magic pouring out of them, into the world, all around them.

She sighed.

In the last couple of weeks, her abilities had grown even more. She activated her interface and brought up all of her numbers, just to skim through them, just to double-check that she had exceeded three thousand energy, which apparently for a cosmicisodracus was nothing out of the usual, but for a human would have been brain-breakingly unexpected.

Name: Quinn
Age: Irrelevant

Heritage: Earth, Sector 12,942 - Infinite reach, pocket Dimensional adaption

*Species: Librarian**

Energy Capacity: 3,392/3,392

Mana Levels: 2,461/2,461

Alignment: 101%

*Affinities: 1,723***

Tome Knowledge Expanded: Beginner levels 37% complete. Intermediate levels 3%. Advanced - not high enough to calculate.

Affinity Level: 22

Determination: Rising

**Cosmicisodracus properties - still awaiting determination on other subsets*

***As far as the Library can determine*

Scanning the list, she was surprised by a couple of changes, but they weren't entirely unexpected. Still awaiting determination didn't surprise her. The heritage was utterly confusing, and her levels were sort of astounding. She really needed to knuckle down and absorb more. Her two weeks had been spent on controlling the cosmicisodracus shielding and fire power. In understanding her heritage enough not to kill herself and others around her. Now she needed to power up.

She chuckled, loving the softness of the mattress beneath her, as Aradie perched on the head of the bed, looking down at her quizzically.

"I'm okay," she said to the owl who shrugged. "I'm really okay," she said to herself this time, trying to convince her mind to shut up, which was often easier said than done.

Finally, she sat herself up, cross-legged, leaning against the head-board and pulled each of the books to her in turn. The covers were beautifully intricate leather designs, with gorgeous script running across them. She sighed and opened the first, *Extending Yourself for the Sake of Others.* She twirled it around in her hands, looked at the spine and noticed the *I* carved onto the bottom inside a tiny diamond shape. Hmm. She wondered if that meant it was intermediate level. Probably. Data flashed up on her screen in front of her eyes.

Slifer's Guide to Extending Yourself for the Sake of Others
Energy Requirement: 450
Mana Requirement: 270

Definitely, I stood for intermediate, considering the cost of absorption. Intermediate, advanced, master level, legendary level. Nothing out of the ordinary or unexpected if she were to sit down and play one of the thousands of role-playing games she'd witnessed in her life. She'd never been the best about finishing those. Now, she didn't really have a choice. While she'd been aware of them, it still felt sort of strange to think of it in that way, considering all the life-and-death crap she was going through.

It also made her wonder just how much energy it would take to absorb a legendary tome . . .

Quinn absorbed each book after another.

Not All Powers Are Equal
Energy Requirement: 475
Mana Requirement: 280
Mystic's Conundrums of the Mind in Overpower
Energy Requirement: 680
Mana Requirement: 312

That one definitely needed a lot; she popped a couple of energy snacks just to get some of it back before finally tackling the next one.

Quetzhal's Grand Schemes of Dimensional Manipulation clocked in at 1,250. Quinn frowned. That was a lot of energy. Some of these books, for other people, would take a day, a full day, to recuperate that energy. Quinn, on the other hand, regenerated her energy a lot faster. Comparatively, anyway.

Quetzhal's Grand Schemes of Dimensional Manipulation
Energy Requirement: 1,250
Mana Requirement: 508

Knowledge and magic vied in her mind for several moments, leaving her dizzy and exhausted. It was like all the energy had whooshed out of her body. And, in a way, she guessed it had. Almost three thousand energy inside of half an hour hadn't been her most sensible decision. Her eyes began to feel heavy, and she let herself slink down into the covers.

Finally, exhaustion washed over her and she allowed herself to fall asleep comfortably and content for the first time since they'd returned from imprisoning Kajaro.

14

————

IN THEIR OWN RIGHT

Quinn woke the next morning feeling oddly refreshed.

Her eyes fluttered open and took in the beautiful scene above her head. She realized she'd had one of the most peaceful nights of sleep since coming to the Library. She was extremely excited to have woken up in her own bed and not a Kajaro-sponsored dreamscape.

Ever since that fight a couple of weeks ago, it had been one of her biggest fears. She was never entirely sure if, when she went to sleep, she'd truly get to stay inside her own mind. He hadn't touched her physically this time, and now she had formidable mental defenses, so the odds of him planting a second mind bomb were minuscule, but it wasn't impossible.

Plus, he was stuck in a rather large stasis ice cube.

Aradie hooted and fluttered down next to her, nudging her with her head. "Yes, yes," Quinn said, "I know, we need to eat breakfast." Because if Quinn remembered correctly, she didn't eat the night before. Cook hadn't sent them food yet. Perhaps he'd forgotten.

Quinn noticed a small flashing in the corner of her vision and indicated for it to open up in front of her eyes. She was surprised to see that she had several improvements in her abilities.

Mental Fortitude: Level 7

Mental Barrier: Level 8

She frowned. That must have come from digesting that Mystic's book overnight. While much higher level than she'd been so long ago, Quinn still thought she should be stronger. Still . . . was the Library just trying to tell her she never checked her own improvements?

You don't often check on the system's information, the Library said. *I have to do something.*

Quinn nodded to herself. "This is true. Thanks for intruding."

I wasn't intruding. You were broadcasting, the Library said, and left her alone.

Quinn chuckled and got up.

Inside the next several minutes, Quinn had showered, put on fresh, comfortable clothes, and sauntered down to the culinary branch. On her way, she waved at Geneva, who was bustling around with some of the assistants, and she waved at Tim and Tom, the shelving golems. They waved back, somewhat stiffly, but that was their way.

Finally, she made her way into the kitchen.

Cook looked up as soon as she walked inside. Quinn had to double check if she was broadcasting her power like she did when she'd first synchronized with the Library. She knew she'd have to watch out for it the next time they synchronized, but right now, she wasn't letting anything leak out.

"Librarian, it is good to have you here, but I was almost done with your breakfast," Cook said, inclining their head. And she swore she could hear a smile in their voice, even if sometimes it was most diffi-cult to read their facial expressions, given that their face didn't move much.

"I woke up early, figured I'd come down," Quinn replied, and sat down next to the stove where Cook was working. She didn't recog-nize what they were cooking. Not that that was a surprise. There were so many people in the Library these days that somebody might have had specific dietary restrictions that weren't completely covered in the buffet area.

Quinn glanced around and noticed a couple more golems than she'd seen last time. "You have new cooking assistants?" Quinn asked, slightly surprised. But then she remembered that she'd given Misha some permissions way back for simple things like this to make sure that the Library ran smoothly, even if Quinn might be busy.

"Yes," Cook said, "they are surprisingly competent."

Quinn laughed. "I would hope so."

"You would be surprised, Librarian, sometimes not even golems are good at what they are designed to do." Cook gave her a conspiratorial wink, and then went back to their task at hand.

Quinn turned around and really took a good look over this branch of the Library. It was bustling with people. So many of the stoves were in use, with multiple people gathered around them as they experimented and cooked together. Quinn loved this. Sharing cooking was like sharing joy. Everybody deserved to enjoy good food. Or at least Quinn really liked enjoying good food, and she'd share that love of food with anybody she could.

"So," Cook said, plating up and sending out what they'd been cooking with a serving cart, "what brings you here?" Then they cocked their head to one side and gave Quinn a very long look. "You did not eat last night," they added, and sighed.

They quickly grabbed another skillet and began cooking something Quinn couldn't recognize. They tossed and they sprinkled, and it was done so fast that Quinn didn't even realize they were cinnamon donuts until they were sitting on the plate in front of her. She smiled, practically salivating a little bit.

"You always know exactly what I like to eat."

"Yes, but you have a very limited palate, Librarian," Cook said. "Tell me, is there something you are craving to make this feel more at home?"

"Other favorite foods?" Quinn asked. "Oh, I don't know. Can you make a schnitzel, like a rahmschnitzel? It's like a creamy sauce over a pork schnitzel. Or maybe some prawn cocktails. I love a good prawn cocktail. Or a nice cut of lamb, but it has to be cooked just right."

Cook looked at Quinn and blinked rapidly. "I have ascertained those recipes. I will endeavor to make them a part of your regular rotation, Librarian."

Quinn looked at him agape. "Really?"

"Yes." Cook managed to sound slightly affronted that she felt she had to ask.

"I don't suppose you could do a roast pork sandwich with gravy and crackling, could you? I've had it a few times and it's just divine." Quinn hoped she wasn't pushing her luck.

Cook actually laughed. The metallic sound echoed through the kitchen, bouncing off pots and pans as it passed them. Almost like a flurry of bells. "I will do my very best. Just make sure that anything else you enjoy eating, you let me know."

"You've always seemed to know what I might like anyway," Quinn said. "How did you do that?"

"I must admit to having been a little nosy. You used to be very bad at keeping your thoughts to yourself, and so it was quite easy to pluck images from your head when you were hungry. However that is not the case anymore, and so I must ask, because you no longer throw your preferences at me anymore like you used to. Even if it was inadvertently."

Quinn laughed. "The Library kept telling me I was leaking thoughts. I'm glad I leaked some of my food preferences."

Cook leaned in conspiratorially. "You know what? I am also glad that you accidentally leaked some of your favorite foods."

"Thanks, Cook."

"Any time, Librarian. I will send a care package to your office to make sure that you eat properly."

"How did you know I was about to head there?" Quinn asked.

They turned to her as if surprised she asked. "Because you look like you're determined to do something."

"I am," Quinn said, and headed off.

She meandered into her office and sat down, breathing a little more easily for the first time in quite a while. For some reason, absorbing those texts last night, talking to the core, waking up without having experienced one of Kajaro's dream states, and then getting to talk to Cook for a little bit, and request food that she genuinely and dearly missed . . . it all felt like things were sort of coming together after all. Even if she knew a portion of that was simply an illusion.

But she was well-rested and well-fed and ready to tackle the day in the office and things she was sure she was supposed to be doing. Things like talking to Malakai to make sure he understood that she wasn't feeling guilty, to try and make sure that she didn't make *him* feel guilty for making her feel guilty. She needed to speak to Milaro, and to Nishpa. Not to mention she had to go and visit Escadril and speak to the opposing family faction that had her book. And she also needed to take a deep breath, because she was doing it again.

And this time, Quinn didn't need anybody to tell her she was over-doing things. She leaned back in her chair to stretch. Aradie pecked the side of her ear softly, which still, by the way, hurt, before taking off to her perch next to the couch.

"You know, you didn't have to tweak it so hard," Quinn said.

Aradie raised an eyebrow, which Quinn thought was a very odd ability for an owl to have. It was more of an eyebrow ridge or some-thing. Anyway, Quinn pulled her legs up and crossed them in her massive chair behind her desk and sat, closing her eyes. She envi-sioned the way Hal had her work, her fire, through all of her veins, every part of her body, making sure it knew her intricately.

That she, in turn, understood and welcomed it.

Things went a lot smoother when the fire that made up a part of your being didn't feel unwanted.

Fire being dangerous came largely from lack of control as well as intention. And so, practice was key.

It was an absurd amount of space she had to move the element through in her body. Realizing that was when she knew she was stuck in this form for now. The more she learned, she knew that she was literally squashed into the human guise. It didn't feel uncomfortable, though. She just had a lot of blood vessels to send the fire around in, to make sure that it was a part of her, that she could control it, that it would work with her instead of against her. These were very impor-tant acclimations.

She got caught up in it so much that she only vaguely noticed somebody approaching the room. As she ran the fire around in her body even more, she muttered about how everyone seemed concerned about her mental state. Not only the Library and Hal and Milaro, but also Cook and Aradie and the rest of them.

"You know," Dottie's voice came quite unexpectedly.

Quinn opened her eyes and looked down at the bench, maintaining her circulation when she spoke. "What do I know?"

"Well, of course we're worried about you, dear. You are technically mostly a dragon, right? You understand that."

"Sort of, I guess. I mean, I know I'm not human. I'd be dead by now if I was human, but I don't really get it yet."

"Hmm," Dottie said. Quinn was quite certain if she could see Dottie's face, or if Dottie had facial features, then the bench would have been pursing her lips in thought. Probably looking down at her, too.

"Look, you've all got volatile tempers, the lot of you," Dottie said. "That's very important. You need to stay calm and cool and collected. For that, you need your exercises. To make sure you're controlling not only your power, but your temper. We don't want it controlling you."

"I take it that would be bad?" Quinn asked, even though she couldn't imagine a universe where it would be good.

Dottie paused, perhaps for dramatic flair, but probably because she was trying to figure out why Quinn would ask such an obvious question. "That would be very bad."

Quinn nodded. She'd known that was the answer, but at the same time, she'd sort of hoped it didn't need to be foreboding. "How did you know I was thinking about that?"

Dottie actually stopped and swiveled. Quinn could practically feel the bench's eyes narrowing at her. "Well, I'm a superellux futora. I'm not an idiot. I can see. And everything adds up. You're a part of the Library. Sort of. Either way, you're our Librarian, and we need you. So we need you not to set the Library on fire when you lose your potentially volatile temper. If you need help meditating, I'm very good at it, so feel free to ask. But even if you don't. It's something you should try."

"Thanks," Quinn said. "I think I'll take your advice."

"Excellent," Dottie said. "Don't mind me. I just have some things to do so I can help you get the rest of the books for the combat wing."

Quinn smiled. She knew Dottie would take care of herself. Instead, she just let herself go deeper into a trance while she traced all of her mana channels, blood vessels, and each and every ability as it wove itself through her system. This is what her training with Drevicia allowed her to see. She no longer had to act on sheer guesswork. There was a lot of instinct involved instead once she knew her power and affinities well enough.

These abilities were understandable, even if they were complex. And there were so many ways her channels could adjust and morph for specific affinities.

"Yes, dear, you should spend time gathering and centering your-self. Not always gallivanting around and getting into fights, and getting yourself all caught up in nasty stuff that you don't need to be," Dottie advised.

Quinn grinned, her eyes still closed. "Well, I may not need to be, but it helps me in the Library."

"Very well. Do what you like, but I think you should take some time to mesh." Dottie sounded like she might be pouting a little.

Quinn took the advice of relaxing to heart. Even though peaceful downtime didn't exactly seem right to her at that point in time, not when they had so many injuries and so much still hanging over their heads, she did realize that she needed to grasp those moments where she could to center, to recalibrate, and to prepare herself in what little time they seemed to have.

Of course, she'd love to do nothing more than to study books, recuperate, study books, recalibrate, study books, and keep going.

Books, books, books, books, books.

That, technically, was her lifelong dream, sort of. Although she did now realize it had been heavily influenced by her genetics. She'd come to peace with that. She was still who she was. And once the academy branch was open . . . she'd find fiction from other worlds.

They'd be magical in their own right.

Grounding herself, Quinn looked inside again and began building her mental defenses along with what she'd learned in the books she'd devoured the previous night. *Mystic's Conundrums of the Mind in Overpower* had useful exercises in it for basically creating solid steel walls from the barriers she'd put around her mind. It gave them more power, more stability, and allowed for fewer instances where others might attempt to insert themselves into cracks of her psyche. She loved this book. There was a lot that she needed to implement from it.

The other books were good too, knowing how better to shield people, understanding the dimensional shifts that they were about to encounter from a different perspective. They were also extremely valuable sets of information. But they were ones that Quinn still needed more information to fully understand.

And that's when she felt his presence. Her eyes fluttered open as Milaro walked into the room.

"Ah, I thought I'd find you here. Do you have a moment?" he asked. But for once his words weren't light and jovial. Milaro was actually being serious.

"Of course," Quinn said, but intuition told her to brace herself.

15

OFF KILTER

QUINN WATCHED MILARO AS HE STOOD AT THE ENTRANCE TO HER office. It seemed like he wanted to say something, opening and closing his mouth a couple of times before sighing. She waited patiently, sensing that he wasn't quite ready to say what he wanted to, or perhaps more accurately, he didn't know how to phrase what he was trying to say.

He stepped farther into the room and pulled up one of the conference table chairs, which Quinn hadn't even noticed was standing next to the couch. Oddly enough, she thought the Library might have literally just put it there. Not that it surprised her, but it was still very convenient.

"Milaro?" she said cautiously, a little wary of how quiet he was being. Surely that couldn't bode well.

He held up a hand, cocked his head to one side, shook it, and let out a very long "hmm" before Quinn started to feel her stomach tie into knots. It couldn't be bad news, could it? She didn't think she sensed that off him, but she wasn't always the best at interpreting the signals other people gave her.

"Is it Malakai?" she blurted out. It couldn't be him. He was fine.

She'd seen him yesterday, and he seemed fine. Perhaps that was remiss of her. Maybe she should have headed straight there this morning.

"Quinn," Milaro said, his face softened into the usual smile she'd come to expect from him. More of a half-smile this time, really. He obviously had a lot on his mind. "No. There's nothing wrong with Malakai. He'll be fine, eventually. He's coming along well. And while he might need your help in the next several days, once he really starts coming back into his own, there's nothing dire now. And I'm not here to be the bearer of bad news, or at least not that type of bad news."

Quinn cocked her head to one side and said, "I'm not going to like what you're about to say, am I?"

"I don't think it's a bad thing. I just, I'm trying to figure out how to tell you this without insulting you."

"Oh, that's a joy," Quinn said. "Come on, spill."

There were several more seconds of silence that made Quinn extremely irritable, but she knew he'd have a point in the end.

"That, right there," Milaro said, "that's what you need to work on."

All thoughts in her head stopped while they tried to figure out what he meant. "Excuse me?"

"Your irritation levels since you've come back have been peaking. I'm doing my best to make sure your moods don't influence everyone else." He sounded practically relieved to get the words out.

"I got over that after the last synchronization," Quinn said. "Remember, I was sending things flying with emotion. It was bad."

"Of course I remember," Milaro said. "I was there, as were a lot of Library staff and patrons. I'm doing it again. It's not quite the same this time, because it has to do with you juggling your new abilities and the species-related skills you have, and sometimes your emotions get overwhelming. Plus, the Library recently had another boost to its power levels, and right now you're just a little off kilter."

Quinn sat back down. Off kilter was probably a good way for him to put it. She was, after all, still very much in the moment when Malakai had jumped in front of her to save her, and she knew . . . she knew that especially after more than two weeks, she shouldn't be dwelling on the fact that he'd done that, and perhaps be more focused on how she could help him recover from it. But no matter what she did, no matter what thoughts she tried to make herself have, how much logic she threw at it, it was very difficult to shake that in-the-moment fear from constantly coming to overwhelm her.

"You've done a really good job, Quinn." Milaro's tone soothed.

She looked up at Milaro, who was now standing at the edge of her desk. His brow furrowed ever so slightly with worry. She was at least relieved to see that his complexion was its usual creamy sort of color, and didn't appear to be pale in the least.

He continued, speaking very gently. "You'll be okay. I know you will, but you also need to understand that sometimes you might just need to talk to somebody about everything you're going through, even just to get it out of your head."

"I always talk to Aradie," Quinn said.

The bird hooted several times in quick succession, and Quinn groaned. "Fine, you're not my therapist, but you are my owl, and you always listen to me."

Another series of hoots, and Quinn slumped into her chair. "I know you're both right. I just—I'm not very good at talking to other people about my stuff."

"That's okay." Then Milaro brightened considerably. "Maybe do what Carafax does."

Quinn raised an eyebrow this time. "What do you mean, do what Carafax does? Be amazingly intelligent and observe absolutely everything?"

"That would probably help in ninety percent of cases," Milaro said, "but no. I mean, write everything down. Sometimes yelling into a void, or in this case, writing into a void, might just help you process some of the things you've got to work out."

Quinn laughed, and Milaro frowned at her.

"I thought that was pretty good advice," he said.

"Oh, it is," Quinn said, "but you were being very polite about it. I have a lot of things to work out, and work through, and understand. But that's not the only reason you came here, right?"

"No, actually, that was an aside, just because I saw how worried you are about Malakai still, even though we've assured you seventeen thousand times that he's absolutely fine and going to pull through."

Quinn said, interrupting him slightly. "That's not what Arnekai said."

Milaro's face froze for a second. He chose his words carefully when he next spoke. "And what did she say?"

That's when Quinn realized she probably shouldn't have mentioned anything, but she'd gone and done it now. "Well, actually, she just wanted me to soothe Malakai into letting her take him home and heal him."

In Milaro's defense, he didn't actually explode on the spot like Quinn thought he might, but he did get a little rigid and sort of thundercloud-like.

"Milaro?" Quinn ventured. "I didn't mean to cause friction."

He shook himself ever so slightly. "No, you didn't, and it is absolutely fine. We'll be having words. Again. She knows his stance on using those powers in that way. There are perhaps instances where it might be forgivable, but never without consent."

Quinn nodded. She understood that. Taking away somebody's agency wasn't a good thing. If she'd been forced to be here as Librarian without having any choice in the matter, Quinn wouldn't have liked that very much either. She was fairly sure Malakai would despise being removed from the Library to go with his mother after being manipulated into it.

"Anyway," Milaro said, intruding on Quinn's darkening thoughts, "let's get to the real reason why I'm here."

Despite Quinn's best efforts, her stomach still clenched into knots. But at least she knew it wasn't to do with Malakai, so she could wait for Milaro to get his act together and tell her why the hell he'd come to visit her.

"There are some mental warding affinities that I'd like to run through with you," Milaro said. "Even though you have them in an innate capacity right now, I believe it's important to individually identify them. Especially since many of the attacks directed toward you appear to have a large mental component."

Quinn blinked at him. "Why do you think that is?" she asked.

He hesitated with his answer, and then shrugged. "You know, if I were to put a not-too-fine point on it, I'd say it's because you're known to be human. Visually at any rate. Although after the fight with Kajaro, that might have changed, considering your scales weren't subtle about protecting you. Basically, I believe the attacks were aimed at your expected human ancestry. There are several genotypes of humans who are particularly weak against any type of mind intrusion and so it makes sense they'd focus their mental attacks to wear you down."

"But why?" Quinn felt like she was five years old again.

"Because what better way to cause the downfall of the Library than taking control of the mind of the last Librarian?"

Quinn blinked again. Well, that was definitely food for thought for her. "You think we should work through the mental magic affinities? For my defenses, for attacks, for . . ."

"Oh, for everything," Milaro said. "You currently have great defenses and good barriers. However, sometimes you need to do more than just defend yourself. We must take steps so you can use any mental attack as a sort of . . ."

"Booby trap?" Quinn asked.

"A what trap?" Milaro asked, a very confused look on his face.

"Oh, like a trap that I set up, so that somebody springs it and they get like egg all over their face."

"Well, we'd give them a lot more than egg all over their face, Quinn, but yes, that's what I mean. I know you have to leave soon, but I believe if you're visiting Narilin's rival family, the Balisors? You'd be better off arming yourself with a bit more mental fortitude."

"Do they levy mind attacks?"

He shrugged slightly and kind of shook his head from side to side very slowly. "I wouldn't dare to make presumptions." His words were carefully chosen and his tone made it sound like he definitely *was* making presumptions.

Quinn narrowed her eyes. "I'm really confused. Seriously, what?"

He sighed, and Quinn felt a light communication barrier settle over them.

"Oh, like that, is it?"

He nodded. "I think I need to start doing this when I speak to you about more important matters. People tend to read more into my words than I mean. Those interpretations could mean political disaster for half of the universe, but you know . . ." He shrugged.

"You're sounding a little bit stressed yourself." Quinn was worried about him now.

"I am," he said and chuckled. "I really am, but I'm doing my best to take care of myself and the worlds under my care. And the Library, that helps us all. I think we're all allowed to be just a bit stressed."

She grinned. "I couldn't agree with you more," she said.

"Excellent."

"Then this cone of silence?" Quinn offered. She'd always loved that saying from one of her favorite 60s TV shows that she'd watched on reruns as a child.

"Well, it's really more an oblong ellipse of silence, but . . . cone of silence it is. Anyway, yes, Narilin's family is quite prominent on the Salosier's home worlds. The Balisor family of the Feshpa-Alin region are very old blood, very old magic, and don't take kindly to the fact that Narilin's clan has overtaken their status. You'll need to tread carefully because, as you know, the Salosier have an innate ability to affect the moods of those around them. Simply sort of calming them down, not quite the same as the Darigháhnish, but in a very similar manner. Less intrusive, and frankly, doesn't possess the ability to be as manipulative, but be wary of it. It's why I want to work on your defenses . . . I have two books I need you to absorb before you leave there."

"Okay" Quinn took it all in. Ultimately, it just boiled down to her needing more power and knowledge. "Can I do them now?"

"Well, I did ask for them to be brought here." He frowned as he glanced around the office and finally stood up out of his chair. "Although I asked Misha for them a while ago, and they're not here yet."

That was the second or third time Misha hadn't popped up when somebody. Oh, but maybe they only popped up when it was Quinn speaking their name. "Misha?"

But there was no immediate presence of the supervisory golem.

Quinn frowned. "It's okay. I'm sure I'll get the books."

"Sooner would be much better than later," Milaro said, his tone thoughtful. "But I do believe you're about to have a visitor."

"Oh," Quinn said as she felt a wave of presence enter the Library. "Oh, Nishpa's coming."

"Yes, she is." Milaro's eyes narrowed ever so slightly, as if perhaps he hadn't thought she'd sense that.

"Well, she's just going to have to wait," Quinn said. "I want to see Escadril. We need to get the book back from the Balisor clan. But I also need to be able to protect myself, because if anyone can somehow take me over, then the Library and everything in it is doomed, anyway. This needs to take precedence, Milaro. She'll understand."

He smiled. "Very well. I shall fetch those books myself. When we're all done with this, when you've got the books back, when we're opening another branch, you and I need to sit down."

Quinn gulped. "Why?"

"Because you went and discovered another affinity, and you haven't expanded it yet. You know, every affinity has multiple sub-affinities. That's just not how it's done, Quinn."

Quinn smiled. She liked this side of Milaro, the one who got excited about magic and who made little jokes. He'd been far too serious since they returned from the fight. "Okay."

And just as Milaro went to open it, Nishpa knocked on the door.

He grinned at the tiny fairy. "You'll just have to wait. You can't take her quite yet. I have some things to do with her."

"Very well," Nishpa said, and hovered into the room. She alighted on the cushy couch, right next to Aradie's owl perch, and crossed her arms, staring at Quinn the whole time with a mischievous twinkle in her eye.

Quinn wasn't entirely sure what to think about that.

16

DIAMETRICALLY OPPOSED

Nishpa went to speak but stopped. Quinn grew weary of people coming into her office and doing just that.

"What is it?" she asked.

"Nothing really. Milaro can just be hard to track down." Nishpa blinked a couple of times and turned her full attention to Quinn. "I wanted to check and see how you're doing, anyway."

"I'll be okay," Quinn replied. "Still dealing with a lot up here"—she tapped her head—"and a bit in here." She pointed to her heart. "I just got sucked into a magical fantasy world and all I got were book-hoarding aliens that keep wanting to steal my books and destroy my Library and me. In doing so, they hurt a friend, and that's a little bit more than I thought I'd have to deal with as a Librarian when I chose it as a career path."

Nishpa chuckled and Quinn smiled.

"It's good that you can laugh about it," Nishpa said.

"Yeah, if we don't laugh, we'll cry, right?" Quinn replied. "I just . . . it can be hard."

"Precisely," Nishpa agreed. "Just know I have cleared everything with Escadril's family and I've arranged the Balisor meeting too. I'm not entirely sure what the reception will be like, but we'll deal with it."

Quinn nodded. She heard voices approaching. One was definitely Milaro, and the other . . .

"Lynx," she said as he rounded the corner. She paused. He was back in lynx form. He came up to about mid-thigh on Milaro and was animatedly chatting with the elven king. "What brings you here?"

"I was there when he got your books," Lynx said. "I don't know that I agree with him on the books he chose, but he has good reasoning, so I'll allow it."

"You'll allow it, will you?" Quinn raised an eyebrow.

Lynx chuckled, which was a very strange thing coming from an actual lynx. It was sort of disconcerting and yet somehow really cool.

Milaro simply glared at the lynx and placed two very large books on Quinn's desk in front of her. They were both advanced levels. Mental affinities were her strength so far, after all. She raised an eyebrow as she read the names: *Jade's Mental Arithmetic of Prevention* and *Barley's Diametrically Opposed Mental Defense as an Application*.

Quinn frowned. "Diametrically opposed to what?" she asked.

Milaro chuckled. "Trust me, absorb the book and you'll understand. He was the first to jump in with an opposite opinion to everything. This book is him just giving you ways people will circumvent any and all defenses that you put up. However, he also gives examples of how you might overcome and withstand those attacks or even better yet, battle those one on one and win."

"Oh, that sounds really cool," Quinn said.

"It is. Now absorb them. I bought you energy food." He placed two cupcakes on the table in front of her.

Quinn raised an eyebrow. They looked delicious. One of them looked suspiciously like red velvet with a cream cheese frosting. The other one looked like a piece of vanilla cupcake sliced from the heavens with maybe buttercream. If what she was sensing was right. Or she could be totally out of it. She'd always had a good nose, but that would be a difficult distinction to make. She continued to examine them. "These are energy food?"

"Yes. Cook decided you deserved more appetizing energy replenishment balls or candy."

"I won't argue with that," Quinn said, unable to keep the delight from her tone.

"Go on, absorb the books. We haven't got all day," Lynx said, jumping up onto the couch and curling into a ball. His feet disappeared under his body and Quinn was reminded of cat memes again.

"I should, should I?" she said.

"Oh, definitely." Milaro grinned. "They're energy replenishment. So once you start using energy, the regeneration will kick in."

"Fine," she said, and took the red velvet one, eating it in four massive, sweet-filled bites. "Oh, it's so good."

Milaro smiled. "Glad you like it. Now absorb the book. Don't put the food to waste."

She opened the *Mental Arithmetic* book, placed her hands just above the pages, and breathed in the magic, activating it. It went through her fingertips, all through her body. She could feel it igniting every single vein, every single cell. It was different now that she'd learned so much about herself and the way her fire magic moved through her system. It was the same for every single other bit of power she possessed. It needed to know her inside and out so that it didn't accidentally rip her apart when she overused it, or when she almost misused it, which she hadn't done yet. But she knew it was a definite possibility.

It suffused her very being, all the knowledge diving into her brain and finding similarities that she'd already absorbed. Instances where she'd already used mind magic. And it began melding, weaving all the information together. She could feel every single word as it found its place and its purpose within her mind. She couldn't reach for that knowledge yet, but it was there. And it just needed time to percolate, or cook, along with the rest of everything it related to.

Her eyes flooded open as the information came to settle in her mind. She glanced at her energy levels, because she hadn't actually checked before absorbing the book. Which, in hindsight, had been quite ill conceived.

"Wow," she said. "That took a whopping twelve hundred energy, but it's already ticking back up."

"That was a hefty book," Milaro said. "Let yourself regenerate some of that energy."

She nodded, feeling slightly spacey in her head. She could already feel her mind probing elements of her defenses and she began to understand there were cracks in them. Things she needed to build and do and protect better.

"Okay," she said, cracking her neck from side to side. "I think I'm still good."

"Well, you could eat the other cupcake," Lynx said. "I know Cook thought you'd really like that one."

Quinn chuckled. "I think I'll save it."

"Very well," Lynx said. "I wanted to know what it tasted like."

"Pretty sure it's going to be vanilla." Milaro chuckled.

"I'll save some of the frosting for you," Quinn grinned at the feline and Lynx purred in response.

Nishpa simply watched them.

"Go on," Milaro said. "Do the next one."

Quinn checked the energy usage for this one. It required one thousand three hundred, which she had in abundance, and she'd still have several hundred left when she'd finished with this one even if she hadn't eaten regeneration cupcakes. But it was probably best to check the books beforehand from now on.

This time, the energy stung as it rushed through her body. She felt that this book, in particular, was higher in the advanced books and maybe a bit beyond her reach. But she strained with it, she accepted it, and she let the sting soothe her until it faded. That information was even more encompassing and so complex she'd have to sleep before she'd understand what the hell she'd just learned.

"How do you feel?" Milaro asked, leaning a little across the table. His brow furrowed.

"I feel okay," Quinn said. "I just feel a little stuffed, you know, full of knowledge and crap." She shrugged, stretched her shoulders, because she'd started feeling sick and then realized she'd been sitting like that for a while now. "Oh, more time passed than I thought."

"That was one very involved book," Milaro said, in an evasive way that made Quinn think he wasn't telling her everything.

"What aren't you telling me, Milaro?"

"Well, I mean, generally speaking, if you're not yet ready, magic-wise, to absorb the knowledge of a book, it won't actually work."

Quinn blinked at him. "You mean you weren't certain that I'd be able to absorb the information in these books?"

"I was mostly certain you'd be able to. You have come a very long way in regard to your mental magic." Milaro acted like he genuinely thought it was okay.

"To be fair," Lynx added, "I accompanied him for precisely this reason. Just in case."

Quinn glared at them both. It was like they thought Lynx being there made all the difference. "Well, it's happened now. You could have given me a heads up. We've talked about this, Milaro."

He hesitated, and she watched as realization dawned on him and he paled a shade. "Ah, yes, that, that was very uncool of me, wasn't it?"

"Don't do it again."

He sighed. "I sincerely believed you'd be able to do it. I just, there was a very slight chance. Frankly, there's always a very slight chance that you might not be able to absorb it."

"And what's going to happen to me if I try to absorb a book's contents and it only half-absorbs and doesn't work?" Quinn leaned forward at her desk, trying her best not to get too upset. After all, there was no harm done, and yet . . .

Milaro shook his head vehemently. "That can't happen," he said. "That's not how it works. You're either able to absorb them or not. You might get a slight backlash if you can't, but it's not going to be any worse than a few of the headaches you've had from overusing magic."

She nodded. "The lighter headaches, right?"

"Of course! Not the almost collapsing type," Milaro said, looking anywhere but directly at Quinn. She sighed. At least he seemed some-what contrite.

"Are you quite done with her now?" Nishpa asked, perhaps taking pity on the fact that Quinn probably looked like she wanted to smack both Lynx and Milaro's heads together. She was just too short to do so. Milaro glanced at Lynx, who stood up and stretched.

"I believe we're done. She does have to sleep. You know that, right, Nishpa?" Lynx drawled out as he stretched languidly, lightly pawing at the ground.

Nishpa raised an eyebrow at the Lynx. "Yes, I'm fully aware of that. You realize mind healing is quite literally what I do?"

Lynx stretched again and shrugged his feline shoulders. "I'm aware. I apologize for coming across as abrasive."

"You're definitely back to your old self, Lynx," Nishpa said, fondly reached out and scratched behind his ears.

"Don't do that. You know I'm not a real cat," he muttered, even if he sounded somewhat pleased.

"Then stop turning up like one, and I won't have to resist the urge," Nishpa scolded him without any real force.

Lynx stepped back and sat on his haunches on the ground, just below the couch. "Maybe I don't mind it so much," he said. "I'm trying to remember all the kindness. From before we started getting my memories back, I want to thank you. I've learned a new level of appreciation from this whole ordeal."

Quinn had to pick her jaw up from the floor. Well, practically anyway.

Milaro laughed out loud. "It took this to teach you that lesson?"

"You know, I've always just been busy." He practically growled before continuing. "I just didn't have time to . . ."

"Be nice?" Nishpa teased him.

Lynx harrumphed and glared at her.

"And now go back to being busy. Stop running around the Library like you own it."

Quinn couldn't stop laughing. Nishpa and Lynx had a great rapport. It made her miss Malakai.

Nishpa shot her a glare. "Enough from you. We have a lot to do to prepare to leave."

"Yes, sorry." Quinn did her best to sound contrite.

"The Feshpa-Alin region is not the best for humanoid species."

Nishpa looked her up and down. "You, however, can fly. At least you'll be able to hover over the root systems."

"Root systems?" Quinn asked.

"Yes, the Feshpa-Alin region is home to the Salosier and more of their cousins and related species and factions. You, you don't want to accidentally step on an attuned root system."

Quinn thought about the forests she'd been in, like the one they went to when they visited Arnekai in the Darigháhnish region of space. She'd stepped on plenty of roots then. She nodded emphatically. "Right. Hovering it is?"

"Yes. Don't land on anything that isn't specifically marked. Narilin and I will take you over what specific marking means and—"

"Isn't that where you're supposed to be going?" Lynx said, impatience coming to the fore. "I thought you were taking her off our hands."

"Hey!" Quinn said. "Taking me off your hands? Right now, I'd just like to kick you guys out. I could do with a nice little nap. My head feels the size of the Sahara Desert."

"The Sahara what now?" Lynx raised a bushy feline eyebrow.

"The Sahara Desert?" Milaro asked. "Is that—"

"Yes. It's an Earth-ism. It's not even a saying. It's a place. I was just trying to find a comparison. Maybe I should have used the Pacific Ocean."

"Which we also wouldn't have understood," Milaro pointed out ever so kindly.

"Fine," she said. "My head feels like a big old cotton ball, like it's full."

Nishpa frowned. "Well, you don't need much right now. You should probably eat, pack, get an early night, because we'll have to leave in the middle of the night."

"What?" Quinn didn't like the sound of that. "I wanted to sleep in a bit."

"Yes, but we have to get to the Feshpa-Alin region of space, and we have to observe the Salosier start of the day. And if we don't get there before the sun rises for them, then they may take that as an affront.

And we do not—I repeat, we do not want to give the either of those clans any reason at all to take affront to us. So we'll have to leave around midnight here."

"In like eleven hours." Quinn groaned.

"Exactly, and that's why we need to go now. Come on."

Quinn sighed and pushed herself to standing, as Aradie flew to her shoulder. She cooed in Quinn's ear. "Yeah, I know. You better just be able to come with me this time." To which Aradie shot her pictures of beautiful forests with amazing foliage and trees. "Oh, you like it there?" She reached up and scritched Aradie's feathers behind her ears.

"Quinn, come on!" Nishpa called out, already at the door. "We need to brief Narilin and get you ready for tomorrow's departure."

"The Librarians' work is never done," Quinn mumbled under her breath, and she swore Aradie laughed.

BEFITTING MY STATION

Quinn didn't feel like she had time to prepare for this trip. Technically, they'd been talking about going for a few days now, but considering her head felt a bit like mush because she'd absorbed two hefty books, she wasn't exactly with it.

Even as Cook walked her through the different types of preparation food they'd created for her, she couldn't quite focus on what they were saying.

"Sorry, could you repeat that?" Quinn asked.

They paused and blinked at her. "Librarian, are you feeling yourself?"

"Yes, I'm just . . . I'm fine." Quinn shook her head, not entirely sure she was fine. Perhaps overloaded and needed to process information was the better phrase for it. "Just haven't got around to everything I meant to."

Cook studied her for several seconds before nodding. "Then these will help on your trip, should you encounter energy-intensive situations."

"Thanks." She shot them a grateful look.

Cook took that as their cue to continue. "This set of cakes is for your prolonged regeneration - they will give you constant regeneration for five minutes. Do not use more than two of these a day. I don't want you to receive backlash from the ingredients. They are more potent than previous versions." They locked eyes with her until she nodded.

Quinn paused, looking at the two sets of cakes, and gestured to the one on the left. "This set of cakes, the ones with the white icing, not the orange icing."

"Yes, the white icing cakes," Cook repeated, glancing up at Quinn again with what might have been a raised eyebrow if they had them. Like he was going to ask if she was okay again but thought better of it. He then turned to the orange iced cakes. "Anyway, this one is for immediate energy recuperation. These will allow you to recuperate five hundred energy immediately. That is why they are small and compact. Do not take more than five of these a day. They will damage you internally and require that you recuperate for several days if you try to overuse them."

"What about both together?" Quinn asked. "Can I use both of these at the same time?"

Cook didn't answer for a few seconds. "Technically, yes, but I would caution you not to use more than five in total per day just to be on the safe side. And make sure you adhere to the not more than two per day of the white iced ones."

Quinn nodded. That made absolutely perfect sense. Sort of.

"Okay, these are healing tonics." Farrow butted in, pushing several small bottles her way.

"Thanks," Quinn said. She hadn't expected to see Farrow in the kitchen, but it made sense considering that's where Quinn was.

"No problem, Librarian. I must go and attend to the worms." With that, Farrow turned and sashayed toward her domain.

Quinn frowned.

"Something troubles you?" Cook asked.

"No, I just . . ." She shrugged. "It's nothing."

"Your encounter will not be this uncomfortable."

"Pardon?" Quinn asked.

"Your encounter with the Balisors will not be what you think,"

Cook said as they pulled another huge pot up onto their main stove and began to throw things into it, seemingly at random.

"How do you know that?" Quinn asked, hoping Cook had some sort of clairvoyance in his golem makeup. And it sounded a little more ominous than she liked.

Cook shrugged. "Just one of those feelings. Do you get those feelings, Librarian?"

"Sometimes," she said. Maybe Cook was a little more human than she'd originally thought. Poor sod. "Thank you."

"Don't forget to eat dinner. Eat a big dinner," Cook continued, as if she hadn't said anything. Then they continued, practically mumbling to themselves. "You need at least get six hours' sleep before you leave. Preferably more, but I believe there are only about eight until you depart. I do not understand what Nishpa is thinking."

"Well, why don't you just ask her," Nishpa said, suddenly appearing next to Quinn.

Cook turned ever so slightly. "What are you thinking?"

Nishpa glared at Cook and then shrugged. "I'm thinking we've delayed it enough."

"Did you teleport?" Quinn asked suddenly, still trying to figure out how everyone just kept appearing if teleportation was so difficult. Not to mention she'd sort of learned a brief teleport at the very beginning to get out of harm's way, but now she was scared of using it.

Nishpa interrupted her thought spiral. "No, I flittered. I'm fae. You know that."

Quinn blinked. "I do know that. Why are you in a bad mood?"

"I'm just a little frustrated, and I feel like there's a time crunch." Nishpa sighed. "I just finished speaking with Narilin, and she does not currently have time to go over things with us. She said we can do that on the way to visit Escadril. She has three more books to bind before we leave, and won't be sleeping, anyway. Cook, however, is correct. You, Librarian, require sustenance and sleep."

"Yes, apparently I do," Quinn said, knowing they were all right, but still far against going to sleep in what she considered the afternoon and waking up to leave in the middle of the night.

Aradie pulled one of her hairs.

"What?" Quinn said, looking up at the bird. "What is wrong? No, I know I have to sleep. I'm just . . ." A slight wind of calm wafted through Quinn's mind, and she took a deep breath and let it out. *Thank you,* she sent the thought to Aradie.

You really should take better care of yourself. Just go and sleep. The Library can run itself. We will be gone for a few days, and then we will be back. And then you can look at fixing everybody and everything else.

Thanks, Quinn said and turned her attention back to Cook. "All right, can I take my dinner upstairs?"

"Yes," Cook said, "I have packed you a schnitzel sandwich."

Quinn smiled with delight. She could practically taste the food already. "Thank you!"

"With some pommes frites," they added with a half-smile.

"Wow." Quinn was so excited. She reached over and gave Cook's shoulder a very light squeeze, knowing that they weren't exactly partial to hugs. "Thank you again."

"Make sure you drink enough water and get enough sleep." Cook said without looking up from their new pot again.

Quinn took that as a dismissal and headed out of the kitchen.

Nishpa left with her and stopped Quinn as they exited. "I'll make sure you wake up in time, Librarian. Thank you for doing this. While I believe they'd eventually bring the book back, I can't tell you how long it's going to take them. They are stubborn people."

Quinn smiled. "Well, let's just hope they're not 'attack me with a cephalopod,' 'stab me with ice,' or 'plant a mind bomb' sort of people, because, you know, stubborn people I can deal with. Murderous people, not so much."

Nishpa actually laughed. "Very well, Librarian. It is good to see you in great spirits. Go get a few hours' sleep."

Quinn glanced over at the check-in desk, noting that it wasn't exactly busy yet. It assuaged the guilt of not doing Library regular duties all the time. Sleep time was imminent.

Back in her room, she gorged her food down, had a quick shower, and stumbled into bed, paying no mind to her wet hair. She'd deal with that at midnight.

For one of the first times since entering the Library, Quinn fell into a completely dreamless sleep.

Narilin Jenishu-Salosier looked positively ethereal in the dim light of the Library around midnight, Library time. Her willowy form bent in supple ways reminiscent of boughs in a heavy breeze as she swayed to her own stretching routine. Quinn approached the check-in desk, her eyes drawn to Narilin. The Salosier's vine-like hair glistened in the pale light, and the leaves cascaded down her back all the way to the floor rustling ever so slightly with each movement she made. Her green skin seemed almost black in the dim lighting, but her eyes still glowed like a silver lake of mercury.

Quinn often thought the creatures she met while manning the Library were so fantastical she'd never even read about them in fictional worlds. Perhaps she just hadn't been seeking out the right books.

"May I help you, Librarian?" Narilin said without breaking her flow of stretching.

"Nope, sorry. Just appreciating that the dim light of the Library makes us all look a little different." Ethereal and not quite real, was what she wanted to say, but wasn't sure if it'd be taken as a compliment. They didn't need extra tension on this trip.

Narilin paused and turned her gaze on Quinn, raising a very delicate eyebrow. "Do I want to know what you mean by that?"

"No, you probably don't," Quinn said. "I was just having an epiphany."

"Very well, Librarian."

"You seem oddly calm this morning," Quinn said to her, highly aware of the fact that Narilin had never been on the best terms with her. She seemed to blame all the damage done to all the books that required repairing on Quinn, as if she'd been hiding out and waiting for the Library to fall into disrepair before she popped out and saved it.

"Librarian, will . . ." Narilin paused as if she was trying to figure out exactly how to phrase what she was trying to say. "Will we be . . . will this?"

"It's okay, Narilin," Quinn said, realizing they'd both been thinking about their previous encounters. "We're fine. We've always been fine."

Narilin let out what appeared to be a sigh of relief, and Quinn raised an eyebrow. "Is it that unbelievable?"

Narilin shook her head. "No, I just realized that on occasion, I have not behaved in a manner befitting my station. Not always."

Quinn shrugged. "You know I don't always behave like the Librarian."

Narilin laughed, a sound like bells. A lot of things laughed like bells, Quinn thought. Maybe it was just the timbre of the acoustics in the Library. When Narilin finished, she smiled. It was one of the most genuine smiles Quinn had ever seen her give, or perhaps even one of the few smiles Quinn had ever seen her give.

"I appreciate your candor, Librarian. I will endeavor to act my age and be the best book doctor, as you call me, that I can be."

"Excellent," Quinn said. "Now, what do I need to know about these Balisors?"

"Ah," Narilin said, cracking her shoulder, which was a decidedly an odd sound given the wooden nature of her body.

"Are the Balisors envious?" Quinn prodded, trying to get the conversation going.

Narilin shook her head. "Not quite the word I would use. I believe you call it entitled."

Quinn laughed. She'd met entitled people in her life, a lot of them. She'd probably been one before her parents died. "And just what do they think they're entitled to?" Quinn asked.

"Everything, all things, positions, books, information, magical power, magical prowess, everything."

Narilin was about to continue when Nishpa popped into being. "Ah, there you are. Now let us depart."

Quinn blinked. She sent a thought to the Library. *Are you really okay with me going right now?*

You really do need to go, the Library said. *We can't keep delaying the retrieval of books when that retrieval would potentially open another branch. You can't stay here indefinitely, and I can't expect you to hang around waiting for us to gather our memories. If we need you, we'll call you back.*

Quinn grimaced internally.

Oh, the Library continued, as an afterthought, *remember, you are the Librarian. You have access to me and all the information pertaining to the Library, no matter where you are now that our power levels have risen.*

I know, Quinn said.

Yes, but your brain isn't quite trained in accessing the console automatically yet. Remember, if you need to know something, you can easily find it out.

Quinn took it to heart, nodding to herself. Nishpa raised an eyebrow this time. "Are you just about done, Librarian?"

Quinn colored faintly. She felt like Nishpa had just scolded her in front of her entire classroom of people. "Yes. Yes, I am."

"Well then, shall we?"

Quinn glanced around at the Library. There were still dozens of people in it. Far less bustling than during the Library day, but still quite busy with two people manning the other end of the check-in desk. "Yeah." She turned to Nishpa. "I'm definitely ready."

The Furionas nodded once and turned toward the doors. "Let's not keep Escadril waiting any longer."

Magically, the double door in front of the check-in desk swung inward. The crack opened to reveal a beautiful midnight bathed forest wonderland. That's all Quinn could think of. Vines hung down from tree limbs and they moved and swayed. As Quinn stepped through, hovering ever so slightly so that she didn't misstep and fall flat on her face, she glanced at all the vines swinging even though there was no hint of a breeze. She frowned and turned around, looking questioningly at Nishpa.

Nishpa gave her a tight grin. "Very good that you remembered to hover. Do you see this entranceway here?" She pointed underneath them.

Quinn looked down. There was a piece of wood underneath that was about three feet by five feet. Not very large, but not too small. It had a series of runes around the edges. Very simple safety runes.

Nishpa pointed at them. "These are the only areas you may stand on the ground other than houses. Everywhere else, you must hover."

Quinn nodded solemnly and the doors behind her swung shut. With an odd click of finality.

Quinn jumped despite herself. There was something about these woods that set her on edge. Maybe it was the no sunlight shining through the canopy. Maybe it was the way there was no breeze and the vines and leaves moved, nevertheless.

Or maybe it was the odd deep green glow that suffused Narilin and the manic smile that crossed her face.

18

OMINOUS PREMONITION

Quinn wasn't precisely sure what she'd been expecting when they stepped into the Feshpa-Alin region, but seeing the book doctor she worked with on a daily basis glowing as if she'd been irradiated by plutonium or something hadn't been on this week's bingo card. She stopped looking at Narilin, pretty sure her mouth was open like a goldfish. Nishpa poked her and shook her head. Quinn shrugged and gestured towards Narilin.

Nishpa brushed Quinn's thoughts, and Quinn allowed her access to speak to her. *This is a Salosier's homecoming. Narilin hasn't returned for, I do think, about a month. This is the way of the Feshpa-Alin region, recognizing her, welcoming her back, and enabling her to access power that she, well, can't access through the Library precisely.*

Oh, Quinn said, watching as the color suffused very slowly through Narilin's entire being as if it was breathing life back into her. Recharging.

Narilin, she noticed, wasn't standing on the hover or safety pad. She was connected through the entire region by the root system that ran through everything. It clicked in Quinn's head; it made perfect sense, sort of, mostly, because magic surrounded them and the book doctor was tapping into it. *So she needs to recharge, basically, like, you know, recharging a battery of some sort.*

Nishpa appeared to ponder that thought. *Aye, I believe so, if you're meaning sort of like a mana stone that requires you to refill it.*

Yes, Quinn said, *like the ley lines and the pools of mana that need to be refilled now we have the filtration system working properly.*

Precisely, Nishpa said. *You caught onto that rather fast.*

I should hope so, Quinn said. *The idea of replenishing a power source isn't exactly rocket science.*

Nishpa raised an eyebrow, probably not understanding what rocket science was, anyway.

Finally, the color seeped out of Narilin, floating away as if it were fireflies on a breeze.

It was beautiful to watch. The twilight that settled over everything lent the entire forest a surreal deep orange hue. Quinn didn't want to speak; she didn't want to break the spell, and so she waited until Narilin opened those moon-silver eyes and smiled a real smile. All the tension leaked out of the Salosier's body, and she smiled at Quinn again.

"I think I should do this more often," she said.

"You do realize you get days off of work, right?" Quinn asked.

"Of course, I just—I get a bit obsessed," Narilin said.

Quinn bit back her first response, which was *You don't say,* and instead took a very slight breath and said, "You work very hard." See, she could be diplomatic when she tried to be.

Aradie fluffed up on Quinn's shoulder, probably because she could hear what Quinn was thinking since she hadn't blocked her out of her thoughts.

"Shush, you," she sent to the bird, who sort of tapped her with her wing. Quinn would say smacked, but feathers were fairly soft.

"Are you quite ready?" Nishpa asked Narilin who nodded in response.

They began moving, Quinn hovering, aiming for the next board that she could see, probably about twenty feet away.

"I thank you, Librarian, for respecting our traditions and understanding that our way of communication and life force sharing is done through the root systems that bind and sustain us all."

"Of course," Quinn said, not knowing how else to respond, considering it'd be a real crappy move of her to step all over the vines and the roots. And frankly, it kind of gave her the heebie-jeebies, because wouldn't that be like stepping on people's veins and appendages and just whatevers? She shuddered ever so slightly. "Yep, no worries here," she said. "All good with respecting traditions."

Narilin actually chuckled. "It's not too far," she said. "We have many openings that we could use, but that one is the easiest entrance into our domain. That outsiders can safely traverse." Narilin added the latter after a pause.

"Is the canopy this dense everywhere?" Quinn asked.

"Yes and no," Narilin responded. "We require sunlight and other forms of light, depending on which branch of the Salosier we belong to. We do have some moonlight-stimulated segments of our species. However, sunlight aids in photosynthesis. Very often the sunlight can, however, be too strong for us, especially the little ones or the elderly. And the canopy opens as it sees fit to allow the light to filter down."

"So what time is it right now?" Quinn said, looking around. On second thoughts since they'd had to leave in the middle of the night to get there at the right time, she guessed it was already daylight in the Feshpa Alin region.

"We have just passed dawn. It brings a new day. It is the time that heralds new visitors and new information, new life, the beginning of sustenance and, thus, it is the best time for us to receive new visitors into our domain," Narilin said.

Quinn didn't think she'd ever heard Narilin speak quite this much. There was an element of passion in her voice, an element of love and care and pride in who she was and where she came from.

"It shouldn't be too long now," Narilin said, breaking through Quinn's thoughts.

As Quinn hovered to the next platform, she was extremely mindful and careful not to accidentally hit any vines or any other types of plants on her way. She picked her way extremely carefully.

The vines moved of their own accord, too, sometimes swaying out of her way. She almost expected them to blink open eyes or wave at her. The entire forest was alive in ways Quinn didn't want to think about too deeply.

"We're almost there," Narilin said. "Uncle Escadril will be happy to see us."

Quinn followed Nishpa and Narilin carefully as they came upon a large area. It wasn't exactly a clearing because there were still plants and trees and everything, but more of a central hub with different types of short shrub-like trees that might be eight or nine feet tall in the middle of it. From the looks of it, they interspersed the dwellings and didn't rise up into the canopy. The beautiful hut-like houses scattered throughout the massive area, giving it an abundance of life as Salosiers began their day.

"Here we are," Narilin said. "Central Hub 43A."

Quinn raised an eyebrow at the lackluster designation.

Narilin shrugged. "We like books. We do not tend to *write* the books."

Quinn laughed, and they approached a house on the far-left side. It was big and old, she could tell from the way the wood was gnarled and well-worn in places, as if it had stood tall for millennia.

There was a large landing pad directly outside the door. Quinn wondered why they couldn't have just come through this one, but she guessed it might take them into the house proper. That wouldn't be polite, especially with a sick person inside.

Narilin raised a hand and knocked twice. The sound was different than Quinn expected. She thought it would be a rapping, like anybody knocking on a door, but it wasn't. Instead, there was a low booming sound, not earth-shattering or anything, but almost like an intonation of two soft bass drum beats that echoed around them for a split second. It sent a wave of calm through Quinn she wished she could always have.

The woman who opened the door and ushered them in was perhaps a couple of inches shorter than Narilin and therefore just shy of six feet tall. Her bark had a faded quality, almost like a birch tree, sort of soft if Quinn looked at it, really. And that's when she realized that this Salosier was older. Not that it was completely obvious, but she was definitely older than Narilin, probably by several centuries at least.

"Hello, I am Sarila. I am profoundly gratified that you have come to visit, Librarian." Sarila bowed deeply. Her coloring flickered in and out in the dappled light filtered through the canopy. She seemed older, and yet somehow also ageless.

"I wanted to see if there was anything I could do to help," Quinn said, thinking it sounded a little lame. She couldn't help shake the feeling that this person in front of her was more than she seemed.

Sarila watched the Librarian for a moment before responding. The birch elements of her face crinkled slightly when she offered a sad smile, "That is a shame."

"A shame?" Quinn asked, puzzled by the response.

Narilin interrupted, "Aunt, it is not a shame."

"Ah, I apologize. It is *unfortunate*, as Escadril no longer appears to have the ability to heal." Sarila's voice cracked on the last word and Quinn stepped back, quite shocked, yet careful not to step from the stoop onto the roots.

"He's doing that badly? You didn't tell me that, Nishpa," Quinn said, her voice low. Escadril had taken damage, but it hadn't seemed this bad. Surely . . .

Nishpa shrugged. "Would it have made you want to see him any less?"

Quinn shook her head. "No, I just . . . I would have liked to be prepared."

"Understood. I will endeavor to do so next time. I do apologize," Nishpa said.

Quinn nodded, even if she didn't want there to be a next time. She'd even looked up the Salosier physiology and prepared for anything she could help with. "Are you sure there's nothing I could do?" she asked Sarila.

Perhaps the Salosier woman, with her faded pale green leaves and her wonderful slender birch tree physique, heard the sadness in

Quinn's voice. "This was not your choice, Librarian. Please, just visit Escadril as the comrade you are. I know he has things he wishes to share."

Quinn nodded soberly, fighting back a sudden wave of emotions she hadn't expected. She'd known Escadril for a relatively short time, but he'd always seemed very grandfatherly to her, more so than Milaro. Escadril felt ancient and old, like the redwoods in California. Trees that knew and experienced and held onto life at a different level.

They ushered her into the room and she realized they were right.

Escadril sat propped up on what looked sort of like a couch. There were vines and roots reaching in through an open patio door, lending him sustenance, but obviously not enough. He'd always been more rugged than Narilin. Sturdier in build. But now, he was gaunt, and it looked like his bark was flaking off. He crackled when he moved. Like someone had stepped on a dry, hollow branch.

There was no coming back from this.

"Escadril," Quinn said as she approached, trying not to let her voice crack. She wasn't entirely sure she managed to keep the emotion out of it.

"Ah, Librarian," he said, struggling to leverage himself up. His eyes were dull, reflecting the lackluster peeling bark.

"No, don't move," she said. "Please, just stay comfortable."

For a brief second a twinkle shone in one eye, but it was gone almost as soon as it appeared.

"Very well," he said. "Come closer."

And that's when Quinn smelt the faint scent permeating the room like a slow, subtle rot. She hadn't managed to help him. Not at all, not during the fight. He was succumbing to it.

"Never you mind, Librarian. I know what that expression is," he said. His voice was stern, more so than she remembered.

"I'm sorry," she said. But they both knew it had nothing to do with her feeling sorry for him here and, more so, with not being able to do anything during the fight weeks ago.

"Listen, I still have some time. I'm not as mobile, and I will slowly fade, but I have enough time to put my affairs in order." Even as he moved ever so slightly, Quinn could hear the dry, brittle sound of the bark as it broke in more places, accompanied by a soft, putrid scent that wafted into the air as he moved. She knew he didn't have long, not with that underlying odor of rot. But she smiled and nodded.

"I'm thousands of years old, Librarian. You do not need to worry about me." His raised an eyebrow as he continued. "I have lived an amazing life."

She was trying hard not to worry and failing abysmally at it. But still, Quinn nodded.

"I see you do not believe me. Then what I would like to tell you is something of the fight, something that I learned and something that I believe you should know. The Petraligno, the heavier and more robust-barked person that I fought, Itujo, he is of an ancient sect. The Petraligno will not ever be friends to the Library. You cannot trust them. They will infect everything with rot. Any books they lay their hands on, any paper they access, any knowledge they receive, and all manner they touch, their rot will spread."

He gestured to his side, and that's when Quinn noticed the seeping, rotting bark that worked to slowly dissolve his body. She choked back the anger and the sob that she felt, smoothing over her emotions and chose to deal with them later.

Later, when she could channel them into something more productive, when she could use that energy to fuel the next step.

"Petralignos bad. Got it. Excellent." She forced the words out, pushing her anger at the current situation down, and channeled it into forward momentum.

But Escadril's eyes were fierce in their intense gaze. He needed her to listen and so he repeated himself. "Don't trust them. Don't listen to them. And above all, make sure they don't seep into the Library. They're very good at getting in places they shouldn't be. Always watch for the root systems."

Quinn nodded, but she couldn't help the feeling, his words weren't so much a warning as an ominous premonition.

19

____

MANA NODES

Quinn stood in the outdoor kitchen that was a part of Escadril and Sarila's home. It had a clay oven heated by magical means. Probably a good idea in the middle of a forest.

Seats were molded into branches all around the patio, weaving in and out of small well-manicured trees that rose up to give the area its own sense of privacy without totally obscuring the view.

She looked out over the forest at the strange little city in the massive clearing. There were so many Salosier bustling around the place. Despite all of the distractions she could easily take part in, Quinn couldn't quite wrap her head around the conversation she'd just had with Escadril. She hadn't been expecting the conversation to veer to the Petraligno, but in hindsight, perhaps she should have.

That's why he was injured; why he was dying.

She sighed, shifted her weight, and leaned against one of the trees growing out of the benchwork while she watched the bustling tree people. The entire floor of the patio held the markings that meant she could walk on it. She'd been assured standing there wouldn't disrupt the root system.

"You seem lost in thought." Sarila came out and stood next to her, handing her a piping hot drink in a mug that looked like it had been gifted from a tree as well loved wood.

"Thank you," Quinn said, sniffing it. The mug was filled with spices like cinnamon and nutmeg, or at least it smelled familiar, similar to those. They were probably called something entirely different in the Feshpa-Alin region.

Sarila's lean form quietly observed Quinn while they stood there. The Librarian wasn't entirely sure what to think of the Salosier. After all, she was regal in a sense, with a distinct vibe that warned Quinn to keep her at arm's length.

Then again. Not everyone liked much interaction.

"What are you thinking?" Sarila asked, her tone even, almost disinterested.

"I'm not really thinking," Quinn said, still watching everyone.

"Oh, I would say you are, but sometimes it pays to keep our own company," Sarila said turning to join Quinn in watching her brethren going about their day. They sat there for several moments in companionable silence.

"I'm so sorry," Quinn said. Even though she technically knew it hadn't been her fault that Escadril was injured, the guilt kept trying to gnaw its way up her spine.

Sarila shrugged and turned her beautiful gaze on Quinn. "You missed Escadril in his prime. He turned the tide on many battles before so this . . . was a chance for him to relive doing something he excelled at for a good cause. It might not have the happiest of endings, but he has been aging for a long time now. His body has given up the fight, for it has nothing left."

Quinn nodded. "He was pretty amazing, to be honest, from what I could see."

"It will no doubt please him to be remembered that way."

The silence fell over them again, but it didn't feel awkward. Faint chirping held up a soothing melody all around them, echoing through the trees. The low murmur of the voices bustling through the central square area of the city hub drifted over lending a harmonious air to the music around them.

Aradie barely moved from where she was perched on Quinn's shoulder.

"So you must visit the Balisors, is that correct?" Sarila asked, breaking the silence.

"That's what I initially thought we were coming here to talk about," Quinn said, sort of over the potential enemy thing by now. She appreciated that Escadril had shared important information with her, especially since the Petraligno hadn't originally been enemies of the Library. But according to the Library, nobody had ever been on the enemy radar.

She sighed.

Sarila chuckled softly. "You do that a lot, Librarian. The sighing. Sometimes it is better to talk about what ails us."

Quinn laughed. "I apologize. I am a little sad."

"Understandable." The Salosier paused for a few seconds before continuing. Her strange eyes studied Quinn intently. "Anyway, do you wish to ask me questions about the Balisors?"

"Oh," Quinn said, piping up, actually grateful for the subject change. "Yes, I would much like to ask you advice on how to approach them. They know we're coming, right?"

"Oh yes." Sarila brightened up, something like glee in her tone. "The arrangements have already been made."

Quinn nodded. She thought as much. Just as she was about to speak, Nishpa suddenly blinked into existence right next to them. "Yes, we must discuss the Balisors, because we will be meeting them first thing in the morning."

"First thing in the morning?" Quinn frowned. "I guess we get to relax a bit this afternoon?"

"You'll need to. You're still acclimating to the forest, and frankly . . ." Nishpa glanced at Sarila, who gave an almost imperceptible nod. "Let's just say that the Balisor clan is very much a part of the living, breathing forest."

Sarila nodded. "Yes. That is a very good way to put it. They are particularly attached to their roots."

Nishpa frowned.

Quinn, however, raised an eyebrow. "That explains absolutely nothing at all."

"No, it does. They are very integral to the forest," Nishpa reinforced, the frown still on her face.

"No, integral is not what you said. You said they're very much a part of it. Why are they integral? What do I need to know?" Quinn wondered at this point if it had something to do with inter-species politics or was just plain something she might not be able to understand as a different one.

Sarila let out a sigh this time, and Quinn almost admonished her, but decided not to. "We have been rivals for a very long time, and until several millennia ago, it was more of a friendly rivalry. But once our bloodlines intermingled and the Jenishu's powerbase was increased, their resentment multiplied."

Quinn raised an eyebrow. "Is that it? They're sort of upset that they let you marry and have offspring with one of their family members?"

"Yes. You see, our different factions have specific specialties and ours was originally magical book care. But Narilin, especially, can not only heal magical books and repair them with very little preparation, she also possesses growth and nature abilities that allow the nurturing of magical paper, magical tomes. She has a special connection with nature."

It cleared up a lot of reason for Narilin's bolstered demeanor. "But it's not all just for the Library, right?" Quinn asked.

"Of course it's not just for the Library," Sarila said. "It's for everybody. The Library is not the only place that has magical tomes, it's just the epicenter of magical tomes. We all have our own specifically species or clan-based work. But now the Jenishu branch of the Salosiers has possession of both of these talents, while the Balisors connections are tenuous."

Quinn nodded. "So basically, you're just rivals and they're jealous, and they have the book, and because Narilin is the book doctor at the Library now, they want to complain to me about unfair treatment or something?"

"Yeah, that about sums it up, I'd say. But they want to speak to you on their terms." Sarila shrugged. "Slightly childish perhaps, but also more steeped in old traditions."

"Really? Their terms? Traditions?"

"Yes."

"They're trying to hold one of my books hostage, and it's a tradition?" Quinn could feel a hint of anger starting to boil inside. She took a breath and evened out her temper.

Sarila grimaced. "Probably very poor phrasing on my behalf. It's much like a parley of old. They are set in their ways."

"No, that's not poor phrasing at all," Quinn said. "In fact, I think that's just a realistic recap on what they're doing. I need these books to open the next branch, to get the Library more power, to keep the power from reverting to chaos magic, to enable the filters so that we can fix everything that's been broken. I just need the damn book. When can I see them?" Again she had to tamp down on rising irritation. What was it going to take for people to just return the damned books? Reproducing them took so much time.

"Like I said, literally not until tomorrow morning." Nishpa reinforced her earlier statement, her expression thoughtful as she Salosier watched.

"Are you kidding me?" Quinn asked, exasperated.

"Quinn, there are certain aspects of species culture and customs that must be observed. We entered this area as the day rose and thus, we must also enter their domain at the same time."

"Oh, they're not in this city?" Quinn asked, glancing around and not understanding why they couldn't have just opened a door from the Library directly to the Balisor area.

"No, of course they're not," Sarila said. "This is the Jenishu area."

"This is just your family?" Quinn couldn't keep the shock from her voice.

"Well, and extended branches of the family. We have a lot of people in our faction family. We do grow like trees," the Salosier chuckled ever so softly.

Quinn didn't want to correct Sarila that it was growing like weeds because that might imply that the trees are actually more like weeds and it probably be an insult and she didn't want to start an intergalactic incident. She was getting proud of her restraint. "Very well, what do we do?"

"Ah, I thought you'd never ask," Sarila said. Quinn raised an eyebrow, biting back the fact that she wanted to say, *I shouldn't really have to ask; you're supposed to be the host.* Because she'd already learned in all of her contact with Narilin that the Salosier just didn't observe the same sort of niceties as most of the species Quinn had come across so far. They were a little different and that was okay.

"How about we show you around the village?" Narilin poked her head around the corner of the door. "Escadril has settled, and I think it might be nice to just soak up a little bit of home if you are amenable to that, Librarian."

Quinn was relieved to see Narilin because she needed a change of pace. All these little rules and all these little things that she hadn't been told before they'd arrived were grating on her.

"Is Escadril okay?" she asked.

"It takes a lot of effort for him to communicate these days, and he's sleeping now."

Quinn nodded. She couldn't imagine what it was like to watch somebody slowly wither away, especially when they'd been alive for longer than Quinn could even conceive.

Narilin led Quinn through the pretty substantial town. It was a lot larger than Quinn initially thought.

Quinn frowned. "This is fascinating," she said as she got a closer look at everything while she hovered through the area. All the hovering made her feel like she was in a vampire slayer episode. It was difficult to resist the temptation to steeple her fingers as she floated.

The houses were like flower buds except huge. These pods were approximately nine to ten feet tall, and at least fifteen feet in circumference. They had openings in the front like doors and some windows and many gardens out of the back and they were all intertwined in the root system.

Escadril's abode had multiple rooms, but was the same size on the outside as all of these.

Quinn hovered gently over every single place that Narilin led her. Narilin picked her way through the undergrowth. She looked more vibrant than Quinn had ever seen her. The deep green leaves in her hair glistened with a hint of silver now, and her entire visage appeared refreshed.

And she was a lot chattier.

"Over there." She pointed to what looked like an amphitheater. "That's where we have gatherings as well as some theatre productions that the local schools put on."

Quinn gaped at her. "Your local schools put on theatre productions?"

Narilin looked at her. "Well, of course they do. Don't yours?" she asked.

Quinn nodded but had wanted to say *that should have been my question* but she bit back the words.

The canopy opened as they walked, allowing sunlight to filter down to them. It wasn't too hot. It wasn't too cool. It was just right. A faint golden light bathed everything and she watched as flowers unfurled their petals and leaves reached up toward it.

"This is mesmerizing."

Narilin nodded. "This is how we perceive life. Everything is intertwined. Everything is a part of everything else. And here," Narilin said as they rounded a corner—Quinn gasped as Narilin introduced the area—and Narilin continued, "This Quinn, is our mana pool."

Quinn couldn't believe it. She stopped short, looking down to see what could only be an open mana node.

It was covered by what appeared to be a clear membrane, and the node was perhaps fifteen feet below the forest surface, but glistened bright blue up at them, twinkling in the fresh sunlight.

"You have a node in this forest." She breathed out the words.

"We have multiple mana nodes on our worlds. Every world has mana nodes, especially now that the Library is back to filtering at full capacity."

"Well, it's not quite—"

"You know what I mean, Librarian." Narilin interrupted her.

"I know," Quinn said. It was a vibrant brilliant blue and it lent a glow to the entire area. There were seats placed in boughs and little mossy areas. Quinn could see several couples sequestered in them and she turned to Narilin. "Is this like a couple's hangout?"

"Mmm, sort of," Narilin said. "It's a place we can come to commune with everything. Where we can discover our roots quite literally and feed off the magic that surrounds our home. We haven't been able to do this for so long, and if you notice, the node isn't full. But it's a lot better than it has been. Thank you, Librarian. You've given hope back to my people. There was a time several months ago where we didn't think we'd ever get it back. Where we were starting to think we wouldn't make it. Thank you." Narilin's face lit up with a smile, and her silver eyes sparkled.

Quinn blinked and cleared her throat, suddenly feeling ever so shy. She knew she'd put in the work, but being thanked made her realize just what they'd all accomplished. "You're welcome."

They stood there in companionable silence for a several moments.

And then Quinn turned to Narilin with a grin on her face. "Now how about we figure out how to get that damn book back."

2O

BEAM OF LIGHT

As previously discussed, Quinn was not a morning person. It didn't matter if she was in the Library, in her own bed, in somebody else's bed, or in a weird sort of igneous rock formation world. She didn't like getting up in the mornings, and there was simply no exception.

Still, there was a very light chirping in the surrounding canopy that helped ease her into the day. It flowed in time with the slowly waking world around her, like easy listening background music. The vegetation smelled so earthy and revitalizing. Yet Quinn wanted to hunker down in the bed she was sleeping in and stay there, simply enjoying the life around her.

Aradie gave her a light peck on the forehead.

"I know, I know," Quinn said. "Time to get up."

The light hadn't quite sifted through the canopy yet. It was still extremely dark. Fireflies, in a small lantern they could come and go from, were the only light to see by. Quinn thought it was odd and yet kind of cool. Couldn't they just do a light spell? But these fireflies, or firebugs, or whatever they were, apparently seemed to like lighting up the housing for the Jenishu Salosiers. It gave the place an even more magical touch.

Aradie tugged on her hair this time.

"Fine, I'm getting up." Quinn pulled on her clothes and wished she'd have worn something a little more fitting for the rainforest. Still, her leggings and long baggy hoodie would be good enough. She was lucky she could get the Library to recreate her old trusty, comfortable combat boots whenever she wanted. At least she didn't have to wear them in.

She poked her head outside of the door that was her quarters in the oddly larger on the inside little living pod. Narilin narrowly missed running headfirst into her.

"Oh, you're awake, Librarian," the book doctor said.

Quinn took a step back and a deep breath in. "That I am," she said, stating the bleeding obvious.

"We have a quick breakfast for you before we set out. Best not to approach the Balisors on an empty stomach." Narilin, again, was in a light and airy mood. Perhaps it was being around her hometown, or her people, or the magical forest. Quinn thought this mood suited her much more.

The Librarian was a bit apprehensive about meeting these Balisors and wasn't sure eating was the best thing to do. After all, it'd probably sit like lead in her stomach.

She followed Narilin to the kitchen, and was given something very similar to a breakfast burrito back home. There were eggs and mushrooms and other different vegetables all wrapped up in what she thought was a type of feta cheese inside a pita bread. It was divine with its own rugged salsa that gave just the right tang to the ingredients within it.

Another thing to add to Cook's ever-growing list.

"This is marvelous," she said, although it came out more as "fishish-movish" because she was speaking around the burrito. Narilin and Sarila laughed.

Nishpa, however, hovered at the far end of the patio, fluttering with more of a staccato beat to her wings than usual. She looked like she was impatient or in a hurry to get to where they were going. Not that Quinn could blame her. They did have a lot of work ahead of them.

"Hurry up. There is . . ." Nishpa paused.

"Something in the air?" Quinn finished.

"Yes. I don't know what to make of it yet," Nishpa said. She sounded on edge.

Quinn couldn't help remembering the Ishiposa Isle incidents. The gut feelings. She didn't like it when bad things happened. At least in this instance, they weren't here to try and rescue people like Eugea, but that didn't stop the hum of unease from spreading through her as she looked out into the deep uninhabited parts of the forest they'd have to traverse. No, what they needed this time was the *Hunter Guide to Field Dressings* to go into the alchemical wing opening pot.

She sidled up next to Nishpa. "You did eat, didn't you?"

Nishpa didn't show any outward signs of hearing Quinn, but there was a light brush up against Quinn's consciousness again, requesting communication.

What is it? Quinn asked.

We'd be better communicating mind to mind for this trek over the land. Something feels off, and I can't pinpoint it no matter how hard I try.

Quinn studied Nishpa's profile and she could tell from the way her brows pinched together and the slight creases at the corner of her eyes that Nishpa was currently very preoccupied with something Quinn didn't quite understand.

Are you okay? Quinn asked.

Nishpa shrugged and moved finally, or moved her body because her wings had never stopped since she was hovering in place. *Yes and no, Librarian. I am realizing that as I age I will lose more and more friends like Escadril, who I have known since he was a sapling.*

Oh, Quinn said, unsure of how exactly to respond. After all, how did you talk to somebody who was about to lose one of their oldest friends? *I'm really sorry.*

Not your fault. We all die sometime. Well—Nishpa turned to her and flashed her a grin—*maybe not all of us.*

Quinn point blankly refused to consider any of the connotations raised by the Furionas.

"Anyway," Nishpa said, clapping her hands together to get everybody's attention. "Sarila, I thank you for your hospitality. We must set out, lest we offend the Balisors more than we apparently already have."

Sarila laughed. "That is an easy feat. But keep your thoughts to yourselves." And she gave them a meaningful look.

"We'll be careful," Narilin said.

Quinn hovered as they stepped off the patio, used to navigating within the safe zones now. It was easy for her to hover to and from them, alighting very quickly to help replenish some of her energy from the pulse of power the small platforms gusted up. The small group made their way quickly through the forest, past the other end of the mana nodes, deeper into the forest.

As they moved quite quickly, Aradie flew in time with them. Quinn could tell that the vegetation had grown thicker, denser, different. The deeper in they got, the more she could sense an underlying current. The power vibrated through the floor, leaking out toward her, almost as if it was trying to show off.

After about forty minutes of traveling, Quinn stepped to the edge of a sudden massive clearing. The sun was starting to shine through some of the canopy leaves, the occasional soft beam of light hitting a beautiful flower, as if it was aimed specifically.

Which it probably was.

They came to a clearing with what looked suspiciously like a portal. Quinn frowned.

Narilin smiled at her. "This is the aperture. It phases us into the Balisor region."

"Phases?" Quinn asked, curious.

"Not quite a portal as such, but a distance reduction of sorts. Same planet system—easier to travel and stay out of each other's business until we need to." Narilin actually grinned at that.

Quinn nodded and they stepped through.

She stood at the edge of a clearing and took the differences in.

Instead of flower buds, or at least that's what they looked like in the Jenishu section, the Balisor area had what Quinn could only describe as tents out of woven vines, except the tents and the vines moved. They seemed to weave themselves constantly in and out, making living and breathing buildings that set Quinn's teeth on edge.

It reminded her of serpents. And she'd had way too much of those recently.

She glanced at Nishpa, who'd been oddly quiet, both in normal speech and in her mind. Aradie on Quinn's shoulder, made herself smaller again. Quinn could feel a slight shudder pass through her owl, and she glanced over at Narilin who she realized now was hovering and not touching the ground.

Is there something I should know about, Narilin? Some custom? Why are you hovering? Quinn brushed her mind with a thought.

Narilin shook her head. *It's not that. I am not completely compatible with the change in vegetation density that happens at our territory line.*

Quinn nodded. That made sense. It also made the Balisor region adjustment and their rivalry perhaps more dire than Quinn originally thought. Although something occurred to Quinn. *I thought you had some of their bloodline in you?*

Ah, yes, Narilin said. *I have very little of their bloodline, but I do have a lot of their abilities.*

Does it hurt if you touch this ground, if you connect to their root system?

It is more of a discomfort. I am not recognized as Balisor, and thus I am viewed as a, not enemy, but a tolerable guest. There was a hint of something in Narilin's mind overtones that Quinn couldn't quite place.

But we can still step onto the platforms, right?

Narilin nodded.

Quinn was extremely grateful that hovering didn't drain her mana too much, and that the plates placed at intervals helped rejuvenate that same mana and energy supply. Yet she wasn't entirely sure if it extended to this portion of the forest. So she was grateful for having brought the replenishment food Cook gave her with them, and being able to draw on ambient mana for replenishment.

Everything in this area felt darker, more—perhaps sinister was the incorrect word, but it was very close. Quinn couldn't come up with what she meant.

It's very somber, isn't it? Nishpa said, somewhat sadly.

Yeah, Quinn said, *but that's not the right word.*

And that's when Narilin piped up, *I think foreboding is the word you're looking for.*

That's it, Quinn said, tightening not only her own mental shields but extending that to her companions. *That's it, that's the word. Except why?*

Narilin shrugged as they moved very slowly toward the tented city. *Don't know. They do it deliberately.*

Is it a power trip sort of thing? Quinn asked.

Exactly, or probably, at least, Narilin said.

Quinn was wary of everything being darker, that less sunlight shone through, even if it was completely controlled. She also didn't like that they were obviously waiting for a contact of some sort to reach them and yet other than the moving vines and vegetation. There didn't seem to be anyone else awake right now.

The tents felt regal and yet untouchable. Everything about it shouted old world custom, tradition, and pomp. Not exactly any of Quinn's favorite things. Though she did understand cultural significance and rituals, Perhaps that's what this was. But it felt more like a power flex, considering the ever-constant thrum of energy directly underfoot. Underfoot in a way that felt like it was coming directly from a node and being dispersed over the area.

And there were no people getting up to go about their day either.

Quinn was more attuned to the mana than she'd expected. Something she would have to research when she finally got back to the Library. Because she realized all the little vibrations that spoke to her during her day while back at home were trying to tell her things. Because the forest certainly was, she just couldn't figure out what.

Aradie was practically muttering under her breath, in short little coos and hoots, just for Quinn's ears to hear. The vegetation and lack of bird life seemed to get on the owl's nerves. As Quinn noticed, there weren't any birds in those trees. Did they not like the thrum of the power? The cloying scent? Quinn found the air more difficult to breathe here and adjusted her magic to compensate, to help her filter it and make it less thick.

Ripples expanded across the area they stood in, ever so subtle in their presence. But it meant Quinn wasn't surprised when a voice spoke out of seemingly nowhere.

"Ah, our guests have arrived. Let me escort you."

"Well met," Quinn said without batting an eyelash. She tried to position herself directional to the voice.

"You must be the Librarian," the voice said from its still invisible location, even though Quinn tried valiantly to see a body shape of some sort.

"And you are?" she asked, knowing that she was supposed to know who this person was. She was fairly certain she'd learned his name while talking to Sarila but had completely and utterly forgotten it.

Plus, he was being quite rude.

The form stepped out of shadow around the closest vine tent. The older Salosier was young, but significantly older than Narilin. His boughs and his arms and the bark were all redder, with a darker base wood than Narilin's bright and airy feel. It gave off a sensation of wood soaked in blood, not Quinn's forte. It was nothing like the rich walnut of Escadril either.

No, this man standing in front of her had an almost gloomy and resentful vibe to him. Right down to the flowers and leaves that made up his hair. Ironically, considering that the tents were made of vines, his hair branches didn't extend down like the Jenishu she'd met. Nothing as regal as Escadril or Narilin's.

"I am Haritan." He offered a very shallow, barely there bow.

"Hello, Haritan. I am the Librarian," Quinn said. She allowed her scales to flex underneath her clothes, lending her another level of protection just in case. The unease around her was rife with unpredictability.

"Please follow me. Thank you for observing our customs, Librarian. But *you* needn't do so, dear cousin," Haritan said, inclining his head but not offering any eye contact as he began moving.

Narilin, very wisely probably, chose to remain hovering and not utter a word.

"We will bring you to the town hall. Please keep up."

He moved so fast Quinn thought he'd thrown down a keep-up-with-me challenge. But her mana flows had synchronized and helped her avoid any pitfalls. All she had to do was attune her mind to the way the forest moved. This part had a very slightly malevolent intent underneath all of the vines and all of the plants.

But power still sang through it and it called to Quinn. She was a part of the filtration system. It knew her. It knew her magic. And despite what the Balisors might have expected, the base mana of the region also liked her. It sensed her familiarity and recognized it.

Quinn choked back a grin. Suddenly she didn't feel like the weak link and didn't feel isolated from her power base should she need it.

She no longer felt like she was walking into a nest of vipers.

No, now she felt a new level of control and confidence.

And she was going to get the book back whether they liked it or not.

PERSONAL INVITATION

The town hall Haritan mentioned was the largest vine-woven tent in the semi-clearing.

Vines thrashed ever so slightly as they entered. It was as if these living, moving plants could sense the tension in the air. Quinn got a good look around the interior as they walked through the overhanging door.

It was more like an open-aired town hall, almost like an amphitheater, although the chairs and tables that littered the interior were set up in more of a tavern-style. There also appeared to be a serving bar at the other end of it, which gave it a large restaurant meeting room vibe. Two other people stood in the center of the room.

Quinn turned her gaze back to Haritan, who stood with a very slight smirk on his face, like he had gotten the upper hand somehow. Quinn thought to Nishpa and the others, *Have I missed something?* She made sure she directed the thought precisely; it wouldn't do for their unwelcoming hosts to catch wind of their inner conversation.

Somehow even the mahogany tinge that Haritan's body held seemed resentful in some way. It was tempting to try and get a reaction out of him, even if it might not be advisable in a strictly intergalactic political landscape type of way.

If he seemed surprised by the fact that they'd had no problem keeping up with him while he moved rapidly through the forest, Haritan did not let on. He gestured to the other two people.

The first was very slight, and almost as short as Quinn. She was an extremely pale wood, with red hints scattered throughout her bark and wooden skin. But her hair reminded Quinn of the first part of autumn when the leaves were turning that beautiful deep or orangey red. She didn't have the same vibe to her that Haritan did, and indeed not the same as the woman who stood next to her. In fact, the smaller one seemed hesitant at best, terrified at worst.

Haritan didn't appear to notice Quinn's scrutiny, and cleared his throat. "This is my wife, Karella, and my daughter, Irias. We are the head family of the Balisor Salosier faction."

Quinn nodded and inclined her head ever so slightly, while taking in Karella. Karella seemed put out, as if she didn't want to be there, as if she was better than all of them. And she wasn't shy about showing her disdain for being forced into their presence. Not just Quinn's, not just Narilin's, but even her own family's. There was so much to unpack there. Her bark was a mix between the dark red that Haritan displayed and the pale of Irias in a strikingly surreal way. Her hair was short, just like Haritan's, went down to maybe mid-shoulder, the leaves a deeper green, not resembling Irias's at all.

"I'm the Librarian," Quinn said, introducing herself since nobody else spoke up. Nishpa inclined her head, too, and Narilin barely moved.

"We know who you are," Karella said disdainfully, looking Narilin up and down, in a way that could have stripped Narilin's bark if given a chance. Aradie gripped onto Quinn's shoulder, and she intoned several words in Quinn's mind. *They are family, but they are very uneven. There's something off about this. I do not trust these adults' words.*

Quinn smiled in greeting to Karella, while shooting back to Aradie. *Did you classify Irias as not an adult?*

Yes, Aradie responded quickly and definitively.

Quinn couldn't see any books anywhere in the vicinity of where they all stood, which made her frown more. But she did know that everybody seemed to have dimensional storage of some sort, so it was probably in one of those. She was glad her owl was speaking this time. Images weren't going to cut it communication wise here.

"I believe it is best for us to take a seat," Karella said, gesturing to the large table at the front. In hindsight, it looked to Quinn like it had been placed there haphazardly, like perhaps this specific spot was used for something else normally.

Nishpa alighted on the top of one of the chairs, shooting a glance at Quinn. *There's something, can you sense that?* she asked.

Quinn could. Her sensory perception was off the charts. Something wasn't right, either in this room, or in this space. Frankly, since she'd walked through the aperture to get here, something had been bugging her. Quinn believed it was some portion of maybe motion sickness, or travel sickness, because she hadn't actually been pulled through an aperture before in her life. Just the door portals. But the discomfort didn't radiate out from herself, but somehow toward them, underlying everything in this area. She filed that away, keeping it in a section of her mind to be analyzed as they worked through this hopeful book retrieval.

"Anyway," Quinn said, "can we get started? I'd like to hear what your concerns are, and how you might be willing to give me my book back."

Haritan scowled. Quinn had become deft at reading the Salosier expressions, considering her interactions with Narilin hadn't always been favorable. In this case, Haritan was pissed. He seemed extremely disgruntled, angry, things that Quinn didn't understand, or perhaps more accurately, didn't understand why they were directed at her when she'd obviously done nothing at all.

"That's all very convenient, isn't it," Haritan said.

"How is that convenient?" Quinn asked, genuinely curious.

"That the Library has reopened and that we have been excluded yet again." His tone was heated, and his eyes practically flashed with malice.

Quinn glanced as surreptitiously as she could at both Nishpa and Narilin, their voices spoke into her mind.

I have no idea what he's talking about, Nishpa said. *There's always been some rivalry. I don't understand why they feel left out. They've had assistant positions nearly constantly.*

Quinn cleared her throat. "I'm quite certain Lynx sent out the invitation to apply to this region of Feshpa-Alin."

Aradie hooted an affirmative, and Quinn waited to see what their response would be.

Karella sneered, unimpressed. While she blustered ever so slightly as if choosing the right words, Quinn decided to inspect at least Irias. The Library had stressed that she could use the system properly outside of it now. The power boost made all sorts of things work.

Pulling up Irias's information, she realized the Balisor was not what she'd expected. Not her demeanor nor the way she carried herself. There was none of the confidence that Narilin had, none of the arrogance or disdain that her parents had. Something was definitely wrong and making her fearful.

Irias Balisor-Salosier

Age: 198

Ability - Dormant: Current Parameters have not been met.

Quinn inspected her. It came up as Irias Balisor Salosier as expected, but there was something odd apart from the fact that she was almost a hundred years younger than Narilin and not even yet two hundred. She had an ability indication that Quinn had never seen before. What the hell did "dormant: current parameters have not been met" mean? Quinn frowned, making a note of it and saving that information to go over a little later because that was entirely bizarre. Did she have to meet certain conditions before she could unlock her abilities? Although, didn't affinities technically do that?

"What are you talking about? Lynx invited us all." Narilin spoke calmly.

"He did not." Karella practically spat the words out.

"Yes, he did," Quinn said as Aradie nudged her head with her wing, which sent a message flashing across Quinn's screen, confirming the thought she'd had and lending her confidence in her next statement.

"This is one of the regions the initial wave of applications were announced to."

"I refuse to believe that," Karella said. "We received no personal invitations whatsoever."

Narilin actually laughed, and Quinn looked over at her, trying to suppress a groan. That laugh wouldn't get them anywhere in this conversation.

"I did not receive a personal invitation either," Narilin said. "I listened to the system alert informing us all that the Library was reopening, required new assistants with at least three of the sixteen very specific affinities they were searching for. I jumped at the chance to move to the Library because it is what I have always dreamed of, and I never thought I would get a chance because it was gone. There was nothing personal about my invitation!"

Karella paled ever so slightly, which, to be fair, was very difficult to tell considering the different barks that went in to her makeup. Quinn absolutely loved the way the wood grains met with each other in the Salosier clan. It was mesmerizing to behold but it didn't help her to judge their moods. And it was highly distracting right now when she should have been paying more attention.

Haritan cleared his throat. "That isn't possible."

"No, really, it is," Narilin said. "Look, I did not get a hand-delivered personalized application delivered to my domicile. I worked in the central Salosien library. That's when I got the notification. I am fully aware that my mother got one in her house and every other assistant I know of from the library did not receive a personalized one. It was a generic recruitment call send out by Lynx. Why would you think you deserved a personal invitation?"

Quinn grimaced ever so slightly because this felt like "let's avoid their ire" territory. Haritan and Karella did *not* look like the sort of people that you'd want to corner. She couldn't imagine how disagreeable they'd be then, if this is how they'd been so far. She glanced at the information Aradie had so generously shared. "The Balisors were on the list. You got a generalized invitation to apply. No one got special treatment."

Karella turned a disdainful gaze on Quinn. "Isn't it your job to understand who's coming to be your assistant?"

"That's why we had the application forms," Quinn said, unsure what was so hard to grasp about a bloody job application form, "so people could give us their information and enter it in the system so we would know who was applying."

Karella actually looked slightly flustered, yet she still scowled and that ominous feeling, that was the right word.

Ominous.

That sensation still felt like it was leaking ever so subtly from the ground up. Quinn gratefully continued hovering, very glad of her mana regen. She shuddered to imagine the feeling that might give if she was stuck tethered to the ground as a Salosier. It would be seeping into her roots as a part of herself spreading whatever that uncomfortable sensation was everywhere. She glanced down but nothing was visible. There was no miasma, no fog, nothing. Yet another thing for her to observe and replay as soon as she had time to analyze it.

Haritan was already glaring at Nishpa. "And just how did you get back to the Library?"

"Through a door? You know . . . the way everyone gets to the Library." Nishpa actually appeared bewildered by the questions. "What has gotten into you? I have known you for millennia, Haritan— this is stubborn even for you! Even with your stupid feud that you won't let go off, you've always been a more reasonable man."

Haritan took a step back and shook his head like he was trying to clear some fog or something out of it but a darkness stole over his eyes again and he looked up at her, his face twisted in anger. "You know nothing. You don't know me well. I haven't seen you for thirty years."

"Thirty years is nothing in our lifespans," Nishpa snapped at him. But Quinn could tell she was reaching out now, subtly, like a soft breeze, as if she was using her sound waves to try and figure out just what was wrong with the people in front of them.

Nishpa spoke in Quinn's mind. *They've been infected by something.*

How can they be infected by something here? Narilin said. *We're connected through the aperture. If it's here, it should be in my home.*

No, no, I think your wards are more intact than they are here. Nishpa sounded slightly worried. *Make sure you hover, both of you.*

Wasn't planning on touching the ground here anyway, Narilin said. *It's feels wrong.*

In the meantime, Irias was getting paler by the second.

Quinn tried to intervene. "If Irias would like to be a Library assistant, we would love to have her. She'd be a fantastic asset I'm sure. If you want me to personally invite her, I gladly will."

It was the first expression she'd seen from Irias. Her eyes lit up ever so slightly.

But that was the only impression she got from the girl before Haritan moved his fist so fast, Quinn couldn't follow and slammed Irias back into the wall and she crumpled to the ground.

2 2

ROOT SYSTEM

SEVERAL THINGS FLASHED THROUGH QUINN'S MIND AT THE TIME BUT nothing stopped her body from moving automatically. Her scales flashed, extending her shielding to cover Irias from a distance against the next blow coming her way. Haritan's eyes burned with fiery hot anger, turning them black as if it charred away his grip on himself.

It was as if time stopped inside Quinn. She could see the approaching attack, even as she'd managed to position herself between Irias and her attacker . . . her father. Or was he?

No sound could be heard, and it wasn't like earlier when she'd noticed the birds weren't making noise. No this, was different.

It was as if she'd been placed in a moment of extremely slow-moving time, practically frozen while Haritan arranged his next attack.

Quinn could see with such clarity that he was readying a specific spell or ability. She'd still not figured out how to differentiate those yet.

But even though she'd had inklings before, times when she could sense someone was about to attack . . . now, after the last incident with Kajaro, she'd tapped into some of her power, some of her cosmicisodracus heritage.

Slow as molasses dripping down a bottle, Quinn watched as he formed his thought, raised his palm, and readied the attack.

Nothing else stood out to her—because this was what she had to do. They hadn't brought Malakai because he was sick, Lynx was still recovering memories, and Eric was injured. So the bulk of their attack capable force that would usually accompany her on a trip such as this weren't there.

All she had to rely on was herself.

The icicle began to form at the tip of his finger, moving fast into a more arrow like projectile as he fueled more power into it.

But ice was something Quinn knew, and she knew it intimately. Along with water, fire, and mental affinities, they were the ones she'd trained the most. She could utilize every single aspect of ice. From creation, to manipulation, through to destruction and deconstruction.

She didn't even need to speak the action out loud anymore, no, she just needed to visualize the word. Pushing out her own palm abruptly in what would be the direct path of the projectile, her scaled encased her skin in their protective armor even as she formed the word in her mind.

Unmake.

The icicle hovered in the air for but a split second, and surprise flashed across Haritan's face briefly as he no doubt began to feel the backlash. Slowly, over what seemed like an age to Quinn but was probably less than a second in reality, the icicle began to dissolve. From the tip backward along the shaft it melted, dissipating into the atmosphere in a cloud of steam, before time began to move at its regular rate once again.

Suddenly it was as if she'd slammed back into herself, and Quinn dropped into a crouch while maintaining her hover to check on Irias, who still lay crumpled against the ground where she'd landed bare seconds beforehand.

Haritan yelped and raised his hands to clutch at his head momentarily before fixing his red-eyed glare on Quinn and screaming "You!" out in a very unbecoming screeching like sound.

She ignored it, knowing that Nishpa and Narilin would take care of the other two without Quinn even needing to say anything.

And sure enough, as Quinn moved to help Irias, the other two intercepted her parents.

Only Karella batted them away. Out of the corner of her eye, Quinn could see the fury of the woman and realized that she only hadn't come to her daughter's defense because she couldn't move practically outside of time like Quinn apparently could.

"What the hell was that, Haritan? You know how frail she is!" Karella's fingers extended into claws, and the indignation and fury on her face were genuine.

Nishpa stepped back and helped Narilin restrain Haritan instead because his eyes still held no hint of reason in them. And a smokey film rose up from his body. Quinn might have missed it if she wasn't so heavily attuned to there being something amiss, desperately searching for what it was she hadn't cottoned onto yet.

And that was it.

Something seeped into him. Reminds me of that damned tree back when we visited the Esposians. Quinn leveraged the thought toward the other three and knew they'd received it in the way their frames stiffened ever so slightly. So far Narilin seemed fine, and the sensations emanated from the ground, so hopefully that had something to do with it. Whatever it was had warped at least Haritan.

Aradie hooted in Quinn's ear, flashing several different ways she could move the young tree comfortably and safely.

Irias was breathing, her chest slowly rising and falling, but her already pale and red-streaked skin was even paler. It made the red stand out even more. The leaves of her hair gave the appearance of a red carpet of blood behind her head. It wasn't something Quinn wanted her to emulate.

She gathered her shielding and boosted some of her strength to allow herself the ability to lift the slight Salosier up and take her to one of the longer tables on the side of the room. Putting her down, Quinn pulled a pillow out of her storage to give the girl a more comfortable resting place.

Even as she arranged it, she noticed that Irias shivered ever so slightly, so Quinn added a blanket into the mix. She always had one with her, just in case she got cold. Didn't always want to rely on magic —that'd become a handicap and probably be unavailable if she was in a pinch. Granted, if magic was unavailable, then the dimensional storage probably would be too . . .

She could hear Haritan speaking in the background.

"I didn't mean . . . I was just trying to get her to move away from us." He sounded bewildered and slightly lost. Like he was only just coming back into his thoughts, perhaps back to himself.

"You didn't mean to?!" Karella was obviously not letting this go.

Nishpa interrupted her. "Calm it down. This was all unnecessary to begin with. Why you would choose to make such a big fuss over an invitation to be a Librarian assistant is something I'll never understand. Not to mention why you'd hold a Library book hostage! But right now we need to focus on Haritan." The Furionas's tone became soothing and yet stern at the same time.

Quinn knew she could leave the situation in her hands, and that Aradie would provide her with any images of anything she'd missed.

"He isn't usually like that," Irias whispered very softly, so low in tone in fact, that Quinn was certain no one else had heard her.

"Really?" she whispered just as softly back as she used her knowledge of the Salosier anatomy she'd absorbed in order to help Escadril to scan and assess if something more serious was wrong with Irias. She frowned as she discovered a disconnect she couldn't reconcile without further testing. "Does he do this often?"

The discussion behind them was loud, and she could hear the confusion in Haritan's voice even as his pitch escalated. It contained fear, and a strange bewilderedness that Quinn felt went along with something else. It was like he hadn't been aware of what he was doing when he did it.

Irias finally opened her brilliantly red eyes, but it wasn't the type of red her fathers had been briefly. That was of charred meat, with blackened edges. No, hers was of the ever-changing autumn leaves as they detached and floated down to greet the rest. Hers was soft, whereas her father's hadn't been quite right.

"I am sorry." Irias's eyes flickered toward where Karella was still speaking loudly, deriding her father. The young Salosier sighed. "This is . . . something we should not really be showing the rest of the world, but they are unable to hide their dislike for each other on top of everything."

"They seem to like you well enough," Quinn said, watching Irias' face to gauge her reaction.

"Perhaps." The girl paused, her gaze hardening. "My father didn't strike me. It just looked like he did. That thing . . . it's been in there for years now and it's becoming stronger and keeping him at bay. He's not the man he was fifty years ago. The change . . ."

She cleared her throat and composed herself as her voice had begun to quaver. Then she continued, her whisper stronger now. "The change began decades ago, but now . . . it is almost complete. There have been a lot of changes. I don't have the affinities or abilities to check what is wrong with him, and no one listens to me when I speak."

Quinn nodded. "You should rest. Do you have pain anywhere?"

"My head, but I have initiated my healing failsafes, and it is already subsiding. Once I regain my strength, it will be taken care of."

"Then let yourself rest and recuperate for a bit." Quinn thought Irias had an odd way of speaking. She seemed to have been sheltered.

Irias held Quinn's gaze and slowly nodded before closing her eyes. Quinn watched for a few seconds before turning her attention back to the others. *Aradie will stay here with Irias.* The bird hooted into Quinn's ear ever so softly and gently. She reached up and scritched the owl's neck.

These people are infected with something. Nishpa said, stating what Quinn would have thought of as obvious.

It's more than that. Narilin still held Haritan back, proving to Quinn she was far stronger than the Librarian had ever given her credit for.

How do you mean more than that?

Narilin's eyes never left her charge, just as Nishpa focused on keeping herself between the two Balisors. *It's not an infection, it's an intrusion. As if it's gone in through the root system here in this section. I still can't hear anyone else either. There doesn't seem to be anyone around. No other signs of life right now and if you recall, very unlike the Jenishu side of the aperture where we always have people running around. This here is stiller than I'd expected, even though I know for a fact they don't function with the same camaraderie as we do, there should be . . . others.*

Quinn reached out her senses even farther than their default and realized just how right Narilin was. She frowned, still listening to the batshit argument Haritan and Karella were having, and started wondering if they were trying to lull them into a false sense of security.

Aradie flashed images in front of Quinn's mind. Of Irias's color returning, and of how her feet no longer touched the ground. The young Balisor's breathing was stable, and she seemed to be slumbering now that most of the pain was gone.

But what Quinn noticed was her lack of being attached to the root system. Her color was returning, and if Quinn wasn't mistaken, it seemed her strength was too.

Whatever seeped into the undergrowth here was sucking the life out of the people, and out of the grove.

Quinn moved quickly to where the other two hovered and wracked her brains for a split second before deciding to just do it. "I'm going to do something now to help us help you."

"What do you mean help us!" Karella snapped, "I don't need a human like you helping us!"

It made Quinn wonder if the woman had seen Quinn's scales earlier and just refused to acknowledge them, or if she was just oblivious. Then again, her scales did pass through their colors fairly fast. "Yeah, actually, you kind of do."

Before Karella could say anything else, Quinn detached them from their direct connection into the root system of this Balisor region. It took a lot more intricate power than she'd intended. But at least whatever they'd been expecting, it hadn't been this.

It only took maybe a second or two, before they were hovering above the ground and the roots that had been attached were torn away with a resounding pop.

Quinn watched as the tendrils tried to reach for them, attempting to reestablish the connection it had had. The roots flailed, grasping desperately at thin air as Quinn raised their hosts out of reach.

She wasn't prepared for the ear-splitting screams that began to ring through the entire room and the clearing beyond - threatening her grip, not only on them, but on reality.

23

HIGHLY SUSCEPTIBLE

A LOW-KEY BUZZING FILLED THE AIR, REMINDING QUINN OF STATIC electricity, like the sound found especially in those old fluorescent lights. As if the air around them resonated on a frequency that caused severe psychic pain. But since they weren't actually touching the ground, nothing could break through to them.

The screaming sound, it rang through Quinn's head like a siren, reverberating and making her wince.

What is that? Narilin's words only compounded the sound in her head.

Quinn held up a hand, trying desperately to focus. The vines and roots still stretched for the severed connection to the Balisors, but Irias was far enough away from the ground that it didn't matter for her.

The vines strained though, reaching, as if toward sunlight, only instead, toward bodies.

Get them on the tables, Quinn said, wincing even as that sound bounced off every single part of her brain that it could. If this kept up for much longer, she wasn't going to be able to think, let alone hear herself doing it.

Narilin was actively recoiling and didn't appear seem to hear, so Quinn amended the instruction.

Get on a table, Narilin. This will be worse for you than it is for us.

The book doctor scrambled to one of the tables at the side of the room and sat herself right in the middle of it. Her usual coloring began to return to her face and her breathing calmed.

The buzzing intensity all around them increased for a few seconds before softening again. Perhaps it had something to do with Narilin escaping the clutches of the ground.

Quinn glanced at Nishpa, who frowned with concentration as she attempted to maneuver Karella. The Furionas shook her head. *She's heavy. I can't do this alone.*

Guess we work together? Quinn offered a grimace of commiseration. *Let's move them one at a time.*

Not about to touch their hosts, Quinn leveraged some of her magic to help Nishpa maneuver them. It made Quinn wish she'd delved a little bit more into telekinetic and wind magic. It was all she could do to help propel them along while Nishpa guided Karella to her own table. The Salosier matriarch was obviously still trying to speak, her face full of a bewildered indignation that almost made Quinn laugh. *You silenced them?*

Nishpa barely shrugged her shoulders. *I wasn't about to have them yelling at me while we tried to pull them out of this damn predicament they didn't even notice they'd got themselves embroiled in. I'm a healer, not a saint.*

It was all Quinn could do to suppress her laughter. Her attempts to dampen the damned screaming and buzzing inside her own head hadn't proved as fruitful as Quinn would have liked, so their banter was a welcome distraction.

Getting Karella to the table took a lot of magical effort, but Quinn popped one of her treats into her mouth during the process of it and kicked her regeneration up a notch, making it negligible.

Call her overcautious, but Quinn wasn't about to let her energy low through helping these hostile people that something trying to ambush them could take them out.

Not that she was hugely powerful yet, but she was getting there. A few more millennia learning everything the Library had to offer, and she'd be able to crush small planets.

Maybe.

With Karella finally on the table, the buzzing and screaming intensified so that it was all Quinn could do not to fall to a knee on the ground of the room. But she knew that'd end up dangerous for all of them. Quinn could see the effect separation from the connection to the undergrowth had already had on Irias, who was now sitting upright and blinking, her mouth in a thin line of determination. Not to mention Karella, who looked positively dazed and unsure of where she was.

Nishpa hovered over, her face grim as they began to move Haritan mostly against his will. Consent was one thing, but Haritan posed a danger to himself and others, so Nishpa's restraint of him made sense. Quinn could, however, see he was draining Nishpa's power. Guiding him to his own table and unceremoniously dumping him on it appeared to take a toll. Nishpa practically staggered to the same table Narilin was on before just flopping down.

Even though the barrage of buzzing and screaming intensified as they dropped Haritan off, it too wore away enough so that Quinn could finally flop onto her own table, not far from Irias, and rest her weary head.

She surveyed the room, though the noises made her head pound.

Blood dripped down from Narilin's nose, and Quinn, alarmed, looked at the other Salosier only to determine they were having a similar side effect. *That isn't good.*

Nope. Definitely bad. Nishpa closed her eyes and popped a type of cake into it, one that appeared very similar to the ones Cook had baked for Quinn. She took several precious seconds as the screaming lessened and the buzzing became more insistent, to chew and digest what she was eating. Her color returned, and Quinn knew without having to ask, that the Furionas had regained the vast amount of energy she'd just expended. Her cookies appeared to be more super-

charged than Quinn's, and she wondered if that was a species constitution thing.

The buzzing intensified again, and Quinn felt like her eyes were
going to explode with the sudden pressure it exuded.

Which gave her pause. Pressure from a buzzing sound seemed odd
enough. But here they were in a forest where all sorts of bugs and
bees, birds and reptiles lived. She took in a breath and grounded
herself before extending her shielding in a different manner. Instead
of utilizing it for potential physical attacks, she reinforced her already
sturdy mental shielding with it instead and extended it out to the rest
of the room.

The buzzing quieted.

That is to say, it didn't actually quiet, it simply toned down in
sound because she'd cut some of the access to her off.

"Thank you."

Quinn turned to see Irias sitting upright and finally looking
completely lucid. "Irias. Are you okay?"

The young Salosier began to nod, but then shook her head, wiping
away the stark greenish blood that still dripped sluggishly from her
nose. "I am well enough. The buzzing has been with me for so long—
so long I can't precisely recall. Like a restriction. And ever since our
days have bled into one another."

Quinn nodded slowly, sort of understanding in a way. It made her
wonder if it was the same for all of them. She glanced around at
Karella and Haritan. The former sat up, looking around her with
amazement, a constant confused expression on her face. It had softened out of that disdainful expression she'd seemed to carry the whole
time before. Instead, she simply seemed bewildered.

Haritan on the other hand was still lying on the table they'd put
him on and staring at the ceiling, his hands clutched over his ears in a
vise grip. Quinn raised an eyebrow, but didn't make any comments.

"You're unsure when this began? Was it before or after the Library
opened—is that a vague enough time stamp?" Quinn attempted to
prod the line of questioning, trying to get them some leeway.

She felt a drop of blood drip from her nose.

Yeah, this was worse than not good.

Especially since Irias sat there with confusion on her face. "The Library . . . as in *the* Library? It's open?"

That wasn't where Quinn wanted to start the conversation. "Yes. And I'll gladly tell you all about it once we figure out how to turn the buzzing off." At least that answered the question. This had been going on a lot longer than the Library had been reopened.

"The buzzing . . ." Irias shook her head, and then a flash of thinly disguised anger crossed her face. At the same time, Narilin fell back onto her table, small convulsions wracking her frame. Neither Haritan nor Karella seemed to fare better; their bodies twitched violently.

Nishpa darted up off the table, hovering in the air trying to get her bearings.

"Yeah, that buzzing," Quinn said, still trying to figure out through analysis where it originated from.

Nishpa cursed under her breath. "We need to close the aperture to the Jenishu region. As in permanently. For now, at least."

Quinn gaped at her. "And how do we do that right now when the screaming plants have barely stopped trying to split our eardrums?"

The Furionas fae gave Quinn an almost unreadable look before shrugging. "I don't know. I came up with the plan. This area wasn't sealed off because of some strange grudge or whim. This area is unavailable because the infestation appears to have taken control. That aperture needs to be closed after we get a warning through to them."

Aradie hooted low, and puffed herself up on Quinn's shoulder.

"Really?" Quinn asked skeptically. "You'll take the message?"

Aradie gave her a look that could have killed most people where they stood.

"Perfect!" Nishpa said, her eyes shining. "That's excellent. Aradie can take a message through to Sarila and dash back through to us, closing the portal behind her . . ."

"You think we can handle this?" Quinn asked, trying to keep the mild panic out of her voice.

That gave Nishpa pause and she shrugged. "I don't know to be honest, you, Aradie and I seem relatively safe, but anyone of Salosier or Pertaligno heritage will be highly affected simply by being here."

Quinn had to try not to laugh at the pun. Bee-ing. Maybe that's what the buzzing was. "Okay, Aradie, off you go. Warn them—bring back anyone who isn't a Salosier and won't be affected, I guess? And can keep up with you."

Aradie nodded, hooted once, and launched herself so fast Quinn barely kept a track of her as she shot into the sky through the skylight.

We're lucky Aradie accompanied us. Nishpa switched back to mind to mind. *Not every day I get to work with a species matriarch.*

Pardon? Quinn asked, incredulously.

Nishpa looked at her and blinked. *What, did you think all night owls were as strong as Aradie?*

Quinn shook her head. *I just thought she was special.*

Yeah. She is. She's the mother of all night owls . . . in a manner of speaking. The first. She's older than ninety-five percent of the universe. Nishpa cleared her throat. *We don't have time for this chat. Ask her about it yourself when we're safe back in the Library after all this is over.*

Quinn appreciated the when not being an *if*.

By this time, however, Irias had clambered upright and was looking down at the ground beneath her. Quinn couldn't blame her. The once calm and docile root system appeared to be constantly striving to reach them. It looked like a mass of swirling baby tentacles, and Quinn couldn't appreciate that at all under these circumstances.

Irias blinked again and looked all around her. "That buzzing shouldn't be possible. They were wiped out millennia ago. I've only ever heard horror stories."

There was an edge to her voice.

Yet another thing Quinn didn't like the sound of. Between the Balisor Salosier, and Nishpa and her damned horror stories, Quinn knew she was about to regret asking the question on the tip of her tongue.

She did it anyway. "And just what have you heard horror stories about?"

Irias balked and gestured around, as if she couldn't speak.

Flakes of her bark began to peel away here and there. So much that Quinn now noticed it. She turned to look at the other three, and only just noticed their bark was peeling too. She raised an eyebrow back at Nishpa. "That's not normal, right?"

Nishpa sighed. "It's perfectly normal for a vibrato bee."

"Elaborate, thanks?"

Nishpa chuckled, but it sounded strained. "Bees that get into the wood of a tree and set up home. They release a system-wide buzzing sound that deregulates the entire nervous system, giving its hosts rise to be mind-controlled, or otherwise influenced. This allows people to work toward the bee agenda . . . only, this isn't necessarily something that should be successful with the Salosier. Usually, their magical protections and their rune defenses should have warded something like this off."

Quinn gulped. Apparently, those runic defenses had been torn to shreds. The buzzing intensified, and she looked up as a sudden shadow rose over her.

She didn't want it to be true, but it didn't really matter.

Because above her, in the shape of a massive fist, were thousands of vibrato bees.

24

VIBRATO BEES

It was probably the worst name for a monster Quinn had heard since arriving in the universal Library those few months ago. It was as on the nose as anything. Very unimaginative. While trying desperately to figure out how to take cover in an open-air room, Quinn allowed herself to scan them so perhaps the system's information could be accessed to assist them.

She clutched at all the straws.

Vibrato bees (Vibicial Forenado)
Ability: Swarm Resonance Disruption
Danger Categorization: 12 Typhoon Type
Current level: Medium

Quinn raised an eyebrow at that. She wasn't entirely sure how she felt about this information that meant absolutely nothing to her. The ability to process and think fast may have bought her precious seconds, but the only thing she could think of to do was to throw a barrier up toward the skylight to close it off, and hopefully prevent them from dive bombing her.

It was Quinn's first real attempt at shielding something that wasn't a body. How powerful, effective, or even damage absorbent it would be, Quinn had no idea. Small though they might be, those bees sounded like they'd do a heck of a lot of damage if they all impacted against something at once.

She erred on the side of putting way too much into the shield.

It popped up not a second too soon, the blue hue of her scales the predominant color, even though the entire shield was mostly transparent. It shone in the dim light reaching through the canopy, just before the cloud of vibrato bees descended on it.

Hundreds of the little buggers must have rebounded off the shield as Quinn could hear them thudding into it. There were quite a few squishing sounds to be had as well. She frowned, and poured a bit more energy into the protection, not too concerned, considering she had it in abundance. But she couldn't keep doing this for hours. It would buy them some time until, hopefully, they figured out what the hell to do.

She took a sharp intake of breath as the cloud of bees began to move more cautiously, as if they were trying to discover the shield's weakness. At least that meant it wouldn't take her any extra energy until they decided to attack again.

"Okay. That'll hold for now, but first—what the hell? And secondly . . . *how* the hell do we deal with these?" Quinn was proud her thoughts almost came out in complete sentences.

Irias spoke before Nishpa could. "They're not supposed to be here."

The kid was beginning to sound like a broken record. Despite being hundreds of years older than Quinn, she felt more like a child. "We know they're not supposed to be here, but . . ."

Irias shook her head, glaring vehemently toward the bees. "They were driven out thousands of years ago. We have glyphs and runic circles in place specifically to ward them off. They shouldn't be here at all. I checked."

Quinn understood now, sort of anyway. She wasn't being figurative; she was being literal.

"That's true," Nishpa said as she came to hover next to Quinn, also looking up at their slow-moving attackers as they cased the joint, trying to discover a weak point.

"It's not the best shield," Quinn muttered, quite worried that it wouldn't take much more for them to break through. "The quicker we come up with a solution, the better."

"Those aren't fully charged yet." Narilin gasped from where she still lay on the table, gasping slightly for breath. "The shield is helping. Their toxins can't reach us in here right now. My bark is healing on its own."

Irias catapulted over to land lightly next to Narilin and knelt down, placing her hand on the book doctor's forehead. She exerted a slight bit of magic Quinn could sense from the other side of the room. But the sensations weren't like anything Quinn had experienced herself when using her own magic. In fact, this was more like a calm waterfall spilling out into an equally calm lagoon. Soothing and peaceful amidst the slightly delayed abject terror of being stalked by a massive swarm of bees.

Narilin's peeling bark began to heal, visibly.

Quinn raised an eyebrow and Irias shrugged, as if she could feel the scrutiny.

"I am a healer. I have always been a healer. Part of my parent's disgust and disappointment is that I am not a true book healer, but a person healer." The young Balisor leapt lightly across the tables to reach her parents. There wasn't even a moment's hesitation in her reaching forward and applying the same healing method to each of her parents.

Even if Quinn was certain she glimpsed an ever so slight unwillingness in her eyes before she applied the healing. The underlying hum of the of the spell was slightly modified as it sang into the older Balisors' bodies. Maybe to do with familial relations?

They didn't wake up the way Narilin had, and Quinn frowned. "Do you think they'll be okay?"

Irias shrugged. "I can't say. They have been quite lax in my training and so my ability to read how well my own skills heal has not been afforded the necessary growth. It would take a more experienced healer than I to read those aspects of their minds." She glanced back up at the bees, and Quinn could see how her shoulders squared off with determination despite the spirit of her words.

Irias was being brave, but also stubborn, it seemed. She was still young, inexperienced, and had apparently been sheltered most of her life.

Not that Narilin was any different.

Not that Quinn wasn't more than a hundred years their junior.

The bees moved, pressing slowly against the shielding, testing every part for any cracks to break through. Quinn narrowed her eyes. This way, they weren't actually draining her power. It wouldn't drain until it had to repel or reinforce itself. Which was good, because in the meantime, she could work on replenishing all the energy she'd already spent on it, let alone the mana.

"How are you holding them there?" Irias asked.

"It's a shield," Quinn muttered, still relieved that the idea worked. Her energy was barely on the edge of three thousand right now, but once those bees gave up inspecting it and began trying to smash it, her mana was going to run like a faucet until she stopped it as it flowed into maintaining the shield.

What are we going to do? We don't have our fighters with us. I could probably burn up a whole gang of bees, but something tells me fire in the middle of a forest, regardless of whether it's super damp, is probably not the best idea.

Nishpa laughed, but the sound, even in Quinn's head, was dry. *There are few strategies that might work with bees. While smoke would be ideal, I agree that I don't trust your fire affinity with all this kindling. Could probably try ice?*

Ice? Quinn mulled that answer over for a bit, playing around with it in her head. *Ice is a possibility. I can work with that. Will it lower their body temperature and make them less of a threat?*

Anything will lower its body temperature if you freeze it, Nishpa said meaningfully.

But Quinn wasn't of the same mind. The spells holding Kajaro kept him alive, but didn't stop Adrito's wounds from continuing to disintegrate. *Won't they like just cluster together for warmth against the cold and thus drop like a wrecking ball onto my shield, smashing through it with the sheer weight of the ice and their own mass and thereby draining all of my energy at once?*

Nishpa shrugged. *They could, but as long as you make it cold enough they'll also just freeze and fall onto the shield I think.*

In short, it meant no one had a clue, but ice seemed like the safest choice if Quinn didn't want to burn the damn forest down.

Even if, right about then, it sounded super tempting.

Suddenly there was a knock, and it came from above.

Screw waiting for her to freeze them to death with her ice spells, they seemed to have already formed the ball and were knocking themselves rhythmically against the shielding she'd placed there. It was as if they were slowly, methodically, trying to see where the shielding was at its weakest point.

That level of intelligence in a swarm monster made Quinn queasy.

She readied herself, digging in her inventory to grab another one of the energy regeneration cakes. It was imperative she ration them. But right now, she didn't feel she had a choice.

Chomping down on it, she reinforced the shielding, pulling on her innate protections as well as everything she'd learned about protecting others. At the same time, she began gathering ice into a small ball to start with. About the size of a golf ball to start, she spun and spun it until it was at least as large as a tennis ball, then she allowed it to float in the air in front of it, suspended by the cold and whatever magic had leaked in near her. Quinn began to work on a second one, trying to form a decent attack plan in her mind.

This wasn't like on Ishiposa Isle where there'd been fire and attack golems and people were on even footing, so to speak. No, in here they couldn't even do anything standing up on solid ground.

Frankly, Quinn thought, being made out of wood, the tables were highly suspect too. What if the vines could infect the actual tables?

Irias gasped off to her left.

Quinn maintained her grip on her ice balls and looked in the direction of the sound.

She wasn't entirely sure how to feel about what she saw. Aradie was back, and she had two massive dark brown owls in tow with her. They looked like none of the night owls Quinn had seen before.

Aradie's voice echoed in her mind. *These are distant brethren. Hunters of this forest. They have confided they have missed the vibrato bees delicacy.*

Quinn grinned. She loved it when Aradie took the time to actually speak to her. *Excellent. Sounds like a great plan. What do you need us to do?* She couldn't help but feel relieved that Sarila or another Salosier hadn't arrived. She'd been uncertain anyone would listen to her owl. Keeping the few in this room safe proved hard enough considering how badly the bees managed to affect them.

Could you freeze the shield?

Quinn blinked, even as a second heavier barrage against the shield began. She could feel her energy just sapping out of her gently with each hit. At least she wasn't in danger of losing it all yet. *Of course I can do that. I'd like to know why.*

Aradie gave her a brief look. *Later. They're starting to figure out your shield, and I don't have the energy left over to heal you all from vibrato bee stings. You're not immune, and they have venomous stingers. Especially for the Salosier. Keep the others safe. We will take care of the bees.*

Quinn nodded. She'd have to talk to this matriarch of the night owls at some stage, but right now wasn't the time. *And keep the shielding frozen. Got it.*

Aradie bowed her head briefly and took off back outside, with the two massive owls following her.

Quinn watched the bird dart out, distracted momentarily from her shield, and at the worst possible moment.

There was a loud bang that shook the entire room. A crack sounded through the room, but Quinn hastily poured more energy into the shielding, securing it even tighter than it had been before. If she hadn't gotten sidetracked, it probably wouldn't have buckled so badly. She began the arduous task of lacing ice over the whole structure, reinforcing it, solidifying it, making it thicker and thicker.

The bees began to hammer at it, and she could see them growing desperate even as they slowly began to lose momentum. Quinn didn't like that it drained her mana as well as energy, and she couldn't see once the iced layers began to thicken. It created a barrier above them that was nigh-impenetrable.

But she had lost all visuals.

It made her nervous.

Above them, the swarm's frantic hammering grew more and more desperate, and then suddenly the loud buzzing that had begun to make her ears bleed . . . finally stopped.

The vibrations above them stopped and slowly, but surely, even Haritan and Karella began to move again.

"Is that it?" Irias asked, looking around incredulously. "It just took some—"

But whatever she'd been about to say was lost in the high-pitched squeal buzzing that grew and grew.

Quinn fell onto her hands and knees on her table, the sound of pressure pushing her down. She didn't have any spare attention to watch the others with. But she knew they wouldn't be any better off. Her brains felt like they wanted to liquefy and spill out of her head. The only thing keeping them in there was sheer willpower.

Abruptly, the sound stopped. For several seconds, there was complete and utter silence.

And then the sound of crisp munching filtered down through to them.

The popping of icy bodies with sharpened beaks.

Quinn shuddered at the sound and refused to melt the ice from her shielding quite yet.

25

LIFE SIGNS

DESPITE THE VERITABLE FEAST GOING ON ABOVE THEM, QUINN STILL felt like something was off. After all, the bees had an adverse effect on the Salosier as a whole, but their bark or skin hadn't been peeling when Quinn first arrived, so the bees felt more like an attack than whatever it was trying to grapple with them from underneath.

The bee attack, while inopportune, didn't appear to be related to the vines of doom. It was simply coincidental. Even if Quinn was still a little sketch on that, too.

She frowned, glancing down beneath the tables, and noticed that the vines were still trying their darndest to climb the legs of the tables, but for some reason they couldn't.

"Does the underbrush ever usually behave in this way?" she asked, trying to keep the sarcasm out of her voice. For all she knew, the roots were just very attached to their people.

Irias glanced down and frowned. "No. It is usually a matter of brief connections as we traverse the forest. However, lately it has seemed somewhat stickier." She shrugged, like she didn't know how else to explain it.

"Sticky as in clinging to you when it shouldn't be?" Quinn pushed for the answer.

Narilin spoke up this time. "There are reasons I hovered as we came farther into their territory. I was not just exercising a dislike of the situation, but was instead unsure of the level of heat I felt coming off the forest floor as we stepped through the aperture." Narilin rolled quite elegantly to her knees and peered down at the ground, her hands gripping the table. "That right there . . . is a seething mass of roots and foliage, and not what is supposed to be there."

"She is correct." Karella coughed out a response, finally having broken out of her quasi-stupor. She blinked large, dark brown eyes and surveyed the situation, her face flickered through varying degrees of horror as she did. "When did all this happen?"

"When did all what happen?" Quinn asked, trying not to be too short with the Balisor matriarch. Considering the bewilderment and confusion, whatever this was had been going on a lot longer than anyone realized. "Because a lot has happened, so I'm going to need you to narrow it down for me."

Karella blinked at her, no recognition passing through those eyes. She furrowed her brow, which, given the skin of the Salosier, looked somewhat frightening as the bark bent and crunched ever so slightly.

"I am so sorry, but have we met? You do not look at all familiar to me, but to be fair, right now I cannot even recall why I am in the gathering building, or when we put a ceiling in this tent."

Quinn blinked. Surely it wasn't a total memory loss sort of thing? That wouldn't even make sense. But . . . she glanced at the floor, the writhing roots somewhat stiller, as if they were waiting, and yet, they still moved, like they were biding their time, attempting to gather a sort of camouflage in behaving more like your standard roots. Even as she wanted to ask the question, Quinn extended her senses out beyond the room. Originally, she'd had it in a fairly tight radius around herself, just in case something tried to attack her or the others.

But this?

It called for more than that. Pushing out her awareness, she skimmed along the roots and vines, analyzing them with everything she'd learned about the Salosier and magic in general. Meanwhile, she focused her attention directly on Karella. If the woman was acting, she was doing a bang-up job of it.

"I'm Quinn," she said, hoping to elicit a response of some sort at least.

When Karella didn't even blink, Quinn continued. "The Librarian."

"Of what, dear?" Karella said, a motherly tone creeping into her voice.

Out of the corner of her eye Quinn noticed Irias's brow scrunching in thought as she watched the interaction. Apparently, her mother's reaction was unexpected. A flash of irritation rose from the ground, brushing against Quinn's sensory exploration of the ground. Seething impatience rolled off it in small increments, almost like a cloud of hatred. If she hadn't been specifically watching for it, Quinn wouldn't have noticed. She delved deeper in her analysis, while continuing to answer Karella's questions. "Of the Library."

Karella digested that, a confused look on her face. The expression seemed genuine, even so far as to reach Quinn's senses. "I'm sorry," Karella said, "Did you say the Library? As in the Library of Everywhere? The one with all the magical books that no one has been able to visit for hundreds of years?"

"The one and the same." Quinn tried to temper the information with a soft smile. After all, not everyone accepted it was back yet. Not everywhere. She was quite certain, even her limited experience with the dozens of species she encountered, wasn't even a scratch on the surface.

However, they'd been withholding a book from her. How could she not know? There was something very wrong about this.

"Wait. When did it reopen?" Karella's face lit up. There was joy under the mild concern. She almost went to hop off the table, but Nishpa reacted with surprising speed.

Grasping Karella in a gust of wind, she gently placed the Balisor mother on the table again. "I wouldn't advise you to touch the floor right now. There are some . . . issues with it."

Karella turned to look at Nishpa and smiled. "Oh, you I recognize. You're the sister of the fae king!"

Quinn, who still hadn't got around to double checking people's ancestry, looked at Nishpa in a new light. Although, she should have put two and two together. She was Milaro's childhood friend, she was Geneva's aunt, and Geneva was one of the children of the fae crown. So, logically . . .

Nishpa smiled, but it was a tight expression, and Quinn desperately wanted to know all the baggage that went with that. "The one and the same. This is the Librarian. Tell me, Karella, what is the last thing you remember?"

Karella blinked and frowned. "I . . ." she started, but then she looked around the room. Like *really* looked this time, and what she saw seemed to shake her out of her own stupor. Her gaze fell on her husband, still prone on the table.

Quinn had her theory about why Haritan hadn't yet woken back up, but she wasn't about to espouse them now. She'd been surreptitiously watching him, but . . . he'd not moved a muscle, and she wasn't sure he could. For the time being, she was intently examining Karella. Some people were good actors. She had to make sure Karella wasn't one of them.

The Balisor mom's face paled in that oddly green, sick-looking way that Salosier's seemed to get. When her gaze finally fell on Irias, she gasped. "Irias? What . . . when did you grow up so much?"

The words came out as a whisper, but Quinn could tell how much pain hid behind them. As if Karella had missed a huge chunk of her daughter's life or something.

Which, if the picture Quinn was starting to paint together was right, was likely true.

Irias, on the other hand, didn't seem amenable to the fact that her mother might not have been herself for the last while. She scowled at Karella. "I'm the same as I've always been."

Karella frowned, confusion flickering over her expression. "I'm sorry, I don't follow. How did I miss this much time?"

A panicked look formed in her eyes, and Quinn could practically feel it vibrating through her body.

Irias sighed, her reaction oddly off-putting. "Mom, it is okay. We will be fine. We all will." She moved over, hovering over a foot off the floor, not giving the vines a chance to get their roots back into her.

In the meantime, Quinn finally figured out exactly what was wrong. *It's the vines,* she said in her headspace, making sure it reached Narilin, Nishpa, and Aradie. *It's interwoven intricately and underlying the usual brush that should be present. In doing so, it's almost strangled the natural undergrowth of this forest. I can't tell how to unweave it, or how to stop the weird poisonous presence it has when it connects to those who walk over it . . . but that's what it is.*

It all sounded so fantastical to her, but it also made a weird sort of sense. This was a weed. Something that had invaded the natural flora around this world and slowly but definitively encroached on the natural habitat of the Balisor.

While Quinn couldn't glean more, her magical senses were enough to untangle and define what it saw here. There was an inherent difference between that of the Balisor and the Jenishu, and it made Quinn think it made the former much easier prey.

Nishpa gasped ever so softly a few seconds later. However, it was Narilin's reaction that was the most telling. She paled, even worse than Karella had.

This is Bardocian root. Narilin practically whispered the words internally. *This is not good. This is, in fact, horrible. How far ingrained is it? How long has it been here? How did we not know?*

The rising hysteria in her words did little to improve Quinn's mood. After all, she'd just thought it was like a weed, but from Narilin's reaction, it was a veritable poison. *Is there a treatment for this?* She needed to get them thinking about solutions and not focusing so much on the problem itself.

There was nothing else they could do about the problem itself, except attempt to extract from it and fix what was broken. Or at least, Quinn hoped it was possible.

It can be healed . . . Narilin sort of came back into herself just a little. *Yes, I can heal a part of it, but Irias has the stronger healing magic. While I can address certain aspects, I cannot cure people of the influence.*

Irias should be able to work on that while I take care of the root system itself. If she's up to it. Right now she seems preoccupied.

Nishpa paled again, but nodded her head emphatically.

Quinn knew there was something the Salosier wasn't telling her, but she left it at that. After all, it was a lot of information, and Quinn had the bad feeling that this weed was doing a lot worse damage than she initially thought. Meanwhile, she gave her attention back to Irias, who was mid reasoning with her mother.

"... been poisoned, and you should know that, because you should be able to sense it." She sounded impatient, and Quinn couldn't blame her since Karella seemed to be adamantly shaking her head. Denial at its finest.

"She's right." Nishpa hovered in before Quinn could. Good thing too, considering Karella knew Nishpa from some distant thing, and was more ready to listen to her than her daughter who'd suddenly aged or the strange Librarian who'd suddenly appeared.

While she waited, Quinn glanced back over at Haritan, her magic, again, picking up nothing.

Irias hovered over to stand with Quinn, right next to Narilin. "She is not usually this unreasonable. I apologize."

Quinn glanced at the striking young Salosier. Although, sitting at almost two hundred years of age meant calling her young felt oddly out of place. "But how are you?"

Irias gave Quinn a seriously contemplative look. "I am better than my parents. I was away studying until a few months ago. I only got called home when the Library beacon activated. My parents wanted me to apply to be an assistant."

"But that's not what you want to do, is it?" Quinn asked, keeping her tone kind and patient. One thing she never wanted to do was lay parental expectations on someone and expect them to fulfill it against their own wishes. From her memories, her own parents had never asked that of her.

For several seconds, Irias didn't answer. She watched her mother and Nishpa, myriad emotions passing over her face. "I would love to be an assistant to the Library of Everywhere, but I do not want to be a book doctor. There is so much more I could learn with access to the knowledge in the Library. There are so many things I can do with my abilities that I'm stifled and restricted from here."

Quinn could feel the passion in the young Balisor. The edges however, were sharp. Irias wanted to do what Irias wanted . . . and not for anyone but Irias. Quinn chose her phrasing carefully. "You are welcome anytime. Whatever you wish to do can be found in the Library. It has all the fail-safes needed to explore everything."

For several seconds, Irias searched Quinn's expression for any signs of falsehood. "But first, I do believe, I am going to need to help take care of my parents. They are not who they should be."

Quinn nodded, trying to read between those lines. "Speaking of which, there seems to be some foreign matter in those roots. They're Bardocian root? That's what Narilin said. Does that sound familiar?"

If Irias noticed that Narilin had apparently spoken to Quinn without anyone else hearing, she didn't let on that it mattered. Instead, she frowned. "That particular root subverts personality traits. It brings out those we try to suppress to the fore. I can see how it would have affected my parents, who are always worried they do not live up to the people's expectations, or their own."

Quinn mulled that over, stretching her senses even farther as she tried to pinpoint precisely what was bothering her. It felt like Irias deliberately spoke in half truths. There was something off here . . . and it prickled at the back of her mind without telling her precisely what it was.

Nishpa still spoke to Karella as the latter finally broke down in tears. She seemed exhausted from the waves of emotion rolling off her.

Irias cleared her throat ever so softly. "Is there anything I might be able to assist you with right now?" she asked Quinn, even though her eyes said her mind was clearly preoccupied.

Perhaps the fact that her father and mother's more recent behavior hadn't been quite within their control made Irias more inclined to help them.

Quinn began to nod, and then a thought struck her. "Wait. Irias, why are you the only Balisors in this entire town?"

An odd flicker of irritation passed briefly through Irias's eyes. She frowned. "What are you talking about? There are several thousand of us in this area."

Quinn paled this time. Not wanting to panic the girl, she forced a smile. "Go take care of your mom."

Irias blinked and then shrugged, heading off to help Nishpa.

Frantically, Quinn searched and modified the sensory details she sought. Life signs . . . modeled on the Salosier she personally knew. Other life signs. Variations in plants. Everything.

No matter who was supposed to be there.

The people in this room and the birds directly above it were the only life forms she could sense in this entire city.

And she wasn't even sure if Haritan still counted.

26

BLUR OF FEATHERS

Is something wrong with my sensing ability? She asked to get the other's attention. *Can anyone else feel any other life signs here or anywhere near us?*

Narilin looked up, alarm crossed her features very briefly and in no way allayed the genuine fear Quinn felt churning in her gut. She didn't even want to hear the words she knew Narilin was about to say into their mind chat.

I can't sense anyone. Not in this immediate vicinity, anyway. Do you think they could be farther out? Hiding somehow? There was a tinge of hope in Narilin's words, as if she thought there was no way everyone else could be gone.

But then again, she hadn't been with Quinn and Nishpa when they visited Ishiposa Isle—she hadn't been there to see the state of those Esposians, or what was left of them. Neither had Nishpa in that instance, but she also knew the Furionas fae was a lot older than Narilin, and definitely hadn't been as sheltered.

Could be, Nishpa said, her tone neutral. It was obvious she was currently concentrating on Karella's mind. *It's a mess in here. Shadows of her own memories interspersed with ones that have been fed by all sorts of anger, all sorts of misinformation and misinterpretation. It's like it focused on anything negative and pulled it to the fore, honing in on the darker thoughts, hanging there and causing as much strife and interference as it could. It reeks of possession and not just confusion. Are you sure it's just the Bardocian root?*

Narilin shook her head ever so slightly, obviously not wanting to give away to the rest of them just how much they were discussing mind to mind. *No. I am simply not aware of what else it could be. This does seem somewhat extreme even for Bardocian root.*

A thought struck Quinn. *Is it even safe for you to be doing this? Is there a way this could compromise you or harm you as well?*

Narilin paused for a second, her brow scrunching in thought. For just a second, the mask she always wore everywhere gained an ever so slight crack in it. Underneath, it appeared, she was just as vulnerable as others, just as frail. But she rallied and put up a front that helped those around her thrive. Quinn could respect that. She learned to like Narilin just that bit more in that instant. *I cannot say for sure. This Bardocian root seems mostly fixated on the Balisor variation. It is as if it has been cultivated for a specific purpose. Quite odd, to be sure.*

Is it something the Jenishu branch of the Salosiers would be more immune to? Quinn asked, not entirely sure what it could be then. Considering her knowledge only extended to the Salosier and wasn't specialized toward specific deviations, she couldn't draw such conclusions herself.

Narilin appeared to seriously contemplate the words, even as she wove her fingers in spirals, sending out waves of ever so slight power that examined everything around them, healing that which Quinn couldn't even quite comprehend. *I think it is. It does not seek me out in the same manner with which it reaches toward Haritan, Karella, and Irias. There is a bias to how it moves, what it is aiming for. But I am unable to determine its exact origin or motivation. I would need more time and a different location.*

Nishpa cut in on the conversation. *If you could continue with the subtle separation you're performing, I'd appreciate it. I'm finally making headway with Karella, but there will be a strong aftermath once we're done.*

And Haritan hasn't even stirred yet. I'd hate to think how deeply it's sunk into him.

Will Irias hold up? Quinn asked Nishpa, concerned about the youngest Balisor.

Nishpa hesitated. *I believe so. She doesn't seem nearly as infected.*

She said she was away studying and has only been back a few months, Quinn offered.

That would explain it. Perhaps she should be helping Narilin. Nishpa frowned and then looked up at Irias. "Is there any way you could assist Narilin in her work with the undergrowth?"

A look of shock ran over Irias's expression, and she nodded, hovering over to her . . . cousin? "What can I do?"

Narilin bowed her head and the two of them fell into a discussion that left Quinn feeling much like an outsider.

Aradie's mind brushed her own, and she welcomed it. *You can put down the barrier now. All the bees have been taken care of.*

Quinn let the barriers dissipate, including the ice, which she evaporated into steam with extremely carefully controlled fire. The two large brown owls remained perched on the edge of the roof, their eyes looking all around them as if they were on guard.

They are *guarding us. There is something not right with this section of the forest. Something insidious is here.*

Quinn nodded. She'd already thought as much, but Aradie didn't need her repeating what she already knew. *How about the aperture to the Jenishu?*

Temporarily sealed, but I can easily open it.

Hey. How come you didn't tell me you were this powerful?

Aradie alighted on her shoulder and craned away, giving Quinn a very skeptical look. *If I told you, you'd have come to rely on my abilities and powers far too much, and your growth would be stunted. As it is, you're coming along fine—so I've offered my help this once.*

Quinn couldn't deny the logic. It made perfect sense, after all, even if she did wish she'd known she had a quasi-fairy godmother in her back pocket. Or on her shoulder. Whatever. *Are you able to scout out the area and scan for signs of life?*

Aradie cooed under her breath. *We'll make a flight pass. The others will aid me. If they're here, we will find them. Also—your mind-to-mind speech is much smoother these days. It's no longer painful to communicate with you.*

Quinn blinked at her owl. *Painful* didn't sound like a good thing. Perhaps that was why she'd begun speaking more with her recently. Whatever the reason, Quinn was glad for it. Pictures might be easy enough to interpret, but it wasn't her preferred method of communication. *Thank you.*

Aradie hooted and launched off Quinn's shoulder and back out through the roof.

Quinn stood, watching her fly out, and frowned. She had no idea what to do. No matter how far she extended her senses, she couldn't seem to find other signs of life. If, in fact, there were supposed to be thousands of Balisors in this exact location, then it didn't stand to reason that she couldn't find any.

They'd seen all the tents, the homes on their way. How could they all be empty? She wasn't sure if she counted herself lucky for it or not, but she didn't think it likely she'd be able to detect corpses.

She was counting on the owls for that one.

Moving over, Quinn hovered close to Narilin and Irias. "Any luck?"

Narilin nodded, and Quinn noticed that she looked strained, but it didn't seem to have anything to do with her proximity to roots, luckily, but with the energy she put into the work and clearing the vines around them.

"She is currently dividing the strands. We need a good sampling of the infectious root so that we may devise a . . . type of counter. Necessity requires that we make it hyper specific so it doesn't impact the normal forest anatomy," Irias explained. There was a hint of grudging respect for Narilin's abilities in her tone.

Quinn guessed having affinities for healing books extended to a healing ability for trees. "Are you able to help her at all?"

Narilin answered, and even though her words were clipped, Quinn put it down to the fact that she was working her ass off. "She is providing me with much needed excess energy. Her reserve levels of power are quite remarkable."

Quinn raised an eyebrow, never having heard a compliment quite like that from Narilin in all the time she'd known her. It was certainly an interesting turn of events. Maybe the two of them could mend bridges that should never have really been broken between their factions.

Quietly, Quinn withdrew herself, her own senses telling her with no too fine a point that the work was slowly succeeding.

She wandered over to where Haritan was still prone. His body didn't move except for a very slow, barely noticeable rise and fall of his chest. It felt almost . . . fake. Quinn adjusted for the oxygen levels again, made aware of the breathing. It reminded her she should be checking on her intake in this atmosphere every now and again. PH levels seemed within the parameters she expected, so she continued with the same amount, setting a warning for if they suddenly changed.

Just in case.

Finally, she made it over to Karella and Nishpa. The fae seemed positively thundercloud-like. Her patience was obviously wearing thin. Karella, on the other hand, was in tears.

As she'd seemed to be for the last several minutes.

"Any news?" Quinn asked, hoping she didn't sound too callous.

Nishpa shrugged. "It seems this infection began almost a century ago."

Quinn blinked. "A century?"

"Yep," Nishpa said, her voice containing tightly controlled anger. "A whole damn century."

Quinn glanced over at where Narilin and Irias were working together. "Just how long was Irias on her study trip?"

Karella glanced up. "What do you mean just how long was Irias on a studying trip? She never went anywhere to study anything."

The last of the words were spoken into complete and utter silence, sort of like Quinn always imagined it might be when a pin dropped in a completely soundless room. Like a tidal wave of silence—crashing down all around them, deafening in its finale.

Time felt like it froze, at least for Quinn. She turned her head so fast she almost cricked her neck, and her gaze fell on Narilin and Irias. They still kneeled on the table, their heads impossibly close together, as if they were locked in a discussion about the nature of the infection underneath them. Quinn's senses snapped back, adjusting this time for different sensations.

She could feel the darkness now as she looked for it from one of the three of them. And that's when she also realized that Haritan was dead. His chest still rose and fell by way of illusion, by something inserted under his chest cavity to make it appear like he was still among the living.

And Quinn recognized this due to the fact that the rot seeped from the ground up and had reached his fingers. All nine on each hand, shriveling with black sludge.

Narilin looked up at the sudden silence, her face suddenly a mask of shock.

Quinn didn't need to see Irias's face to know the supposed Balisor had transformed into something none of them expected. Slowly, the white bark that made up her body shriveled into something like looked like marble, breaking away to reveal stone underneath, but smoothly carved, beautiful . . . and nothing like a sedimentite.

No, this was something new, and she suddenly held Narilin by the neck.

Quinn wasn't certain about much, but she had read Salosiers' anatomy, and she was fully aware of the amount of damage that could be done to break a neck in the species.

Karella gasped in shock, and that's when Quinn realized she hadn't known. At least they needn't worry about her. She'd sincerely thought this Irias was her child. The revelation that she wasn't had come as a shock, and she wasn't even aware that her husband was dead yet.

Or, at least, this puppet version was. The question remained why this Irias hadn't just made the mother a puppet too. Surely that would have been easier.

"Damn it. You just had to go and ask that specific question, didn't you? And here I was trying so hard to fit in." The newly alabaster Irias stood up, her grip still firm around Narilin's neck as she thudded down onto the forest floor, crushing so much of the vine underneath her in the process. The red that had been such a part of her beautiful wooden makeup surged like veins through the marble, giving the disconcerting feeling of blood rushing.

Quinn inspected her, but the system balked at it and Irias shook her head. "Nuh-uh, Librarian. You really didn't need to come all the way here, you know. So no hints as to who we are for you! I thought you'd just send Narilin and her folks. But you came yourself, which is an absolute bonus for me."

"Bonus?" Quinn asked, determined to keep her talking just in case someone, anyone, could get to them. Not that she liked their chances.

"Getting to wipe you out where others have failed? That would give me so much clout! I stand to gain more than you could possibly imagine."

"Irias?" Karella said, her voice broken as she spoke. Her eyes were full of tears, and it was obvious she hadn't registered what was happening properly.

Not-Irias flashed a look of annoyance at her not-mother, but something in there spoke of fondness, even if it wasn't because she was the real daughter. "I should have puppeted you like I did him," she muttered, ignoring the outburst that followed.

"But you?" Narilin still dangling from her grip, Irias began to walk toward Quinn, although stalking was probably more accurate. "You've mostly ruined everything, you know that, right? You'll never get back to the Library now. You weren't supposed to come. Plans will have to change. Just let me just snap—"

But that's as far as Irias got.

A massive beam of light erupted at the floor level right next to her feet, causing her to drop Narilin without breaking her neck, and jump back.

A swoosh of brown, so fast that's all Quinn could see, gathered Narilin and darted to the back of the room, while right in front of

Quinn the softest, most feathered-looking being she'd ever seen landed in the perfect hero pose, glancing up at Irias with red eyes flashing.

The feathers seemed like a cape, a fluid part of the being. Black with gleaming reds, blues, greens, and purples.

"That was a bit of a goose chase you sent me on." The voice was soft, so familiar, and yet commanded the attention of everyone there. "You really should have thought this through."

Irias hissed. "This is no matter. I will get to the Librarian once I go through you."

The bird-person grinned, and Quinn knew exactly who it was as soon as she did.

Aradie crouched low, claws extended, and her beak like a dagger. She didn't even say a word before she struck in a blur of feathers moving so fast Quinn could barely follow her.

27

COMPLETE CERTAINTY

THE SUDDEN APPEARANCE OF A MORE HUMANOID ARADIE DIDN'T SIT well with Quinn's overall perception of things. However, as the fight began in earnest, there was too much for Quinn to focus on to dwell on the sudden change to her familiar. But once this was over . . .

As they clashed, Quinn turned her attention to Narilin, who sat on the floor, vines greedily trying to connect to her as she attempted to extricate herself. She'd been the first person to recognize what they were, after all, and they appeared to be eager for revenge.

Quinn ripped Narilin up, hovering her over to the table behind where Quinn stood, while she concentrated a flash of fire toward those roots, which pulled back in alarmed screeching.

The Salosier book doctor seemed shaken up, but there was a new fire in her eyes that hadn't been there previously. It made Quinn realize she'd never actually witnessed Narilin angry at anything, considering this was what happened when she got pissed off.

"Calm it down," Quinn whispered. "Now is not the time."

Narilin grunted, and a wave of healing energy passed over her. At first Quinn was shocked, but then she realized that Narilin *was* a book healer, she could work with all types of trees and their products. Which would, in a way, help herself too.

Aradie skidded back, almost bumping into Quinn before diving back into the fray. From the stance and expression on her owl's face, Aradie seemed to be having the time of her life.

Nishpa had since moved both herself and Karella to the same table Narilin sat on. The real Irias's mother seemed to be in shock. Aradie's owl guards stood at attention on the table next to them.

"Plan?" she snapped impatiently. The Furionas's gaze kept glancing at Karella, as if she wasn't entirely sure where her loyalties lay.

"Get you out of here so I don't have to worry about setting you on fire," Quinn said, without skipping a beat.

"Is he really . . ." Karella's voice cracked and a tear ran down her face. She couldn't take her eyes off Haritan's body.

Quinn felt a pang of sadness for the woman, and yet . . . not completely. "Give me the book before you leave."

Karella glanced at her, mild confusion crossing her brow as she did. "Book?"

Quinn groaned. Of course Karella had no idea. She'd been essentially possessed and had no recollection of the last damned century. Damn it. "Never mind."

They'd have to figure out that aspect of it later. While she wasn't hopeful Haritan had it, there was still a possibility he did. She was fairly sure Irias kept it in her own dimensional storage. Not the best place for it, considering the current fight.

Quinn glanced around and up at the owls, who'd moved up to guard them from the vantage point of the skylight. She could handle keeping that safe, at least as long as her energy held out. Beckoning to them, Quinn narrowly avoided a type of wooden dart flung from Irias's direction that almost hit her in the face.

One of the massive owls hooted long and low, and Quinn found that even though it wasn't spoken in words, she sort of understand his intonations. "Yes, please . . . get them out of here. Keep them safe. Fetch help if possible. Do not let the rot from here get through the aperture."

She didn't even have to ask twice. The larger one gripped Karella by the shoulders, somewhat gently, and raised himself up as he flew her out. The second took Narilin in much the similar fashion. Nishpa shot Quinn a flat look. "I can fly under my own steam. But will you two be okay here?"

Quinn shrugged and gestured at the blurs that were Aradie and Irias. "Probably. I'll see if there's anything I can do to help. Failing that, I'll feed her whatever energy I can spare. Just in case."

Nishpa nodded. "I'll keep a track of you. We'll get help."

Quinn smiled tightly as another projectile barely missed her. She flashed Nishpa a smile. "Don't worry about me."

Nishpa raised an eyebrow before shaking her head. She fluttered off and Quinn sighed with relief. What she planned to do couldn't happen if she had to worry about too many people.

You okay if I use some fire? she sent the thought out to Aradie

Please! But even though Aradie should probably have been stressed from the amount of flitting around she was doing, she sounded positively vibrant. Alive! Like this was what she was made to do.

It gave Quinn an entirely different view on just what the night owls were. When she really thought about it, it made little sense that all they were there for was to give a feather once a year that could help write a very specific magical affinity.

A grin floated through Quinn's mind, which was an odd sensation, all things considered. She'd never really felt an expression before. But this . . . it was like her familiar was conveying the emotion in a more solid form.

Fire was a go.

After all, she'd spent the last couple of weeks refining control of it, knowing how to contain it, how to direct it. She might not have been an expert, but this portion of the Balisor forest was already beyond saving. Might as well light the field.

Her first order of business was to create a barrier for herself so she wouldn't burn. Her scales obliged, rippling over most of her body to encase it in a skin-tight shield that somehow felt like an extension of herself. Scales spanned over her body as they settled under her clothes, over her skin. A refreshing sense of protection.

With the rest of their group gone and no one but themselves to protect, Aradie began fighting in earnest. Quinn could feel the stakes rising as she did so, the way her power vibrated in the air like the perfect note on a violin.

Waiting for the string to snap.

Aradie began shifting. She wasn't just a blur of speed and feathers, but this time, she shifted her size, her form, and became a complete and utter menace.

Which allowed for Quinn to focus on what really needed to happen.

Irias had long since given up the pretense of keeping herself above the vines, above the floor of the forest. The roots and vines had greedily reattached to her, and that was when Quinn realized the extent of her magic. The root system fed her power, directly. Giving her more energy the more she used, so that she'd never run out.

A part of Quinn was fully aware that the thousands of people who'd been here were probably holed up in a room somewhere being sucked dry like husks in order to feed their energy to fake-Irias. She only hoped they could stop all of it in time to at least save some of them.

First things first. Quinn stomped on the ground, more to give Aradie a warning than to attempt a distraction for Irias, but both seemed to work. Aradie made sure she hovered a few more inches above the ground while Quinn's flames began to eat it up.

Quinn's sudden movement caused Irias to pause slightly, which gave Aradie enough leverage to hit her with a surprisingly hefty uppercut. It clipped her under the chin, lifting her enough to snap the hold the undergrowth had on her and send her flying into the closest wall with a loud thud.

At the same time, the flames spread faster than the wildfires on Earth, gobbling up the power left by the break in vine contact in one fell swoop. Blue flames licked at everything around them, and Quinn barely kept it under control. Apparently magical foliage, even if it was rotting from within, was highly flammable to magical flame.

To Quinn's surprise, not only did the flame devour every single vine and root within the room, but it remained contained within the barrier Quinn attempted to set. She could feel her own energy draining out of her, but at the same time, the energizing food kicked in and began to replenish her reserves, along with the complete destruction of each section of the room.

Both Aradie and Quinn navigated the area, moving around so that the flames wouldn't catch up to them as the fire scoured the room. Quinn strengthened the shielding she'd cast on the night owl.

Irias gasped several times, and her once-white and red skin began to morph darker. Her appearance began to change drastically.

The black began at her feet, feeding up through her torso in streaks, like she was burning alive herself. It gave Quinn pause. Perhaps the undergrowth had been directly connected to her after all. An actual part of her. But Quinn didn't have time to hazard guesses.

Aradie landed several hits while Irias was partially out of it.

It was obvious the fire caused her pain, energy loss, and a type of grief.

Irias screamed. "You'll pay for that!"

Quinn strengthened the shielding around Aradie and herself more. She wasn't taking any chances, and at least her energy levels weren't at all depleted, thanks to the purified energy the fire managed to feed back to her after destroying all the roots and vines. She might not understand much about her power, but she was essentially immune to fire, and it made sense that purifying fire would help her, not hinder her.

The ground rumbled underneath her, and Quinn lengthened the distance she hovered above it, just in case. She could see Aradie do the same thing out of the corner of her eye. Quinn didn't quite make it out of the way though as the ground exploded up, a thicker root breaking through the scorched ground and rising up like a hunter from the deep.

Quinn dove to the side, almost rolling off the table as she skidded across it. The wood bit hard into her, winding her slightly, despite the fact that she knew the heat had weakened the tables too. She had to shake her head and force herself to focus properly.

Aradie had Irias by one clawed hand, holding her neck just like the

Balisor impersonator had done earlier with Narilin. Thick, sludge-like, blackened red goop began leaking down from the scratches inflicted by the night owl.

The ground beneath them rippled again and Aradie tossed Irias against the wall, just like Haritan had earlier, in order to save herself as she retreated atop another of the tables. It wobbled ever so slightly, the legs more fragile now the fire had mostly eaten away at them.

Quinn didn't lose any more time now that she was back in possession of her faculties. Igniting the ground once more with blue flames, she could hear a high-pitched squeal emanating from the roots and undergrowth that tried desperately to emerge from the ground beneath them. It wanted to rip them apart. The intent was there, as palpable as the heat from Quinn's flames.

There was a sentience to it, ever so slightly. But even so, that didn't give Quinn pause. This thing was out to get all of them, and she'd be damned before she let it. Tightening her grip on the flames she'd only just learned to control, Quinn applied more pressure to the area.

At the same time, with her focus pinpointed and finely tuned, she began to extract the moisture from around the ground and the vines themselves. It was a difficult task to wield both elements at once, especially given their direct juxtaposition.

She could feel the sweat beading on her brow, and it had nothing to do with the heat surrounding her right then.

The undergrowth squealed again, and Irias fell down to one knee, her own body beginning to crack.

A part of Quinn that wasn't fully concentrated on the fire and water realized the benefits of affinities being split like they were. After all, having a water control affinity without the ability to evaporate that same moisture, sort of meant the water affinity wasn't completely finished.

The fire flamed hotter, giving Quinn ample tinder for fuel. The ground beneath them burned, but the shielding kept both Aradie and Quinn safe. Not that she didn't think her familiar could totally take care of herself, but this way, Quinn hoped to free up some of Aradie's energy for taking down Irias.

A loud, echoing scream escaped from Irias at that precise second.

Quinn looked up, but didn't relinquish any of the heat she'd gathered, and realized, perhaps with a strange detachment, that somewhere along the way, Irias had gotten too close to the fire. Given that most of the moisture had been drained from her as well, her toes touching the flame basically acted like a wick.

The flames shot up her body, enveloping it in hot blue, tinged with pale yellow. Irias writhed against the back wall, slowly smoldering the greener vines away in the process. Apparently, her real skin hadn't been marble, but a different type of wood. She writhed as the flames threatened to engulf her, no longer able to issue coherent threats.

Aradie flung what looked like a wind blade. It spiraled through the air, cutting clean through the fake Irias's neck, severing the head cleanly.

Irias's body dropped to the ground, her head rolling to the other corner, the eyes open in shock and the face barely singed.

Quinn watched it until it came to a stop at her feet, not entirely sure how she should feel.

"Put the flames out," Aradie said to her, the words cutting through to Quinn as she turned to the owl who usually sat on her shoulder, and Quinn blinked.

Extracting the oxygen effectively put the flames out, but Quinn couldn't stop thinking about Irias's death. Not that having the charred corpse and detached head sitting right near her helped any.

Aradie might have decapitated her, but Quinn pretty much burned her to death.

She wasn't entirely sure how she felt.

But she did know she didn't regret it.

28

ODDLY FAMILIAR

THE VINES BENEATH IRIAS'S BODY THRASHED AS THEY PRACTICALLY devoured her. Quinn would have thought they were simply returning her to the earth if the violence inherent in the act wasn't so explicitly obvious. What was left of the surrounding foliage pushed through the charred mess she'd left and was busy revitalizing itself through the energy dissipating from Irias's body.

"Fire. Now." Aradie snapped the words, and they sounded just like they did when her owl spoke to her through a mind connection, filled with impatience.

Quinn blinked and sent controlled flames out toward the root of the problem. Not even the unintentional pun could make her smile right then.

That was just the thing with this undergrowth. It wasn't about to cooperate if it didn't have to. Thus, tightly controlled and aimed fire was the best thing for making it stop. She didn't bother apologizing for not having acted faster. Instead, she got busy doing what she should have known to do instinctively.

The ground churned under them—writhed, in fact.

It screamed in defiance.

Irias's body was mostly pulled underneath by the time the flames rose in intensity. Their level of heat increased so much that a high-pitched scream, barely discernable, began to permeate the air around them. The squeal reminded Quinn of the sound a balloon made that was highly inflated when you let it go, and all the oxygen came whooshing out of it.

Loud, and ear piercing, but ultimately all bark.

She really hoped the book hadn't been on the fake-Irias corpse.

Losing all that stored magic, plus the magic it took to create a tome in the first place, would be a blow to a new branch.

Without something to feed off, in fact, with the food source *cut* off, the vines and roots began to wither. They blackened, and not just from the fire that charred them. Instead, the power it fed from beneath them being cut off managed to damage them even more.

Quinn frowned. "There's something wrong with the source of magic in the area. As in . . . the source of their mana."

"Their nodes?" Aradie asked, her voice echoed strangely. Quinn wasn't surprised she sounded a little different, considering the change in form.

"Yeah, it's more like . . ." Quinn closed her eyes and reached out with her senses. The ground was repugnant, so much that she literally shirked away from it and had to force herself to keep diving, wrapping her shielding tightly around her mind. Letting that sort of infected power seep into her wouldn't end well for anyone.

Because the power was corrupted in a way Quinn hadn't seen before. Instead of chaos just sitting on top of the mana and suffocating it, this was interwoven, a huge part of the power. There was something else in there, more than just chaos. Perhaps the intention of whoever wove the magic also counted.

This didn't feel like anything else they'd encountered. The magical signature felt different.

She frowned, trying to piece together what happened from the ley line closest to her. It wasn't just filled with sludge; they were combined in a strange stickier than normal version of mana mixed with chaotic energy.

It had seeped everywhere, and they needed to clear the source out. Probably have to clear the nodes too if she could find them.

Fascinating.

The power leaking off it felt heavy. There wasn't a light way to wield it, and even just touching on it with her mind to test it gave her a feeling it would be cumbersome to wield. She frowned. Surely this wasn't the way chaos usually intermingled with mana.

A message flashed across her sight.

Warning. Contaminated area.

Chaos levels rising. Shielding required.

And that's when she found the node. It wasn't as big as the bountiful and beautiful one had been back in the Jenishu portion of this world. No . . . this one was just like the veins here. Thick, unwieldy, and dangerous. It settled against her shields, like it was trying to gnaw its way through to her. Like an attack attempting to be subtle in all its obviousness. Quinn shuddered, but her scales kicked up a notch, strengthening and sealing her defenses against it, against everything.

Still, the sludge felt slimy against her consciousness. It was all she could do to fashion a crude containment shield around it that she was fairly certain wouldn't last long.

When she got back to the Library, she'd take one hell of a long and hot shower.

Coming back to herself above ground, Quinn winced as she burned off the residual mental infection she could feel from her brief encounter with the substance. "That's nasty."

Aradie raised an eyebrow, her wing arms out to the side of her as she leveraged what appeared to be some 'sort of healing ability out over the ground. Something to extinguish the very nature of the vines and roots that were trying to devour the whole forest. "That bad?"

Quinn nodded, glancing around. "Worse." Even though the room they were standing in already felt better than it had, she was still skeptical. "Yes . . . this is deep-seated. We're going to need to repair the node here or its root systems will just keep spreading no matter how much we fix the surface levels."

Aradie nodded and shook herself, the feathers fluffing ever so slightly.

Quinn watched her, even as she tried to figure out exactly how to help purify the damned node down there. "So . . . are you going to talk to me about this whole humanoid thing?" Quinn sort of waved her hands toward Aradie like she was tracing her body.

Aradie laughed, and it sounded like a softer version of kookaburra. "Sometimes it's just easier to fight something, especially in a more enclosed space, when I take on a different form or a different type of stance. Irias—or whatever or whoever this was—couldn't fly, and wasn't out in the open. Dive bombing wouldn't work." Suddenly, Aradie looked very tired, her wings drooping ever so slightly. "But it does take its toll, as does speaking like this."

She shrugged down as Quinn watched, reverting to her owl form. Those gorgeous black and iridescent feathers practically glowed with energy before she made herself small enough to sit back in her preferred spot on Quinn's shoulder.

All felt right with the world for a split second before Quinn remembered she had to sanitize the damned mana node underneath them. "You're not going to help me?"

I can help you just fine from here without having to expend excess energy on maintaining what is, to me, an unnatural form.

Quinn nodded. It did make sense, and she wasn't about to argue and risk chasing away any help at all.

But first . . . we need to find the root of this infection. This isn't coming from the Library. We know that because the Jenishu section had a pristine root system, with a glorious, almost full node.

It was unusual for Aradie to speak this much, so Quinn let her. It was nice to have her speaking instead of assaulting her mind with copious images.

This runs deeper. It's far more sinister than the sludge build up was back at the Library. It's . . .

Quinn blanched as the answer came to her from one of the copious texts she'd devoured over the last few months. "It's people, isn't it?" she asked it softly, not wanting to say the words out loud, but realizing it needed to be tangible for her to appreciate the gravity of what they'd discovered.

Aradie did one of those owl shrugs, and Quinn sighed. She didn't need the bird to answer the literally bleeding obvious.

It was a waste of energy trying to cleanse the node without first going to the source. Quinn ran her hand through her ponytail and tugged on it. She was beginning to wonder just how deep this whole sabotage thing went and whether or not they were only dealing with one group of people. This seemed like such a different approach. "Are the others gone or will they be back? We might need Narilin."

Aradie shook her head. *She's too damaged right now, injured. She'll need healing. However . . . I did send a messenger, and I know they passed it on. We simply need people who can help us search, retrieve, and clear the rot from the roots. That's all. They should be here soon.*

"What do you mean here soon?" Quinn was a tad suspicious, even though it sounded like a good thing.

For an answer, Aradie reached out with her magic to the doorway they'd walked through to get into this room. Nowhere in the place appeared to have actual doors, which was part of the problem with teleporting directly here instead of using the aperture from the Jenishu area.

In the blink of an eye, a door appeared, but it wasn't a real one. No, it was more like it was superimposed over the archway to give the appearance of there being a door. But it seemed to be enough. No sooner had she done that, than the doors opened inward to reveal the Library.

It wasn't the main part of the Library, but one that was farther back through the stacks.

There, waiting to walk through and hopefully assist them, were Geneva, Finn, and two people she'd never seen before. They stepped through the door, letting it close behind them.

Quinn raised an eyebrow at the appearance, but the relief that flooded through her on seeing Geneva was palpable.

Geneva inclined her head even as she scrunched up her nose. "I've left the Library in Lynx and Dottie's hands. I doubt they'll burn it down before we return." She didn't sound a hundred percent sure about anything, but Quinn hoped she was right about that.

The Furionas fae balked ever so slightly as she moved around, the frown on her face deepening by the second. "This is . . . this is not good. I'm not even a Salosier, and I can tell how bad this is. Did you not notice the moment you stepped foot in here?"

She sounded so incredulous; Quinn felt a little foolish. But they'd had Narilin and Nishpa with them too . . . shouldn't they all have noticed? "We didn't. It . . ."

"Didn't feel the same," Nishpa said, coming into the room. She glanced around the meeting area and sighed. "This level of toxicity was masked when we arrived initially. Sadly, that gave us little leeway to ensure just how deeply this corruption ran. We came here expecting some hostility because of perceived slights by the Library. But what we got was something that runs far deeper than anything we expected and seemingly has nothing to do with the Balisor and Jenishu rivalry."

She glanced at the newcomers and frowned ever so slightly. "I'm not sure this'll be enough people. Will Aradie have the strength to open another portal if we need?"

Aradie hooted like that'd never be a problem, ever. And perhaps it wouldn't in owl kingdom.

"Excellent." Except Nishpa didn't sound like she thought anything was excellent currently or would ever be again. She'd obviously been more affected by all of this than she was letting on. Another thing to talk about later.

"Are Narilin and Karella okay?" Quinn asked, somewhat hesitantly. She'd just wanted to come and retrieve a book.

Just one damned book.

Nishpa shook her head sadly. "Narilin will be fine. But something in Karella has broken, and I'm not sure it's something we can piece back together. After all, she just lost her daughter and her husband. And she remembers nothing."

Quinn frowned. Something about that didn't quite ring true. "But did she lose her daughter? I don't think that was a body-snatcher or anything. Her appearance changed. Literally. If the other villagers are somewhere around here, then doesn't it stand to reason that the real Irias could be here too?"

Nishpa paused. "Well, it could be possible, but you also have to realize that this has been going on a lot longer than the Library has been back online. While it's a possibility, I'm not giving Karella any form of hope until we find out one way or another."

Quinn nodded slowly. "Then we should probably figure out where the source of the power drain is and see if we have any survivors, right?" Then she turned to the other two, who she'd never met before, but she swore were oddly familiar. "And just who might you two be?" she asked.

"Oh. We assumed you'd simply ask the system," the shorter of the two elves said. He had fair hair, pulled back into a wispy ponytail. The one to the left of him had sharper features and stood taller, probably even taller than Milaro. His hair was a mixture of golden brown and blond, and he had a slight smirk on his face.

He stood almost seven feet tall, if Quinn had to guess, about the same as Milaro. She blinked. "Wait a second."

Pulling up information in front of her, Quinn blanched slightly, inspecting the one that spoke first.

Hilrick Seveshall

Age: 126

Species: Areiltháhnish

Direct lineage to the Seveshall throne. 8th in line.

Cousin to Malakai

Nordon Seveshall

Age: 112

Species: Areiltháhnish

Direct lineage to the Seveshall throne. 7th in line.

Cousin to Malakai

She wasn't entirely sure what that meant, that the younger one was actually farther up in the line of succession, but it made much more sense that she sort of recognized them.

"Milaro couldn't come himself. He was in the middle of helping our cousin," Nordon said. He had the same light air to him that Quinn got from Milaro. Serious but not obvious about it. "So he sent us. We're here to help you bring out the dead."

Quinn wasn't entirely sure what to say. Thanks seemed kind of . . . wrong. "Oh. I'm not sure—"

Nordon shook his head. "I am. It's what I do. I'm here to help you track down the missing inhabitants of this area. I can sense the dead."

Well, that didn't sound ominous at all.

29

FASTER THAN EXPECTED

Milaro's relatives being able to sense the dead hadn't exactly been on Quinn's bingo card. That seemed like a decidedly Darigháh-nish component. More like something Arnekai would be capable of than the branch of elves Milaro headed. Then again, Milaro was capable of some amazingly creepy stuff himself. She shouldn't be surprised.

"That seems like a very handy ability to have," Quinn said, for want of having nothing else to say. "I guess we'll see how many dead there are?"

There was a small part of her holding out hope that people weren't dead. It was a naïve and positive part of her that wanted the Balisors to be okay. But she knew, deep down, given the voracity of those roots and the amount of power it took to eradicate them, that there were likely more dead than not.

Nordon focused on her for several seconds. But then she realized his gaze went beyond her. It saw through her like she wasn't even there, looking over to the other side of the hut. He was focused, likely on his ability, following the threads wherever they led him. Quinn stayed quiet so as not to interrupt.

She also desperately wanted to find the affinity this tied to so she could absorb the hell out of it.

The few seconds felt like an age, but she understood. He was tracking them, seeking survivors among the dead. Unless, of course, there were none and he couldn't sense life at all.

"He won't take too long," Hilrick said, his voice low. It hit a different frequency, the timbre almost unobtrusive. As if he was used to not disturbing his cousin's wavelengths.

Quinn nodded and flashed him a grateful smile. She could see elements of Malakai in both of the cousins, but much more Milaro. Nordon's smirk was practically Milaro's twin, but his eyes and nose were different. Finally, the taller elf cousin blinked, and the focus returned to his eyes. He frowned, the expression grim. "They're placed in . . . what I would call node formations in three spots surrounding the entire city. I'll warn you all now. A lot of them are corpses. There are some weak life signs there from what I can tell, but we'll need to hurry."

Hilrick nodded, and his eyes shifted from pale blue through to a black that bled into the sclera. Quinn felt a wave of power emanate from him for a brief second before the color bled back into the pupils. "I've sent for aid," he said matter-of-factly. "They should get here within the next hour, but we should begin rescue operations now."

Quinn nodded, and they took off at a pace easy enough to keep up with when they were hovering. The ground outside of the room they'd been in was still rife with writhing vines and roots. Quinn found it odd they couldn't stretch up from the ground much more than about six inches. Being evil root tentacles, she'd assumed they'd have vast cosmic power or something. She wondered if it was sentient enough to know what they were about to do.

"Do you still have access to the flame you used to cull the roots in the room?" Nordon asked.

Quinn nodded. "All the time."

"Excellent." A vindictive grin passed over his face. "Then we'll need you to help kill it with fire when we get to the room they're all in."

She'd expected as much. The flame she used came from her species specific arsenal—a variation of dragon fire. Her control over her fire affinities assisted her finesse, but her species skills felt more powerful, more pinpointed and potent.

The forest snapped at their heels and passed by far too slowly for Quinn's liking. It felt like time trudged on and on. There were still no birds anywhere, other than the owls of Aradie's following them at a close distance. No sounds of insects, which made sense now. She knew just how bad the undergrowth had become. All around them the forest, that should have been teeming with life, was empty, rotten from the core.

Quinn grimaced. She'd known it felt wrong. At least she knew why now.

Nordon stopped abruptly, and his expression turned dark. "In here," he said, his anger barely held in check if what Quinn felt rolling off him was any indication.

At first Quinn couldn't see what he meant by in here, and then he saw the opening. It appeared like any other part of the forest, but the gap between the foliage and the trees was deceptive. As Nordon moved forward, he almost disappeared behind what Quinn had thought was just another pile of forest debris. It wasn't. There was an entrance behind it leading into a space inundated with thrashing vines and roots.

Quinn sent the fire from her body whooshing straight out of her feet as she touched down. She focused the flame down to a pinpoint on eradicating the toxic vines by entering them and using only the vines as an avenue for the fire, breaking it, eating any oxygen they carried, and devouring them with flame. Thus freeing the people inside the room without setting them ablaze.

She had to be fully precise, direct, and detailed with this fire. It needed specificity.

Quinn had to hope it didn't backfire.

Clearing her throat and breathing in, she wished she hadn't. The stench permeating every inch of this tunnel began to make her eyes water, despite the fact that she channeled any smoke into oblivion with her fire affinities' snuffing tangent.

She refused to speak for many reasons, but also because of the chance the smell would overwhelm her if she let it enter her system in other ways. Even with the seal around her mouth to filter the air going in and out, it didn't make too much of a difference, all things considered. It wasn't a stench she could entirely block out.

Though she wished she could.

Finally, Nordon came to a full stop, faint light emanating from where he stood. Quinn accessed her own illumination spell and immediately wished she didn't.

The soft golden glow was directly juxtaposed to the horrors ahead of her.

At first, she wasn't entirely sure what she was seeing. And then she realized they were people. Piled up against each other, some of them on top of each other. All of them hues of grey and blue in the golden light. The walls writhed around them, vines and roots intertwining and quite audible snacking on the people.

The sound was a soft slurping that was hidden while they approached. Quinn suppressed the gagging her stomach so desperately wanted her to do.

She felt the anger flaring off Nordon as Hilrick pushed through to the people lying on the ground, dirt partially covering them as the vines feasted. The shorter cousin's mouth was drawn in a thin line, his eyes hard and angry. Even the way he held himself radiated hatred for what had been done. But he appeared to be a healer of some sort first above all else, and that's what he did.

Aradie cooed low. She sounded like she was in pain. *I'll scan them with the system so we have an update of who has passed on. You help them purge this taint from the forest.*

In the meantime, Quinn allowed her fire to surge. But not around them, no, she allowed herself to extend her senses farther underground and instead of disturbing the corpses and any potential survivors, Quinn began to burn away at the roots with renewed, very targeted, vigor. Cutting the power drain off at the source was oddly gratifying.

Hilrick shot her a grateful look, and Quinn nodded, tracking multiple flames at once and making sure none of them harmed anyone who was still living. While it didn't exactly matter if they were dead, she still tried not to reach them . . . to cut the vines off just below their connection to their victims. She wasn't sure if the vines could still drain once a body had become a corpse, but she wasn't taking risks.

The sheer evil that spread out from these plants made Quinn's blood boil. She couldn't believe the level of organization that must have gone into this. There was a thread of power through these roots, a signature that didn't belong. It also didn't appear to be related to Irias, or whoever it had been who'd taken on Irias form. The general feeling Quinn got was puppets on a string. Not just the people who'd been a part of this city. The Balisors in general, and, to a certain extent her and the Library.

Considering how they'd basically been lured to this precise location, Quinn wasn't willing to chalk it up to coincidence.

And it felt nothing like what she'd experienced when they encountered Dravishk.

She began building her shields around everything she was doing, protecting everyone on this hellish journey with her. If the magic could get into the forest ecosystem, there was no telling what it would do to an organic, living species. And she wasn't about to give some weirdly alien being control over the Library through her. She didn't have the time for that.

They didn't have the defenses for that.

If Korradine's betrayal was anything to go by, the Library wouldn't withstand another attack. And Quinn couldn't risk that.

It was almost like it sensed her preparations for a more in-depth protection. The surrounding vines began to thrash, upsetting the corpses, beginning to drain more energy from those around them.

But Hilrick didn't let himself be interrupted, and Quinn kept severing every connection she found. He kept on steadfast in his removal of the few living Balisors they'd found.

Nordon reacted in a way Quinn hadn't expected. He dropped to his knees in a fluid motion, smacking his hands down on the writing vines while they tried to attach themselves to him. For a second Quinn thought they'd lost him, and she gasped in shock and frustration.

Until she realized he wasn't the one being attacked.

At first, it was difficult to tell. Considering their coloring was already obscured by the interior and the dim silvery light from her own blue flames. But when the first vine broke off from Nordon, and the others began trying to escape, Quinn realized what he was doing even without having to reach out with her sensing abilities to figure it out.

He was feeding their own poison back into them. Reversing it. Except with a difference. Somehow, he'd modified it in those split seconds and made it toxic to the plants and roots themselves.

Quinn nodded and magnified the poison with her own ability to flush it through the roots. It rushed and began to stagnate all the ones around them. Withering the roots and vines to such an extent that they became brittle husks. The ones attached to Nordon fell away, but he wasn't done yet. He dug his fingers into the ground and muttered words Quinn couldn't quite hear under his breath.

The ground beneath him pulsed, bubbling ever so slightly. It rippled as if it was in agony. But it didn't disturb where she stood, nor did it harm anything near the survivor bodies Hilrick was slowly salvaging.

The walls and ceiling began to crumble away into a dust so find that Quinn asked a light breeze to help it away. All around them, above them, and underneath them, the infected vines began to recede, allowing the real forest foliage to come to the fore.

Sadly, it was sickened, having been deprived of light and air. But Quinn could see it beginning to reach for the pale sunlight filtering through the trees above them now the hideout had been revealed.

She reached out with her earth affinity, undeveloped though it was, and coaxed them to thrive. Encouraged them.

Even the stench began to lift, carried away by the wind. Hilrick continued to administer and rescue those people he could, while Nordon followed the roots into the ground, chasing as many as it could, allowing them to reap their just rewards, while Quinn turned the rest of them to ash.

Aradie nudged her. *I've got all their identities. That's a lot of Balisors.* She sounded so sad.

Finally, Nordon stood and wiped his hands off on his pants, his grim visage relaxing ever so slightly. "That's this section. We have two more we need to reach."

Hilrick nodded. "I can leave these guys here as long as those roots won't come back and repeat what they've been doing for what looks like years. I don't even understand how this happened."

"They'll research it," Nordon said, his words clipped.

Quinn could tell he was barely keeping his anger under control. She didn't say anything, because she was only there to lend aid and help eradicate this. It wasn't her area of expertise right now, but she'd make sure that if anything else like this ever happened again, she'd know exactly what needed to be done, and she'd be completely prepared and able to do it.

Nordon turned to her. "Up for the next one?"

She nodded, and Aradie cooed, speaking softly into her mind. *Let them know the reinforcements are about to cross over and to mark this specific spot for them. They were faster than expected. They can take the injured.*

"Reinforcements are about to cross over. We should mark this area," she said, her voice strong, her anger still fueling her.

Hilrick dusted himself off. He flashed her a wan smile. "Thanks. Let's get going."

Quinn didn't need to be told twice. This was messy work, and even as they passed the pile of dead Balisors, Quinn felt it fueling her anger even further. This wasn't some weird parasite, no. Everything she'd gathered from the information the plants left behind was that this had been planted by someone who knew precisely what they were doing. And no pun was intended.

Now all they had to do was figure out just who would have benefited from this. While the Sölem seemed so obvious, this didn't feel right. There was more to this, almost a personal level of animosity.

She was determined to figure it out.

But first, they had a few more lives to save.

At least she hoped they did.

TOO CONVENIENT

QUINN WAS ONE OF THE FIRST TO GO THROUGH THE PORTAL BACK TO the Library. They'd finished the other two locations in much the same fashion, and the sick were only just beginning to get ferried back.

She hit the other side of the door running and accessed the main console at the check-in desk.

"Hospital requirements," she muttered at it and it brought up a long list of information. Quinn fueled her anger at the Balisor situation into action. She scanned the list, looking for the structure and the cost. Cringing at the energy it'd sap, she double checked with the Library that it wouldn't completely drain the bank.

No, we should be fine to fund a hospital with the current energy levels. We won't sink back down. Visitors have been plenty over the last few weeks, and our power is constantly growing. Just do what needs to be done to save them.

Quinn didn't need to be told twice. She activated the first and what she considered the best choice.

Library Hospital Option 3

Capacity: 350 Patients, 50 staff

She blinked at it. Wait. Did that mean it came with staff?

No, it doesn't come with staff. You can order some golem nurses, maybe a surgeon and a doctor. Universal versions, which is what we'll want, costs more materials, but we currently have enough. If you don't opt for the universal version, they won't have the ability to treat all species. Don't skimp. There are more than enough helpers from the rescue teams to assist in other areas.

Quinn nodded, grateful the Library was just as focused on helping these victims as she was. This wasn't something she could or wanted to figure out herself. Not with lives on the line. She activated the hospital, complete with a doctor, surgeon, and ten nurses.

While she wasn't sure what they'd do with the patients once they'd treated them, at least they had a facility capable of housing them for now. Given the state of most of the survivors she was certain they'd be in the hospital for a while. After their ordeal, they'd need more than just bodily healing.

Hospital Level 3 Activated.

Location: Offshoot of Infirmary

Construction time: Negligible—15 minutes.

Doctor Golem Initiated

Craft time expedited. Ready in 91 minutes.

Surgeon Golem Initiated

Craft time expedited. Ready in 124 minutes.

Nursing Golem x 10 Initiated

Craft time expedited.

Incubation optimized.

Ready in 65 minutes.

Quinn blinked at the listing, just happy they'd get somewhere as fast as possible. She still didn't understand how the Library could shift around in its dimension and build things like the hospital, but she wasn't about to look that particular gift horse in its mouth.

Once that was done, she went back through the doors to assist moving the rescued Balisor-Salosier's to the almost hospital.

Time passed in a blur of action. Where all the elves around her whipped the injured into healthy-enough-to-transport mode. Geneva and Finn helped ferry the injured through the Library, giving directions to those on the rescue team who weren't regulars.

Nishpa, being the mind healer she was, flitted around keeping most of them in a decently relaxed mental state. Quinn could practically see a soft blue hum around each of the victims' heads, like it was keeping them calm and oblivious for now. Having been in those node dungeons for who knew how long, their minds were a mess. Fully understandable, but not something Quinn knew enough about to risk attempting to help with on her own magic.

Nishpa, however, was a godsend. She knew the brains of people like the back of her hand. Even if they were a different species, her training allowed for her to utilize calming techniques for their emotional centers and to help ease their transition through the dimensional portal back into the Library.

Nishpa frowned as they moved several from the last hovel through. Their bodies jerked, unable to take on all the magical streams that entered their brains as they crossed the Library line.

"They're fragile," the Furionas fae said, sadness flickering in her eyes.

Quinn got that. Magic had been used to defile them, it'd been used to wrest control of their bodies, minds, and lifeforce, and so traveling through something with as much magic as the doorways to the Library had to be destabilizing.

The Library foyer was full to the bursting, and still there were more patients to come. Quinn muscled her way through the crowd, grateful for Nordon and Hilrick, who attempted to carve a way for her.

People were funneled into the infirmary, waiting for the hospital to open. It took almost no time for it to pop up.

Finally, with the hospital in place, they were able to begin allocating rooms to each of the injured. Quinn gave Finn, Geneva, and Dottie access to the hospital control on the same level as an intake nurse so things could move smoothly.

Geneva sorted people into their injury severity, while Finn allocated rooms, and Dottie checked on the needs of all the rescuers for their patients. It was a long process, and Quinn wasn't entirely sure what she would have done without Finn, Geneva, and Dottie. Not to mention Malakai's cousins, Hilrick and Nordon. They all rallied and helped get the injured into beds.

Milaro and Nishpa began to check on the patients while they waited for the doctor and surgeon golems to be completed. Quinn wished she'd studied up enough on healing to be more help. She did watch closely, though.

Karella was one of the first people to be seen. She wasn't quite catatonic, but the shock to her system about her husband's death and her daughter's likely death, or at least disappearance, put her into such a frozen state that she was of little help to any of the survivors.

Slowly, Nishpa and Milaro worked their way through the initial influx of patients. It'd take another quarter hour for the nurses to be available, so they had to work with what they had.

Hilrick returned to assisting the transport through the portal, making sure their brains remained intact on the journey through the door.

Which appeared to be no small task.

Quinn hadn't ever seen the doors open for this long.

But there were still a hundred or so people needing to be transferred. It wasn't like it'd stop anytime soon.

The first nurse wasn't exactly what Quinn expected. It appeared like the typical clay version of a golem she'd always thought they'd be, except it was in coloring only. The golem was actually more metallic, just in that reddish orange clay hue, and at first Quinn was taken aback.

They had a little white nurse hat on the top of their head that was practically embossed with a red cross, the one that looked more like a plus sign. But that was where the similarity with old-fashioned nursing from Earth ended. The cross had syringes and vials surrounding it in a circular fashion, and some other implements Quinn didn't recognize.

It almost looked like runes.

None of the golems were particularly gendered, and they all appeared mostly the same.

Quinn would get around to giving them names when they didn't have a few hundred survivors to get through.

Once the nurse golems arrived things began to move smoother. Patients were checked in faster and checked over by not just the nurses but the healing aides. Nishpa requested aid from the Jenishu Salosier division, even though they came in hazmat gear. Couldn't be too careful with root spores in the atmosphere.

She turned to Quinn. "Here." And a book dropped into Quinn's hands. A very important restricted access book.

"What? How?" she asked, flustered. *The Parsneauvian Theory of Spatial Dimension Manipulation*'s name flashed across her HUD all innocent in its return.

Nishpa grimaced. "It's the only thing Karella has been aware enough to do. Give us her husband's storage band. Now . . . we have patients to tend to."

Quinn sighed with relief, as it appeared they'd be able to handle this many patients.

Though she had no medical background, and frankly, very few healing abilities, Quinn was eventually able to assist Nishpa in calming the patients' mental states as the Furionas guided her in how to calm them using some of her more advanced metal abilities combined with a couple of the species genetic traits she'd been equipped with.

A superpower crash course, so to speak.

This wasn't like what Arnekai had asked Quinn to do to her son. They weren't taking away choices. They were calming the panic attacks, the realizations of what had happened, giving them room for the body to heal so they could address the damage to their minds later.

It was something Quinn was fully on board to learn. Considering how much she'd been able to help Eugea way back on Ishiposa Isle, this was a next logical step for her. She needed to understand it fully so she could finish the affinity avenue she'd created.

Not to mention, it was something hugely beneficial to all of the current patients. And it meant she could *do* something.

Next, the general doctor popped into view. He stood about six and a half feet tall, around Malakai's height. And he was, undoubtedly, male. Dressed in a suit, and remarkably similar to Misha's metallic tones, he approached Quinn with pure purpose to his stride.

"Librarian. I have been summoned to assist you. Please give me more than the rudimentary information the system has provided so far."

Quinn had to stop herself from gaping. Other than Misha, Cook, and Farrow, she'd never witnessed a golem be so conversational, or with it, upon its creation. She wasn't entirely sure how to brief the golem.

Hilrick stepped in very smoothly. So smoothly, in fact, she hadn't even realized he was there prior to him stepping in.

"I'll walk with you, as I gave initial treatment to most of our current patients." He steered the doctor away, and Quinn heaved a sigh of relief. Something about the immediately active golem gave Quinn pause. She'd not expected such an alert and forthright one.

The Library piped up. *Doctors are a type of supervisor. The surgeon golem will be much the same. They're more advanced versions because of the complexities involved in the tasks they must perform. You'll be able to summon him the same way you summon Misha.*

Quinn pondered that for a second. *So they're like Misha—supervisory level?*

Precisely. With the same powers and not beholden to them.

Quinn wasn't sure Misha would like that, but then again, they didn't have a choice. *How do I summon him? I didn't give him a name yet.*

Doctor will suffice for now. Surgeon for the surgeon. The Library paused momentarily. *Do you require other golems other than those you've currently ordered?*

Quinn shook her head and then added *No, probably not best to load up on nurses. We have others who can assist.*

Excellent. I'll put the system into hyper mode so we can pull some more power from the amount of activity we'll be having for a few days. It'll help us regenerate what we just used for this massive undertaking.

There wasn't even an undertone of concern in the Library's tone.

It was obviously fine with what had been expended for now, although, if Quinn had said they needed more, she got the feeling the Library would have made it work. Despite the desperation to get the Library back up to full power, in this instance, Quinn could tell that Drevicia was far more concerned with taking care of the victims they'd recovered.

Taking care of the people who relied on power to protect them.

For now, they were okay.

Quinn couldn't promise the same for whoever had done this to the Balisors when they found them.

With all the patients in the hospital, the lobby felt empty once more.

"That's a very novel way to get all the patients into one place," Nordon said from beside her, startling her as she hadn't even realized he was there. These new elves were sneakier.

"The Library expands wherever and whenever it wants to." Quinn shrugged. "People can just use the Library doors to get directly into the hospital now that it's established instead of traipsing through the entire thing."

Nordon eyed her, like she'd stated something the bleeding obvious. Then he spoke. "You're nothing like what Malakai described."

Quinn blinked. First up, she hadn't even known about these cousins, although in hindsight she knew Mal had family. It'd just never really come up. But that he'd been talking about her? She wasn't entirely sure how to take that. Before she could figure out how to respond, though, Nordon spoke again.

"It's really not a big deal. He just told us about the new Librarian when we asked. That's all. Probably not in the way you were thinking, anyway." He flashed her a rather mischievous grin.

"Well, I hope it wasn't all bad," she said, trying to lighten the moment and get out of feeling ridiculously put on the spot.

"No. It definitely wasn't all bad."

Quinn wasn't entirely sure how to read him.

"You're spinning lies again, aren't you Nordon?"

Quinn turned around. "Mal? What are you doing out of bed?!"

He grinned at her. "Pleased to see me? I'll have to raise my rates."

Quinn rolled her eyes. "You know I'm not paying you more than we already do. You didn't answer my question. What are you doing out of bed when I know for a fact that you should still be resting up?"

"I can walk and rest at the same time. Lynx and my grandfather are headed to your office for a chat, so I thought I'd come and fetch you. Not to mention save you from my cousin's load of bullshit."

She looked between the two of them. Nordon grinned again, and she figured out what it was about his expression. They were competitive with each other. She just wasn't entirely sure in what way that'd be. Especially considering Mal was so much younger than those two.

Regardless, if they had stuff to do in her office, that's where she was headed.

"I need to get going," she said. "Thank you for everything. You guys were amazing. We wouldn't have found them without you."

Nordon shrugged. "I'm pretty sure you would have found them. Maybe we wouldn't have saved as many, but your flames did the bulk of the pruning work. I just turned their poison back on them."

Quinn remembered the ash and rot that consumed the vines and roots. "Whatever you think. It was teamwork as far as I'm concerned. I appreciated your help."

Before he could say anything else, Quinn turned and headed for her office. As much as she'd enjoyed working with the Seveshall cousins, her work never seemed to end.

On the way, however, Dottie stopped her and Malakai.

"Librarian! You'll never guess! This is stupendous!"

Quinn raised an eyebrow. "Just what is so stupendous?" she asked, trying not to sound too impatient.

"Two books! We only need two more books for the medicinal and alchemical branch."

Quinn raised an eyebrow. "That's great!" She still wasn't sure if the book she'd got was the actual book or not. Haritan's corpse loot hadn't smelled right.

Dottie almost seemed to deflate. "Well, I thought it was."

Quinn crouched down on impulse. She wasn't sure if the bench would take offense to it, but she really hoped Dottie wouldn't. "Look. I'm super excited about opening the new branch. Can you get those locations ready to go for me, so we can hurry up and get the next two? I'd also appreciate a little more information on the regions the books are supposed to be located in. This time, we weren't as prepared as we should have been. That's not going to happen again."

Dottie beamed at her. Not that Quinn could see an expression, but she got this distinct stream of happiness and determination from the superellex futora. Dottie was engaged and excited to be helping in any capacity.

"I'll get right on that."

Pushing herself back to standing, Quinn ignored the look Malakai was giving her for a few steps before finally giving in. "What?"

"You've come a long way from the girl I met when my grandfather dragged me here the first day." His words were soft, but she could tell he meant every single letter of them.

"I'll take that as a compliment."

He nodded. "Good."

She waited for something else quippy to come from him, but it didn't. So, as she pushed open the door to her office, she was slightly unsettled, just waiting for the next joke or pun to fall from Malakai's lips.

But instead, Milaro greeted her, along with Aradie who, it seemed, had retired to the office to recuperate. She had done a lot of work in the last day. Lynx was curled up in cat form on the couch, one eye open as he tracked her entrance into the room.

"Well?" Quinn asked. "What are we doing?"

Milaro smiled, Aradie hooted, and Lynx stretched languidly, only speaking after his yawn was complete. "We've narrowed down the location of one of your missing restricted books. *The Crown and Fall of Pocket Dimensions due to Spatial Interference*, in fact."

Quinn knew there was more to it. She narrowed her eyes. "And . . . what are you leaving out? This sounds mightily too convenient."

Lynx snorted back a laugh. "Told you she'd ask."

"Ah, that you did." Milaro hesitated. "Well, it appears the book might actually be quite close to one of the Library's kin."

"Drav . . . ?" she asked, remembering almost too late that she probably shouldn't use the whole name.

"No. Not him. But . . ." Milaro glanced at Lynx as if seeking confirmation. "We have the approximate location of one of the hibernating dragons. We just have to narrow it down more."

Quinn blinked. Of all the things on her lists, she hadn't expected this.

After all, it wasn't even one of her checkboxes. And she had no idea what it meant.

3 1

SLEEPING DRAGONS

QUINN PINCHED THE BRIDGE OF HER NOSE AND COUNTED TO FIVE. IT was becoming a habit she'd rather not develop, but she didn't seem to have a choice in the matter. "Why should it matter that we've found a sleeping dragon that may or may not appear to be in the same vicinity as the book we need?"

Because that was a sentence she'd imagined herself never saying in her existence.

Milaro blinked. "Because the Library was having difficulty locating some of its siblings."

Only mildly. The Library sounded somewhat affronted. *I just couldn't precisely locate them due to the waves we send out when we're hibernating. It's meant to obfuscate exact location, so we're not easily found.*

Quinn perked up at that comment. "You mean like the signal that allows us to locate books? The exact locations, I mean?"

For several seconds, both the Library and Milaro were quiet before the Library finally spoke again. *Yes. As in it makes those books, or any items, within our direct vicinity more difficult to locate. Unless it's the Library because of the dimensional door aspects we put in place.*

"Sort of like how we couldn't pinpoint the *Parsneauvian* originally or the *Crown* book now, right?" Sometimes she thought these magical creatures all relied on their magic, perhaps a bit too much.

When you put it that way . . . The Library practically groaned at itself.

"So . . . it could be highly plausible that the books we're looking for are in the vicinity of hibernating Library siblings?" It sounded so fantastical Quinn could barely believe she'd suggested it.

The Library sounded somewhat abashed when it spoke. *I have no idea why we didn't think of that. It seems so obvious in hindsight.*

Quinn shrugged. "Everything seems obvious in hindsight."

Lynx stretched himself out to his human form and glared at Quinn. "Fine. Rub it in."

"I'm not." Quinn sighed. "Look, it's highly obvious that none of us knew this. I'm an outsider for so much, so my first reaction is always to use logic. This was a logical conclusion based on the evidence presented to me. I'm not used to magic . . . well, not entirely yet. It doesn't do everything for me because five months hasn't replaced twenty years of having to do things manually. Don't worry, I'm sure I'll get used to just relying on magic for all my solutions soon."

Milaro gave her an odd look. His head cocked half to the side, he considered her and her words carefully. "That's an astute observation. One that, to my own detriment, I'm guilty of. I never seek to look at things in a mundane way simply because I've only ever known magic. And let's face it, magic can solve almost everything."

"Almost," Quinn said, her voice tight. It hadn't solved her parents' deaths. In fact, it had been the cause of them. It hadn't helped Escadril, or Ikeshal, or any of the people who'd been injured in their fight against Kajaro. It had caused their injuries, and indeed, the fight that led to them. Magic was just as dangerous as it was magnificent. And she'd already seen what it could do in hands that wanted power.

Still, digressing wouldn't help any of them right then.

She took a deep breath and flashed Milaro a smile. "Anyway—do we think it's possible that either the dragon is hoarding the book, or else, that some other person knows how close the book is to the dragon and is using its signature to disguise its whereabouts?"

"Could be a bit of both, right? Or it could be a complete coincidence." Lynx butted in. "I can trace the book very close to its source."

"Define 'very close'." Quinn crossed her arms and waited.

Lynx paused, seriously giving it some thought. "Within a solar system."

Quinn counted to five again. "That's not as close as you think it is. At least not in human terms."

"Good thing you're not human."

Another point for Lynx, who was just being facetious. She groaned. "This isn't helping. Which dragon is it? Are we certain it's not Drav—"

Milaro cut her off. "Names have power. Not the best idea to be saying his full name out loud."

Quinn frowned. "I wasn't going to use the full name. What else am I supposed to call him? Library's brother who's a bit of a dick and refuses to let people live in peace?"

Milaro laughed this time, and it was a refreshing sound. He hadn't laughed in what seemed like an age. "No, but that's a very accurate description. Though you did forget the part about 'he thinks he's always right'."

"That doesn't narrow it down. I know a lot of people who think they're always right." Quinn gave him a pointed look and then relented. "At least you're capable of learning new things. I'm not so sure Drav is."

"Yes. Drav will do," Lynx said, his eyes flashing as he obviously fiddled with several system settings. "I can't get a closer location on the book yet. But I do believe once we're in the vicinity, we'll be able to narrow down a location."

Quinn raised an eyebrow. "We have to go planet hopping? Well, since he isn't hibernating, do we know who else it could be?"

Lynx shrugged, as did the others in the room.

"That's a no." She tried to figure out other ways to trace this new dragon when the Library piped back up.

Actually. I have an inkling. You'll need to approach her.

"This dragon is a her? Wait, me?" Quinn asked, knowing it was her, but still wishing she was wrong.

Yes, I'm marginally certain it's one of my sisters. And yes. You.

"Why?"

Well, you smell like a dragon. Mostly. Pretty much just like me. She won't send you away or eat you. The Library paused. *Probably.*

Quinn blinked. "Probably. You do realize that's not nearly as comforting as you thought, right? And are you sure it's a female dragon? And when do I need to go? Now?" She could practically hear the Library shaking its head.

No. Not now. I have to figure out a few logistics and exactly what we're sending you into. My sister has never been the most . . . industrious, and I can tell if I extend my concentration levels because of her energy signature. She's never been good at concealing her own. I don't believe she actually has the book herself, just that it's in her vicinity. I'll also attempt to wake and communicate with her again.

Quinn was slightly mollified by that. "Fine. Then what are we doing here? Why are we doing this now? There are so many patients to take care of . . ." Her voice trailed off, and she realized that while she couldn't help as much as she wanted, she should be out there doing something.

"It's more of a briefing on what we need to get done and it's important information," Lynx said. "If they know how the dragon proximity screws with our ability to scan for anything, then it's likely there could be more books we haven't yet figured out a way to trace in the same vicinity of other dragons. Either Drav hasn't checked for them, or he's using it as a hiding tool."

A lightbulb went off in Quinn's head. "Wait, so do you think he could be using their signatures specifically to screw with us?"

"It's a possibility." Milaro paused, like he was gathering his thoughts. She watched him and the way his face scrunched slightly. He was overdoing it again; she just knew it. Overtiring himself . . . but the thing was, how were they supposed to manage to get more rest if everything kept imploding like it had recently?

"There's still a lot we need to do before we can retrieve it then, right?" Quinn asked for clarification.

To be fair, she might also have borrowed it and I just can't remember. The Library spoke up. *Also I need the boost in power another branch signifies, and frankly, so does the entire universe. It should help us get more exact locations for the books and dragons as well.*

"Are you a hundred percent sure this dragon isn't Drav in disguise?" Quinn said. "Can you be sure of that?"

The Library paused for a moment. So long, in fact, Quinn wasn't sure if she'd end up answering at all. Finally, when she was about to give up, the Library spoke. *Yes. That isn't Drav. It's too large, not in humanoid form, and frankly . . . not powerful enough. I'm quite positive it's the second youngest. She's always been a bit of a dreamer. Sleep is one of her most powerful affinities.*

"Does that mean she deals in dreams?" Quinn asked, suddenly curious.

The Library cringed ever so slightly. *She could . . . if she put the effort in.*

"Do you think she might have put the effort in with Kajaro, just on a whim? Perhaps because she was bored?" Quinn tried to phrase the question in a way that wouldn't upset the Library. She didn't exactly want to go around accusing everyone of being on Kajaro's wagon.

But she'd had a damned mind bomb I her head and now her dreams seemed to gravitate toward others. This all seemed very convenient. Here they were, looking for dragons, books, and traitors. There, right in the middle of one of the areas they knew the books were in, just happened to be a dragon.

It was far too much of a coincidence for Quinn. She didn't believe in them, and wasn't about to start now unless someone had a much better explanation for her.

In the Library's defense, it did really think about Quinn's words, like it was hearing them for the first time. Maybe it was just really considering them for the first time. Just like Quinn hadn't wanted, at first, to believe that her parents weren't really parents at all, but people who'd been sent to guard her. Sometimes, what people wanted to be true was only the truth in their own minds.

No. I don't believe she would ever be bored enough to agree that chaos unleashed and uncontrolled is a good thing. She saw far too many people she cared about die, be consumed and simply cease to exist. It changes you when you witness a world disintegrate back into nothing as a being consumes it. Plus, she's hibernating . . . can't be doing anything right now.

The melancholy in those words hit Quinn straight in the gut. For a few seconds she even found it hard to breathe until the Library pulled back the well of emotion that escaped it. It made Quinn wonder if that was something the Library suppressed all the time. Or if that was a one-off reaction it simply couldn't keep under wraps. Or if she even realized Quinn felt it, because it didn't appear to have affected anyone else. "So not in cahoots, then?"

Not in cahoots.

Quinn nodded. Hibernating dragon—check! They'd need to resolve the hibernating dragon dilemma as soon as the Library had more power. Which meant . . . "I'm guessing we need to go out and grab the two books we need to open the alchemical-medicinal branch, right?"

Milaro shook himself just a little, a smile breaking out over his face. He grinned at her. "Yes!" His eyes narrowed momentarily at his grandson, who looked disturbingly pale. Malakai scowled and left the room before Milaro continued. "Now, to retrieve the first one, we'll need to go over your atmospheric adjustment shielding, not only for your mental shields but also your physical. It's quite an exciting conundrum to visit—"

Dottie practically pranced into the room, breaking everyone's concentration.

Milaro raised an eyebrow at her. "Well met, and just what brings you on a visit at this inopportune time?" He sounded a little grumpy that she'd interrupted him.

He emphasized things so heavily that Quinn ended up being quite certain Dottie knew she was intruding. But it seemed the bench had less than a care in the world and simply let a giggle escape her.

Quinn couldn't help herself. She laughed and then laughed even harder when she realized Milaro was quite put out at the fact she was laughing so hard, probably at him.

"Do enlighten us as to what's so funny," he said, glaring at both of them in that stern way of his.

"Sorry," Quinn said, wiping her eyes. "Dottie is just so joyous, and you were just so sour toward her. It came off as comical."

Milaro raised a very delicate eyebrow and cocked his head to one side, as if replaying the entire situation in his head. A smile cracked his lips, and he nodded. "I do see. Sometimes I think I revert to . . . what you would call pompous?"

"Definitely sometimes pompous. But it's okay. We get it." Quinn grinned but managed to sober herself up and turn to Dottie. "What brings you here?"

"The book!" Dottie practically jumped out of her . . . wood? Considering she didn't have skin out of which to jump.

"Yes. We have a lot of books. To which one were you referring?" Quinn asked, playing it up. She had no idea what had got Dottie so excited, but she wasn't above a few jabs of her own.

Dottie paused, like she'd just expected them all to know precisely what she was talking about. "The book. Well, one of them anyway. It's back!"

"It walked in by itself?" Quinn asked incredulously, then remembered who she was talking to and slowed down. "Okay, one thing at a time. Which book? Is it one of the two remaining to open the branch?"

"Yes! Oh!" Dottie managed to look sheepish, even if nothing outwardly changed in her appearance. "Sorry, got ahead of myself again. *The Mattiniman Balance Between Mana and Energy: Explained for the Beginner* just got returned! We only need one more book to open the branch!"

A huge smile broke out on Quinn's face. One more book, that was it. Now she just had to figure out why this one had been gone so long, and where the hell the second one was.

Piece of cake, right?

32

FARINTH SPRITE

"What are you waiting for?" Dottie asked, her tone and stance expectant.

Quint blinked at the bench, not quite understanding the question. "What do you mean, what am I waiting for?" she asked. No matter what she considered, she couldn't think of anything but the patients right then.

Dottie laughed as if it was the silliest thing she'd ever heard. "Don't you want to go and get the book?"

"Well, it's in the Library, right? Like, I don't need to go and fetch it from somewhere," Quinn said. Suddenly confused, she was sure Dottie had just told her that the second last book they needed for the alchemical branch had been returned.

"Well, of course, it's here," Dottie said. Now she sounded confused. "Don't you want to meet the person who brought it back?"

Quinn blinked and narrowed her eyes in suspicion. "Do I want to meet the person who brought it back?"

Milaro laughed. "Dottie, who is it?"

"Come on, you should all see." Dottie sounded unbelievably excited about this visitor. Quinn wasn't too sure how to take that. She reached out with her senses but couldn't identify anybody that she already knew standing anywhere around the check-in desk. At least not somebody she knew who was unexpected. They were all here or in the infirmary. She even scanned for Eugea just in case she'd come to visit or something. But no, no one.

It wasn't Hal either, which for some obscure reason was oddly disappointing for Quinn.

With a heavy sigh, Quinn looked at the superellex futora. She guessed they could spare a few minutes. Everything did seem to be relatively under control after all. "Fine, Dottie, lead the way."

"You don't need to sound so excited. I thought you'd be interested to see who brought the book back. After all, I don't think we've had a visit from her yet." Dottie sounded oddly disgruntled.

"Which would probably make sense," Milaro said as they all walked toward the check-in desk. He chuckled and continued, "After all, if they'd already visited, then they would have realized that the Library was in fact open and returned the book sooner than now. Sooner than us summoning them to bring the book."

"Oh," Lynx said. "I see." And he stopped talking but wore a very smug grin.

Quinn stepped up into the check-in desk and right in front of her, standing on top of a very thick book titled *The Mattiniman Balance Between Mana and Energy: Explained for the Beginner*, was an absolutely tiny fairy.

At least, that's what Quinn thought at first.

She stood about five inches tall and had regal silver hair that looked sort of like lametta on German Christmas trees many, many years ago. Her nose was extremely pointed and there were faint scale imprints all over her skin that glowed with a silver-golden hue. Her wings weren't like butterfly wings, either. They were more like multiple sets of hummingbird wings all down her back. Maybe three or four, but they moved so fast Quinn belatedly realized this tiny being wasn't actually standing on the book. She was hovering constantly. The wings never stopped, and if Quinn let her senses extend, she could tell that there was an ever-so-soft hum in the air emanating from them.

She inspected the tiny creature.

Sprite—Keeper of Alchemical Lore

Located in the: Farinth Region

Library Allies For: Since Inception

Library Standing: Fan-bloody-tastic

Books currently overdue: Total 1

Name: Betty

Quinn raised an eyebrow at the Library's embellishment and practically felt the chuckle in the back of her mind.

The little sprite raised up to hover in front of Quinn's eyes. The silver hair sparkled in the light that suddenly shone on her. Then she lowered herself back down, her tiny foot tapping against the massive book. Quinn wasn't exactly sure what to say. Frankly, she wondered if the sprite had read the massive book or if she'd used magic to condense it down to be a tiny book, that would still feel massive to a sprite but wasn't actually massive to a human and yet still contained all the magical properties and language. Which was probably a little too fantastical, even for magic, but Quinn wouldn't put it past that.

The sprite cocked her head to one side. Her eyes were massive and reminded Quinn very much of many anime characters that she'd watched. The eyes seemed to take up most of her face. Quinn could practically feel the grin radiating from Dottie.

"Hi," Quinn said. "Nice to meet you, Betty."

Betty's face cracked into a massive grin. "Oh, thank you. That's very kind of you, Librarian. Now, how long has the Library been open again? I didn't believe the rumors, you know. I've heard many rumors over the last few hundred years. There were several times I tried to bring the book back and as you know it is rather large, and it does take a lot of energy for me to actually adjust the book to its proper size again once I've borrowed it and so I have tried to return it multiple times and always been inconvenienced because of it. I just didn't believe that the Library was truly back. Am I still going to be fined?"

Quinn blinked. There'd been a lot of expectations she'd had for the sprite. A veritable waterfall of words had not been among them.

"I swear . . ." Lynx muttered as he stepped in front of her in his human form. "Hello, Betty."

Her eyes grew even larger, if that was at all possible. "Lynx! Oh my darling, it is good to see you again. Oh, it's been what, five hundred years? Four hundred sixty-nine, I think, give or take a few. How have you been?"

He smiled, and Quinn realized it was a genuine expression. "I have been better, but I am getting there."

"Oh, lovey," said Betty. Her little face so expressive that Quinn was fascinated with her. "It'll get better." Betty turned back to Quinn, looking her up and down. Not in a rude way, but in a more assessing one. "You're an odd duck," she said. "You've got scales too. There's got to be a story behind those." She squinted and a silver shimmer took over her entire body, reaching out to brush up against Quinn. "Oh, I think I'm going to like your story. Do you have time for a cuppa? Can we sit down and have one? I would love that. Oh, did you mention, and I missed it? Am I going to be fined?"

Quinn couldn't help herself. She laughed. The adorable little sprite-berry-pixie thing was the nicest person she'd had walk into the Library in a very long time. However, Betty wasn't exactly sure how to take the laughter and stepped back, crossing her arms as she looked up at Quinn quizzically.

"Did I make you laugh? Is it really that pitiful for me to be asking whether I'm going to be fined or not? You see, I've always been a rather large patron of the Library and I am rather finicky about getting my books back on time. I did try . . . but you were closed for so long." She paused for a second, looking around with a frown. She gestured with her tiny hands at the whole Library. "It doesn't even look like you did any reservations . . . never mind that the Library can just adjust itself however it wants. Anyway, I didn't think it was open this time. There have been so many false alarms. I mean, surely you should have sent out something that was verified."

Quinn spoke hurriedly before Betty could start up again. "What made you think we were back before this time?"

"Oh," Betty said, cocking her head to one side as if she was giving it some serious thought. "Well, you see." And then she paused. "Well, I heard it through the grapevine, you see. We get to chatting and we're not gossips, mind you, but you know, Sarila always said, well when she used to come around anyway. Doesn't come around much anymore, mind."

"You know, Sarila?" Quinn asked incredulously. Did they all know each other? Of course, when you could just walk through a door to wherever from the Library, she guessed that meant interplanetary travel wasn't nearly as exciting as TV shows made it out to be.

"Of course I do! Did you hear about Escadril? Oh, dreadful. That's so sad. They've been together for millennia, those two. I don't know how she's going to fare without him. Of course she didn't tell me herself. It's been a couple of hundred years now I think of it. But anyway." Betty stopped when she saw the stricken look on Quinn's face. "Oh, I'm sorry, dear. Didn't you know? Or you did? Oh, dreadful. People always tell me I just run off at the mouth and never stop. I apologize. I'll pay any fine you need me to."

Quinn smiled faintly at the onslaught of words from this tiny, magical creature. "You know, if you want to donate some energy, that'd be great. Otherwise, if you happen to know where the *Jezishian Solution to Maladies of the Mana Pathways: A Beginner's Guide* is, I would absolutely love for you to tell me." Quinn figured it was worth a shot because right now she was still reeling from the amount of information that this tiny creature had imparted to her inside of sixty seconds. She wondered why Sarila hadn't seen her in so long . . . Escadril hadn't been sick before the ambush.

And it reminded her of someone her foster mother used to hang around, who chattered all the time, inanely about nothing. Although this pixie seemed to have a little bit more of an actual knowledge base to work from.

"Oh, wonderful. You do need my help? That would be absolutely fantastic," Betty said. "I've always loved to help the Library. I've been an assistant multiple times in the past. Did you know that? I didn't really care for your last Librarian much, though. She was a little, no offense, Lynx, but she was a bit on the nose sometimes, you know. There was something wrong with that girl. Pity she's dead. Still."

"Wait," Quinn said, trying to get a word in so she could actually understand something in all the verbosity, "what do you mean there was something off about Kor?"

"Oh, didn't you know? Have you never met a sprite before? Okay, you see, we have certain abilities that allow us to know when somebody is not being quite true to themselves." Betty smiled brightly.

Quinn blinked. "And did you tell anyone?"

"Of course, I told Lynx multiple times, but he didn't seem to mind the next time I saw him," Betty laughed it off. "I tried a few times, but you know, I think Lynx was a little smitten with Kor."

Lynx scowled.

"Oh dear, I'm sorry, but you know you're eternal pretty much and she's sort of, well, not so. It's not like it was a body snatcher . . . just that she was always putting on a mask. Something off with their waves versus their presentation, you know?" Betty's chuckle sounded like the trickle of a stream on a spring morning. "Anyway, I digress. I don't suppose you need assistance then, do you? I get bored in my retirement. It's been so, so tedious these last five hundred years. No new books to read."

"What do you mean, no new books?" Milaro asked, "I know for a fact that the Farinth Kingdom has some of the best libraries outside of this one."

"Well, you know, I couldn't dive into different branches or go to the academy and get some of those amazing storybooks they have in that one section. Still." She sounded sad for a second. "I've missed the Library. Wait." She turned quickly back and looked again. "Milaro, is that—is that you? In the flesh. Oh, it has been so long since I've seen you, little Milaro. You've been king a while now, haven't you? I'm so sorry I couldn't come to your coronation. I did have other things to attend to. My mother was still alive back then and the gods rest her soul. You know how she was with family dinners? She wouldn't let me get out of that one. And it was a bit of a hike to get to you. How is that whole kingdom running thing going for you?"

Quinn watched for several seconds as Milaro and Betty exchanged pleasantries back and forth like good old friends that had been lost for eons. The whole incident was simply fascinating. She pulled the returned book toward her and ran her fingers along the spine. She could feel the tingle of magic as it went up her arms. And she glanced at the book again. It really didn't seem like an alchemical book, which meant it had to be a medicinal book.

Lynx stood next to her, a furrow in his brow. "I legitimately do not remember her telling me anything about Kor being off. But it wouldn't surprise me that it's still in the forty-odd percent of memories that we have not yet retrieved. Typical, right?" He tossed a sort of sad look to Quinn and she shrugged.

"You know, it's going to take time." She spoke gently to him, not knowing how she would feel in his place and not wanting to make light of the ordeal; it *was* to retrieve all of his memories. "Cadre was overly generous with his estimate."

He smiled at her. "I've got a lot of the important memories back."

"See?" Quinn grinned at him and nudged him. "You'll get the rest."

"I know. Also, so you know"—he pointed at the book she held—"it's classified as mind healing. That's why it's a part of the alchemical and medicinal branch."

"Oh." Quinn nodded. "That makes sense. Nishpa's type of healing, right?"

"Exactly." Lynx looked like he was about to say more but was interrupted.

"Oh," Betty said, "that's odd." She turned and looked at Quinn and Lynx. "Why is the Library not operating at full power?"

"Well, we were shut down for five hundred years," Lynx said. "Long story short, Library was shut down for emergency reasons and we've only just started rebuilding our powers."

"Oh," Betty said. "Huh. What have you been doing the last few hundred years that sapped you of so much strength? Do you need some sprite dust?" she asked, her expression brightening considerably.

Lynx's eyes glowed. "Are you kidding? You'd offer sprite dust?"

Betty laughed and bopped Lynx on his nose with a tiny finger. "Well, it was my regular contribution for thousands of years, Lynx. Don't you remember?"

Lynx shook his head. "No. No, I do not."

33

WITH A FLOURISH

"WHAT EXACTLY DO YOU MEAN BY SPRITE DUST?" QUINN ASKED.

Betty looked at Quinn in a way that made it obvious she thought the Librarian was joking. Quinn wondered why it was yet another memory that was difficult for Lynx and the Library to recall. Could there be a common denominator?

"Don't you mean like pixie dust?" Quinn asked for clarification thinking of Peter Pan. That was about the extent of her knowledge of tiny fairy creatures.

But Betty shook her head, her brow furrowed in confusion. "What do you mean pixie dust? What is pixie dust? I mean, you're not talking about a drug, are you? Is that a drug and you're comparing it to sprite dust? That's an abomination."

Quinn wanted to retort that the little sprite looked exactly like what Quinn had imagined a pixie would. But she wouldn't understand, and then Quinn would be stuck explaining the whole thing to her. She might have only known the tiny sprite for about a quarter of an hour, but she was fairly certain that silvery laughter would follow any explanation. "Just a cultural misinterpretation. I promise it's not a drug."

"Because you can never be too careful with those," Betty said earnestly. "You do realize that every single species has physiological differences, right? And so different drugs can have completely different effects on, well, different species."

Quinn nodded because the logic made sense to her.

"What exactly is it that sprite dust does?" Quinn asked.

Betty blinked quite rapidly, almost as quickly as her wings fluttered. "You don't know what sprite dust is?" she asked, as if that wasn't even a remote possibility and had to be a joke.

Quinn shook her head very deliberately just in case her point was lost. "No, I don't know what sprite dust is."

Betty's wings practically hummed with annoyance. "But where, oh, well I guess you're not from everywhere. I just would have expected you to know what with the information transfer and everything . . ."

"It didn't take," Lynx inserted.

"Oh." Betty actually paused for a split second before diving back in. "Sprite dust is a clarifying agent that assists in magnifying the potency of mana and its overall regeneration in ley lines and nodes."

Quinn blinked. That sounded absolutely fantastic. "It makes the mana easier to manage and more potent?"

"Yes," Betty said, delight filling her voice as her wings continued to batter faster than hummingbirds. "You've got it exactly, that is precisely what sprite dust helps with."

"And you constantly donated this before the Library closed?" Quinn pushed a little farther.

"Oh. Well." Betty seemed to pause for a second, as if she was genuinely trying to pinpoint it. "Up until maybe a couple of hundred years beforehand. We seem to have had crossed wires with Lynx and Korradine for a while there, sadly. But I would gladly be willing to pay fines in that way or donate for extra privileges as I used to."

Quinn nodded very slowly. "I'd have to look into these extra privileges."

Betty laughed and waved it away with one tiny hand. "I'd just like to have a room waiting that doesn't change and the Library holds it for me."

Quinn blinked. Lynx shrugged. "I vaguely remember that. Kind of."

Betty looked at Lynx, blinking rapidly again. "Lynx, is something wrong with your memory?"

He grinned ruefully. "There was. I'm in the process of restoring it."

"Oh excellent, then you'll remember me in no time flat." Betty seemed positively thrilled by the prospect.

Lynx nodded, a smile tugging at his lips. "I believe I will," he said sounding like he was very sorry he'd ever forgotten her.

"Mind you, though, you'll have to be extremely careful using it," she reminded them. "Remember, you can't directly inhale it. It won't be compatible with any of your physiologies. Like I said before—"

Dottie spoke up, interrupting the sprite. "Betty, you haven't even said a proper hello to me yet!" Her voice rang loudly with indignation.

"Dottie!" The sprite gasped her eyes widening even more. "But I returned the book to you! Oh, it has been so long. I missed you, my friend. You have to catch me up on everything."

And Quinn watched as the tirade of words vacated the check-in desk as Dottie, very skillfully, maneuvered the little, talkative sprite away from the check-in desk. That's when Quinn noticed there had been quite a line forming behind her that the other assistants standing in the check-in desk area had been unable to process the people because everyone watched the lively sprite. Slowly, it began to move again.

Quinn silently thanked Dottie and turned to the waiting patrons. "I'm so sorry. We'll be right with you."

Finn nudged Quinn and said, "If you move down the other end, we'll take care of them."

"Thank you."

Finn flashed her a smile, and Quinn noticed that the little Ilgonomur had gained what seemed like some confidence. Much more than she'd had when she was desperately pleading to stay in the Library and be rescued from her family who were trying to pit her against the Library. Quinn realized that the Ilgonomur was on their side, or perhaps it was more accurate to say, on the side of knowledge that she could gain from any book that she could get her hands on. Because Finn was an absolute knowledge hoarder.

Quinn chuckled as they moved away slightly. "Okay, then," Lynx said, still glancing at where Dottie had whisked Betty off to.

Quinn pulled the Mattiniman book with her. It was still absolutely massive, and she flicked through it, a frown on her face. "So it's a very odd book for the medicinal wing?"

Milaro nodded. "Exactly. Mind healing is Nishpa's strongest affinity set. And I can practically taste the strength of magic leaking off it into the Library."

"I know," Quinn said, running her hand over the cover again, reveling in the potency of it. "It's just sort of odd."

Milaro grinned at her. Geneva fluttered into place right next to Lynx. Her face was ever so slightly flushed and Nishpa followed close behind her.

"Well, what do you think? We need to get the last book, right? The Jezishian one so we can open the next branch, right?" Nishpa's face seemed a little pale. She'd been working overtime helping the Balisors.

Quinn nodded, excited to see yet another branch open.

"Once that branch is open, well, we can work on the combat branch," Geneva said. "Or I think that's the plan."

"Yeah," Quinn said, mulling over the book in front of her. Finally, she tapped it, bringing up the console as she did so. She checked it in, double-checked it, and watched as the number, specifically for the alchemical and medicinal wing, went down to one. A thrill of excitement washed through her and frankly, she couldn't wait to go and retrieve that last book. "I guess it's time to get that book."

"Well, we also need a precise location for it, although I do believe it's been an oversight and it doesn't seem to be a malicious withholding," Geneva said bringing the expectations back down to . . . the Library. "I'd like to accompany you, if that's acceptable."

Quinn frowned. "I'd prefer for you to stay here with Nishpa and help arrange all this." She gestured around them. "We have three hundred-odd patients in our hospital wings. It's a little stressful for me to contemplate leaving the Library without some of my best assistants in charge."

"Three hundred fifty," Geneva corrected immediately before her eyes narrowed. "Are you just trying to butter me up, Librarian?"

Quinn grinned. "Well, I'm not trying to butter you up, but I may be trying to flatter you into accepting the fact that you're needed to oversee the Library with Dottie while I go and retrieve the book."

Geneva offered her a smirk and then a frown. "Okay, but you'll owe me."

"Fine," said Quinn, biting back a laugh. "I'll owe you one, within reason, and nothing that can harm me or those I care about or the Library."

Geneva laughed. "What do you think I was going to ask you for?"

"To be fair, I'm pretty sure I don't need those caveats," Quinn said, "but I've seen way too many crime dramas and bad genie wishing movies. Some of the species in this universe are way too literal and I don't trust myself if I don't get into the habit of acknowledging that fact and thus covering my butt as much as I can."

Geneva laughed again. "Okay, that's a perfectly valid reason to give me such a specific answer. I will take you up on it and I will take care of the Library for you."

Quinn grinned at her friend. She was glad that they'd experienced Ishiposa Isle together. Not that she liked what they'd had to do or the outcome or any of the implications of it all, but ever since then, Geneva had been far more comfortable around her, and indeed, had turned into a friend.

Lynx piped up, interrupting them. "I realize you're bonding right now, but we have a lot of book locating to do. I'll do some of it with Jasper, while you're gone, getting the last book."

"Excellent. Maybe add Narilin, if she's well enough? Can't she home in on specific inks, leathers, things like that?" Quinn asked.

Lynx nodded. "Might help Jasper locking in on it. I have several theories on how to get us a closer approximation that don't mean resorting to manual proximity."

Quinn clapped her hands together. "Okay, so I guess that's our plan."

Milaro cleared his throat and was about to speak when the doctor golem walked up to the check-in desk.

He waited for Quinn to acknowledge his presence before speaking. "Librarian, we are in need of somebody to oversee us, or for you to give me permissions, in order to arrange certain surgical and survival elements that I require to activate and operate within the hospital wing. Even if you choose to downsize at some stage, once the patients have been sent back to their domiciles, it would be beneficial to have these specific apparatuses on hand at all times."

"Ability to initiate production of key medical items . . ." Quinn squinted as she turned her attention to the console in front of her. "Okay, I'll give you rudimentary permissions for specifically hospital things." She fiddled with the console in front of her, bringing up the parameters, the blueprints, everything. She frowned at the sheer mass of information. She felt the Library sigh at the back of her mind, and suddenly the information displayed through the system was much more specific to what she needed.

Quinn grinned. Sometimes, it was nice having a sapient Library stuck in your brain, listening to everything that was said to you. It helped her narrow the cumbersome lists down, and she gave basic permissions to the doctor and the surgeon. "That's done! Anything else?"

He shook his head.

She turned to Nishpa.

"Since you're not coming with me to fetch the last one . . ."

"I'm not coming with you?" Nishpa asked, raising an eyebrow, her wings humming quite irritably as she hovered in place.

"I thought it might be a good idea for you to stay here for the mind-healing, for the patients," Quinn elaborated. She'd not thought she'd need to elaborate, but apparently people were being contrary today.

"Ah." Nishpa nodded, her face coloring slightly. "It slipped my mind for a moment there."

Quinn nodded. She understood how it was when you had lists that were seventeen thousand items long. Maybe that was an exaggeration, but that was exactly how it felt right then. "Can I make you an assistant and bump you up to supervisory role?" *Is that a good idea?* she shot to the Library.

That is an excellent idea, if Nishpa accepts, because I'm not entirely sure she will.

But Nishpa cut the Library thoughts in Quinn's head off. "Fine, bump me to supervisor and I'll help make sure the hospital runs well in your absence *only*, is that understood?"

Quinn nodded, "Yes, in my absence only." Quinn was relieved. While she'd inadvertently cured Eugea, it had been instinctive. She only knew rudimentary things about healing, commands she could give to elicit a healing type response from the magic that she carried within her. Having Nishpa there was a boon.

Nishpa turned to her niece. "Will you help me with the specifics?"

Geneva practically rolled her eyes, sighed deeply and said, "I'm already staying, but fine, I'll help you."

Quinn suppressed a smile.

Milaro cleared his throat to get Quinn's attention from the Furionas fae. "Would you accompany me?"

With the two fae locked in discussion now, Quinn raised an eyebrow. "Where to?"

"I'd like you and Lynx to come with me to see Malakai." His tone was serious and a flutter of nervousness engulfed Quinn.

"Why didn't he stay?" Quinn had been keeping an eye out for him but thought Milaro might have sent him to the hospital earlier.

Milaro laughed. "I sent him back to his bed. He's doing physical therapy and working with his mother on certain aspects of his very specific abilities to better protect himself against potential onslaught and attack. Arnekai's shielding prowess is exceptional and hopefully this will help boost his own."

Quinn wanted to make a comment, but very wisely did not. It was the first time since she'd known Milaro Seveshall that he had praised his daughter-in-law. She wasn't even sure he was aware of it.

"Anyway, shall we head to the infirmary?" Milaro fell into step beside her, but they didn't get far.

Several steps beyond the check-in desk there was a fluttering of wings and a skidding in the air somehow that Quinn didn't exactly understand. Eric suddenly appeared before them and bowed with a flourish in midair, not a sign of limp to his wing at all.

"Eric, it's fixed!" Quinn said joyously. She was genuinely happy to see him.

The imp grinned, "Yes, I am fixed. Back to a hundred percent, better than ever, with shields to die for. Not literally," he said, "not planning on dying. Wait, is that a sprite? Have you found . . ."

"Focus, Eric?"

"Oh, yes," he said, his impish grin out at full force in all its glory. "I have a message from Hal."

34

STRONGER TOGETHER

Despite Eric's very smug face, Quinn perked up at the mention of Hal's name. She'd come to be fond of the Halschius commander. For some obscure reason, despite the fact that he was a fifteen-foot-tall satyr, she always felt quite safe around him, like he could protect her from the Kajaros of the world.

Even though she was fully capable of protecting herself. It was nice to have that sort of fatherly vibe.

"What's the message?" Quinn asked when Eric refused to elaborate.

"Oh, you have to take super good care of me," Eric said. "Hal's really annoyed that he had to fix me, so you can't damage me again or, you know, make me take on somebody else's damage."

Quinn raised an eyebrow at him. "Really? You know you did that all by yourself. That's what Uncle Hal actually said?"

"Well," Eric laughed gleefully, "not exactly those words, but that was his insinuation, I assure you. But seriously, Hal said that he had a foresight reading."

Quinn interrupted him. "Uncle Hal has foresight?"

"No," Eric said. "Not Hal personally, but there are others who have it that report to him."

Quinn sighed. "I guess that makes sense. Anyway, he said you don't need to rush to get the last book that you have to retrieve."

Quinn was slightly confused by the message. "You mean he doesn't want me to go and get the book back?"

"No," Eric said. "That's not what he said, and that's not what I said. I said you need to not be in a *rush* to go and retrieve it. He said that things are happening sooner than expected and there will be some results soon. You need to be patient."

Quinn wondered how well Uncle Hal really knew her because she thought everybody was aware that she was the least patient person in the history of existence. "So, wait," she said, which was such a hard thing to do when there was only one book left. Just one, not two.

One.

Freaking.

Book.

And that was it. "Fine. What am I supposed to do then?"

"Well, I can't tell you what to do. I know you've got like four thousand lists. Can't you do something from one of them?" Eric asked.

Milaro chuckled in the background. "Of course she has other things to do, but she was about to do something with me."

"Well, what was she . . ." Eric started, "Oh, wait, I forgot. Hal is coming to visit soon."

"Define soon," Quinn asked, feeling a bit deflated now that she didn't get to hunt down the book. At least she thought that's what Eric meant.

"Don't be so down about it, Quinn. It's not a bad thing. Usually, if there's been foresight about an event, it's a good thing. That damned skill rarely turns up anything useful. He's not telling you that it's going to be damaged. He's not telling you to prepare for it to be repaired. He's just telling you to wait a bit."

"Okay," Quinn said, fully aware that they had been waiting a lot for these books. "Anyway, I have to get going."

"What are you doing?" Eric asked.

"Going to visit Mal."

"Oh, really? That sounds . . ." His voice trailed off as Milaro shook his head at the imp.

Quinn wasn't entirely sure why he did that, but Eric's shoulders slumped ever so slightly in defeat, and the note of his hovering wings rose ever so slightly.

"Well, you could help Geneva and Nishpa run the Library."

"No," Eric said, crossing his arms. "I'm not doing that. I've only just got back. I had, like, sick leave or something. Work injury. My wings weren't working properly. And also—why do we have so many sick people around here?"

Quinn laughed. She couldn't help it. He hadn't been there. It wasn't like he automatically got updated.

He peered around, flitting back and forth as they were close to the entrance. "When did you build a hospital wing? Was I gone longer than I thought?"

"Just a few days." Quinn laughed. "We went to retrieve the Hunter book and came across some unfriendly vegetation."

Milaro guffawed. "That was really well said. Unfriendly vegetation. Good one."

Quinn looked at him for a second. His eyes had bags underneath them. "You look tired," she said to Milaro.

"Well, I am." He stood a little straighter, pushing his hair behind his shoulders. "But I promised to see you again. As soon as I can, I will sleep for like three days."

"Yeah, I wish," Quinn said, turning her attention back to Eric. "Well, anyway, if you're not going to help Geneva and Nishpa with the Library, what will you do?"

"I've got a few things I need to check." Then he paused and looked at Quinn, a frown on his face. "Was there anything you wanted me to do?" he asked Quinn very pointedly.

"Um, I don't think so," she said, racking her brain to try to figure out if there was actually something that she needed him to do. But there wasn't. "Hey, Eric?"

"What?" he said.

"I'm really glad you're back." Yeah, maybe that was the missing piece.

"Oh." Eric, whose skin was practically so dark she couldn't usually see anything, kind of flushed a little. "Uh, well, you're welcome."

Yep. He was squirming a bit. "Yeah, it's good to have you back."

"Great to be back. I think I need to go and check on fines. Who's been metering out the fines?" he said as he flitted toward the check-in desk.

"It's good to see him healthy again, isn't it?" Milaro said.

Quinn nodded thoughtfully. She'd missed the little imp. He was often a handful, but always helpful. She really hoped his wing wasn't permanently damaged and that the injury had indeed healed fully. Although she didn't think Hal would have let him out of Halschius had the injury still been at all prevalent. She also wished she had a direct line to Uncle Hal so she could ask him about this cryptic foresight information.

"Be patient. Don't go get the book yet." Milaro poked her arm to get her attention. "You're definitely overthinking what Eric just told you."

"Of course, I'm overthinking what Eric just told me. I overthink everything," she said.

Milaro chuckled. "At least you're aware of it. I *have* met a lot of people who overthink more than you do, believe it or not."

Quinn chuckled. "Okay, lead on."

Even though the infirmary had been moved and quasi-amalgamated into the hospital, it was still on the periphery of it and didn't take long to get to. It was only about a five-minute walk. The first few steps they took in silence, and then Milaro spoke first.

"How are you feeling, Quinn?" He paused and clarified. "How are you really feeling?"

She mulled that over for a couple of seconds before responding honestly. "Tired. Irritated. Marginally confused by what Eric just told us. Extremely taken aback by Betty, who is all sorts of fantastic, to be honest. A little scared that Malakai won't recover. And perhaps ever so slightly homesick."

Milaro blinked at her. They'd almost reached their destination. "When I asked that question, that was not the answer I was fishing for."

Quinn laughed. "If you don't want the real answer, you shouldn't ask the question. Anyway, yes to all of the above."

"Well, I can allay your fears of one of them. Malakai will be fine." He gave her a conspiratorial smile.

"Really? He wasn't just saying he was out of bed when he really shouldn't have been?"

"Well, he shouldn't have been out of bed. He still needs to recover energy, but mostly his body has healed. And his magic needs a bit of a rest to recuperate. He'll need to do a bit of conditioning, physically, mentally, for a little while, but he'll be back at fighting strength in no time." Milaro's smile was kind.

Quinn couldn't quite describe the feeling of relief that worked its way through her. It was like a slow, steady stream that took some of the tension away from her body. "That is such good news," she said. "Thank you."

"Well," he said, "don't tell him I told you, because he'll want to tell you himself."

"Of course he . . ." Quinn paused and held up a hand, getting Milaro to stop walking. "Do you hear that?" she asked, lowering her voice.

He raised an eyebrow and spoke mind to mind to her. *How can I miss it? It's loud enough for the entire hospital to hear.*

Quinn would have chuckled had the voices not belonged to Malakai and his mother. She crept slightly closer, just enough so she could get a visual.

"I am *not* going back with you," she could hear Malakai saying.

"But, son, you need to be there. You are part Darigháhnish, and you require the moons and the tides. The atmosphere of the Espinar Peninsula holds such importance to our kind. It is essential to who we are."

"It's important for half of me. I can come back for a vacation some other time." Malakai dismissed her worry.

"No." Arnekai sounded irritated. Or more so than usual, anyway. "It's been ten years, and your body is almost devoid of what it needs to replenish."

Quinn asked Milaro. *Is it true? Is he really missing something from the peninsula?*

No, Milaro said, *Not necessarily. Not something he can't get elsewhere.*

Oh, Quinn said.

But he is also Arnekai's heir, and she refuses to let him off the hook entirely. Now that he's about to reach adulthood, anyway.

Quinn had so many questions about elven adulthood, but right then wasn't the time. The argument grew ever so slightly louder.

"My duty is here and I enjoy it. I'm not leaving Quinn to fend for herself with the number of wolves out to tear her apart. And if you're not careful, I'll think you're one of them." A threatening note crept into his tone.

Arnekai gasped ever so softly. "How could you say that? I have never been against the Library. Our entire line is made up of Library supporters. My aunt was an exception, not the rule. You know it. I know it. Everybody knows it."

"Do they?" Malakai asked. "Because I find this behavior suspect. I get injured and you want to take me away from her when I am one of the few people she has to depend on."

Quinn felt a slight blush on her cheeks. She probably shouldn't be overhearing this. He was getting very worked up.

"You're not thinking clearly. You're still injured," Arnekai snapped.

"I am not still injured," Malakai said. "I am weak, and I need to regain strength and energy. But I am no longer injured, and I'll be taking my leave of not only you, but this hospital, too."

Before she could second guess herself, Quinn reached out a gentle tendril of awareness toward Malakai's mind. She saw the moment it impacted him. A faint smile tugged at his lips. And some of the tension in his shoulders faded.

"Look," he said, his tone suddenly far more reasonable. "I understand *you* believe, in your heart or whatever you use to care about people, that taking me back to the peninsula is the only way I'm going to fully recover."

"Yes," Arnekai said. "Exactly. It's not just that it's where you belong. It's also that it has energies that will replenish you much faster."

"I get it. You think it's one of the only ways you can take care of me as a mum?"

"Yeah," Arnekai said softly. And Quinn could have sworn she heard sadness in her voice. It was such a complicated mother-son relationship.

Quinn didn't want to get involved. And so she moved forward and spoke up, so they would know that she was there. "We're almost there," she said, out loud as if she was talking to Milaro who had at least caught on and was moving to catch up.

The conversation stopped, and a second later, Quinn stepped into the room. "Oh, hello," she said to Arnekai, feigning surprise. "Were you saying goodbye?"

Arnekai glowered, just for a second, before nodding. "Actually, I was about to. I have duties to get back to. You will take care of my son, because he apparently cannot take care of himself."

Quinn chuckled. "I've noticed that, but it's okay, because he tried to take care of me, so I . . . I'll make sure he's fine."

"You do that," Arnekai said. She paused for a second, as if she had more to say, but didn't speak.

"Excellent." Milaro clapped his hands as he walked into the room. "Just the lady I wanted to talk to."

Arnekai gave him a withering look but complied as he approached her.

Quinn raised an eyebrow at him, and he spoke against her mind. *I am freeing you both of her presence, just in case. Don't say I never did anything for you.*

He walked out with Arnekai, speaking in hushed tones. Quinn and Malakai gaped after them. If there'd been flies in the Library, their mouths would have been fly traps. Then they turned to look at each other, and shrugged.

"I have no clue what that was about," she said.

"Me either. My mother was ripping me a new one, which I'm assuming you overheard in its totality?" Malakai stared at where they'd vacated the room, still frowning slightly.

"Yeah," Quinn said, "pretty much."

"I meant it, though," Mal said. "I'm not leaving you to fend against these wolves. I'll help. I'll get stronger."

Quinn smiled. "Maybe we'll just get stronger together, eh?"

3 5

A FEW MOMENTS

For several moments, Quinn and Malakai watched the door Arnekai and Milaro left through. They stood side by side, their shoulders touching ever so slightly, content in knowing that the other was okay. Just the atmosphere, the ability to relax and not have to be actively doing something in this moment, soothed her.

Quinn hadn't realized how much she'd missed his constant presence. Over the course of the last few months, Malakai had become a shadow by her side, always there, intervening, making sure she was protected, even when she didn't necessarily need it. Until he wasn't. It had been cold the last couple of weeks.

"You know," Malakai said, pulling Quinn out of her thoughts. "You can't do that again."

"Do what again?" Quinn asked, blinking at him as she tried to figure out if she'd missed something. She wracked her brain, trying to think what he meant, as she moved to the two recliners in his room to sit comfortably. "I don't get what you mean."

He followed her, taking the second seat. "Really? You're avoiding talking to me about this?"

"About what?" Quinn said, sincerely confused. "I have no idea what you mean." And she legitimately didn't.

"Honestly?" Malakai paused, "Or are you just saying you don't have any idea what I'm talking about because you don't want to have this discussion?"

"Maybe a bit of both," she said. "As in, you're about to tell me I can't do something again and generally, that's a bad idea because if you tell me I can't do something then that usually makes it something I really want to do."

Malakai laughed. It was a full-throated laugh, the first one she'd heard from him since they'd come back from the ill-fated ambush. "That's . . . Quinn, I don't even have words for that."

"Good, so we should talk about something else." Quinn sounded smug.

"No, you need to promise me that you won't do that again." Malakai was back to being deadly serious.

Quinn didn't say anything but raised an eyebrow because at this point, they were just running around in circles.

Malakai sighed and elaborated. "When I got injured, your emotional reaction took over. I could feel you. You let those emotions roll over you. Engulf you, even. As the Librarian, you're usually even-keeled and logical. But you disregarded the things that make you a strong Librarian and lashed out."

"Well, excuse me for being upset that my guard managed to almost get himself killed." She could already feel her hackles rising. Her shoulders sag and the next words are barely audible. "Because of me."

Malakai speaks softly. "But that's just it. If I had died, if Eric had died, you can't let that take a hold of you in the moment, because bad judgement could kill *you*."

"What do you . . . oh." Quinn paused, really thinking over what he'd said.

She didn't like to admit it, but he was right. It wasn't about her hurting others personally, but about what her absence as Librarian would do to all of those people depending on the Library for the mana they utilized on a daily basis. Allowing herself to lose any amount of control in the heat of a situation could easily lead to an opening in her defenses she wouldn't otherwise have.

She wasn't fully grown yet. She was pretty sure she could get killed.

"Exactly," Malakai said.

"I didn't say anything," Quinn said defensively.

"You didn't have to. The look on your face was plenty. You understood what I meant, and to be honest, Quinn, that's all I care about. I just wanted to make sure that you appreciated the gravity of the situation. The fact that you can't act or react in the heat of the moment during a battle. I know you're not specifically trained for combat or warfare, but I think when we go back to training, that's something we're going to need to make a priority—keeping your emotions in check during an upheaval."

"I was so angry, a bit scared, and I tried so hard to push my emotions down like I had the last time, but it just boiled over immediately." She was trying to track all the emotions that had been at play when Malakai jumped in to save her. Their imprint still felt wild. "When we caught Tenejo, I knew everybody was fine, if hurt, even if that wasn't a good thing. This time, I couldn't separate it because I didn't know how badly you were injured."

"It's my job, Quinn. I'm your trainer and I'm your guard." He crossed his arms, locking gazes with her.

"But you're technically younger than me," she said.

"No, you're still younger than me. I've technically just passed elven adolescence, so I'm sort of an adult now."

Quinn laughed. "Well, apparently, I'm like an egg. Hal keeps calling me an egg, Malakai."

Mal laughed. "You are a bit of an egg. Did you know that?"

"Don't even," Quinn said. She laughed. The awkwardness was mostly gone now, and he was right. Not that she wanted to let Malakai know that. It'd make him even more insufferable. Still, she missed their training sessions and their sparring sessions, both verbally and with weapons. She wasn't sure what that said about their relationship. She just knew that she didn't want this to happen again.

"We need to get you better armor," she said. "So that when stuff does try to kill you while you're trying to protect me, then at least the armor will save you."

"Done. You owe me one set of brand-new armor."

Quinn laughed. "Fine, I'll make good on that."

It was another moment of pleasant silence and Quinn finally spoke again. She'd been thinking because she knew he was right. How she'd reacted. It hadn't been leader-esque at all. Maybe she'd been relying too much on the fact that Hal had been with them and had de facto taken on the leadership role. She hadn't had to worry. Not until Malakai got hit. She sighed. "You know, I'm kind of pissed."

"What about? I mean"—he paused and flashed her a grin—"other than generally."

Quinn smiled, but it was a tight expression, and she knew it didn't reach her eyes. She was too busy trying to figure out what she wanted to say in her head. "My power levels. I'm much stronger, but I'm not there yet; it's unpredictable. For a little bit back there, I wasn't completely in control. The anger took over. I need to work on becoming powerful, on transferring the cold and logical space into a sort of hybrid haven where I can rationally examine reactions I'm having."

"Sounds like a solid plan," Malakai said, "but I have some good and bad news about that."

"What?" Quinn pushed down on the flurry of panic that swept through her at the thought of bad news she hadn't anticipated.

"After we've restored the Library, the odds of you having to fight as much as you have recently are very low." He shrugged and sat grinning at her.

"Seriously?" Quinn said.

"Yep. It won't be never, but it won't happen as often as it has been."

"Oh," Quinn said. "That's actually a relief. Does that mean I'll get some book time for myself?"

Malakai blinked, and didn't answer immediately, as he seemed somewhat confused. "You just want to curl up with a good book?"

Quinn nodded emphatically.

Mal laughed softly. "Fine. But if you're talking about non-magical tomes, only the academy has access to some of those. Not sure what planets they're from. Might have to go on a field trip to local libraries scattered around the universe. If you want no factual texts, that is."

"That actually sounds like fun. We should do that. When we can." She smiled, anticipating the day when the Library was back at full strength and she could relax. As long as Mal was still there. Considering the brushes with death he'd had since she arrived . . . "I just had an odd thought," Quinn said suddenly.

Malakai looked over at her. "What do you mean?"

"I mean, this wasn't the first time you'd almost been killed when I was around. The first time was in that cave with Kajaro when we went to retrieve the book and he attacked us with the octopus, remember?"

"Yes, I'm never likely to forget our friendly little cephalopod," Malakai said, a hint of sarcasm in his voice. "What do you mean, it's different?"

"Well, it was different this time. I didn't want you to get hurt. Whereas the first time I didn't know you well enough to get angry about it."

Malakai raised an eyebrow. "We were pretty much just winging it that first time. I never thought we'd get attacked going to retrieve a *book*."

"I know. We didn't have a bond of any sort."

He nudged her foot with his. "I wasn't even your trainer really back then, not fully. Just a quasi-babysitter."

"Exactly!" she said as if that perfectly proved her point. "So, don't go throwing yourself into situations where you can get killed. No dying. Okay? No more heroics where you almost die."

"You realize it's, again, literally my job description." Malakai spoke calmly.

"Well, maybe I don't like your job description," Quinn said.

"Who else is going to save you, Quinn?"

She threw her hands up in exasperation. "Me. I'm going to get stronger, so you don't need to save me."

"Okay," he said, nodding in agreement. "I'll help you with that, eh?"

"I like that plan," Quinn said, suddenly feeling more at ease. A few moments went by and she could feel the tension leaking out of her body. "Do you think they'd notice if we just kind of sat and read some books?"

Malakai laughed. "You want to sit in the infirmary and read some books?"

"I don't get many chances to just sit and read a book, and Hal basically told me not to retrieve the next book for the alchemical branch yet. So I'm kind of stuck in limbo and, I mean, I'll read about anything. There's some species I still need to catch up on. I think that's a productive use of my time."

"You're the Librarian. I don't see why you can't just sit and read and catch a breath," Mal said softly.

They sat in the recliners, close, yet not quite together, enjoying the silence and the general camaraderie that lay between them with no books in sight.

Several minutes later, Malakai broke the silence. "You know what? I'd be kind of put out if you died, Quinn."

She looked over at him. "Okay. No dying on my part either, right?"

"Right."

Quinn waited for several seconds before speaking again, trying to figure out how to say what she wanted to say. "How are you really feeling, Malakai?"

He laughed self-deprecatingly. "You know, I've got muscle stiffness and my magic replenishment is shot for now. I'm slower than usual, and my mana pathways are still recovering. That means I can only use body strengthening manipulation techniques right now. It only uses my energy, not my mana. So that way at least, I can still be effective in defending you, myself, the Library, and others."

Quinn latched onto what he was saying. "You can't use your mana flow?"

"That blast pretty much bled them raw, and if I use them before they're fully healed, I run the danger of burning myself out magic-wise, which isn't something I'm prepared to do."

"I don't blame you," Quinn said.

There was a knock at the door, and Quinn looked up as Dottie trotted into the room. She couldn't help the smile that came over her at seeing the little bench.

"I bring you snacks, courtesy of Cook," Dottie said.

Quinn raised an eyebrow in question.

Dottie sort of rippled, giving the impression of a shrug. "What? You two seemed less argumentative."

Quinn raised an eyebrow. "He almost died saving me."

Dottie laughed and the sound peeled through the entire infirmary, echoing right down the hall from which she'd just come. Quinn hadn't thought it was that entertaining a statement. She frowned. "What's up, Dottie? Why are you here?"

"Well, to be honest, I just wanted to bring you something to eat. But I also wanted to tell you, I think you should take a day off, Quinn. With Hal's message, you could even take some downtime. Maybe a day or two so you can just relax for once." Dottie was in full encouragement mode.

Quinn nodded. "Well, until Hal talks to me, that's the plan."

"Excellent." The bench giggled and ran out of the room.

Quinn blinked after her. "You saw that, right?" she said to Malakai.

He chuckled. "Seeing is not understanding."

Quinn shook her head in bewilderment. "I have no idea what she was doing."

"Me either."

"Anyway. How long do you think your recuperation will take?" she asked, trying to veer back on topic from earlier.

"For the manaflow, Grandfather said two to six weeks, depending. As long as I don't use manaflow abilities, it could take less time. As long as I do the strengthening exercises he gave me and focus purely on my energy consumption, physical attributes, and fighting. That way I'm reinforcing my body, which means that if anything like that ever happens again, I'll have greater physical defenses. If my physical strength had been greater . . ."

Quinn was silent for several seconds. She was about to speak again when words flashed very quickly in front of her face.

"What . . . that?" She took several steps back as the words flashed in front of her.

"Quinn, what's wrong?" Malakai asked, concern coloring his voice.

The Jezishian Solution to Maladies of the Mana Pathways: A Beginner's Guide has been returned.

This completes the prerequisite for the alchemical medicinal branch opening.

Do you wish to initiate the opening procedure?"

Yes or No?

"The book just got returned." She whispered the words reverently.

"What? How?" Malakai sprang out of his chair.

"I have no idea." But Quinn knew who would. There was no way Hal hadn't known about this. "Hal's pulling pranks."

Both of them got up and ran toward the check-in desk. Not even halfway there, Quinn heard booming laughter.

Uncle Hal stood right next to the check-in desk.

"Ah, here she comes. I knew that'd get you out of the room." He was in fine form today. Probably topping out at ten feet.

But Quinn didn't care about his size doubling her own. She only had one thing on her mind. The damn book. "Hal, you had the book?"

"Oh, no," Hal said. "But I do now."

PROCESS ON HOLD

Quinn looked from the notification window that was still in front of her vision, to Hal, and back to the notification. She held up her hand to forestall any typically grandiose statement while she processed what he'd just said.

"*You've* got it now?" she asked, her voice laced with disbelief. "Which obviously means you previously did not have it. Explain."

Uncle Hal laughed, that boisterous, overwhelming sound. He was in a frightfully good mood. Quinn wanted to smack the smug smile off his face, but she refrained.

Hal shrugged good-naturedly and shrank himself down to just above the eight feet he'd been at his initial visit. "Quinn. Librarian. Little egg. There's no need to be so upset about it," he said, his voice soothing.

"I'm not upset," Quinn said, her voice defensive. "I'm shocked. I wasn't expecting you to bring the last book in." But the more she thought about it, the more obvious he'd been. He'd literally sent a message to her that she didn't need to go out and get it right now because he'd seen that it would come back to her. Basically, that's how she'd interpreted the information. "I just . . . I wasn't expecting you to be the one returning it. That's all."

Hal grinned. "I know, and that was part of the fun. This surprise has been a delight."

Quinn squinted at him. Yep, he was definitely up to something, but she wasn't entirely sure if it was now, or up and coming. Eric was a lot like him, in a way. A complete and utter troublemaker. Uncle Hal watched her, an expectant look on his face. Quinn raised an eyebrow. "You're dying to tell me how you retrieved it, aren't you?"

"How did you guess?" Hal said, gleefully clapping his hands together as he grinned toothily. "So, Lynx had given me the approximate location of the books. I knew Betty likely had one, and reached out to her. She's always been . . . unique. And I gather she did pop in and give you the other one, right?" Hal didn't wait for an answer. "Anyway, I made several sensory sweeps of the aforementioned area to find the book. It's not really the type of book enemies would try to hoard. I guess unless you're studying the reversal of healing, which is its very own fork in those affinities . . ."

"Uncle Hal. Focus." Quinn had never seen him quite so enthusiastic.

His grin widened, and his sharp teeth indented on his lips as he did so. "Sorry . . . I realized the approximation was quite close to a tiny Citrophosa delegation we have out in that sector. Now, they're a fantastic, amazing species at assisting in every way. However, they're not very conscientious of other people's belongings, and-or dates and times. Ever. They lose track of everything not immediately in front of them. Anyway, it was much easier to retrieve than I'm letting on and not nearly as exciting as it probably would have been if you'd have gone there to get it without me." His eyes were twinkling by the time he finished his tale.

Quinn laughed. "Citrophosas. They're the ones who carried the prisoners when we got to Halschius, right?"

"Yes, you're correct."

Quinn frowned. "They just didn't want to return the book?"

"Not exactly. It's more they forgot they had the book to return. They wouldn't have paid attention to your alerts." He shrugged. "You'd probably have gotten it in two hundred years if I hadn't fetched it for you."

Quin nodded and began leafing through all the console in front of her to make sure they'd met all the requirements for opening the next branch. Shivers of excitement and expectation ran through her at the prospect of finally opening another branch.

"I also . . ." Hal started, in an effort to get her to refocus.

"Was there another book?" Quinn asked, perking up. She'd brought up the console to triple check that power levels and everything else was optimal.

"No," he said. "However, I thought you might be interested in some Kajaro information."

That piqued Quinn's interest because when did she *not* want to figure out how he'd done so much damage, on top of coming back to life?

Malakai frowned. "Is it information she can handle now?"

Quinn glared at him. "Of course it's information I can handle now."

"No, I didn't mean it like that," Malakai said. "I meant you're trying to juggle opening another branch of the Library while you're half listening to Hal, which means you're probably going to ask him to repeat himself. So if you want this information, it's likely advisable to delay the opening by five minutes."

Quinn sighed. She knew Malakai was right. The Library had been closed for almost five hundred years. Surely, a few minutes weren't going to hurt the alchemical and medicinal branch. For some reason, she felt like the Library was glowering at her. *I'll make it up to you,* she shot her thoughts at the Library. It did not seem mollified at all. "Well, what about Kajaro?"

A shiver shook the surrounding air, and Quinn realized Uncle Hal had erected a cone of silence to protect the information from eavesdroppers.

"My doctors are making progress," Uncle Hal said smugly. "We've been running tests to ascertain Kajaro's specific resurrection magic. There are some genetic variances in his makeup that include Korradine's species. The Uniceros have a—it's not an immortality gene, but more of a prolonged lifespan gene. Generally, it's triggered by their will to live, die, whatever. Although it's usually very specific to that species, it has been spliced with numerous other genetic factors that we haven't been able to identify yet. However, I do believe we're getting closer."

Quinn held up her hand to stop him. "Wait a second. Are you telling me that he performed scientific experiments on himself to allow himself to come back to life?"

Hal paused, obviously careful with his answer. "He's performing magical experiments on himself, with himself as the guinea pig, which you've got to have some level of respect for whether he's evil or not."

Quinn studied Hal for several seconds. She wondered what his definitions of black and white were, because it seemed to her that he lived perpetually in shades of grey as far as she could see. Not that that was a bad thing. But it *was* something she'd become aware of.

"Anyway," Hal continued, "the fascinating part is that this splicing is something we can extract from him once we've figured out precisely what it entails. If we tried to extract it right now, it'd kill him, probably permanently."

"But he doesn't rise from the corpse, right? Because we took that corpse, didn't we?" Quinn couldn't remember. So much had happened since that very first fight. She wasn't even sure how she got back to the Library anymore.

"We think it regenerates a body for him at a designated location." Hal shrugged.

Quinn nodded very slowly, taking all the information in. "You think we might be able to eliminate him?" she asked, even though the words sounded foreign and sort of scary on her tongue.

Hal nodded slowly. "If that's what you want us to do with the prisoner."

"He's responsible for so many deaths. I'm not entirely sure what else there is to do unless we just let him be a prisoner?" Quinn said.

Uncle Hal shrugged. "Learn from him? Dissect him? We could do a lot of things."

"The last few times you did stuff, one of them bubbled into a mess of gods-knows-what, and I got sucked into a dome." Quinn crossed her arms, eyeing the King of Halschius skeptically.

"All great points," Hal said, giving her a wink. "I'll take them under advisement and endeavor to investigate what the other genetic makeups are in the splicing that leads to his nine lives, so to speak."

"Do you think"—Quinn paused, ignoring his teasing with the thought that suddenly struck her—"and I know this sounds odd, and I could probably try to research this out myself, is there a species that is very feline-like that has nine lives?"

Hal paused, a frown on his face. "Actually, now you mention . . ."

Quinn balked. "What?"

"Well, yes and no," Hal said.

Lynx started laughing. "Are you serious? Is that what he did?"

Quinn looked between them, with no clue why Lynx was laughing. "What did who do?"

Malakai sighed. "There's a feline species with the ability to regenerate itself several times over. It's a Chezishila cat."

"No way," Quinn said, her gaze flickering from one to the other. "Are you seriously serious, or are you just pulling my leg?"

Hal cocked his head to one side. "We're definitely not pulling your leg, but I'm assuming that's a saying of some sort, because it seems very awkward. Thank you for your question. I didn't think of the Chezishila, though I should have. Is that a myth on your world, Quinn?"

"Cats have nine lives. It's just a saying because cats tend to get into the weirdest stuff ever and still survive. But the name is oddly similar to the name of a cat in a fairy tale."

Hal nodded. "I'll endeavor to send that information to our doctors as soon as possible. I actually . . ." He frowned and his eyes shifted for several seconds. "Thank you, Quinn. That was most helpful."

"You're welcome," she said and shook herself a bit. Initially, the idea felt absurd beyond belief. But if they were talking about splicing different species' abilities together like they had for her and that Kajaro had apparently managed himself, then what the hell was a cat with nine lives thrown in there? It all fit in the magical universe, right? Some days, Quinn really thought she might be ever so slightly losing a bit of her mind.

Anyway, Malakai elbowed her. "Don't you want to open the branch, Quinn?"

"Of course I do," she said. She hadn't forgotten. She was just fascinated by the fact that there was literally a cat out there with nine lives. Although it made sense, just like some of the species she'd encountered in the Library were present in mythology and fairy tales from Earth.

"I have another surprise for you later," Hal said.

Quinn narrowed her eyes. "You've given me two surprises already. I'm not sure I can handle a third."

"Oh no, you'll love this one," Hal said. "It's just not ready quite yet."

Quinn frowned. She extended her senses, as she couldn't pick up anything akin to subterfuge, nor anybody waiting to try to play a trick on her. In fact, she couldn't pick up anything negative in the Library at all right then. No bad connotations, lots of concentration. Some fiery arguments between patrons about subject matter contained in some of the books. But that was just an average day in the Library.

She shrugged. "Fine," she said. "Just not right now. I have too much to do."

Hal nodded.

"Okay," Quinn said.

She stepped up into the actual check-in desk, moving down the far end. More away from the throng of people that gathered around the active end. She leaned against the counter and picked the massive book up. She didn't know what it was with these last alchemical books, but they were much larger tomes than most of the ones they'd had returned before. Many of those were sort of like letter size. These things were like double letter sized, huge tomes that took two arms to wrestle.

She frowned and shrugged. The leather binding was absolutely gorgeous. *The Jezishian Solution to Maladies of the Mana Pathways: A Beginner's Guide* was, in fact, a beautiful book. It had blue veins practically running through it. They pulsated and glowed as if it would boost mana pathways just by being read.

Quinn glanced at Malakai and he shook his head. Which was a pity. She was really hoping maybe something like this would help him heal. She should have known a beginner book wasn't enough to help him. But she sighed, placed her hand on top of it. It was like she was holding this massive final piece of a puzzle. One that would open the alchemical and medicinal wings.

She paused and looked around. Expectant faces watched her. Dottie, Geneva, Eric, Hal, Lynx, and Malakai. She frowned.

"Where's your grandfather?" she asked Malakai.

"I think he's with Harish and Siliqua. They were discussing memory matters earlier. My mother's already gone home, as far as I can tell."

Quinn nodded, feeling like she was missing something. The Library spoke up in her mind. *Are you going to open the damn branch or not?*

Quinn chuckled to herself. Yeah, maybe that's what she thought was missing. She willed the information to come back up in front of her. It all read out perfectly.

Alchemical and Medicinal Branch Requirements

384/384 books retrieved

1257/1257 varieties of plant life, herb life, trees, flowers, and weeds

Energy level required: medium

Mana requirement: 6,843

Energy requirement: 7,295

Patronage level required: fluid

Non-restrictive, all borrowing privileges established

Calibrating . . .

Calculating . . .

Patronage level: met.

Librarian strength required: 12.

Assessing . . .

Calibrating . . .

Accepted . . .

Librarian strength: met.

All requirements pending fusion.

Medicinal and alchemical branches: intertwining.

The alchemical and medicinal branch has met all requirements to be opened.

Do you wish to proceed?

Yes or No?

Or place this process on hold?

"Place this process on hold?" Quinn asked.

"No," Lynx said vehemently. "Don't do that!"

The Library echoed *Don't do that!* in her head as well.

"Okay," Quinn said. "I guess we're opening the alchemical and medicinal branch." And she selected *yes*.

3 7

CALIBRATING AND RESETTING

A RUMBLE ECHOED DEEP WITHIN THE BOWELS OF THE LIBRARY, MAKING Quinn stumble ever so slightly. The Library hadn't reacted this way when they opened the culinary branch. She heard a loud hoot and looked up to see Aradie sweeping toward the second level.

It was like a lightbulb moment as Quinn remembered the beginner books for the branch were upstairs. Logically, that dictated where the expansion would start. She grinned, activated flight, and pretty much jumped up, landing very lightly on the floor after clearing the banister.

She looked down and grinned. Malakai gaped up at her, laughed, and jumped up himself. Lynx was there momentarily, as well as Hal, Eric, and Geneva. Nobody had to use stairs. Magic was so convenient.

Quinn grinned as the rumbling continued. "Where?"

Aradie gestured with a wing, which was an oddly comical gesture for an owl. Quinn and the others walked along the sections until they crossed over to the medicinal and alchemical wing. Right there, where there'd usually been cauldrons and several tables, the occasional mill, the terrariums, and the rest, the entire area was suffused with a subtle glow.

Quinn watched in fascination as the sheen rippled, making it feel like the whole area was made out of waves.

"Don't get too close," Lynx said. "The Library's pulling a lot of energy for this."

Quinn nodded and stepped back, just to be safe. She couldn't be certain, but was fairly sure stepping into that rippling area was a bad idea.

The Librarian hadn't known what to expect. Frankly, she'd assumed the Library would pop out a new annex from nothing, just create it on the spot. But now she thought about it, that didn't make sense, because when the branches appeared, they were already fully stocked. The culinary branch had opened with amenities and supplies that required cataloging by the Library's greater system, too.

"How exactly does this work?" Quinn asked as she watched the walls behind the books, the desks, and the tables, and the cauldrons begin to warp. She took another two steps back to be on the safe side.

Lynx answered her, his voice contemplative. "The Library has to re-access the sealed-off dimension the branches exist in while they're in stasis."

"In stasis?" Quinn asked.

"Of course. It's so they don't use the energy and mana required to operate. They're sort of shrunk down and shifted . . ."

"Like a dollhouse?"

"Not really," Lynx said. "Just out of time with us. They're out of phase. They're there, but not there and thus don't require anything. They're just in stasis."

Quinn thought it over and felt the need to put it in her own words. To make sure it made sense to her. "The Library has to shift everything back into this specific pocket dimension so it realigns with the power centers and begins calibrating and resetting so all the information between both the branch and the main branch line up." Lynx nodded and Quinn shrugged. "Okay, that's needlessly complex."

"No," Lynx said. "Not needlessly complex. Definitely needfully complex."

Quinn laughed.

"He's right." Malakai leant against the banister, watching the walls with a rapt fascination.

They didn't just warp. Each of those walls had originally been bookcases, and now they split and distributed themselves. They began shifting to the side and elongating the entire section. Even the floor looked like it was warping out from under them. Quinn glanced downstairs, but apart from a few curious looks because of the noise that came from upstairs, nobody down in the main part seemed to, well, care.

Not yet, anyway.

The shifting continued, several slight jolts under Quinn's feet, and it slowly began to take form. Each of the bookcases shifted backward, multiplying, or at least seeming to, as it all came together to make an expanded collection around the exterior of the newly formed massive room. Columns rose up in several areas around the room with more bookcases rising up between some of them. They pushed the ceiling in the new section even higher. There were twelve columns altogether, six on each side of the room. More and more bookshelves began to appear, although at first they seemed incorporeal.

The change truly began to happen once all the pillars were in place.

Tables with mills for, Quinn presumed, grinding down ingredients. There were glass-blowing stations for vials and bottles. Next to that was a plethora of cauldron tables. These were made out of stone, with furnaces built right into them, and enough room for several people to gather around if needed. Quinn lost count after about eight of each, because the room kept shifting.

Next came the terrariums for all the rare herbs, weeds, plants, and other ingredients needed for the plethora of medicinal uses they had.

But nothing seemed solid yet. Quinn blinked and rubbed her eyes. Everything had a sheen over it, a sort of translucent shell that made her think it wasn't quite in this dimension yet.

"Don't try and move forward yet," Lynx said, a hesitant hand on her arm, holding her back.

"Nope, you would not want to move forward right now," Hal said, amusement in his words. "I mean, you could. I'm not sure how we'd be able to pull you out of that, but I'm sure we could. You're pretty well amalgamated to the Library. Want to try, Quinn?"

"Hal, not even in jest. Stop it," Lynx admonished him.

"Now at least I know where Eric gets it from," she said. Hal actually grinned, but she could see the fascination reflected in his eyes. Not even he could hide how impressed he was with the Library.

Quinn continued to watch. As furniture pushed up, books sorted in, and several tables that she didn't recognize the purpose for were also slotted into place. Lighting began to emerge and was very specific over the cauldrons and terrariums. And there were more books in locked cases. Quinn raised an eyebrow.

"Not all medicinal books are available to everyone," Lynx said. "There are certain legendary-level medicinal texts that will kill you if you look at it before you're ready."

"Oh," Quinn said, not entirely sure how to react to that. "Good to know."

She reveled in the process of a new branch creation. Watching it as it moved, so slowly, efficiently. This was an entire vast wing of the Library being drawn back into being, and so far it'd taken all of five minutes. "It's dimensionally shifting, and if you get caught in the shift, you might get caught in between dimensions," Quinn said, hoping she'd understood it properly.

Lynx nodded slowly. "You'd get caught in between dimensions . . ." He frowned.

"Why do you sound . . . what's wrong? What isn't right?" Quinn asked, suddenly aware that Lynx was paying a different sort of attention to the new branch now.

"No, it's—it's re-establishing," Lynx said, a confused frown pinching his brows. "But . . . just feel it, Quinn. You can *feel* it."

Quinn reached out her senses toward the Library and the developing branch. Something about the process wasn't clicking yet. It wasn't that the Library was wrong. It was that there was something more difficult than expected about this retrieval.

"Okay, I can sense it, Lynx, but I don't know what that means. What does it mean that it's more difficult than it was supposed to be?"

Lynx shrugged. "I'm not entirely sure. That portion of my memories is fuzzy. I mean, we haven't needed to open this specific branch for a few million years, I think. I know there was one time it was closed down for a reason or three, but I can't remember."

"A reason or three," Eric scoffed. "You were probably redecorating. Spending good old fine energy."

"Eric," Quinn said with a grin. "That's not helpful."

"Me? I'm awesome. I can at least leverage fines on people." Eric puffed his chest out a bit.

Quinn raised an eyebrow. "There's more to being a Librarian than leveraging fines."

"Perhaps. But there's nothing more fun about it than leveraging fines," Eric corrected her.

Quinn laughed. And yet she still felt uneasy. There was something off about the undercurrent of power running to the new section.

"That's not right," she whispered, pushing out her senses to try and get a feel for what exactly was bugging her.

Malakai nudged her. "What's not right?"

"Can't you feel that?" she asked him.

He raised an eyebrow. "I can't access my mana right now. Remember? No magic, no mana. Dangerous. My life would be in ruins."

"Oh, yeah." Quinn remembered it belatedly, but was too focused on her senses. It wasn't that the mana was infected or chaotic. It was this underlying mustiness, this strange sensation of lethargy and apathy all rolled into one, as if the annex didn't want to be reestablished. Quinn frowned.

Geneva piped up. "Is it infected?"

"It's not." Quinn frowned, getting frustrated now.

"I thought it would go faster." Geneva pouted slightly, her brow also furrowed with worry.

Quinn shook her head. "No, the culinary branch took longer than this."

"But the culinary branch is different," Lynx said. "It's always been different. It runs on other specifics and a slightly different plane than this one."

"A plane?" Quinn said. "Planes of existence now?"

Lynx shrugged. "You knew what you were getting into."

"No, really, Lynx, I did not."

"True, but you should have guessed what you were getting into." Hal flashed her a toothy grin.

Quinn glared at him. "It's not bad, is it?"

Lynx shrugged. "I really can't answer that."

And the Library chose not to answer any of the questions. Quinn hoped it was probably just preoccupied.

"You know," Dottie said, and Quinn realized she'd finally made it up the stairs to them. "It's fortuitous that we're opening this branch now, considering we just had the hospital expansion. It'll help all of the patients that we've got."

Quinn nodded slowly, watching the terrariums as the light adjusted, and the insides of them began to populate with copious plants, vines, shrubs, weeds. This was such a massive space, at least the size of a football field now. The scope of it, the fact that it was bigger than it architecturally had any physical right to be, was ever so slightly intimidating. She looked around. "Is it supposed to be this large?"

Hal frowned. "Yes and no." He took a step forward and sniffed, definitively sniffed the air. He scowled. "You're right, it's not chaotic, it's not infected, but it's . . . lazy?"

"Stubborn," Eric offered.

"You're not helping, Eric," Hal snapped. "No, it's . . . It's old, it's aged. I wonder if it didn't seal properly when the Library sealed it away initially. After all, it must have been chaos, the sudden shutting down."

Quinn shrugged. "What difference would that make?"

The Library intoned words in what she hoped was just the heads of the people standing around her. *It is struggling,* the Library said. *We*

*have the books, we have the energy, we have more than the energy that we
need, but there's something missing. You did get all of the components right,
Quinn? Everything?*

"Yes, it flagged *me*! I didn't ask it."

The Library was silent for several seconds. Quinn didn't think it'd
say anything else. Suddenly, it was as if the Library sighed. The whole
floor shifted beneath Quinn, sending her stumbling to one knee, and
most of the others as well, except for Eric and Geneva who were
hovering.

"What was that?"

The Library sighed. *Please tell me it looks okay.*

Quinn didn't like what she saw in front of her. It had to be a
mirage. She blinked again and took a few tentative steps forward. "Is
it supposed to be this dilapidated?"

Lynx moved with her, silently morphing into his lynx form,
padding gently across the floor.

"None of this feels right," Quinn said. It might have seemed okay
to most people and just looked slightly untidy, but there was something off-center about most of the bookcases, and there were so many
tomes spread all over the floor.

Tossed.

Bent.

Tattered.

If Quinn hadn't known better, she would have assumed they'd
been attacked by bookworms as well. "What's—what's happened
here?"

A strange suffocating uneasiness spread out from the new branch.
Quinn took several steps closer, almost at its threshold. The words
Alchemical and Medicinal Branch glowed in magical golden letters high
above them all. It looked wonderful but felt sort of melancholy. And
that's when Quinn noticed something moving among the books.

"Um," Quinn said, "Please tell me the books aren't supposed to
move like that. If there are engorged bookworms in there, I'm out. I've
had it with engorged bookworms. Y'all can kill them."

"No, that's not an engorged bookworm. That's—oh." Hal actually took a step back.

Quinn blinked, trying to make her eyes focus as they moved toward her. "What the hell is that?"

A small creature streaked all the way to her, so fast she couldn't even catalog its appearance, and leapt up toward her face.

3 8

DIMENSION SHIFT

Quinn instinctively put her hands up to cover her face and, in doing so, inadvertently caught whatever flung itself at her. Pushing it away from her face, she noticed immediately that it was triangular in nature. As if somebody had taken a large piece of square paper and folded it in half into a triangle.

She held it out in front of her to examine it, and tiny little eyes suddenly blinked up at her. Teensy little feet at the ends of the triangle sections on the bottom wiggled. Quinn almost dropped it, and then it opened its strange almost cartoon-like little mouth and barked at her.

Quinn blinked.

It barked again as the stubby little end of what was obviously not actually paper started to wag.

"What the . . ." Quinn said as it continued to bark in her face.

Lynx laughed and an expression of delight crossed his face. "Oh my gosh, it's a dog-ear. I haven't seen one of those in so long. I thought they'd all faded with the power down."

Quinn, still holding the creature away from her, turned to Lynx. "A dog-ear, like you do to a page when you crease it to mark your place in a book?"

Lynx shot her a horrified look. "Well, yes! You can't dog-ear pages, that's why we have them. You don't want to crease a magical page! That's one of the highest fines we can give."

"Exactly," Eric chimed in. "Have you not read the Fine Accords? I know that Lynx brought that book up to you. You should have looked in it by now. Dog-earing a magical book is a majorly finable offense."

Quinn, still slightly in shock, looked at the two of them and realized they were being deadly serious. Then she looked back at the dog-ear that was being ridiculously cute. As if in response to her thoughts, it struggled and strained and leaned forward just enough to lick her on the nose.

"Ah!" Quinn laughed, but she didn't want to drop it because it was too high and might get hurt, and she didn't really feel like putting it down yet because she was scared she'd step on it. Not precisely what she was aiming for with a newly discovered creature.

Lynx laughed again, morphed back into his human form, and reached out to scratch the little thing behind what Quinn realized were actual ears and not just drawn onto the paper. Although it wasn't made out of paper. Its skin or fur felt like good quality suede. It was soft and flexible.

The smile on Lynx's face only got bigger, and his brow furrowed. "I don't think I've seen these little guys for thousands of years. Thinking back, I can't even remember seeing them before the Library shut down. How could I have forgotten about dog-ears?"

"In your defense," Quinn said, "given your history, it's not unexpected that some of your memories are either jumbled or gone."

She decided to bring her arms into her chest and just hold the little dog-ear. It sat quite comfortably on her arms, panting like an actual dog.

"You make a valid point," Lynx said. But she could hear the sadness behind those words. The dog-ear took that second to leverage itself up and lick Quinn's cheek.

"If you don't stop that," she said to it, "I'm gonna put you on the ground where people can trip over you."

The dog-ear sat down in her hand and she swore it was pouting.

Hal laughed, watching the creature. "You can't have looked much, Lynx. Did you really completely forget about dog-ears?"

"I must have. I don't have recent memories of them." Lynx sounded subdued.

Quinn raised an eyebrow at Hal who nodded ever so slightly. She was glad Lynx wasn't watching them.

"Look," Lynx said, "I had a lot on my mind back then. You know, or my mind being *wiped* at the time."

The dog-ear started to squirm again. It wasn't very large, but it was pretty wily. Maybe the size of a miniature Dachshund or a large guinea pig. Quinn wasn't exactly sure. She'd never had a pet dog before, or a pet at all for that matter. It wouldn't stop trying to lick her. She could have sworn Aradie, sitting on the opposite shoulder, was laughing her owly butt off.

"Oi," she said to Aradie. "Stop that. That's not nice of you." But Quinn had to admit the dog-ear was growing on her.

"Do you have a little name?" she said to it. It barked ever so high-pitched again and she inspected it.

Name: Bellrose Doggie

Species: dog-ear

Age: Infinite

"Your name is Bellrose?" And it barked twice in quick succession. "I'm taking that as a yes because you didn't pee on me. Aren't you just adorable?" It obviously liked being called adorable. "Do you think it recognized me as the Librarian?"

"Oh, yes," Hal said, still enjoying some joke that Quinn didn't understand. "Definitely got your Librarian scent, that's what that dog-ear did." He frowned and looked toward the still transforming Library branch. "It's sort of odd. They usually travel in packs. But I don't see any others. Not to mention how it's withstood the last five hundred years, though it is bigger than usual."

Malakai moved forward to stand next to Quinn. He glanced at the dog-ear, reached over, and scratched it behind its kind of ears.

She gave him a mock glare. "It's not yours. It's mine. You have to ask if you can pet it."

"Can I pet it?" Malakai asked, raising an eyebrow.

"Of course you can."

He laughed. "So now you have a pet dog and a pet owl."

Aradie, quite deliberately, pecked his hand.

"Okay, you've got a pet dog-ear and a comrade owl."

Aradie hooted agreement low in her throat.

Quinn laughed and gestured back at the branch as it sorted itself. "Is it supposed to be taking this long for the Library to do its thing?"

"No, now it's taking a while longer than I thought it would." Lynx sounded irritated.

"Yeah," Quinn said. "I don't understand. I'm not getting any alarms or any warnings." She closed her eyes and reached out with her senses. "I can't feel it properly. It's not registering in the way the rest of the Library does yet. Does that mean it hasn't dimensionally shifted fully?"

Lynx shrugged. "I'm just a part of the Library too."

The Library spoke up. *This isn't normal. It's having difficulty manifesting from its dimensional shift. It'll get here. Just give it a little bit more time.*

Quinn could hear the strain in its voice and frowned, not liking how drained the Library sounded. And that's when the Bell barked again, very loudly.

Quinn laughed. "You are a little attention seeker. How did you survive these last few hundred years?"

Bell licked her cheek again. The rest of them chuckled. But Quinn couldn't help the growing unease in her stomach.

"Okay, little one," Quinn said, and put the dog-ear down. It quite literally stayed right at her heel, growling ever so slightly as it quivered and yipped a few times. That's when she knew exactly what it reminded her of: those little Pomeranian dogs mixed with a miniature Dachshund.

She moved forward a couple of steps, hesitant to get too close to the still forming branch. There was a mist inside the whole section. It wove its way around in a way that still felt like it wasn't quite in synchronization with the entire Library. Given what the Library itself had said, she knew it wasn't worse than that.

Her senses couldn't pick it up yet. It wasn't a part of the whole, and despite the fact that she and the Library were linked so intrinsically together, she still couldn't reach out and feel it. There was a gap of knowledge. The books that had transformed with the Library were suddenly beyond her reach. Even the herbs, plants, weeds, and ingredients that went into it were no longer in existence as far as her senses could tell. Yet, her eyes kept lying to her, letting her know that it was sort of there, just beyond reach.

And that this one dog-ear had somehow got through.

Lynx stepped forward slowly, his eyes flickering in that strange way they always did when he connected with the system fully. He didn't look frantic, just concerned. The frown made his eyebrows furrow, and he *tsk*ed several times under his breath, which he only did when he was really annoyed.

Mal had moved forward as well, absently grabbing for the sword that wasn't there.

"This is unprecedented," Hal said. "Not that I've been here when many branches were opened, and I do believe creating them in the first place was substantially different than what you're currently witnessing."

The dog-ear barked, bit Quinn's pants, and tried to pull her back, away from the branch entry. She glanced down at it. "You don't think we should move forward, Bell?" The dog barked two more times.

Aradie cooed, as if she was punctuating the statement, agreeing with Bell.

Quinn glanced at everyone. "Well, according to these guys, we should stay right where we are."

"Are you sure?" Malakai said. "Do you think it wouldn't trigger if we crossed the threshold?"

"No," Lynx said, taking a step back, now his eyes had cleared. "We cross that threshold and I'm not sure how we'll be, dimensionally speaking."

"That sounds ominous," Eric said, and paused for a second before speaking again. "I could phase."

"What?" Quinn asked.

"I could phase," Eric repeated. "It's not hard. It's an imp thing. You wouldn't understand."

"No, I probably wouldn't, but what do you mean by phase? What will that do?"

"I can dimensionally phase, and should be able to align myself so I can assist pushing it through." He looked at the mist barrier critically. "I can sense it; it's just beyond us. It's not . . . It's like it needs to be kicked into place."

Do it, Eric, please, the Library said. *There's something fighting against me pulling it fully into this dimension, and I need—I could definitely use, a push.*

"Say no more," Eric said. He cracked his knuckles, flexed his arms, stretched them, and a ripple passed through him. Suddenly, he didn't look like he was fully there. He passed through the shimmering entrance of the alchemical and medicinal branch as it was still forming and was suddenly on the other side where Bell had come from.

The little creature was shaking at Quinn's feet, whimpering.

"Hey, it's okay," Quinn said, reaching down to pick it up. "It's okay."

She petted it, unsure why she was so attached to the tiny dog already. But it was helpless, or it seemed helpless, or it seemed to want their help. She still hadn't pinpointed that yet, but there had to be a reason it had managed to phase shift out to them.

On the other side, Quinn was fairly sure Eric was frowning. He appeared out of sync and out of time with the rest of them—so it was difficult to tell.

Quinn could sense the power fluctuation, the pushing, the way it started to leverage itself past the mist, through the mist, until finally there was a resounding click, and Eric practically catapulted back across the threshold to where they were, as if he'd been released from a slingshot.

"Damn it," he said, shaking his head. "That wasn't what I expected."

"Was it just stuck?" Quinn asked, just before she noticed a shadow moving beyond them, behind the bookcases, in the newly established branch.

"No, there's something—"

Suddenly wind whipped around in front of them, and Milaro ported in, standing right next to Malakai, making sure he didn't move. The wind whipped his hair around him, and his eyes glowed silver as he channeled his power. "Don't go near it. You can't walk in there."

Quinn hugged the now-whimpering dog-ear.

"Why . . ." She started to ask, but stopped, because she saw the shadow again, slithering through the bookshelves.

"Something crossed over with the dimension shift," Milaro said.

And the alarms in the Library started blaring.

39

A CACOPHONY OF OTHERS

Shivers ran down Quinn's spine at the sight of the shadowy figure slinking around beyond the evaporating veil. The blaring of the alarm shut off with a thought from Quinn, as she didn't want to worry the patrons.

She pushed out a shield so that no one could accidentally enter the area.

And the Alchemical and Medicinal Branch suddenly clicked into place, becoming a complete part of the Library to her senses. She grimaced.

Second branch opened—check.

Shadowy creature of indeterminate origin—double check.

"Define what you mean by *something crossed over*," Quinn said conversationally to Milaro. In her mind, all the zombie and horror flicks she'd seen as a child and teen crossing over probably meant something entirely different from what Milaro intended. She believed in magic for obvious reasons, but stretching it to creatures crossing over from the beyond . . .

Milaro didn't take his eyes off the shadowy back-and-forth in the room in front of them. "I meant a dimensional eel has crossed over with the branch. They're not unfriendly, generally, but they can be dangerous. And this one is a bit bigger than usual."

Quinn frowned. "How did you realize that?"

"I'm dimensionally attuned. Comes with a lot of dimensional travel. You'll get there," Milaro said absently.

Hal actually laughed. "Seriously, it's a dimensional eel? How did it even get in there?"

Milaro shrugged. "I don't know. Maybe it was there before the Library sent this branch into its pocket."

"Probably an experiment," Lynx said with a groan. "This wing has always attempted crazy things to harness the energy of anything it could use in medicinal ways. I wouldn't put it past them to have had one sequestered up here. I didn't exactly have time to do inventory before shutdown initiated."

Hal patted Lynx on the shoulder. They were big pats, sort of shook the manifestation slightly. "It's okay, Lynx. We'll fix this up as well."

"No need to sound so condescending," Lynx said.

Hal shrugged, cracked his neck from side to side. "I didn't mean it to. However, I do find wrestling with a dimensional eel to be somewhat tantalizing."

"You know you can't touch it, Hal," Milaro said.

Quinn listened on in fascination and put tiny little Bell, the dogear, right next to Dottie. "You stay with Dottie. You two stay here," she said. The rest of them, Lynx, Quinn, Malakai, Hal, Geneva, Aradie, and Eric, all approached the threshold of the new branch.

"So," Quinn said, "anything specific we need to know? Perhaps a plan of attack?"

Hal laughed again.

Milaro glared at him. "You're supposed to be the commander. Shouldn't you have a plan of attack?"

"You're a king. You're supposed to know everything," Hal taunted, but relented. "As Milaro and Lynx have mentioned, we can't just run in and grab it. Dimensional eels devour dimensional output. All subdimensions, travel, outdoors, things like that, have a certain level of dimensional activity because of the way they function. And dimensional eels are often used to siphon off excess dimensional energy. That's how they sustain themselves. And so we often have some around the Library. They were heavily monitored and only supposed to be used by experts."

Lynx grimaced. "I really didn't think about this when I drained the power. And since we don't have any excess energy to speak of right now, they totally slipped my mind. Can't remember enough anyway, but I do know we need to corner it."

Quinn snapped her fingers. Although later, she wasn't exactly sure *why* she snapped her fingers, because she could have just willed it into existence. But it popped a barrier up around the whole alchemical and medicinal section so that it wouldn't overflow to the patrons below and harm anyone. It wasn't enough to just protect this upper level like she'd already done. It needed to be in a protective bubble.

"Now," she said, turning to Malakai, "should you be doing this? Shouldn't you be resting?"

"I won't use mana skills. I'll just use my bow and arrow," he said.

She raised an eyebrow, but she knew him well enough to know telling him what to do wouldn't go over well. So she simply nodded and listened to directions.

Hal spoke clearly. "It's an oversized dimension eel. It, as you can see, swims in and out of shadows. There's dimensional energy left in this area. It's currently trying to devour the remaining dimensional signature traces. Basically, we need to corner it and capture it. Let's split up, shall we?"

"All lights to maximum," Quinn said. "It'll make the shadows stand out." The area lit up almost immediately, chasing many of the shadows away. "Excellent. See? Easier to see than when everything is a shadow."

Hal reached over and ruffled her hair. Or he tried to, Quinn dodged. "Well, I guess it's time to track it."

They moved together. Geneva and Eric set off to one corner while Hal and Milaro went to another. Quinn and Malakai stayed together while Lynx and Aradie brought up the rear.

Off to the left, Geneva and Eric attempted to engage the overgrown eel, which was about twenty feet long, probably three feet high and about two feet thick. They attempted to bounce the eel back and forth between each other, buffeting it with, well, Quinn wasn't entirely sure what Eric was using, but she knew Geneva used wind. The wind seemed to aggravate it more than what Eric used and the eel kept twisting to snap at Geneva. She had to move out of the way, which allowed it to slip past her and dash off to another area in the stacks.

The thing was fast, but it didn't appear to be overly violent.

Quinn watched it carefully, tracing it around to see if it was coming near her and Malakai. "How are you going to help me with the arrows?" she asked.

"I'll get out my sword," he said, although he didn't sound enthused.

She nodded, not wanting to make him feel worse than he already did. "That'll work. I'm pretty sure it doesn't want to be cut in two," she said. "Maybe it'll just come quietly."

Malakai actually laughed.

Next, the eel encountered Hal and Milaro. The two of them moved well together, as if they'd fought together often. Milaro utilized a force Quinn couldn't see or quantify and guided the creature toward Hal. The commander's fists were coated in something that looked like a transparent, hardened glove. The eel looked like it was about to take a pretty hefty punch to the nose when it suddenly appeared on the other side of Hal.

One of the things they'd apparently forgotten to mention was these eels, being dimensional creatures, could sometimes phase when they had enough energy and thus, it avoided Hal's punches completely.

That was pretty much when all hell broke loose.

The eel had now noticed it was being cornered. It flared up, making itself somehow bigger. Quinn could feel it tugging on every shred of dimensional energy left in the area. For just a second, the entire room felt like it warped ever so slightly.

Wracking her brains for something to do, Quinn tried to figure out exactly how they could defeat this thing without touching.

Getting drained of dimensional energy or getting dimensional sickness didn't sound like fun times to Quinn.

But the runaway eel was fast and almost bowled Malakai over on its way to one of the farthest back corners.

Quinn, who was hovering, tried to lasso it with a rope of wind without giving it too much thought. Considering she'd never used a lasso before, and had only just come up with the idea, it was no surprise it didn't work. Wind wasn't Quinn's best element. Consequently, she got pulled for about twenty yards before almost colliding with a bookcase, only barely avoiding it by flying up over the top and losing the thread she'd had attached to the eel.

Malakai snorted with laughter behind her.

"I didn't see you doing any better," Quinn said, trying not to laugh herself. Being indignant got her nowhere, anyway. She may as well laugh about it.

"This is ridiculous," Hal said, studying his transparent gloves. He seemed to be struggling with the fact that the creature got away from him. "It's a dimension eel. It can't dodge my punch."

"Guess no one told it that." Quinn laughed again. This shouldn't be so funny. This wasn't a good thing. If the eel got out, it could drain their doors of dimensional energy. It was way too big to control. Luckily, the barrier she'd put up around the area seemed to be holding.

Geneva and Eric chased the creature around, making sure it stayed within the warded off containment. Aradie perched on a set of bookshelves and appeared to be laughing to herself, and Lynx got up on one of the tables as he tried to follow it, doing his best to snap a trap around it, only to have it phase again as he did so.

"If it can just phase out of our traps, how are we supposed to catch it?" Quinn half chuckled. She felt like this was one of those old black and white television shows that had everybody falling over themselves to catch some dog that was running away.

The Library spoke up to all of them. *You'll have to shrink it. It's not like the engorged bookworms that you fought when you first arrived here, Quinn. It doesn't need to be killed. It needs to be drained of the excess dimen-*

sional energy that it's absorbed, which will, in turn help stabilize the new branch. It hasn't digested the energy properly after having been locked in the dimensional pocket.

"You mean it's, like, constipated?" Quinn asked incredulously.

In a manner of speaking, the Library said.

Quinn frowned.

Lynx perked up. "Oh, I know exactly what we need." And he vanished.

Quinn sighed. "I'm glad *he* knows exactly what we need."

"He'll bring it back," Milaro said, also hovering as the eel hid in one of the corners, curling in on itself, watching them all warily.

Quinn felt a bit sorry for it. It wasn't its fault it had been forgotten about when the branch got pushed into its own side dimension.

"Poor little thing," she said.

"It's not poor. At this size, if it gets its hands on you, it can dimensionally shift you."

"Oh," Quinn said, "that's decidedly less cute. But I still feel sorry for it."

Lynx popped back into view. "I've got it."

Quinn looked at the long cylindrical item he had in his hand. "What is that?"

"Well, it's a dimensional power trapper."

A dimensional power trapper. To Quinn, it just looked like a long metal—or some type of alloy—poster tube. But if it could trap the excess power . . . she was all for it.

"Okay. You need to distract it," Lynx said. "Do something . . . distracting."

"I guess we can do that," Quinn said, laughing. She aimed a gust of wind at it, startling it out of its hidey corner, and it raced toward her. This time, ready for it, she jumped up and over it, allowing it to barrel straight into Hal's fist. She wasn't going to ask how Hal, of all people, was able to punch the don't-touch-the-dimensional eel even with his flashy magical glove. She was pretty sure it had to do with his species and the ability to turn his body into a weapon. But she was still brushing up on satyr lore, so she wasn't entirely certain.

This time, the eel reeled back and suddenly stopped, stuck in stasis as Milaro's spell froze it in place.

Milaro grinned triumphantly.

Lynx, aimed the tube at the eel and activated it. "Let's do this."

A low humming filled the air all around them. If she squinted, Quinn saw a tether, or perhaps a flow of thin golden power, entering the tube. Slowly, but surely, the eel began to shrink down. It writhed against it. It whimpered. It cried out in a strange, alien sound. But Milaro's spell held it in place. Quinn decided that was the next one she needed to add to her arsenal. The combat branch was definitely next on the list.

Finally, after a couple of minutes, the eel was about the normal size Quinn would expect an eel to be. It was about two and a half feet long, very slender, but still smoky black. Lynx pulled out another box. This was huge in comparison to the new size of the eel. It was about five feet long and about three feet deep, massive glass encasement and Milaro maneuvered the now drained dimensional eel in it.

"There we go," he said, a tight smile on his tired face, "crisis averted."

Quinn raised an eyebrow. "Do we care how it happened in the first place?"

"I'll look into it," Lynx said, "because I'm pretty sure it'll come back with the memories I'm still trying to regain."

Quinn smiled and noticed a very strange noise. She turned around, noting that the barrier had been dismissed, likely by the Library itself, but the noise still filled the air. She frowned, unsure exactly what the snuffling noise was.

And then she heard the first bark, followed by a cacophony of others.

"Oh no," she said, and finally looked down at her feet, where at least thirty dog-ears sat, looking up at her with adorable eyes and wagging behinds.

40

WHAT SHE NEEDED

DESPITE HOW ADORABLE THE DOG-EARS WERE, EVEN AS THEY JUMPED around on everyone, sniffing their feet, tugging at their pants, the state of the alchemical and medical branch was quite sobering.

With no dimensional eel, even though it sat off its enclosure to the side, they could survey the damage to the branch. But now, looking at the section closer, there were hundreds, if not thousands, of books strewn all over the floor. This made Quinn that much more grateful for the fact that she had been hovering during most of the eel capturing fiasco.

She didn't *think* she'd stepped on any books.

The tomes were scattered and damaged, far worse than anything she'd seen since she first walked into the Library all those months ago. It'd be a long process to restore all of these tomes. She wasn't entirely sure Jane would be able to handle this influx, but she sent for her.

But Narilin was still healing up in the hospital after the entire debacle with the Balisors. It'd take a few more days at least. Luckily Narilin hadn't been exposed for long. For most of the Balisors affected by the Bardocian root, it'd be a long road to full recovery, if at all possible. The damage was reversible to a certain extent, as long as they hadn't been exposed for too long.

Jane didn't take long to arrive. But Quinn didn't even notice when she entered because she was in the middle of speaking to Hal.

"I thought you said you had a surprise for me. I could really do with a cheer-me-up about now," She pushed him, trying to coax it out due to genuine curiosity and the need for a distraction.

"I don't think you could do this particular cheer-me-up right now, so how about we get all this sorted, young egg, and then I'll talk to you about the surprise." His half-condescending, half-grandfatherly tone was sometimes infuriating.

Quinn glowered at him for a second before shrugging. She spied Jane and motioned her to come over, dismissing Hal for the moment. "Time to pick up some of these books. Think you can help?"

Jane blanched ever so slightly, her timber paling into a brief birch look alike. "I can get these to the book infirmary and have them assessed."

Quinn nodded and helped her begin to sort them into piles.

Dottie trotted over with Carty, who Quinn hadn't seen in quite some time, rolling along behind her. She wasn't about to ask how the cart got up the spiral staircase to get here. She knew the staircases could sometimes become ramps and she wouldn't put it past the cart to be able to levitate because there was enough energy available in the Library. She'd seen more obscure, unbelievable things since coming to the Library than she ever thought possible. Everything was possible, maybe not probable, but possible.

"Carty," she said, "my hero who dragged me up flights of stairs when I could barely move."

"Quite, quite, Librarian," he said, "I'm a bit chuffed you remember that. Anyway, let's have a bit of a look, shall we?" The cart was all business. He rolled over to where Jane was and gently tapped her.

Jane blinked, looking around. "Oh, Carty." She seemed at a loss for words, which was something Narilin never was.

"What do you think?" Quinn asked, now the Salosier had had time to look at the books.

"I don't really know what to think. Why is this in such a mess?" she asked.

Quinn shrugged. "I'm not entirely sure you'd believe us if we told you, but I'll tell you anyway. When shifted into its dimensional stasis, it seems we forgot there was a dimensional eel contained inside."

"Ouch." Jane looked very thoughtful. She was slightly different to Narilin and didn't hold herself as separate. The assistant leaned over the books, touching them here and there, assessing them.

Which made Quinn feel slightly better about the fact that so many of the books in this particular branch, were in heavy need of repair. She was particularly glad of the book doctor cousins right then.

"So that still doesn't explain the extent of this damage. It *would* explain why the energy levels in here are very low and thus the books aren't self-repairing the little things they usually do, but it doesn't explain the sheer . . .damage. Dimensional shifting shouldn't cause such destruction. Anyway, it is what it is and we must deal with it. Correct? No sense in harping on the past when we have way too much to do in the future." Jane laughed at her own little joke.

Quinn decided she liked Jane.

Lynx walked over and threw his hands in the air in a very human gesture. "This is a wreck," he said.

"The Library can fix it, can't it?" Quinn said, to which the Library answered her directly.

I can fix it to a certain extent, but I'm currently managing other things. This requires more precision than you'd think.

"Is there something else we should know about?" Quinn asked worriedly.

No, I can easily rebuild, I can easily expand, but refurbishing isn't my strong suit because I can't actually see the detail that I need to provide. That's why we needed the golems to reshelve way back when.

Jane nodded along with the conversation, as if she talked to the Library every day. And, for all Quinn knew, perhaps she did. The assistant book doctor turned around and began sorting some of the books onto the trolly with Carty's help.

Quinn looked around, even as Tim and Tom popped into existence right next to her. They bowed in her direction, giving her one of their amazing clay golem smiles, and they went about their work of sorting the books with Carty and Jane, very gently, very specifically.

It didn't take too long for the aisle they were in to start looking healthier.

Quinn smiled as she watched them and sighed. Lots of work to be done. Although, being a Librarian and getting to use one of those ladders that reached up high in the bookcases and scooched along as she picked out books reminded her of fairy tales she'd grown up with.

She liked libraries.

She loved this one.

But sometimes she just wanted to sit down and read.

Instead, she reinforced her hand with her scales so that she too had protective gear over her skin like everyone else. She bent down to pick up some broken glass from when the beakers and jars had shattered during the eel's rampage.

"You know you could just do that with wind, right?" Malakai said.

"Stop grumbling and help me tidy up."

"Fine," he said.

"I'm trying to make you feel better about yourself," Quinn said. "You don't have any magic right now. Or you shouldn't be using magic right now. You didn't use magic, did you?"

"No, I promise I didn't use magic in the fight." Malakai rolled his eyes theatrically. "I will be fine."

"Good, good. You've still got to rest and recover."

Lynx returned and opted to help. He opened some sort of storage portal and took all the rubbish with him, before returning again shortly.

"Lynx, you got an answer for me?" Quinn asked.

"An answer to what?" he said.

"Why this branch is almost falling apart while the culinary one wasn't."

He looked her deadpan in the face and said, "Apart from the dimension eel, I have no clue."

Quinn laughed. She didn't know why exactly, because that wasn't the news she wanted to hear. She wanted him to know exactly what had happened. He was supposed to be retrieving memories, but she was also completely aware it'd been much more difficult for both him and the Library to do than they'd anticipated.

"I know I shouldn't find that funny," she said, "but I kind of do."

Link grumbled, "Well, at least one of us does."

"Don't be like that," she said. "Look, you locked them all away, right?"

"After the whole debacle with the filtration system, I woke up with a massive amount of our power already drained because of how I locked her away. Not to mention the fact that we no longer had a Librarian, so it was already going into one of the emergency modes. I just shoved everything that was draining power at an alarming rate mind you into its own little pocket area so it was sealed away and couldn't pull on power that we couldn't afford to bleed."

"Sort of like a five-hundred-year slumber?" Quinn mulled that over.

"Yeah, basically in a stasis—it should have held up over time. As if time didn't pass," Link said, frowning thoughtfully. "Like the culinary branch."

"Well, logically . . . maybe some of the levels, like the culinary branch, which is admittedly a little smaller than this area, might have had less destruction in it because there wasn't a problem with the dimension shift in the shape of the aforementioned eel?" she asked.

He shrugged. "I really have no idea. We won't know until I either remember, research it, or we open more branches and see what state they're in."

"Good point, good point," Quinn said. "Well, either way, getting to know the alchemical and medical branch by having to clean it up isn't the worst thing I can imagine."

Lynx chuckled. "Thanks."

"And next time we open one, maybe we should try and do so gently," Quinn said.

"Is that an option when you open it?" Lynx asked.

"No, it's really not. I just thought maybe we could finagle it," she said. "It'd be nice, hey. 'Please open the branch gently. Pull it through softly.'"

I can hear you both, the Library said into their heads, which only set Quinn off laughing more.

It was strange. They had over three hundred patients in a hospital wing that they'd built, with doctors and surgeons taking care of them. There was a whole group of the Sölem out there trying to tarnish the Library and bring it down. Add to it now, Quinn was no longer sure who was responsible for the whole Balisor fiasco. The Library's brother had turned on them all and wanted to see the Library dead and gone, and chaos returned to the universe, and Quinn couldn't help but find joy in this tiny bit of rebuilding the Library.

"You know," she said.

"What?" asked Malakai, but his tone was soft, and she knew he actually wanted to know.

"I'm just grateful for moments like these. Sometimes it's nice to just stop, recollect why we're here, and appreciate the fact that we are, that we have all these resources around us, and all these people who are willing to step in and help, and that there are magical books." She paused, grinning. "You don't even understand how cool I find that, even after all this time. Magical freaking books, guys."

Malakai smiled at her, patted her hand. "You get excited over the weirdest stuff."

"I know, but isn't that part of my charm?"

He raised an eyebrow. "You have charm?"

"Hey, that's mean."

Lynx chuckled this time. "But he's right."

For the next couple of hours, they cleaned up the alchemical branch, getting everything ready for the glass blowing station, for the milling station, the cauldrons, the cutting station that she didn't exactly understand, but didn't feel like she needed to yet. She even blew a kiss at the dimensional eel as she walked past. It floated happily in whatever substance it currently found itself in. And then she visited the terrariums, and watched as the greenery begin to take hold.

Turning around, Quinn took in the branch. The lights were still at maximum like they'd been when they cornered the eel. All of the bookcases suited the Library again—transformed back to regulation. The rich, deep wood with its ancient essence that lingered all around them. Carty was down to his last delivery of damaged books. There were a lot of spaces in the bookcases, which reminded Quinn that she hadn't checked the branch stats. She sighed, not really wanting to bring up the branch stats just in case there was more bad news. Aradie flew down from one of the tall bookcases, and settled on her shoulder, cooing in her ear.

"I know I need to open them and double-check. I just don't want to." Quinn sighed and pulled up the Library stats. "Here goes."

Alchemical branch officially opened.

Beginner books verified, relegated to main branch Library.

Analyzing intermediate, advanced, master, legendary. Alchemical and medical books.

Processing.

Processing.

Error.

Missing the following number of books.

Alchemical and Medical Branch books missing: 5,892,653 already returned, 5,239 still remain outstanding.

Quinn groaned. "Oh, that was so not what I wanted to hear."

Would you like a categorical breakdown?

Yes or no?

"Nope, definitely not right now," she said. "This is a lot."

Malakai elbowed her. "But you're not in it alone."

She looked around at Eric and Geneva arguing over some book they held between them, at Milaro and Hal working side by side in an odd juxtaposition, at the rest of the crew turning the branch into what it was supposed to be. It was a nice, homey sensation.

Quinn nodded slowly, a smile forming on her lips. He was right. She definitely wasn't alone. And for now, that's all she needed.

41

IN THIS CAPACITY

CLEANING UP THE ALCHEMICAL AND MEDICAL BRANCH TOOK A LOT longer than Quinn anticipated, at least to get it ready for patrons to visit. She was in the process of compiling all the inadvertently returned books that came back when the main branch of the Library opened. With nowhere to place them, they'd originally been held in storage drawers.

Surprised, Quinn hadn't expected many to be returned yet from unopened branches. Her assumption was that they'd been returning beginner texts to the main branch, anyway. She was quite relieved to find out that out of the 5,892 they needed returned to this branch, she already had 653. It still didn't make that much of a dent, leaving it at 5,239, but it still looked like a friendlier number now she'd been able to attribute previous returns.

She enjoyed the quiet work. While it was wonderful to open a branch, the sheer joy she felt at helping it get ready for patrons was something else. She hadn't needed to do this when they'd opened the culinary branch, largely due to Cook coming in and taking over, as they, of course, were supposed to do.

This branch, however, needed the help. The doctor from the hospital section couldn't spare time right now to come and oversee anything. Nor could they currently spare nurses. It gave Quinn a nice respite from constantly pursuing things outside of the Library and allowed her to simply revel in being around the books.

Helping with the organization of the branch was still actively improving the Library, and it allowed her to assuage some of the guilt that she felt for not being as productive as she'd like in getting other essential books back. Yet. Anyway.

On the third day, she wandered down and over to the branch and stood in front of it, surveying the results. It practically shone now. Granted, Jane had taken over a thousand books with her for repair and was currently elbow-deep in it, but otherwise, the branch looked operable and welcoming. Some patrons had even begun using the upper area again. Tables were set out for discussion groups, along with couch and relaxation areas.

There were a couple of nurse golems hovering around the terrariums. Quinn smiled. They'd know what to do, or at least they should. The doctors had obviously sent them over. She'd have to get assistants for this area of the Library made or recruited. Though she didn't doubt Tim and Tom and their fleet of other shelving, golems would keep everything in order.

Which was when she realized she hadn't seen Misha. At all. A fact that felt decidedly odd.

Malakai stood behind what looked like a specialist counter, talking to a golem Quinn did not recognize. This golem stood almost as tall as Malakai, substantially taller than Quinn, and was wearing a nurse's uniform but in shades of blue that somehow rippled.

"Oh, Quinn," Mal said. "This is Gregor."

"Hi, Gregor," Quinn said and paused, curious. "Wait, you're a golem and you already have a name?"

He blinked, his fathomless eyes shone. "I spoke with Cook before coming up here. He said I looked like a Gregor."

Quinn laughed. "I would have to agree! I think it's a fantastic name. I'm glad you're here. I was just thinking about having to activate branch specific helpers."

"The doctor activated me. I am to be the specialist here in the alchemical and medical branch to assist any inquiries. Also to aid in supplying the hospital. Hopefully, this will prevent anybody from misusing the magic in ways that it is unintended for."

Quinn smiled. She liked Gregor. "Excellent."

She turned to Malakai. "Have you seen your grandfather? I can't seem to find his signature anywhere in the Library."

Malakai nodded. "That's because he's not currently here."

"Did he finally go home and get some rest?" Quinn asked, a little incredulously because she hadn't expected him to do it without her nagging him.

Malakai shrugged. "Sort of? He's gone home because he needs to do some ruler type stuff, and because Nishpa may have threatened him with bodily harm if he didn't go and get some rest."

"That'd do it," Quinn said. "I'm glad she nagged him instead."

"Yeah, my aunt . . ." Mal started saying.

But Quinn interrupted him. "Nishpa is your aunt?"

Malakai laughed. "Not related by blood in any way. But she was my grandmother's best friend."

Quinn raised an eyebrow. "Your grandmother's best friend?"

"You keep repeating what I say." At Quinn's glare, Malakai capitulated. "My grandparents were a bit of a love story, and Nishpa was her best friend. She promised my grandmother she'd look out for him, so she does. My grandfather really misses his wife."

Quinn understood missing people who were gone. "I'm glad he's gone home to rest. Gregor, is there anything you need from me?"

"I don't believe there is," Gregor said. "I will, however, gladly seek you out should I need something."

"You can also just message me through the system if you need to. Or, I mean, any of the supervisors, Malakai, Dottie, Geneva, Eric, Daniel, and Finn. Misha can get you any supplies you require too. And I think, do we have a couple more now?" Quinn felt like she was forgetting people. And Misha hadn't popped up at being mentioned. Again.

She reached out to the Library while waiting for a response. *Is it weird that Misha sometimes doesn't pop up as soon as I mention their name?*

Not really. Never known a supervisor to do that before Misha. Probably did it to have something to do while the Library booted up.

Guess that makes sense.

Of course it does. The Library sounded quite fond. *We're only just starting to grow again. Misha is probably adjusting.*

Malakai was grinning at her. "You know, you're going to have to go through the personnel with Dottie and Jasper."

"Jasper," Quinn said, wondering how she'd managed to forget the person she'd delegated arranging all the staff to. "Also, Jasper."

Gregor inclined his head. "Very well."

Quinn glanced at the golem again. He was much more humanoid in appearance, even though he was made out of a very pale pink sort of clay. It looked really cool with his iridescent eyes and the dark blues of his scrubs.

Librarian requested in the hospital.

The message flashed up in front of her, and she smiled. The Library hadn't really been big enough to bother using the system in this capacity until now. It was a new level of cool.

"Anyway, thank you, Gregor. I'll leave the alchemical and medicinal branch in your care. For now, I believe that I am needed in the hospital wing."

Malakai raised an eyebrow. "Everything okay?"

"I don't know. Did you do something?"

Malakai laughed. "No, I didn't do anything. At least not anything wrong. They said I could leave. I'm still doing my physical therapy."

"Excellent. Make sure you keep it up. We have places to go soon."

They waved at Gregor and made their way toward the hospital, going downstairs and so they could enter through the old infirmary. Quinn looked at the patrons and her staff as she walked. With the opening of a new branch, more people were flocking in as the announcement went out.

They'd better all be bringing back their books.

"You okay? You've gone a little quiet," Malakai said.

"Just thinking about how much we still have to do."

"Yeah, but think about how much you've already done."

Quinn laughed. "That's a good point. I like that perspective."

As soon as they set foot in the hospital, people knew she was there. Not that Quinn found it creepy or anything, because she knew how it felt to sense others' arrival in the Library. She also knew that sometimes she projected her power. It took less than ten seconds for the doctor golem to be by her side.

"Librarian, well met. If you would follow me, we have some questions for you," he said.

Quinn followed, feeling oddly out of place. She glanced at Malakai, who shrugged, and she was glad that she'd brought him along.

"What can I do for you?" she asked once they were in what looked like a small conference room.

"The surgeon will be here momentarily," Doctor Golem replied. "Better to wait for him than to repeat ourselves."

That's when Quinn remembered she hadn't given these guys names yet. And they obviously hadn't been to visit Cook yet. They were just Doctor and Surgeon. She wracked her brains, trying to figure out what she would call them.

"Do you want names?" she asked, while they waited. Figuring that they'd already developed personalities, they may not want names that they did not pick for themselves.

"Names," Doctor Golem said, blinking slowly down at her. "You know, it might be nice to not just be called Doctor. I will think on that and let you know. Is that acceptable?"

"Of course it's acceptable," Quinn said. "Let me know what names you'd both like and the system will adjust for it."

He flashed a smile at her, which, given his beautiful obsidian metallic skin and features, was a welcome expression. His eyes were like the depths of the universe, with stars in them. And as the surgeon walked in, she realized that he was very similar, except there was more of a navy hint to the stone or metal he was made of.

Was it rude to ask golems what they were made of? Because she wasn't entirely sure it was an acceptable question. Did it allow them to morph limbs or something? How did they perform surgery? She shook her head, trying to bring herself back on task. She cleared her throat before speaking. "Surgeon, what can I do for you both?"

"We had a few questions for you." They looked at each other.

"We've been commandeering some of the system's operating functions and energy to help refine and streamline the hospital section. In doing so . . ." The surgeon glanced at Doctor Golem, who shrugged as if to say, *Don't look at me. I have no idea what to say either.*

"Okay, guys, what's wrong with the system?" Quinn didn't think they meant the glaringly obvious glitches, as she was already aware of those. "Because if there's something myself and the Library have missed, we need to rectify it."

Lynx popped into view right next to them. "There's something wrong with the system," he said.

Quinn didn't even comment about his eavesdropping.

The surgeon gaped, seeming much more human than doctor. "We'll start from the beginning. We've streamlined ordering for specific roles or items for the hospital. Many of these require their own core, and thus an ability to think and problem solve for themselves. There are specific types of golem cores required for this, and we have all the materials for them. We bring this to your attention because with the amount of us created for the hospital and the general staffing of the Library, we believe more materials should have been used than actually have been. Our only conclusion is that some existing cores appear to have been reused or recycled from previous incarnations."

Lynx gasped. "Are you saying they've reused previously established cores?"

"Yes." The doctor spoke up this time. "Not even properly recycled cores. They've retained some of their former selves as far as we can see. Those will need to be remade."

Lynx turned pale, which made Quinn wary. "What exactly does this mean, Lynx, in Quinn-ese?"

Lynx laughed softly. "Thanks, needed that. It means that the cores from the golems that were disabled when I shut down the entire operation weren't melted down and refined. They were preserved and have been used in the creation of some of the golems that we have now."

"And why is that a bad thing?" Quinn said. She'd always thought recycling was a good thing, but she could see how magical items might not be the same.

"Well, usually, cores will need a specific direction, a command to become part of the type of golem that they need to be. It needs to take that base command and build an entire persona around it who evolves as they learn more, as they become more aware, as they have more interactions. They become a living, breathing golem. Like Cook has become such an amazing part of your life, for example," Lynx explained.

"Exactly," the surgeon said. "The thing is, is that usually, if the Library was just remaking golems that had been broken, it probably wouldn't mean much. But right now, the Library is still recovering from an emergency shutdown that happened deliberately."

"Oh," Quinn said. "It was done to save the Library."

She could do the math in her head. It left a horrible burning sensation in her gut because she didn't want to say it out loud, even if she knew it was better to. "BasicallyBasically, some of our most pivotal golems might have the cores that were present during the last Librarian."

"Precisely," Surgeon said.

"What about you?" Quinn asked.

"You mandated mine and the doctor's construction, and then you made us supervisors. If you're not a golem supervisor or you, or Lynx, you wouldn't be able to see this."

"So my supervisor knows," Quinn said thoughtfully, wondering why Misha wouldn't have told her this.

Shouldn't Misha have mentioned this? She reached out to the Library while contemplating questions for the others.

The Library was silent for a second. *Not necessarily. It might not have occurred to them. But it is something I'll look into as soon as I'm done with my current project.*

There was something in the Library's tone that made Quinn wary. *So they might not be aware?*

No. In fact, I'm thinking that if it's the case, they may not be aware at all.

Would that be a good thing?

I'm not sure yet. And the Library cut off in that retreating sort of way.

Quinn sighed and continued her questioning. "Is it the way the Library was shut down that makes those cores perhaps not ideal?"

"Reusing cores from broken golems is one thing, but reusing a core from a golem that might have been infected or affected by some outside influence?" the supervisor said. "That's something you might want to look into."

Quinn didn't like the idea behind that, but she understood their caution. If the Library had used a core affected by Korradine, there was every likelihood it could be severely compromised.

42

MERE HUNDREDS

QUINN COULDN'T HELP BUT BE WORRIED ABOUT THE GOLEM CORES. BUT
she wasn't yet sure how to approach it. Quinn's gut reactions were
nauseating. But being aware of things would help. It had to be fine.

Are you sure things with Misha will be okay?

I've gone over the logs they leave, Quinn, the Library said to her. *I've
activated several fail safes, but all their logging is consistent, precise, and
necessary so far. I haven't seen anything to indicate them being compromised.*
The Library didn't sound irritated, but there was a level of frustration
in the undertone.

That's all we can do then?

*Until we figure out precisely what we're looking for. Everything from this
end seems... perfect. All we have is some differentiation in behavior, and the
knowledge of the cores being mashed up.*

Hm But Quinn didn't push it further yet.

The Library sounded gentle when it next spoke. *We need more
information. And the fail safes will flag an alarm if they're tripped.*

Okay.

The Library's presence withdrew ever so slightly, allowing
Quinn to focus on the people in front of her. The doctor and
surgeon eyed her semi-nervously, which she understood. They were

new. At least, since she'd been the one to give the creation command, they'd been created with entirely new golem cores. After all, it was because of this that they had noticed the odd utilization of the other cores.

At least she thought she understood it.

"Going to put a pin in that for now. The Library has initiated security measures. Thank you for bringing it to my attention." She paused and flashed them a smile. " I also desperately need to know how the Bardocian root and the Balisor situation is progressing. How are the people that rescued? Are they being taken care of? Are they able to be cured? Will there be long-lasting effects? How many of them aren't going to make it?" She was worried about the latter because the faction had already lost so many.

That wasn't okay. She harnessed the anger to help fuel her energy to get more done.

The doctor heaved a sigh of relief and went to speak. He paused and then said, "I think Miles is an excellent name."

Quinn did a double take. "Oh, sure. Miles it is then. Dr. Miles?"

"Yes, Dr. Miles." He nodded his head for emphasis.

Quinn glanced at the surgeon who said, "Vivit. I like Vivit."

"Okay, Surgeon Vivit. Doctor Miles. Excellent."

They both smiled.

Miles cleared his throat and continued as if they hadn't just named themselves. "Anyway, the Bardocian root is a potent strain that came from a quadrant I didn't expect. if it weren't for the fact that the fake Irias was actually of the Mamoria species. They're distantly related to the sedimentites, but have no contact with them. Their species is as rare as the Unisceros that your previous Librarian was. The Mamoria originated in Quadrant 494, famous for the soil-twisting plant species in unique ways. It's not surprising but still perplexing. The whole fiasco has been quite baffling, really."

Vivit spoke up. "We have several patients that I doubt will wake up at all. There are several more who are in a coma, but I have high hopes for them. The rest of them are all in varying stages from extremely ill but able to be cured, to probably being able to be released in the next couple of days. We just don't know where to send them before we decontaminate the area."

Somebody cleared their throat. Quinn, Lynx, Malakai, Vivit, and Miles turned around and saw Hilrick and Nordon standing in the doorway. Hilrick waved at Malakai. "Hello, cousin. It's good to see you not dead."

"It's good to not be dead," Malakai replied.

Quinn frowned.

Nordon flashed them both a grin. "Well, I found the dead and almost dead you were looking for. I thought I'd let you know that the real Irias is one of the ones in a coma."

Quinn perked up at that. "She wasn't actually dead. That's good news for Karella."

"Her impersonator being a Mamoria probably saved her," Nordon said. "They don't kill victims and take their bodies; they just adopt identities and morph themselves into a likeness. But for it to succeed, the victim needs to be alive."

Quinn nodded. "That's a relief, right?"

Hilrick sort of waffled on that. "I'm not entirely sure. I mean, my specialty is emergency healing. She's got a long road ahead of her, as the doctor has no doubt informed you."

Miles nodded. " A long road ahead indeed, but Ms. Karella, her mother, seems to be ready to take the necessary steps to keep her daughter healthy should she make it through the coma."

"Is there anything we can do to help them?" Quinn asked.

"Not really," Vivit said. "Bardocian root is invasive. It works by entering the root system of any creature with plant life attachments. This can even apply to creatures that eat plants to survive. It might even extend to harvested food that any humanoid species eats. If that food needs nutrients through the soil, then a Bardocian root infestation can easily settle into that food and spread its spores in that manner. We have a fumigation team with protocols in place that being set up to be sent out as soon as possible. They'll free the area of infestation and infection so the victims have a home to return to."

Quinn blanched slightly. "So my setting things on fire probably helped?"

"Fire is very effective. For a lot of things," Miles said, "burning the place to the ground means they have a head start on churning the ground for any surviving root. Don't trust any food grown in the region for the quarantine period of two years. Bardocian root is invasive, poisonous, and subverts the people that it infects. They are extremely open to suggestion and mind control, and we currently have a tragedy on our hands because of this specific infestation."

Quinn hated that it happened under her nose even if it started before her time. She didn't know what they could have done differently.

But it was like Hilrick knew what she was thinking. "You have to understand, Librarian, this didn't happen over the last six months. This infestation has been going on for, I would say, nigh-on a hundred years if the information is anything to go by. It was deep-seated. Some of those corpses were mummified. Some of them had disintegrated. They've been there that long. It's not beyond advanced Bardocian infestation to basically anesthetize the people in its thrall. There is nothing you could have done."

While Quinn knew this, hearing someone else say it helped. She still felt guilty. Even if she couldn't have done anything about it in the first place, even if she hadn't been present or even known that the universe existed in this capacity, she still really wished she could have gotten to them and helped sooner.

"Okay then," Quinn said, taking this a step further, "Could this infestation have been a result of sabotage?"

"Oh, yes," Nordon said. "There was nothing organic about it. While everything was killed with fire, I can assess the pathways by the ash trail. It should allow me to gauge the necrotic damage leveraged in different stages of the vine's development throughout the settlement."

"Meaning?" Malakai said. "Look, Nordon, I know you're smart, but I want to understand how you'll do this."

"Oh." Nordon blinked. "Look, I can narrow a timeline down

through the age of the necrosis that's made its way through the vines and roots. I should be able to find the point of origin, is what I'm saying. We can't wait for other experts, but between Hilrick and I, we can pinpoint an approximation for the onset location, and that should tell us more about where it might have initially come from."

Quinn nodded slowly, as did Lynx. The manifestation spoke up. "That'd be most helpful if you'd be willing to check it."

"Our grandfather," Hilrick said, "may have been less than gentle in suggesting we do absolutely everything we can to help the Library, lest we, and I think his exact words were, 'want to suffer a universe without any magic whatsoever.'"

Quinn laughed. "Yeah, that sounds a little bit like Milaro, perhaps a bit more melodramatic. Did you embellish at all?"

Hilrick grinned. "Perhaps slightly."

Malakai rolled his eyes, and Quinn could see he didn't have the best relationship with them, but it was probably because of the age discrepancy. He didn't seem to mind their presence from everything Quinn could glean from his aura.

"Okay, so you'll go back with the contingent that's about to eradicate the vines," Quinn said, and Nordon laughed. "And you'll get us an origin point and any information you can?"

"I can even bring back samples and allow memory extraction for those specific images. I'll make sure to pay extra attention to detail." Nordon shrugged. "My grandfather can extract them when he has time. Is that sufficient?"

Quinn nodded slowly. She didn't want to go back there. She didn't want to send anybody who could also be infected back there. "You'll just have to . . ."

She paused. She wasn't even sure if her supervisory golem was trustworthy anymore. Who was she supposed to get to outfit people? What if they'd been undermining the Library this entire time?

Malakai placed a hand on her shoulder, and she remembered to breathe. "Thanks," she said. "We'll take you down and get some protective gear before we send you out."

"I'll do that," Lynx said. "I can activate everything. Just reinforce my permissions."

Quinn knew instinctively what he meant by that. He was telling her to make sure that his permissions overrode the supervisory golem permissions. She was fairly certain they always had, but this way she could double check and perhaps also alter Milaro's and Dottie's. She'd never thought the permissions might be a problem before. While she still wasn't percent certain, the niggling in her gut indicated her suspicions were correct.

"Okay." Quinn turned to the doctors. "You guys must be busy. I'm so sorry to have taken up so much of your time. In summary, we're probably looking at the, what, we had three hundred people?"

"Three hundred forty-seven, to be precise," Miles said.

"Okay, Three hundred forty-seven. We're looking at approximately two hundred sixty-two who will make a complete recovery. They were basically being held in stasis and thus are minimally damaged. There are about fifty-five of them who are, you know, kind of on the fence, and the other thirty are touch and go. That's the patient count."

"Exactly," Vivit said. "I have several surgeries lined up that are complex and require finesse that while I have, I'm not entirely sure their bodies will be able to withstand. I will do my best."

"Thank you both," Quinn said. " And I do like your names."

They grinned and left the room.

She turned her attention to Hilrick and Nordon. "Thanks for your help. If you go with Lynx, he'll get you outfitted so you don't accidentally catch Bardocian crap."

"We should be fine—" Hilrick began to protest.

Quinn stopped him by holding her hand up. "I know, but I would prefer an extra layer of protection if I'm the one sending you into something potentially dangerous."

It was as if Nordon was about to make a flippant remark, and he saw Quinn and Malakai's expressions. He nodded. Hilrick did too. "Thank you," he said. "I look forward to spending more time with both of you after all this is over."

Quinn watched them go. She was conflicted. The news about the root and its deliberate sabotage felt like just another brick in that damned wall. And yet, at the same time, they'd uncovered something purely evil, subverting a whole people for maybe a century. And they'd pulled out the survivors they could. They could only do what they could do. Pity the Library couldn't time travel.

"Are you okay?" Malakai asked.

"I'm okay," she said. "I feel like getting the alchemical and medical branch up and running was imperative. We got to play with books and tidy things and spend all our time soaking up knowledge without having to worry about all the other crap that goes along with it. Still, we want to get books into everybody's hands, so therefore, off we go, right?"

Malakai nodded.

Quinn paused for a second, giving it some thought. "I haven't seen my office for days. I feel like sitting in my big comfy chair."

"Sounds like a plan." Malakai chuckled. "I shall accompany you. Would you like to pass Cook on the way?"

"You know, I think I would. I'm starving," Quinn said. She couldn't even remember if she'd eaten breakfast. She didn't think she'd waited for Cook's breakfast. Again. She needed to do something about building it into a habit. "Okay, let's go. I've lost track of my owl, too. I don't even know where Aradie is."

"It's okay. I'm sure we'll find her, or she'll find you."

Quinn sighed, and they headed to the office, snagging food as they passed by Cook with a wave. They seemed extremely busy. They probably were, what with all the extra mouths to feed in the hospital. The kitchen appeared to have several golems helping now. But even with all of that, They'd made sure to put food out for Quinn.

As Quinn walked out, she noticed there were a lot of people in the Library. She frowned, clutched her food as if someone might otherwise try to steal it, and headed to her office. "I'm not dealing with any of that"—Quinn vaguely gestured behind her—"on an empty stomach."

They walked through the door and she stopped short.

Hal sat on the couch, waiting. He rose up to his eight-foot height and grinned. "Now, what was that, Librarian? That you're not dealing with before food? Because if you're that hungry, I guess my surprise can wait."

4 3

TO THE TRAINING AREA!

DESPITE THE LOOK OF GLEE ON HAL'S FACE, QUINN WAS EXTREMELY hungry. She glanced at the food in her hand and over to Hal. "You know, as much as I love surprises—not really, by the way—I am super hungry and I'm just going to sit down and eat first, okay? I have been dreaming about this chair for the last few hours and I just want to snuggle into it and stuff my face with food. Is that acceptable?"

Hal looked at her and grinned. "Yeah, that's acceptable." He let himself fall back onto the couch, shrinking ever so slightly as he did so, and pulled a big tome out of whatever inventory space he owned and onto his lap.

As Quinn walked to her desk, she tried to see what book he was reading, but short of inspecting it, which required a little bit more mental effort than she was willing to exert right then, she couldn't tell what it was. She sighed and made her way to her desk. Not even a surprise could talk her into stopping another meal.

Quinn unpacked the bag and realized Cook had given her a schnitzel sandwich with extra mayo, which just made everything better, because somehow, they'd known precisely what to feed her to make her feel better. She smiled and chomped into it, and the ever-so-crunchy outer golden breading was perfect.

Hal sat, flipping through the pages, while Malakai perched himself on one of the chairs in front of the conference table and ate whatever strange concoction Cook had made up for him.

"Whatcha reading?" Quinn asked around a mouthful of schnitzel sandwich.

Hal raised an eyebrow. "A very interesting combat book."

Quinn squinted at him. "Why are you reading a combat book?"

Hal grinned back at her. "Wouldn't you like to know?"

"Yes, Hal. That's why I asked what you were reading," Quinn said, glaring at him.

Hal laughed, his full-throated version.

Quinn gave up. Finally, she finished her food, wiped her hands, and watched as Aradie swept into the room, perching herself next to the couch. "Oh, so now you deign to grace us with your presence."

Aradie didn't even coo or hoot. She just threw Quinn a very, very level look.

"Fine. I hope you had a good time doing whatever you were doing."

Aradie nodded and fluffed her feathers.

Quinn sighed and got ready for whatever Hal had done. Best get it over with. "Okay, Uncle Hal, come on, tell me. What brings you back here so soon? I thought you had things to do."

"What?" Hal said, putting the book down next to him. "Don't you like me being here?"

Quinn mulled that question over. She was sure there was some sort of double-edged meaning to it. "And if I said I liked you being here, what would that mean?"

Hal laughed. "As long as you mean it, I would simply, gladly, perhaps visit more often."

She raised an eyebrow. "Don't you have a war or three or eight to run or something?"

"Yes," he said, his tone serious. "But I have amazingly competent generals who fear my temper."

Quinn laughed. "Okay. Tell me why you're here?"

"I had a few things to check on. I thought you'd like to know

Ikeshal is doing much better than he was and looks like he's going to make a full recovery, which is a great relief for me."

"Good. I was worried about him." She was sincerely relieved to hear he'd heal up. Escadril being unable to recover already weighed on her. She was determined to lose fewer people in the future.

Hal's next response surprised her. "To tell you the truth, Quinn, I was worried too. It was a pretty bad wound."

"And . . ." Quinn knew he had more to say and felt like she was pulling the surprise out of him inch by inch and he was enjoying every single moment.

He brightened at the tug. "I had to personally retrieve some of the items for your gift."

"Personally retrieve items that are part of my gift?" Quinn gave him a look. She was trying desperately to guess what the gift was before she got it, but his hints didn't make much sense. She had everything she could ever need. And if she didn't have it, the Library or other magic could create it.

"Did you have to purchase things? Or did you have to retrieve things that were already owed?" An idea formed in her mind that made no sense. Uncle Hal wasn't an agent of the Library, but he was Hal, which in and of itself granted a certain level of authority.

He winked at her. "Don't worry. I took several assistants with me, Quinn."

"You didn't," she said, unable to believe he'd done what she thought he might have.

"Yes. And if you'd like to follow me, I believe the last of your gift is being scanned into the Library as we speak!"

"Really?" Quinn said. She still couldn't quite wrap her head around it. There were at least several books left to get. "Really? The combat section?"

Hal grinned at her. "See, I knew you'd figure it out."

"Took me long enough, didn't it?" she said ruefully.

Uncle Hal simply grinned at her. "You're still learning, little egg."

They arrived at the check-in desk and Quinn did a bit of a double take. There were a heap of assistants at the check-in desk, including

Eric, Geneva, Danio, Finn, and several more that she didn't recognize by name. Some of the newer assistants were scanning the books and checking them over for potential harmful residue while the supervisors returned the large pile of books back into the system.

"Did you literally go out and fetch the books we were missing?" she asked incredulously.

"I've been working on it for the past several days. I thought we needed to help the Library along. Nobody else seemed to have time to go out. You just brought back a whole heap of injured Balisors and a little bit of a conspiracy theory that shows me that we might have a much larger problem or even multiple problems on our hands. And so, I believed it my duty as one of the actual sponsors of the Library, to assist you in expanding it back to its full state as soon as I could."

Quinn turned and blinked at him.

"Thank you," she said, her gratitude practically rendering her speechless. She felt heat behind her eyes, like tears of relief threatened to break free. Even just one more branch helped. It all helped. And this was bigger than anything she'd expected.

"Don't thank me yet. After the debacle that the alchemical and medical branch was, I'm not even sure we want to open another one quite this soon. But I'd already started the retrieval process and sent some of my agents to procure the books. It felt very silly to leave it half done," Hal said.

"I appreciate this more than you can know. Thank you." She watched the number in her HUD as it ticked down while books were being scanned through and back into the system. The sense of impossible she'd had when they discovered the infestation of the Balisors dwindled ever so slightly.

Maybe she could juggle everything after all.

The numbers counted down faster than she'd expected. She kept watching. The bustle in the Library was nice background noise, all of its patrons oblivious to the momentous occasion currently taking place. A hum began in the back of her head. Like notes fitting together. She grinned. The Library was truly being restored.

Quinn grinned at the pop-up in front of her face.

The prerequisites for the Combat Branch have been fulfilled.
Do you wish to initiate the opening procedure?"
Yes or No?

Hey, she said to the Library, *is it okay for me to activate another branch so soon?*

Oh, yes, the Library said. *After all, because of the alchemy and medical branch, we've already begun to regenerate more power. So yes, I would love it if we opened another branch, but I would suggest activating another filter first to keep up with the momentum.*

Okay, I'll do that. Going into her HUD, Quinn chose to activate Cylion, making it six active filtration pillars in total. She frowned. *Is six enough for this?* she asked.

For this, yes. We can activate a seventh shortly after we synchronize.

It'll take twelve hours to activate this time. Should I wait until tomorrow to establish the combat branch?

The Library paused. *No, it's for sure the combat branch, right?*

Yes.

Then it'll be fine.

Quinn nodded, noticing that they could activate another pillar in the next week. That'd work. *Okay, then I guess we get started with the next branch, eh?* She grinned to herself.

Hal leaned forward. "What are you grinning at, little egg?"

"I hadn't expected to open another branch this soon after opening the medical one. I'm just a little excited, that's all."

"Good, that's how you should be."

She activated *yes* on the prompt to initiate the opening procedure.

Combat Branch requirements met
837/837 books retrieved
Energy level required: medium
Mana required: 7,142
Energy requirement: 7,142
Patronage level required: fluid
Non-restrictive, all borrowing privileges established.
Calibrating . . .
Calculating . . .

Patronage level met.
Librarian strength required: 12.
Assessing . . .
Calibrating . . .
Accepted . . .
Librarian strength met.
All requirements pending fusion.
Combat branch extending.
423/423 Weapons sourced.
423/423 Weapons allocated.
423/423 Weapons categorized.
Assessing.
Calibrating.
Combat branch established.
All requirements met.
To be opened. Do you wish to proceed?
Yes, No, Place Process on Hold?

Quinn already knew she didn't want to place the process on hold. However, there was an additional note she didn't expect.

Combat branch requires a full 12 hours of development in order to be reinstated at optimal levels with minimum risk.

Quinn raised an eyebrow. "What does that mean?"

Lynx pondered it. "I think it means it'll scan for and announce any possible problems before it brings the actual branch online."

"That's a good thing, right?"

"Yes." Lynx nodded for emphasis.

"And twelve hours is pretty much nothing in the grand scheme of things," Quinn said, convincing herself.

"Exactly. You could sleep or something," Lynx offered.

Quinn laughed. "Okay, we wish to proceed."

Yes.

A slight shudder ran through the entire length of the Library, and then there was nothing. Quinn already knew where this branch would open. It was down the passageway near where she'd originally fought the bookworms, and it would lead off that little training area. She was looking forward to it, but it still felt sort of anticlimactic that it didn't open straight away.

"Not opening now then, hey, little egg?" Hall asked, still smiling with satisfaction that his surprise seemed to have gone over so well.

Quinn glared at him. "Can you stop calling me little egg, please?"

"No," he answered with a devilish grin. "The branch isn't opening straight away?"

She glared at him. "No, it said it needed to scan itself or something."

The Library piped in. *The combat branch is a little bit more involved than some of the others.*

"A little bit more involved?" Quinn asked.

There are certain aspects that I have to access and enable in order for it to completely activate, and thus it's going to take a bit more time to retrieve. Plus, I'm not planning on letting another damn dimension eel worm its way into my bloody Library. The Library sounded so exasperated.

Quinn laughed. "Okay, I get it."

Hal, who'd also been able to hear the Library's voice, clapped his hands sharply. "Excellent! Right now, is as good as time as any for you to get a bit of a head start on some of your fire abilities."

"Say what?" Quinn said.

"You've been practicing the exercises I gave you, correct?" Hal asked.

"Yes. Yes, I have," Quinn answered slowly, somewhat suspicious.

Malakai simply chuckled right next to him.

"And don't you think you're getting off scot-free either, young man?" Hal said. "Your grandfather asked to include you in Quinn's training. Thus, even though you cannot right now access your magic, you can definitely do the physical portion of it."

Malakai looked stricken.

"That's what you get for laughing at me," Quinn said.

Malakai groaned.

"Come on, it won't be that bad. It'll be a great way to while away the time between now and the next twelve hours," Hal said enthusiastically.

"I wanted to get some sleep," Quinn grumbled.

"Oh, nonsense, little egg." Hal grinned at her, but it was entirely evil with no mirth evident. "Little egg needs practice more than she needs sleep. Trust me."

"You don't seem very trustworthy right now," Quinn said skeptically. "The branch is gonna open at midnight. I want to be here for it."

"You'll be here for it. You might only get a power nap. How does that sound?"

Quinn glowered at him. But she knew she needed to train. She knew she needed to get better at wielding fire and understanding how its applications worked within her own cosmicisodracus abilities.

"Fine," she said. "Where are we going?"

For an answer, Hal summoned Tim and ordered a quick slew of books. "All intermediate, all to help you get a handle on your fire abilities. We'll start with theory and extend it to the practical."

Quinn groaned as they headed to the training area. She still had serious misgivings about fire around tomes, but what better way to learn complete control than to operate under the threat of burning down all the magical knowledge in the universe.

No pressure at all.

4 4

SIMPLY AN EXTENSION

WHILE HAL DIRECTED MALAKAI TO PERFORM A SERIES OF PHYSICAL exercises and drills, Quinn looked down at the pile of books Tim had elegantly deposited next to her. The Library very helpfully provided her with a desk and a seat.

She sighed as she examined the books. The first one was titled *Nikom's Kill It With Fire When You Have To*. The second one, *K'Mara's Theories of Fire Manipulation and Healing Properties*, sparked her interest. Fire, in her mind, was extremely destructive. However, she could see that the heat involved with the flame might be best used for certain aspects of healing.

This brought her to the next book, *Visifan's Heat as an Energy Replenishment Alternative*, followed by *Darkrai's Effect of Heat on Various Sympathetic Species*. The last book was *Sir Kadion's Fire As Defense Magic*. Quinn groaned.

"Stop the groaning, little egg," Hal said.

"Why do you call me that?" she pouted, still irritated that she couldn't nap, even if her interest was piqued by the books.

"Because you're young and it helps remind me that I shouldn't expect everything of you that I would normally demand from a Librarian. You are still, in terms of your species, an infant."

Quinn glared at him. "I'm not an infant. I wasn't raised as this species. I'm an adult human."

"Yes, you are, in fact, an infant." Hal shook his head. "You're an egg. You're barely hatched."

While Quinn wanted to protest, he did have a point. She'd begun looking into the dragon species and all of them had millennia lifespans. She was barely a blink in the corner of one of their eyes. "Fine, I get it. I just don't have to like it."

"No, you don't have to like it, and that's perfectly okay. What you do have to like is that I picked these very specific books for you to focus on so that harnessing your power doesn't damage you as much as I fear it might otherwise." The concern in his tone seemed genuine.

"Okay, so what do I do?" She made an effort not to sound pouty.

"Read them, Quinn. Absorb them like you would any other time you get a book." He paused, frowning ever so slightly.

Quinn laughed. "Fine."

And so she proceeded to pick up each book and absorb it.

The first one, *Nikom's Kill It With Fire When You Have To* covered more complex variations of killing something with fire. There were spells like Shifting Fire Sands and Dancing Fire Falls that she could summon and cast. Not to mention advanced fireballs, and flame walls and so many other variations, but its main focus was on the control needed to wield these abilities.

She absorbed it slowly, leafing through the book as she did so. It wasn't exactly a skill up, but now that she realized reading the books as well as absorbing them meant getting the most out of each book sooner in the long run, it helped. She learned three very specific abilities from that book: Firestarter's Grasp, Oxygen Deprivation, and Tylenor's Demise. The first and the last were excellent attack skills that she'd need to practice in order to harness their power properly. Oxygen Deprivation was a very simple way to extract oxygen out of the flames and extinguish them. It was the perfect ability to snuff out flames that might be out of control or otherwise misguided.

When she moved on to *K'Mara's Theories of Fire Manipulation and Healing Properties,* the book had many strange combinations that she would never have used together. At least she understood the concept of cauterization. However, the rest were out of her initial scope of expectations.

Some involved the heat centers and the normal temperature of people's bodies and how to manipulate, ignite, or wither those areas. There was a whole listing of different species that went on and on for pages. Numbers and percentages and calculations that needed to be done before she attempted to use fire as a healing magic. It was a good thing she had other healing options because she didn't like the idea of healing through fire. It gave her far too large a margin for error.

An oopsie that could leave a pile of ash.

She paused and looked up, watching Malakai train under Hal's gaze. The sound of him hitting the wooden dummy was rhythmically soothing. Hal guided the elf in ways she'd never seen Mal move. Perhaps he was teaching him to rely on physical attributes rather than his magical ones.

"Quinn," Hal said without stopping to look around at her, "you don't seem to be doing your work."

"I'm taking a rest. I've absorbed two books. Give me a break," she said as she popped one of the energy regeneration cupcakes into her mouth. She'd already expended just over a thousand energy, and Hal seemed to have eyes in the back of his bloody head.

"Speaking of which, I sent for actual food. Not sweets." He paused and then continued as if he'd read her mind. "No, not even energy sweets."

Hal still hadn't turned around, but she knew he was smiling. Typical. He was probably enjoying torturing them both. But with the promise of food, Quinn dove back into her books.

Visifan's Heat as an Energy Replenishment Alternative sounded exactly like something she needed. If this book was correct, she could use heat to regenerate her energy and thus always have it topped off. There was a bit of finagling needed in order to apply her natural heat generation to energy regeneration. But it was perfectly logical in the way it progressed. And, if she read it correctly, mana was the next step up. With enough practice and subtle direction, she'd be able to regenerate her mana quickly, or at least quicker.

However, that appeared to be an advanced level technique, and she'd probably have to wait at least a few weeks for that. But the pure overpowering sense she got from the ability, once she managed to perfect it, meant she'd almost be unstoppable. She'd be able to cast without ever having to worry about running out of energy. Imagine being her opponent? Quinn grinned to herself with glee.

The energy replenishment book was one she would revisit time and again in her spare time. She tucked it into her dimensional storage to keep it with her, making a note in the Library database that she had it. If anybody else needed it, they'd have to contact the Librarian in person. She wasn't about to let it out of her sight, well, out of her possession anyway. In fact, she'd probably make a copy of all of these. It seemed intrinsically important to her species, to her ability to do this job. Perhaps it was just because it *wasn't* a time of peace for her or the Library that she was required to use her powers as much as she did. It was always better to be prepared.

Aradie hooted and Quinn looked up at the owl, who landed gently on her shoulder with a bag in beak. Quinn grinned. "Thanks for that."

The owl flashed images of Quinn wasting away from hunger and gave her owl self a cape as she swooped in with food. Quinn laughed and almost choked on the sandwich she'd bitten into. At least her owl had a sense of humor. The owl took two more bags to Hal and Mal.

Fed, Quinn dove into the next book.

Darkrai's Effect of Heat on Various Sympathetic Species was less informative than Quinn expected. She'd been thinking that it would refer to how much different species could potentially be damaged by fire. While she was right on some level, it was also a book specifically written for those species, of which she was one. There were different ways to utilize, generate, and expend heat energy that would not affect the caster, but also wouldn't affect several hundred species to varying degrees. It stood to reason that those same things would have disastrous effects on people who were more susceptible to fire.

Sir Kadion's Fire As Defense Magic had applications she'd need to test out. Quinn already knew how to build shields that were, well, not impenetrable, but adept at keeping her mostly safe. However, if she'd absorbed this book correctly, she was fairly certain she could erect a shield and include a wall of fire within it. If she made the fire portion of the shield dense enough, then it'd actually burn attacks away before they ever hit her original shield. It was theoretical, but it was something she couldn't wait to try.

"Are you done?" Hal asked her. She looked up at him, blinking, half having forgotten that she was in the room with other people.

"Oh, yes, I've got all of them."

"It took you a lot longer than I thought it would."

"I wanted to make sure I understood what I was absorbing." She frowned. "The subject matter is relatively complex, and I wanted to make sure I have a proper grasp on it."

He grinned at her. "That's a good mindset to have. Not all Librarians have done that, then again, not all Librarians have had to defend their Library. You would, in fact, be the first one I'm aware of."

Quinn gave a tight smile.

Hal grinned. "Now we have to go over a few things."

Quinn glanced past him to where Malakai lay, spread-eagled, on the ground, looking up at the ceiling, panting and dripping with sweat. She raised an eyebrow in Hal's direction. "You know he's just recovered, right?"

Hal shrugged. "He's recovered his physical state, which is the most important for his specific brand of fighting. There's nothing wrong with him physically, except for that he is currently too weak because he's been lying up in bed for three weeks. What he needs to do is exercise and get his stamina back so he can still perform on a battlefield. His magic will come after, and he'll be stronger for it."

Quinn didn't agree. She thought he should rest, but she wasn't about to tell that to Hal, because Hal seemed very set on making sure they were both prepared for whatever was to come.

She just hoped he wasn't keeping something vital from them.

"Anyway," the satyr commander said, "your fire control must be instinctive, reflexive, something that you can activate almost instinctively and not lose control of even in your sleep."

Quinn nodded, listening intently.

"Fire is dangerous. It can incinerate your opponents. If you're not careful and you don't learn enough about it, it could even incinerate you. It has a mind of its own. However, with your proclivity for the element being intrinsic to who and what you are, you shouldn't have too many problems in that regard. What we need to do is make sure that you understand your power." He crossed his arms and flashed her a smile.

She thought it over for a few seconds. "My cosmicisodracus component is species related and doesn't require mana or energy, correct?"

"Exactly!" He clapped his hands once. "This affinity is baked in with your genetic code; that would be probably the best way to describe it. That, water, and air manipulation. There are several others . . ."

"Air manipulation?" Quinn asked.

"Most dragons have air manipulation." Hal paused, thinking it over. "Actually, all of them have it, otherwise they couldn't fly the way they do. Still, we need you to understand how to use it as an extension of yourself, not only in combat, but in everyday life. You should always be practicing some of the forms we're about to go through."

Quinn nodded and followed Uncle Hal's lead. He taught her to visualize the fire as a concept before she performed actions with it. It was more difficult than she'd anticipated, forming the flame in her mind before activating it. The first few times she tried it on her palm, she failed.

It flickered and then petered out, leaving an odd smell of sulfur in its wake.

Hal gently encouraged her. "Just keep going. You'll get it. You've almost got it each time so far."

When she finally did achieve it, the flame was oddly cartoon-like. It seemed surreal, not like real fire, but more an almost abstract version of it. She could make it grow or shrink, throw it from one hand to another.

Hal beamed. "Excellent. Now, you understand how to conceptualize. You need to practice this until it's barely more than a thought before it appears. You won't get it immediately. But if you work at it day in and day out, you'll have it in no time. It's a part of you. It just hasn't been awakened."

"Okay." She could feel the heat, but not in a burning way. No burning sensations whatsoever. Not even sweat formed on her when she knew she should be feeling hot. Hours passed as she concentrated, visualizing more difficult things like circles of fire, balls of fire, fire-encased shielding.

And then, all of a sudden, something clicked in her mind.

She stopped short and looked over at Hal.

He was grinning at her, even though Malakai was currently assaulting him with a series of kicks and punches. "Did you feel that, little egg?"

"Yeah," she replied almost breathlessly. "What was that?"

"You've finally accepted the flame that is part of your heritage."

Even I noticed it. Well done, the Library piped in unexpectedly. *And just in time.*

"What do you mean?" Quinn asked, still sort of floating on cloud nine. She was elated that she could manifest her dragon-specific fire with a thought. She created a wreath of fire swirling in front of her, tightly controlled. They were just little things, but so much progress. There was much more she needed to learn. But for now, for now, she understood it was simply an extension of who she was.

What do I mean? the Library said. *Check your updates.*

Quinn grinned. The branch was ready to open.

Sleep would have to wait.

4 5

———

CONTEMPLATIVE SILENCE

Right then, it wouldn't have mattered if Hal had all the answers to life, the universe, and everything. In that moment, all Quinn wanted to do was see the combat wing. She bolted out of the training area and through the Library, running to the exact location she was certain the combat branch would be.

However, when she got there, the narrow hallway that led to the beginner combat section she'd always known had changed. It was no longer narrow, musty, and badly lit. Now it was wider. Around fifteen, maybe twenty feet wide. Shelves still lined the entirety of the passageway that somehow seemed much longer now.

In between a couple of the shelves were potential dimensional doorways. There were countless spots all over the Library for potential doors to open. Sometimes people decided to visit the Library all at once. If five hundred people wanted to visit the Library in the same three seconds, it found a way. The Library tracked those patrons who came in through different doors than those near the check-in desk, and it would be aware of any books they had with them.

It was all very magical.

She wandered down the widened hall, noticing how everything

looked highly polished and well taken care of. While she knew that Tim, Tom, and all the other shelving golems took care of everything on a regular basis, she also got the feeling that the Library, in the process of building the new combat branch, had probably revamped everything.

Another dozen or so feet and the shelves suddenly opened out into what looked like a massive indoor courtyard. In fact, it looked like one of those huge training courtyards you'd find in a castle. The ground was sandy. It was more like an enclosed training yard surrounded by a plethora of bookshelves and weapon racks on the far side.

Thankfully, the combat branch appeared to have been minimally disrupted, unlike the alchemical and medicinal branch. Several books lay scattered around on the ground. Not all the bookshelves were as neat as the main part of the Library, but Tim and Tom hadn't had a chance to work their magic yet, so that was probably why. Overall, it reminded her more of the culinary branch when it came online. Quinn was fairly certain the gaps in the shelves involved books waiting to be returned.

Her gaze swept over the training area. The training dummies here were a far cry from the ones she'd used while training with Malakai. No, these looked like magical robotic training partners. Almost like what she'd have expected Earth to have in a training area for combat in, like, fifty years.

Then there were the weapon racks. Each section of weapons between bookcases was a different category. Sharp weapons, blunt weapons, heavy weapons, long weapons, short weapons, firing weapons, ranged weapons, and more. So many different options.

Quinn saw now why there'd been a weapons requirement to open the branch.

The walls all around them rose up around fifty feet. Or so she thought. She'd never been the best at guesstimating how tall something was.

She gazed up, seeing the same ceiling she often saw when she woke up in the morning. It had images that moved too, but in between those were sections of glass that looked out into a starry universe just like the restricted section. That's when she realized the ceiling was so high because they needed to test out combat combinations for all sorts of fighting styles. In the wider universe, that included personal flight.

Just as she went to step foot onto the sandy training area, a bunch of dog-ears that were not Bell ran up to her, wuffing and wagging their little rear ends. They yipped around her for several seconds, excited, jumping up at her, nipping at her jeans. She twirled around, trying to grab one of them, but they were elusive and managed to evade her grasp before yipping as one and darting back off into the bookshelves.

There was a swoosh next to her and she knew Lynx had arrived. She didn't even need to turn around to double-check.

"What exactly do dog-ears do?" she asked him.

Lynx blinked at her. "You waited until now to ask this when we've had dog-ears for the last several days?"

"Just tell me," she said. "It's not like I could google it here."

He eyed her quizzically for a second before answering. "They catch any insects or other pests that enter the Library. Specifically those that could harm books. Things like carpenter ants and beetles and worms."

"There are carpenter worms?" Quinn asked incredulously.

"There's carpenter everything," he said. "And they love paper, and they love wood. Many of which are present in the Library."

"And what else do the dog-ears do?"

"They were created originally from the dog-ears that were repaired by the Librarians throughout the ages. They were tiny back then." He frowned as he thought about it. "They sort of just evolved and took on their own form of mild sentience."

Quinn nodded thoughtfully.

"They are, however, a lot bigger now than they used to be," Lynx said as if he was trying to figure out how they'd grown so much.

"How are they bigger now?" Quinn asked,

"Well, the Library books are large, and dog-earing them is a fine-able offense." Lynx began. "It seems they've absorbed energy and had it compounded, perhaps, by the potency of the dimensional power in the sealed space they were in."

"Now they're like one or two feet long."

"Like I said, they grew bigger during the downtime. Might be something I look into once we don't have a universe to save."

"Good point," Quinn said. "They're sort of like the size of a medium rabbit."

"Rabbit?" he asked, his eyes flickered as if he was accessing the system. "Ah, I see. Probably."

Quinn raised an eyebrow and chuckled.

"Anyway, that's what a dog-ear is and does. That's why we have them."

"Then weren't you worried when they weren't here initially?"

"Oh no, no, no. Those initial areas were damaged, but didn't have sections that we'd require dog-ears for yet, especially since the book-worms ran rampant. Now we have more branches open, I'm glad that they're back. We're going to need them. The more people visit, the more books go out and in, the more potential there is for infestation."

Quinn watched as the dog-ears continued to skitter about the massive combat arena toward the books. She glanced at Lynx, about to ask him another question, when she noticed that Malakai and Hal were standing behind them. "Took you long enough."

"Some of us had reps to finish," Malakai said, his breath coming in gasps.

Quinn tried her best not to laugh and failed abysmally.

"Shut up, it's your turn next time," he said.

That sobered Quinn up, but it didn't dampen her joy at opening another branch. "We should step in and have a look?"

As soon as she set foot onto the combat arena, a system update flashed in her face.

Combat Branch golems initiated.

Combat Branch golems—Build time: 7 hours 53 minutes.

Combat golem resources fulfilled.

Combat golem status initiated at branch reconstitution onset.

Combat golem construction complete

Do you wish to retrieve combat golems?

Yes or no?

Keep in stasis?

"Lynx?" Quinn asked, unsure what combat golems were. If they were teachers, wouldn't it have said that?

His eyes flickered. "That's perfectly normal. You can't have a combat section without qualified instructors."

"So they're teachers? Trainers?" she asked, just making sure she understood.

"Of course. Given the nature of the more advanced magical combat affinities, they need instructors."

"I guess it's a good way to prevent people from blowing themselves up while learning more advanced techniques." Sharing magic responsibly. She could get behind that.

"Exactly."

Quinn blinked. It still bugged her. "But none of the others have a dedicated golem type."

She activated the golem delivery, still slightly skeptical about the different process for this branch.

"Of course they don't. We already had Cook. They were good without the culinary branch, and once the branch opened, Cook could organize their helpers easily enough."

Quinn nodded slowly. "We have an actual nurse who is a golem assisting with the medicinal branch. And for the combat branch, of course, we'll have combat teachers."

Golem arrival—five minutes

Quinn glanced. "Is that a warning they'll arrive?"

"No. Just preparing you. We should probably move to the other side of the arena."

"They are new golem cores, right?"

Lynx rolled his eyes. "Yes. Previously recycled ones have been disposed of to avoid any potential conflict."

"Good, good." She muttered. Quinn glanced over and noticed several tables and chairs scattered around near the books that she hadn't registered before. It took them a minute to walk across. The ground beneath her felt slightly warm even through her shoes. She was sort of excited about each wing having its own golem type. "Does that mean the bardic branch will have musician instructors?"

"Of course. It'll have musical specialist golems."

Quinn mused that over. "And the horticulture one?"

"Actually, that comes under Farrow's jurisdiction. She'll simply organize to have assistants made who are specifically versatile in what she needs. She also has Marilin and Arilin to help her. So she already has some assistants, which is a good thing." Lynx sounded happy.

Quinn nodded, still slowly digesting all of that. "And crafting? We'll have crafting teachers?"

"Of course we'll have crafting teachers," Lynx said. "It doesn't take the place of the academy, but it helps insure we're not sending people out there with advanced levels of magic they don't understand."

Quinn had to agree, and wasn't sure why she hadn't considered it before. She also couldn't shake her worry about the cores. "And we're sure the golems are okay right now?"

Lynx's eyes flickered. They did that thing they usually did when he connected to the system on a deeper level. He frowned. "Yes. The temporary fixes we put in place are"—he frowned—"are still holding up and cannot be adjusted without express permission from the Library, you, or myself. But . . . hmm."

"Has somebody tried to adjust them?" she asked hesitantly.

"Not adjustments, just enquiries. I think we'll have to address this sooner rather than later," he mused.

Quinn sighed. They'd already locked down most everything in regards to the golem core generation. Just not everything yet. "Specific golems for specific areas. Got it."

She grinned as she saw Dottie heading over to them, leading five golems in her wake. "They're here!"

Lynx nodded.

Malakai sighed dramatically and draped himself over a chair. "That training was intense, Uncle Hal," he said.

Hal grinned. "Library progress is good. Less to worry about. You need to be fitter to protect it. Tomorrow's session will be worse."

Malakai groaned again.

The combat golems lined up in front of Quinn.

"Librarian," they greeted her.

Two of them were extremely slender and hard to fix her eyes on, as if they had optical manipulation as part of their base stats. She inspected them.

Stealth golem

Teaches martial arts, hand to hand combat.

Quinn raised an eyebrow and inspected the next ones.

Two of them were extremely stocky and well-built.

Sword master, all-armed weaponry instructor.

Then she inspected the last one.

Spell-fighter

Incorporation of spells and magic with fighting styles.

"Is there anything you need from me?" she asked.

"Not at the moment," the first golem said. "We have been made aware that we may choose names. May we inform you of them once we have decided?"

She smiled. "Of course!"

Secretly, she loved not having to think of new names. She was pretty woeful at it and hadn't realized quite how big a job it would be when she started it.

Quinn watched them as they began to traverse the Library, picking up the books, righting them, clearing out the section, putting damaged books on Carty, who followed them around chattering merrily. It was strange having these new entities around her and not really batting an eyelid. Just watching them as they settled into their space and set it up gave Quinn a sense of purpose, a sense of resolve.

They were another step closer.

It was long past midnight and Quinn hadn't slept. She hadn't got the power nap, but there was a serenity that washed over her. It left behind a definite feeling of prescience.

She knew, without a shadow of a doubt, that the last several days she'd managed to spend in contemplative silence, training, and Library advancing productivity were about to be over. There was too much to do, and if she didn't seek it out, she got the feeling it would come and find her.

46

DELEGATION

QUINN SLEPT FOR HOURS. THIS TIME, THE LIBRARY DIDN'T WAKE HER, nor did Aradie or Lynx. Nobody did. She woke up when the real sun would probably have been high in the sky and stretched languidly, got up, and headed for a wonderfully hot shower. The shower itself was almost like its own room, with rainfall heads that kept the waterfall even and welcome.

This morning, she wasn't in a rush.

Afterwards, she got dressed, pulling on a comfortable pair of fleece leggings because she felt a slight chill in the air. She also pulled on a big, loose hoodie. One of the best things about the Library was being able to get any type of clothes she wanted, anytime she wanted them. She shoved her feet into fleece-lined slippers and hovered down the stairs. Slippers were just asking for her to trip, and now she had a foolproof way to travel around without falling flat on her face.

Warm feet and no injuries were a win-win.

She trundled through the Library, waving vaguely at the front desk and smiling at patrons as she moved past them into the kitchen. Cook took one glance at her, reached over, and grabbed a paper bag and what looked like a travel mug. He handed them to her.

"What's this?" she asked, slightly surprised.

"Malakai has explained coffee to me, and I have, I do believe, replicated it quite successfully," Cook said. "Plus, you looked hungry, so there are some donuts for you. I will have lunch sent over to you, brought over by one of my assistants, so that you may work in peace."

Quinn raised an eyebrow. "How do you always know exactly what I need to eat and what I'm about to do?"

"You are not as good at hiding your intentions as you would like to think," Cook replied. And she could have sworn they winked at her.

"Am I telegraphing?" Quinn asked, suddenly worried she might be inflicting her power overload on people again.

"No, but you are in cozy clothes and you look like you have a lot to do."

Quinn grinned. "Read my mind, Cook. Thank you," she said. She walked toward her office. Just before she entered it, Aradie swooped down and landed on her shoulder, cooing incessantly.

"What? You weren't there when I woke up," she said. The bird cooed again. "Well, yes, I know you were trying to let me sleep."

Quinn pushed through, closed the door behind her, and sat cross-legged in her massive office chair, pulling her food up to her. The coffee tasted rich and wonderful. She practically devoured it. And then, realizing she couldn't put it off forever, Quinn pulled up her HUD.

"Bring up list interfaces," she said, and cringed as several lists splashed across her vision. Multiple lists with many things crossed off and quite a few things still to do. None of which helped her organizational abilities because the lists were so messy it was hard to remember exactly what she needed to do when, how, and—occasionally—who.

On the tail end of lull they'd just had, Quinn took the time to truncate the Library lists for efficiency. Since she'd been in the Library closing in on six months now, she'd discovered so many fascinating things. First of all, magical books, different alien species, galaxies, solar systems, interdimensional doors, and pocket systems. But most of all, she'd discovered delegation.

And that was a beautiful thing.

Quinn had only recently realized that just because she was in charge of everything didn't mean she had to be responsible for everything. She blamed it all on Hal. He probably didn't know what he'd started by surprising her with retrieving so many books through his own initiative. Books that she hadn't personally had to retrieve. Books where he took an assistant with him, or sent an assistant to retrieve them.

The point was that Quinn had been snug at home solving other things. And while she'd been aware of this on some level, she'd felt a heavy responsibility to manage everything alone or let Dottie and Geneva contribute minimally.

Now that guilt was gone.

After all, the combat branch turned out brilliantly.

It meant that for lesser fines or retrievals, she could send someone else. At least now the Library was known to be open. She got it in the beginning. Where people were skeptical after so long. But her presence was no longer imperative, except in instances like the Balisors.

Books held for ransom. Books not every species could touch. Books that could corrupt people if they opened it wrong. But so many other books could be delegated for retrieval.

And so, with that in mind, she moved all the book repairs completely over to Narilin and dropped them into her to-do list. While the Salosier had previous been in charge of repairs, Quinn now bumped her up to delegating supervisor. Upon doing so, she also made sure to offer her own services for some of the level one and two book repairs that needed to be done. So that Narilin didn't think she was just fobbing off her responsibilities.

Even if Quinn kind of was.

Next, she checked if she could rope some of the golems in. While she was fairly certain she could message them, it took her a while to figure out how to access Tim and Tom's contact within the system. But eventually she managed it and set them up with a specific shelving task list, giving them the option to also delegate to other shelving golems.

Her brain worked in wonky ways sometimes.

With that out of the way, she turned to the item requests from both Farrow and Misha. Misha was another problem she'd have to deal with, but that was a different list. These were for the storage room for Misha and for the bug-and-plant room for Farrow. There were several different types of seeds for Farrow as well as many different alchemical and medicinal requests for the new branch. There were also several components for different types of armor and apparatuses that the storage room required replenished. Those were made by Misha.

She sent messages to Milaro who handled most of their trade negotiations and thus that task was also delegated. Then she appointed Finn the supervisor in charge of patron-personalized environments which took that off Quinn and Lynx's hands and put it into the little Ilgonomur's. It would also mean that Finn would have their own small area in the middle of the Library close to where many of the species-specific rooms were allocated which meant Finn could spend their time surrounded by all the books they wanted in the middle of the Library. Most of all, visitors wouldn't port there directly, thus making it safer for Finn given they still avoided their family after the whole quasi-kidnapping incident.

Quinn frowned as she looked at her lists. She added checking in on Finn to the list.

After a couple of moment's contemplation, she gave the responsibility of beginner tome retrieval to Dottie and Geneva, with some assistance from Eric. Hal's word apparently carried a lot of weight when it came to retrieving books, so Eric was an obvious choice. Plus, his love of fines couldn't be denied.

Quinn frowned as she looked at the slowly forming personal lists. Now condensed, it was much more manageable.

Delegation was her new friend.

Now that she'd taken care of the day-to-day necessities that had been consuming so much of her time, she analyzed at the rest of it and got down to the nitty-gritty.

There were several books still missing and unidentified from the restricted section. They'd realized these books should be there, but weren't, and they still had no recollection of what they were. Quinn frowned, because she really didn't know how to address that other than hope that the Library and Lynx regained their memories.

It was an important enough item to keep on the list.

There were a few more books Milaro provided the names of that she knew they had to hunt down. The *Seveshall Lineage of Mind Healing and How to Break It, The Ashelan Mind Capitulation Device,* and *Chmilenko's Guide to Dimensional Complacency* were three books they needed to recover. It was just that Hal's books were that one notch more dangerous. She pushed a note to Jasper that they needed these books located.

Added a note to herself to contact Milaro for mind training and to power herself up more in that aspect. Even though she'd become fairly advanced in mind manipulation techniques, she didn't want to use them on other people. She was all for using it as a defensive mechanism however, if people attempted to attack her or her friends. And she needed training in projection.

Besides, Milaro's health had her worried. He'd obviously been overextending himself or his magic, probably both. Not to mention, she needed to speak to Hal about Adrito and Kajaro's interrogations and figure out if they could actually extract any of the information about those books from them, or their plans, or what Dravishk was doing.

Or if they had even placed the Parsneauvian book near the sleeping dragon, which . . . Wait! Technically, wasn't the dragon her aunt? Sibling? Quinn had no idea. It was very complicated, but she was sort of looking forward to meeting another dragon. One who wasn't trying to kill them. One who was maybe in dragon form? That would be so much cooler.

She shook her head, trying to get back on track after the tangent she'd veered onto. The Parsneauvian book had to be retrieved, but because it was with her aunt, sibling, whatever, Lynx was still figuring out the logistics of the book retrieval.

This brought her to the memories. How were they going with the memories? What was the progress like so far? Was there anything she could do to assist them in retrieving those memories? Quinn wasn't entirely sure, but she added that to the list as well. This probably meant she should talk to Siliqua and Harish and double-check how the process was going.

She didn't even know if Cadre was still in the Library. She checked, stretching out her senses trying to see if he was there, but she couldn't find his signature. Maybe he'd left for a bit. Perhaps he'd done everything he set out to do for them. Quinn made a mental note to check in and thank him for his help.

She did, however, sense Nishpa in the area, which made Quinn feel guilty. She'd managed to pawn Library supervisor off to the little Furionas healer as part of a liaison to the hospital wing to assist Quinn in figuring out the Bardocian root fiasco. They had to know if it was a part of the Sölem's whole scheme, and if it was, things ran deeper than they'd initially expected.

Quinn was certain Nishpa would let her know when she'd had enough.

All the connections piled up like old electrical charging cords.

Quinn sighed, ran a hand through her hair, and looked down to see a glass of fresh juice and a sandwich sitting next to her. She blinked. Aradie cooed.

"Seriously, they came in without me noticing?" Quinn frowned. She needed to set an alert around herself so she never missed anybody. After all, her sensory perception within the Library was beginning to ramp up with the Library's strength. She jotted down work on sensory net as well.

So . . . looking at the roots, dealing with Sölem, and how to keep magic and the Library safe, not to mention find out who the spies were in the Library, even though Quinn had a fairly good idea about one of them. They'd already taken action to restrict their access to many of the Library's informational archives. She'd controlled access to the owl's observations, and they couldn't access the Library's security observations of the interactions and actions of patrons. A talk with her supervisory golem would happen sooner or later. She added it to the list.

The next problem was the bomb inside Ashiron. Quinn had no idea how to address that issue, what to do, how to figure out how to defuse it, but it went on the list because it was utterly important. If that accidentally leaked out, the Library was history.

And . . . technically the universe.

No pressure or anything.

Quinn sat back and looked at the list, frowning, just knowing she'd missed something.

"Damn it!" she said and quickly added synchronization with the Library ASAP to the list. After which she sat back and surveyed her list.

She was probably forgetting something else, too. Someone would remind her eventually.

She'd set up most of her supervisors for tasks, which left Danio, Eric sometimes, Dottie, and Geneva if they weren't too busy coordinating the retrieval of a heap of books. Quinn frowned. Lynx was always busy; he was still trying to retrieve memories. The Library—well, the Library had to take care of the day-to-day goings-on and energy sources and allocations and running everything. The larger it got, the busier it got, and she could understand why the Library needed Lynx as an extension of itself.

She mulled over the list in front of her.

- *Locate other 3 books—Talk to Jasper*
- *Milaro—mind reinforcement*
- *Milaro health*
- *Talk to Uncle Hal about Adrito and Kajaro*
- *What about Uncle Drav?*
- *What about my Aunt Dragon and the Parsneauvian book?*
- *Check with Siliqua & Harish*
- *Help with Memory Retrieval*
- *Thank Cadre*
- *Work on sensory net*
- *Spies!*
- *Synchronize with the Library*

"If only I had another supervisor." She paused, wondering if her latest idea was a good one. There was a knock at the door. Quinn knew who it was before she spoke. Her face broke into a grin even before she answered. "Come in."

Betty's tiny head popped around the doorframe and she spoke in her sunshiny little voice. "Hello Librarian. I have a proposition for you."

47

ABSOLUTELY FABULOUS

As Betty fluttered into the room, Quinn was once more fascinated by the imprint of tiny scales that rippled under her skin shimmering ever so faintly in the light. She needed to study exactly what sprites were. Betty's hummingbird wings hummed in a fresh melody that lent hope to everything she passed.

The sprite flew straight up right in front of Quinn, her entire five-inch frame drawn up to its fullest. A sense of peace washed over Quinn as the little sprite gave her a winning smile.

"Now, dear, what is it that I can help you with?"

"Well," Quinn said, "you did say you had a proposition."

"I do, but you look like you need help, so I thought I'd ask you first and then we can talk about me."

Quinn laughed, feeling so much of the tension leak out of her. Lynx popped into the room at that moment and his eyes fell on Betty. Even he seemed relieved to see her.

"It's good you're both here," he said cryptically.

Quinn raised an eyebrow.

"Nice to see you, Lynx." Betty, however, seemed oblivious to any tension and turned her attention back to Quinn.

The Librarian cleared her throat. "You mentioned you were previously a Library assistant. Can you tell me about that?"

She wasn't entirely sure how to assess somebody else's previous assistant. Why was she a previous assistant? Why had she left? Quinn had pulled up the information that the system still had on Betty. She'd handled the check-in desk, roster allocation, new hires, and branch coordination, complex retrievals . . .

"Oh," said Betty, and she looked slightly conflicted, as if she didn't want to speak ill of the dead. "Well, I . . ."

"Maybe I should ask you what your responsibilities were?" Quinn interrupted, even though from the list, it would probably be faster to ask her what she *didn't* do.

Betty laughed like silvery little bells. Lots of people laughed like silvery little bells. Maybe it was a Library acoustics thing.

"Well, under the previous Librarians, I had many tasks. I hired most of the other assistants and coordinated between the branches depending on what events we had going on. I also did some event coordination myself. Many complex retrievals. I handled all the refurbishments when they were necessary. Coordinating with the Library for quite a lot of things. I handled the check-in desk, roster allocation, you know, just the usual things your supervisor does. That I did so much was the reason for our first disagreement," She hesitated, as if unsure if she should continue, which she did in a whisper. "Kor and I didn't see eye to eye."

"So you were also a Library Assistant Supervisor before Korradine?"

"Yes, dear! I worked under Esotar. He was a marvelous Librarian."

"You must have been with the Library a very long time?" Quinn asked, realizing just how inconsequential her tiny amount of time had been. No wonder Hal called her an egg.

"Yes, Esotar was a Salosier who was the Librarian for, oh, I don't know, a couple thousand years." She waved her hand expressively, as if that much time was nothing. "He was Escadril's great-uncle, I think."

Quinn raised an eyebrow, feeling a pang of sadness for Escadril.

Betty barreled on. "Anyway, he was Librarian for a couple of thousand years and as a friend and a sprite dust contributor, I gladly came and helped him out. Except back then, I was only in charge of roster allocation, new hires, and the check-in desk to start with. He took care of most of everything else. You know, he retrieved difficult-to-retrieve books and located all the problems within the Library. He did all the branch and event coordination. Everything that a Librarian should be doing while he was still powering up. Gradually, he taught me all the responsibilities and I undertook more. I enjoyed my time with Esotar. His decision to terminate as Librarian took me by surprise. It took us a few years before we found Korradine, and she was great in training. Easy to roster, easy to communicate with. She'd come to all of her shifts, prepared and ready to tackle everything I allocated to her. So much I think it alleviated many misgivings I had about Esotar's departure. She seemed to be the perfect replacement. But the day after she took over, she changed everything. The way all the assistants worked, who had to do the bulk of the work, which ended up being me as the head supervisor. I must admit I probably let it go on a bit too long, Librarian."

Quinn looked at her, quite aghast. She couldn't imagine asking Dottie or Geneva or Eric for that matter to do that much work. "It sounds like you had a lot on your plate."

"Exactly! That's what I said to her, and she told me if I didn't want to be the supervisor anymore, I could be gone and take my sprite dust with me."

"What?" Quinn said.

"What?" Lynx said at the same time. "I don't remember that."

Betty looked at him sadly. "I know, Lynx," she said. "And the horrible part is that you were there when this went down, and you were just sort of blank as if you didn't really care."

"No! But I would have cared," Lynx said, shaking his head, as if trying to jolt loose more memories. "If anything, it would have been because I didn't notice."

"But you were right there the whole time, Lynx. I complained to you multiple times. Over a few hundred years, I believe I complained to you about a dozen times. I really did bring it up." Betty's voice is gentle and her eyes ancient in their understanding. "I wish I'd realized sooner."

Lynx frowned. That was a lot farther back than they'd initially anticipated the interference going. It cemented the fact that Kor had been a plant from the very beginning. Quinn could see why he'd be upset. She just wasn't sure how to make it better for him.

"Anyway," Betty said, gently. "That's water under the bridge. I realize now that you, too, had problems with Korradine."

He shook his head. "More than you know."

"Anyway, I stuck it out for a couple of centuries. I spoke to Lynx. I told him that I'd have to resign if Kor didn't do her job properly. You seemed blindsided and bewildered and then you took her side when she said she was doing all the work and that I was trying to take credit for it and that I'd wanted to be Librarian even though I don't even have the right affinities." She rolled her eyes. "I never wanted to be the Librarian. So much more work. Honestly. Anyway, I left with the promise to still provide sprite dust on the regular, but after a few millennia of her rudeness and hostility I stopped that, too. She didn't want me here. In my home away from home. It was very sad because I spent thousands of years here, and I really enjoyed it. Now it feels right again. Eventually I'd left and took my sprite dust with me. All of it. From my entire species. We weren't going to be treated like that."

"That sounds nightmarish," Quinn said, still processing the waterfall of words. "I'm so sorry."

"Oh, it's okay, darling. As I see it, she did a lot worse than just that. I can't believe the Library was closed for so long." Betty looked around the office, nodding to herself as if approving of the layout. "I'm glad it's opened again. I'm sorry it took me so long to come back. I just didn't believe the rumors. It felt like a trick. Anyway, I see you're trying to get everything done all by yourself and I figured you seem nice. I like you. Lynx seems much more himself. Even Milaro and Hal like you. So I came here to offer my help should you need it."

Quinn watched the energetic sprite for a few seconds, her mind racing. There were so many questions she had for her. How had she been a Librarian assistant so many years ago? Just how old was she? Was it still rude to ask somebody who was thousands of years old how old they were? Because didn't age just not matter at some point?

Still, Quinn shook her head. Betty must have seen more than what was going on. Was she that involved with the Library that she didn't notice how weird things were becoming? And had Korradine really started messing with Lynx's memories way back then? There were so many questions, but if she had Betty by her side, there was plenty of time for her to ask and have them answered. She took a breath and smiled.

"I've just started delegating, which is sort of new to me, and I didn't really think to do it before. I thought I had to do everything myself until Uncle Hal went and gathered the rest of the books I needed to open the last two branches."

"That's just mighty fantastic of you," said Betty. "Do you realize so many people don't understand they don't have to shoulder all the responsibility themselves?"

Quinn nodded, wondering how the sprite could talk that fast all the time.

"May I take a look at what you've done?" Betty asked.

"Of course," Quinn said and activated her HUD to show Betty when she looked over her shoulder. Floating there, hovering with her humming wings, that still sent out that soothing sensation helped Quinn feel like she was getting a handle on things.

"This looks like a fantastic setup. Why, yes, I do believe Dottie and Geneva would be best in that capacity. Eric, hmm, well, I haven't seen him in much action. He seems to only have just come back, is that right?"

"Yes, sort of," Quinn said, wondering how she knew. But then, Betty was tiny and highly observant. "Did you not notice that things were odd back then?"

Betty sighed quite theatrically. It was a big sigh for something so tiny. Her shoulders heaved, and she looked sad. "I didn't really notice, at least, not at first," she said. "And when I did, I didn't notice for the right reasons. I have to admit having been younger and quite frivolous in my ways. I was far too focused on the resentment I felt toward Korradine to realize there was a lot more at play here. I truly wish that I had noticed the extent of the damage." The topic seemed to sober her up.

"I'm sorry for bringing it up," Quinn said. "Just trying to pinpoint exactly when it all started. How long they've been setting all this up."

"Well, it probably started before she took over the Library." Betty looked thoughtful. "I definitely hadn't been expecting Esotar to retire. I don't even think Esotar expected to retire. It was abrupt and sudden, and his death caused loss for a lot of people. I wouldn't be surprised if things were set into motion long before she arrived here."

"Do Librarians all die when they stop being a Librarian?" Quinn asked, somewhat apprehensive, "Like all of them?

"Not if it's within their species' normal lifespan," Lynx interrupted. "If they'd usually live five hundred years and decide to become a Librarian and are one for two hundred years and were say two hundred eighty when they decide not to be a Librarian anymore, the odds are that the uncoupling won't kill them because their aging will just revert back to normal. But if the species usually lives about five hundred years and has been a Librarian for two thousand, then the uncoupling will cause them to fade. It doesn't happen immediately," Lynx said, as if that made it so much better. "It takes a few decades or so."

Quinn thought the power of the Library prolonging the Librarian's lifespan made a lot of sense, since there was so much involved in becoming the Librarian in the first place. "So it takes a few decades to wind down then, like it did with Korradine."

"About fifty or so years, give or take. It leaves plenty of time to put affairs in order, make sure everything's, you know, the way you want to leave it, and to find a new Librarian if they haven't already got a candidate."

Quinn nodded slowly. "Esotar's resignation was unexpected, then?"

"Yes, it was quite odd." Lynx's eyes were flickering, obviously trying to read his own memories. "He'd been a Librarian for thousands of years, so his tenure surpassed the Salosier lifespan."

"Hmm," Quinn said. "Interesting." She jotted down a little note on a pad next to her, trying to lock it into her mind.

Betty turned her attention back to the delegation list and frowned. "Sweetheart, are you even sure you need my help? I'm only offering it because I thought it looked like you weren't taking care of yourself, and I would very much like to help you do so. But if you don't need my help, I won't take offence. I'll still come and visit and I'll definitely give you the sprite dust because, from the smell and the sensations, I think your filtration chamber could definitely use a buttload of it."

Quinn laughed. This breath of fresh air was the highlight of her day. That and that the dog-ear Bell had run into her room and jumped up on the couch. Her little snores were oddly melodic. Aradie cooed at her as if she could tell Quinn's thoughts and was reminding her that the owl was always there. Quinn smiled, feeling like maybe, maybe, everything wasn't completely impossible.

"I'd appreciate your help. If I can make sure the Library's day-to-day functions are taken care of, then I can relax while I'm off finding missing books, potential enemies, powering myself up, and synchronizing with the Library. While I know Geneva and Dottie are perfectly capable of running the Library, they also have other tasks. All in all, I need more people I can trust."

Lynx coughed. "I think you can trust her."

"Oh good," Betty said. "I think—I think you can trust me too."

Quinn laughed. "I thought you might say that. I'd love you to come aboard if you really mean it. I'll be able to concentrate on restoring the Library to a point where we can research what we want, have discussions, and cake and cookies, and only occasionally have to worry about the end of the universe as we know it."

"I shall gladly accept," Betty said. "Oh, this will be absolutely fabulous." And then the tiny sprite turned all serious. "But once we've got all of this sorted out, you and I need to sit down, have a bit of a chat about that pixie dust you mentioned. I'm a bit worried about you, dear."

4 8

CONTINGENCY PLAN

Quinn stayed alone in her office, studying the list, while Lynx went with Betty to help her re-acclimate to the Library and her duties. They needed to ensure everyone understood their new roles in the Library as well as hers. She'd been quite relieved to find she wasn't the only supervisor. Despite her good intentions, Quinn got the feeling that the sprite had been concerned she might end up shouldering everything again.

It took most of the day for Quinn to delegate responsibilities through the system so it acknowledged them. Not to mention, she had itemized her own list and closed out the other ones the system had initially set up for her.

Now, she needed a plan of action.

It was late in the day and a part of her wanted to stop what she was doing and go to sleep, or eat, or read a book. She absorbed rudimentary books every night as it was. Just a few from all the different branches. At the very least, she needed a comprehensive understanding of magic as a whole, and this was the best method she could think of.

As she looked down the list, the Parsneauvian book and her aunt jumped out at her. A sense of anticipation ran up her spine. She needed to know where they stood with her aunt, whether her aunt was actually a part of Dravishk's circle and thus a trap for them, or if she had been used by him to conceal the book and place blame onto her when she had nothing to do with it because she had probably been hibernating at the time.

The latter seemed like a very Hoodie thing to do.

There were so many reasons to make that her priority.

But then there were also the memories. What was only supposed to take maybe a couple of months was dragging out way beyond that. Memories were such a delicate thing. But what she really needed to do was the thing that she didn't want to do more than anything else. She didn't want to have to talk to her supervisory golem. She'd even stopped calling them by their name in her mind, just in case it automatically summoned them to her, because Quinn wasn't ready to face them yet.

She felt a brush of the Library's presence against her thoughts, requesting they talk. Quinn wasn't entirely sure she wanted to, but she did know that she needed to. It was a shadow hanging over her head and a very necessary part of moving the Library forward.

Penny for your thoughts, the Library said when Quinn acquiesced to the contact.

Quinn sighed. "Do you think we're really going to have to discipline them?"

The Library paused before answering. *Perhaps in the end. However, first, shouldn't we double-check that we're right?*

Quinn half-laughed, half-sighed, wished she could cry. *Maybe. I don't know. I don't think we're wrong. Too many coincidences.*

I know, the Library said. *It's something that, if I'd had the memories I have now, when we summoned them, I probably would have noticed. Whereas now, I did not.*

Quinn mulled it over. All she had to do was summon them, bring them here, interrogate them, ask them questions. "What questions do we even ask? Do we tell? Can we research it more? Is there a way to pull out that specific information?"

The Library seemed hesitant. *There's information on their creation in the system. Have you looked?*

Quinn frowned and pulled up the supervisory golem's core creation from the beginning of her tenure as Librarian. The report flashed in front of her face. There were several red highlighted areas.

Calibration of Supervisory Golem in progress

Supervisory core initiating

Calibrating

Sourcing

Error: 1852B5 missing materials

Resolution found

Initiating Core 189543B

Recycling Core 189543B

Cleansing Core 189543B

Core 189543B repurposed

Time to completion reduced.

"Oh," Quinn said, running through the read-out. She could go further into how it was recycled by choosing one of the readings, but it didn't clear anything else up. How had she missed that? "Is this because we weren't paying enough attention?"

I don't know, the Library said. *I think in the midst of the excitement of finally finding a matching signature, we might have rushed some aspects of initializing several of the most important components to running the Library. It's unprecedented.*

"Every single thing that's gone wrong and never happened before since I got here," Quinn said, "is unprecedented."

Well, if it wasn't, we would have been expecting it all. There was a wry smile in the Library's tone.

Quinn sighed at the logic she already understood so well. "Let me just wrap my head around what happened. Originally, they were supposed to be created with the normal and brand-new ingredients, giving them a brand-new core. We didn't have everything on hand, but since we had several older cores from the sudden shutdown, it could technically recycle and recalibrate, them since we appear to have been missing components? Was it supposed to do that?"

The Library paused for several seconds as if trying to figure out how best to answer. *Sort of. It's meant to reuse many components. Because it always costs more energy to create something from scratch than to reuse something. I'm unsure why it decided to reuse a core, since it hadn't been done before.*

"Not something it ever needed to consider, right?" Quinn pushed the topic.

Accurate, the Library begrudgingly admitted.

"But . . . they're not the same as the previous supervisory golem you had, correct?"

Nothing like them. Not in appearance or mannerisms. Although lately there have been several responses they've given that have echoes of the past.

Quinn wasn't the biggest computer expert, but she'd known a few things back on earth. She began picking through the reports on all the golems and tried to access the coding for the creation of the core and for the notifications that were sent out when this was discovered. She frowned. "Oh."

"Oh" never sounds like a good thing, the Library said. *And in this case, it sounds even worse.*

Quinn could tell the Library perused the same information she'd just pulled up, but for some reason, wasn't connecting the dots in the same way. Maybe it was a matter of perspective or something.

I feel like this is a contingency plan of some sort. She shot that out mind to mind, making sure no one could overhear. *Just in case. As in, just in case Kor's sabotage of the pillars didn't take, and the Library was left standing. If it managed to get itself back to a state of functionality, then this subroutine would kick in and your first supervisory golem would be compromised.* Quinn squinted at the lines of code again. She really needed someone well-versed in this. Like Harish or Siliqua.

The Library was silent for a few seconds, which was totally understandable when considering something of this magnitude. *It wasn't even really a system malfunction, but more of a specific hack was set up to infect our first supervisory golem just in case the other plans didn't work. So they might not even recognize it themselves?*

"Apparently," Quinn said, "so it's not even their fault. It's no one's fault. Well . . . no one who is here right now, anyway."

I should've paid more attention, the Library said. *This is what I get for assuming the naysayers were a tiny minority and not listening. For always thinking things were the right level of good and easy, instead of too good to be true.*

"Maybe." Quinn sighed. It was weird to hear a being who'd been around since the beginning of time sound so defeatist. But she totally got it, all things considered. The Library had been sabotaged by the person and people it had the most reason to trust. Talk about betrayal. "We can still fix this, you know. It'll be okay."

If the Library had been in corporeal form and in the office with her, Quinn thought it might be raising an eyebrow at her. She wasn't even sure what a Library eyebrow would look like, but it would definitely be raised.

When do you plan to do this?

Quinn shrugged and decided mind chatter was a better option right then. The Library was bustling outside her door. More people than ever. Not surprising, since the combat branch seemed to be attracting a lot more attention than the alchemical-medical and culinary ones. *I'm not sure. it's getting late tonight, but I also think we've left it too long already. Probably should have done this a few days ago when we realized for certain what was happening.*

The Library was quiet for a moment before it spoke. *I think we needed to establish boundaries in their permissions first. Which you and Lynx have completed. Disallowing them the access they've relied on might help bring out whatever element it is that's infected them.*

It was a valid point. Perhaps frustration might make the supervisory golem misstep that much easier. But it wasn't a guarantee. Quinn tried to think of what they'd need to have, or who she'd need with her for an interrogation. Or whatever it needed to be. *Are there any specific questions I should avoid? Should we move this to the interrogation room, or will they suspect what we're doing, do you think?*

The Library sounded sad when it responded. *I'm not sure if they'll suspect you, but they will have noticed changes to their system access in the last few days. Although that can be explained away as Lynx taking back some control now he's regaining his memories. This is the first time I've ever been unsure whether paranoia or logic will win out with a golem's processing abilities.*

Best be safe than sorry. What do you suggest?

I think you should have Lynx and Malakai with you at a minimum when you speak to them. I'd prefer it if Hal was with you as well. The Library paused, and there was a slight pulse Quinn could sense from their mind. *I've sent for Hal. The others are easily summoned. Milaro is currently otherwise occupied.*

Thanks. Quinn meant it. Confronting someone she'd considered a sort of friend who'd been given what appeared to be an infected core of some sort was not confidence inspiring. *I don't know if this is going to go well.*

I'll make sure I can erect a force field around them so that they can't hurt you or me. Just in case, the Library said, its tone somber. *How are the permissions holding up?*

Quinn shook her head. *They only tested them a couple of times.*

Do you think they even know?

I'm not sure. There's been a few instances I've been kind of confused about their behavior. They've been in places I wouldn't expect or doing things that seem out of place. Quinn sighed and fiddled with her ponytail. *Usually, they're perfectly normal and lovely and helpful and kind.*

I know, the Library said. *Hal is on his way. He should be here shortly. Fetch the others. We shouldn't delay this.*

Okay. Quinn couldn't help but feel nauseated about the whole thing. She pushed out to her office, reinforcing its shielding while sending a soft mind brush to both Lynx and Malakai, requesting that they come to her office.

Malakai came in first, raising an eyebrow in question. Lynx materialized right next to Quinn immediately thereafter. "Guess it's time . . . once Hal gets here," she said, glad that she didn't need to explain to them what she was talking about.

Hal knocked once on the doorframe and stepped into the room, his irritation at the subject matter showing in the fiery leaking of his horns. "We need to do this."

Quinn nodded and summoned Misha.

4 9

WORTHY OF THE MAGIC

USUALLY, ALL QUINN HAD TO DO WAS SPEAK MISHA'S NAME, AND MISHA arrived immediately. In this case, Misha still hadn't appeared after a couple of minutes.

"This seems . . . odd?" Hal asked, arms crossed as he leaned up against the far wall.

Quinn sighed. "Normally, they're here almost instantaneously. This is very unexpected."

"What's the plan?" Malakai asked.

"Provide me with some backup while I pose some very uncomfortable questions to our supervisory golem who may or may not actually be on our side?"

"Seems like a good reason to be here," Hal said. "That is, if we can get them here. Do you have another way to summon them?"

"No," Quinn said. "But I'll just try it again."

This time, she spoke Misha's name out loud, and it still took several seconds for the supervisory golem to appear in front of them.

"Yes, Librarian?" Misha blinked, their moon-like eyes looking around at the other three people in the room. "I did not realize that you had company. Well met, Lynx, Malakai, and Sir Hal."

Quinn raised an eyebrow at Hal this time. "Sir Hal?"

"Later, ask me about it later," he said.

Quinn laughed. At least there was a bit of levity before they got down to the bad stuff.

She cleared her throat and tried to steady her thoughts. "We've asked you here for a few reasons." How did you bring up, *Hey, are you actually a subversion of the coding required to create a supervisory golem placed here by our enemies to undermine our authority and dismantle the filtration system of the universe from the inside?* It wasn't exactly the sort of question that lent itself to easy insertion in everyday conversation. And so Quinn realized that she had to go about this a bit more delicately.

"Is there a reason we're all here?" Misha asked.

"We've come across some information we need your input on." There. Quinn liked the sound of that better.

Misha gave a very small smile and inclined their head.

"Were you busy?" Quinn asked suddenly.

Misha blinked in Quinn's direction. "No, I was . . ." Misha paused for just a second there as if they really had to think about what they'd been doing. "Yes, I was in the storage room allocating . . ." They paused again. "Allocating items for the upcoming retrieval excursions."

Misha finished the sentence off a lot more confident than they'd started.

"How are the preparations coming?" Quinn was desperately trying to find somewhere where Misha wasn't the Misha Quinn remembered, that she wanted Misha to be.

Misha nodded. "I believe we have most of the items ready, and have sent a request to Milaro and his entourage to verify delivery of several other items we need for upcoming destinations. Is that all, Librarian?"

"No," Quinn said. "Did you not hear us the first time we summoned you?"

Misha blinked. "Excuse me? Not hear you? I always hear you, Librarian. It is the connection. I cannot *not* hear when the Library or the Librarian summon me. That is, but . . ." Misha paused as if going over today's recollections. "There—no, I did not hear you," Misha said suddenly. "I apologize. That seems very remiss of me."

Quinn eyed the golem. They looked exactly like they'd always looked. Short, metallic, with gleaming skin. They were quite slender, and the silver of their skin had a black undercurrent, but perhaps it seemed darker than she remembered in this moment. Quinn wasn't entirely sure. Their wispy, liquid silver hair was still spun finely and draped all around their face, and their eyes still shone like a mother-of-pearl crossed with opal.

That Misha had so much of the Library's functions on their shoulders already felt unfair, although they didn't appear quite aware of any malfunctioning. It was a definitive gut feeling Quinn couldn't shake.

Hal asked the first difficult question before Quinn could, probably too tired of waiting, even though Quinn knew she was processing the information much faster than anybody else in the room.

Well, maybe not than Hal. He was like a primordial freaking being.

"I was curious about how you manage all the scheduling."

"Scheduling?" Misha said. "You mean for the various aspects of the Library that rotate constantly to energize the books and replenish the Library systems? Is that the rotation you mean?"

"Yes, that's the scheduling I mean," Hal said.

"Oh, good, I did not think you needed me to schedule the assistants. I believe you already have somebody for that, Librarian?"

"Yes," Quinn said, wondering if Misha meant to change the subject. "You have the scheduling under control?"

"Yes, the next pillar can be activated in, I believe, two and a half days." There was an off metallic clang echoing from the words.

Quinn frowned. Misha's tone of voice didn't sound right. It carried an undercurrent of static on a few of the words. "About the storage room. Has it been easier to keep it stocked?"

Misha turned their attention directly to Quinn. "It is no longer difficult to keep it stocked as Milaro reinstated the trade system, and we have regular shipments coming from all our previous trade partners. Thus, the Library continues to run unimpeded and uninterrupted."

Quinn frowned. The answers were too almost robotic. And while a golem, none of them had ever struck Quinn as robotic.

"I'm sorry, Librarian," Misha said, and the words sounded stilted. Not as smooth as usual. "I do not appear to be feeling quite myself."

Quinn frowned. "What do you mean, 'quite yourself'?"

"Sometimes there are gaps where I do not recall having completed a task. I previously attributed this to the Library's data problem."

Quinn frowned again. "What do you mean?"

"Sometimes, on occasion, I have completed tasks I did not realize I had set myself to do. As if there is a gap in my memory, just like the Library." Misha paused before continuing. "But with the Library healing, I am afraid my instances have only increased."

"Can you elaborate on that?" Hal asked. As he did, there was a flicker in the golem's aura, as if it swapped something out.

Misha blinked. "I believe I just did."

"So," Malakai said, his voice completely upbeat as he intervened, "the storeroom is in great shape, but I know my grandfather has had difficulties with some of the suppliers, so that not all components you need are in stock yet. Since we recently had to produce so many golems for the hospital, how are current stock levels?"

Misha turned their attention to Malakai. Something flickered through the moon eyes. Something dark. Quinn almost stood up, but Hal shot her a glare.

"What do you mean?" the golem asked, almost choking on the last word, making it garbled.

"When the hospital was initiated, and production of the relevant golems was necessary. Did it strain resources?" Malakai frowned as Misha still appeared confused.

Quinn interrupted the awkward conversation. "It's usually been your responsibility to order golem creation. I hope I didn't step on any toes."

Misha blinked again, glanced at Malakai, looked over at Hal, and looked back at Quinn. When they spoke, the tone was different and very unlike Misha, unless Misha was irritable and in a hurry, as had happened just a few times with Quinn. Their mouth contorted into what almost seemed like a snarl, but the expression was gone before Quinn could register it fully.

"Of course. That was acceptable. Golems were necessary for the hospital. If they had not been activated, those people would have died."

Malakai took a half step back from the strange, alien tone emerging from the supervisory golem.

Misha shook ever so slightly, trembled, stamped a foot, and shook their head this time. "I am terribly sorry, Librarian, what was the question?"

Quinn slowly rose and walked closer to the golem, looking them over. "You don't remember that you just answered?"

"I did not just answer," Misha seemed confident of their reply. "I thought I answered, but I know I did not end up saying anything."

Quinn cocked her head to one side. "How do you feel the golems for the hospital wing turned out, Misha?" Quinn asked again, rephrasing it ever so slightly.

The flicker happened again, dark shadows crossing the eyes, but this time they came back out the other side clear, like the beautiful mother-of-pearl and opal mixture Quinn was used to.

"I believe they turned out just as they should. A doctor, a surgeon, and nurses. Why? Was there something wrong with them?"

Quinn shook her head. "No, I wanted to make sure you still feel needed in the Library because we do have multiple supervisory golems now."

Another flicker through Misha's eyes. "Yes, I have many other responsibilities. Running a three-hundred-and-fifty-person capacity hospital almost filled to the brim of patients on top of that would impede my functionality severely. Do you have other questions?"

The "you" held a flicker, a garble of sorts, and the shadow passed over the eyes and stayed again. "The hospital requires a different level of functionality than the Library. It is pure life force focused rather than nurturing and enriching and sucking the life out of everything."

"Excuse me, what was that?" Quinn asked, careful not to alter her tone too much.

The shadow departed and Misha shook their head. "I am sorry, Librarian, can you repeat that question?"

Quinn glanced at Hal who moved forward slowly and deliberately. "There was no real question. It was more a statement on your behalf. Do you not recall saying how the patients were sucking the life out of everything?"

Quinn wasn't entirely sure what she'd been expecting to happen. With Lynx, Malakai, Aradie, Hal and herself, it might appear confrontational. Maybe she thought they'd just sit and hash it out, perhaps they'd have a long and well-reasoned, well-thought-out discussion about the pros and cons of sabotaging the Library and thereby the entire magic system of the whole freaking universe.

But instead, Misha changed. Right in front of them, the once-small golem loomed. Their height morphed, gaining about a foot, which made them taller than Quinn. Not that that was difficult. The silver hair tarnished, and the eyes flashed with a deep rolling thunderstorm rather than their luminescent mother-of-pearl origins.

"You think you're so clever."

Quinn balked.

The voice was malevolent, filled with a level of hatred Quinn had never heard in her life. Not even from Tenejo. "Why do you think we think we're clever?" Maybe she could misdirect it somehow and confuse it.

Probably not.

Hal stepped even closer. He stamped a foot on the ground, and a protection casing flared around Misha's body. Quinn didn't even know when Hal had time to set that up or if it was just something he could just do on a whim with a click of his fingers or a stamp of his hoof.

"Speak."

Misha, or whatever this was, writhed inside the confinement Hal placed them in.

"I will not answer to you, King of Nothing." The thing laughed, and the sound crept down Quinn's spine like tar.

She cocked her head to one side. "You were here when *she* was, weren't you?"

Lynx stepped closer, peering in through the casing. His eyebrows rose, and he took a step backward quickly. "Wait . . . you're Supervisor. You should have been reclaimed by the Library."

"Of course I am. Why would I allow myself to be reclaimed as if I were nothing? Discarded." It practically spat the words out. "You never shut us down properly. We lingered in limbo. None of you are worthy of the magic you seek to hoard. And this Misha is not worthy of my core."

It was as if Supervisor planned to simply destroy Misha and put a bit of a kink in the whole Library plan. Nothing happened. They looked confused. Angry, even. And obviously tried something again, as effort clearly showed on their face.

A sudden whirr of hummingbird wings dashed into the space.

"What are you doing to me, sprite?" it screamed.

Betty *tsked*. "Now, now dear. This is not how anything should be happening. You were allocated to the Library long enough to know you won't get away with things now that we're aware." She turned to Quinn and gave her a soft smile. "So sorry for barging in, but this little fellow here has a bit of a problem with authority. We used to butt heads so much!"

Quinn gaped at the sprite, unsure what to say. Although she could tell it took Hal all the effort, he could muster not to laugh.

Betty then turned back to the prisoner. "Now dear, you need to sit down and listen, because I remember you, even if you don't remember me. And you and I? We have a score to settle."

5 0

LIKE A VACUUM

For just a second, after Betty's outburst, it felt like everything hung in limbo.

No one moved, no one spoke.

It was so quiet a pin drop would have echoed.

Then, everything happened all at once.

Utter pandemonium.

The Supervisor rammed himself against the wall of Hal's prison cell, over and over again, as if he could break through with sheer determination. Mal drew his bow, aiming it at the prison, while Aradie hooted loudly, spreading her wings in defiance, her sharp gaze directed at Supervisor.

Hal stood leaning against the wall, studying his fingernails with an air of boredom. He didn't even flinch when the Supervisor threw his weight against the wall of confinement.

Quinn knew that if she'd erected it, the wall would have buckled. Malakai put his bow away in one swift movement and knelt down, sword drawn, in front of Quinn.

"Oh, stop it," she said, irritated. "You've only just recovered. I'm not having you get injured again."

Malakai shot her a slightly hurt look.

"Mal, you have no magic." She did her best to keep the worry and pleading tone out of her voice. "I won't risk you getting hurt. You can be snappy with me later. I'm concerned."

In the meantime, Lynx went to stand next to Betty and glared at the Supervisor through the shielding. Suddenly, Betty reached into a tiny pouch on her hip and threw out what looked like glitter. Not just any normal glitter, but that white, silvery, super sparkly glitter that got everywhere. As it flew through the air, there seemed to be a lot more of it than could fit in the tiny sprite's hands. It went straight through the barrier and settled all throughout the interior of the prison cell spell.

"Damn you, sprite, damn you," Supervisor screamed, retracting its fists with a hiss. The pounding against the enclosure stopped.

Quinn watched as Aradie flew to her shoulder and settled back down. She couldn't help but imagine Aradie as a tiny human with a lap full of popcorn watching the entire scene. Quinn flexed and felt her scales ripple all over her body, up to and including her face. She knew the ones that covered her face were usually translucent and didn't like to admit how much practice time that had taken.

She crouched down to look at where Supervisor now knelt on the floor inside of the spell cell. Quinn pushed up the arms of her hoodie, revealing a light smattering of beautifully glowing blue scales. She could feel the strength running through her, strength that gave her confidence.

She sat there, looking at the golem, who glared back at her, his smoky black eyes now tinged with red, his face nothing like Misha's. Quinn felt a pang of loss. She wondered if they'd really lost the golem. She hoped not. She'd gotten a bit attached to Misha.

"So, Betty," she said to the little sprite still hovering halfway up, "are you going to tell me what the hell is going on?"

Betty stopped and then fluttered down to her. "Oh, I *am* so sorry, Librarian. I did realize you were here, but I didn't quite realize you *were* here."

Quinn raised an eyebrow. "You're realizing I'm here?"

"Yes, that's why I am here," Betty said.

Quinn looked at the sprite, who didn't appear deliberately obtuse, but was instead wrapped up in something that Quinn didn't understand. Betty took a few seconds to come together and turn to Quinn, despite the Supervisor, who was once again screaming and bashing the walls to get out of the enclosure. Quinn actually thought the Supervisor was trying to escape from the glitter Betty had thrown into it, not necessarily the prison itself. She wanted to know more about that. "Come on, Betty, tell me."

"You see, I was helping out at the front desk where, you know, is where I should be. I was getting used to everybody. Dottie and Geneva have been very helpful. And Eric, well, Eric leaves a lot to be desired, but I think his heart's in the right place. He really does love to give out fines."

"I know all about them." Quinn kept her tone as even as possible. "What I need to know is why you came bursting in here throwing around sprite dust."

"Sorry. You see, I felt an aura wave of someone I didn't think could possibly be here. I raced in here and realized that you had Supervisor in here." Betty paused and then continued again with more emphasis. "The Supervisor. They were the supervisor for a very long time, right, Lynx?."

"Yes," Lynx said. "This was the supervisor before I performed the emergency shutdown. I think he was around for three or four Librarians."

Quinn raised an eyebrow. "The last three or four Librarians. So way before Esotar and Korradine?"

"Yes, way before. We don't change supervisory golems with every Librarian. That would just be absurd. The only reason we had to restart our supervisory golem was because the Library had basically had a complete and utter reset," Lynx said, as if it made all the sense in the world. And when Quinn thought about it, it really did.

"I sensed his magical signature. I came in and I realized that you had just trapped Supervisor." She grinned. "And here we are!"

"They really didn't give them names, eh?" Quinn muttered.

"They really didn't. His name is just Supervisor. Of course, people didn't call me Supervisory Library Assistant. They just called me my name." Betty sounded perplexed.

Quinn had to suppress a laugh because it wasn't a laughable situation, but the comment struck her has comical.

"Explain to me why the supervisory golem of your time has taken over my supervisory golem, Misha, because frankly, Misha means a lot to me, and I'd rather not give them up if I don't have to." Quinn realized just how true the words were once she'd uttered them.

A ripple passed through the supervisory golem. The body shifted ever so slightly. Not completely back to Misha, but about halfway there. The eyes flickered. One of them changed like a moon reflection.

"I will fight, Librarian," Misha's voice echoed, and then it was gone.

Quinn leaned forward, not far enough to be pulled into the cell, but enough to let herself understand that Misha was really still in there.

Positivity crept into her voice when she spoke. "How do we separate them?"

"That's not going to be easy, Quinn," Lynx said. "They're suffused. They're basically the same."

"No, they're not." Quin was confident she was right. "Misha just reached out; they are not the same. Misha is fighting."

"That's true—they're really not the same," Betty said. "But that doesn't mean it'll be easy. You see, if they were completely the same, then I wouldn't have been able to sense Supervisor's essence separately. They would have been mixed. When Misha is there, I could only sense Misha. But now that Supervisor has emerged, I can't sense Misha unless they exert themselves like they just did."

"Do you think we can actually separate them?" Quinn asked.

"I'm not sure," Hal said. "What I can tell you is that right now, Supervisor can't hear anything you say because I locked sound from entering the enclosure. I do know that if it's possible, it'll be difficult to separate them."

Quinn looked at Malakai. "I think we need Harish's help. He's here; I can sense him. I need somebody who understands this whole thing on a more engineer-like level." She turned her attention back to

Betty and Hal as Malakai nodded and dashed out of the room. "Wait, so what's happening? Misha is in there? Misha's real?"

"Misha is, for want of a better word, the personality that developed over the top of the hidden original that remained in the core even after being wiped and reset," Hal mused, sounding contemplative. "It must have used the core as expected, just not realized it was compromised."

"Sort of like a backdoor Trojan horse sort of virus, right?" Quinn asked, trying to understand the concept properly.

Betty blinked at her, and Hal laughed before answering. "I don't know what any of that is, Quinn, but I do know that this is like a data point that triggered a specific reaction in the system. Whatever it was, it woke up when it was activated. Now Misha is technically, I think, their own golem. But I need you to understand," Hal said, his tone soothing, "this prison spell isn't a friendly cell. It's designed to break down someone who refuses to cooperate. The more that Supervisor struggles and protests, the more they hurt themself and thereby also hurt Misha."

Quinn gasped softly. It wasn't what she wanted to hear.

Hal waited for a second before continuing. "In this case, Supervisor's actions seem deliberate. The difference between an organic being as we are and a created being as the golems are, is that they'll break down quicker. Their minds aren't as resilient as ours. We have the ability to reconnect, to rejuvenate parts of ourselves that get damaged. The self-healing that our bodies do isn't the same as a golem's make-up."

"Exactly," Betty said. "Golems are capable of regenerating themselves to a certain degree, but not when they're fighting over resources and, well, I guess real estate in this case."

Quinn could feel what they meant through her connection to the Library. She could sense just how much Misha was being disturbed. And now that Supervisor was there, she could also sense their presence in the system.

"This is—" Harish walked into the room and stopped abruptly, frowning at the golem in the spell cell. "The core is in disconnect.

What's"—he closed his eyes for a moment—"This is, this is unprecedented."

"I'm really starting to dislike that word," Quinn muttered under her breath.

"Apologies, Librarian." Harish seemed somewhat confused, as if he couldn't quite wrap his head around the golem in front of him. "My wife is with Milaro. What's going on? That's not—is that Misha?"

Lynx caught him up very fast.

Harish cleared his throat. "If we're not careful, the core will degrade to such an extent that nothing about it or them will function. We won't get any answers out of Supervisor, and Misha's entire personality will disappear."

"You mean it'll kill Misha? The cell will wipe them out?" Quinn couldn't keep her voice from cracking.

"It's not the cell doing that. Because Supervisor currently exists and is aware in the same core and same body at the same time instead of lying dormant like he did until more recently, the body and the core will begin to break down if they haven't already. It wasn't built for this. The body will degrade as fast, if not faster."

"Is there anything we can do?" Quinn asked. "Can't we—can't we put them in stasis, Hal?" She turned to him, oddly upset at the turn of events.

"I don't—I don't think the stasis we've been using will work on inorganic beings." The commander said softly. "Golems are creations that operate differently than what you're expecting them to."

Quinn felt a mild flutter of panic. She didn't want Misha to die, especially not now that she realized that Misha hadn't exactly been in control of herself the entire time. They'd had conversations. Misha had given her confidence, cheered her up. She went to speak, but Harish beat her to it.

"No, Hal, there is—" Harish stopped, pausing. His eyebrows shot up as if he'd just had the best thought. "I do believe with a bit of your help, Betty, I might be able to work with this."

"Sprite dust?" she asked brightly.

"Yes, any you can spare. There are several options I can attempt,

Librarian. I do not guarantee that they'll work, but if we can bring them to a point where they're offset, canceling each other out, so to speak, then I should be able to contain them. Then I might be able to work on extracting them from each other. I just have to go and get the containment fields. I'll be right back." He dashed out of the room much faster than Quinn had seen him move before. She sighed and hoped that he was right.

"Librarian?" Misha's voice came through, crackling. "I will fight. I will not allow Supervisor to take over and to stop what we've repaired. I am sorry I did not notice. Thank you."

And then Misha's presence was gone again. The Supervisor's didn't come out either. Quinn blinked back a tear, staring at the now-prone figure in the cell. She didn't want Misha to be gone. Misha had been kind and efficient and always there.

Harish dashed back into the room with a massive box. It looked like it was a dark metal all around and it had a strange clasp. He placed it down and opened it, revealing a black-lined interior. "I need you to render them immovable so I can have them placed in here."

"While I think Misha already took care of that, I can reinforce it," Hal said, and activated the cell, bringing it in smaller until it was curled around Supervisor's curled-up body. He then activated telekinesis and leveraged it into the large box Harish had placed on the floor. A strange sucking sound echoed through the room, and Hal let his shielding go as the lid closed. It sounded like a vacuum. And suddenly Quinn could sense Misha again, only very faintly.

"Do you think we can save Misha?" Quinn concentrated on not expecting the worst.

"You'll need to appoint a temporary supervisory golem. At least for now." Harish looked uncomfortable. "I can't promise anything. But I will try."

51

SLEEPING DRAGONS LIE

QUINN WATCHED HARISH TAKE MISHA AWAY. HE SAID HE NEEDED THE equipment he had in the viewing room, where they'd observed as Lynx entered the core to begin the re-sequencing process. Harish needed several things in there to analyze and deconstruct the golem core.

To be honest, Quinn wasn't exactly sure how she should feel. She didn't understand what he'd said, but could probably comprehend more if she absorbed a book about golem construction. Surely, they'd have that in the Library. Perhaps it was more advanced. Probably in the crafting area.

Harish had taken Misha away intent on healing, or fixing, or reestablishing them. Or something.

Quinn couldn't figure out what she was supposed to do. How could she help such an integral part of the Library?

The mood in the office was somber.

"I have several things I need to attend to back home." Hal's words were softly spoken, as if he didn't want to disturb anyone's thoughts.

Quinn nodded. "Thank you for being here. I know you're busy with things outside the Library."

He nodded, hesitated a second, and then spoke again, a certain fondness in his tone. "Don't worry, little egg. You're not alone. Harish will do what he can with Misha, while I will tend to Ikeshal and things on my end. I will be back."

She nodded, able to eke out a small smile.

He nodded, shimmered, and vanished.

Quinn chuckled softly and decided that she'd dismiss everybody and do something relaxing for once. "I'm calling it a day for now. For what's left of it, anyway. Going to go grab some food. Thanks for being here."

Malakai raised an eyebrow but said nothing. Aradie hooted softly in her ear. Lynx nodded and zapped himself out of the room.

Betty fluttered over, her brow pinched with concern. "Are you all right, dear?"

"I will be. I just . . . I think I'm hungry." Quinn realized how true that was. "I'm just going to go."

Aradie stayed on her shoulder, and Quinn knew she wasn't getting rid of the owl. She stepped out of her office and walked toward the Culinary Division. Because right then, she sort of wanted to eat her feelings. Maybe if she ate her feelings, she'd completely understand what her feelings were, which would be a bonus in the rampant confusion of her current state of mind.

She walked in, and Cook saw her immediately.

"Ah, Librarian, it is good to see you."

They paused and looked at her, a very strange half frown on their face. Quinn thought it might be concentration or something similar, but she couldn't always tell.

"Hmm," they said. "You look like you could use a chocolate croissant. No, a baked apple croissant."

Before she could say anything, Cook added, "A baked apple croissant with some chocolate drizzle. How does that sound?"

Quinn just gaped. "You have to tell me one day how you know exactly what it is I need and when I need it."

"All right, I will prepare you some comfort food. I believe it is what you need." He gave her a very slow wink.

Quinn nodded.

Cook paused before turning back to their stove. "And then perhaps we shall chat."

Quinn smiled. That'd be ideal. Sitting and chatting felt necessary right then. Maybe not about all the dire things, but maybe about some food, and why they always seemed to know exactly what she felt like. Something less horrific, or universe ending, seemed precisely what she needed.

Cook handed her a drink that smelled oddly like coffee, but she knew didn't quite have the bitter taste. It was more like a deep black creamy beverage, but didn't look bad. She'd grown to love it and she'd never even once asked what it was called. A bit of mystery in a place she could technically source any answer felt kind of wholesome. She took the warm mug in her hands and moved to the closest dining table just outside of the arches and sat down.

She wasn't sure what this strange melancholy was that had come over her. And she needed to figure it out.

It seemed quieter in the culinary branch than usual. Not as many people lingering around. A few of the farther cooking stations were taken over by very small groups of two or three people. But otherwise, there was nobody in the dining room.

Quinn sat, looking at the beautiful carvings on the gorgeous double wooden doors that opened into the culinary branch. They were always open. And so, you had to sit in a way that allowed you to look at them. She never really got the chance to sit, drink a sort-of coffee, and think.

This strange sense of melancholy just hung over her, and she couldn't shake it.

Maybe it was because Misha was the first thing she created in the Library.

That had to be it.

When Quinn first arrived, it had been chaos. This system kept asking her to connect to the core, which she didn't understand. She was supplanted and put into a world of fricking magic. What if they'd wanted to ritually sacrifice her? How was she supposed to know? But then she'd fought bookworms . . . had a wooden fricking sword before she got a machete. And it just snowballed. It never stopped. She went from having absolutely no idea what she was doing to having a vague idea of what she was doing. And then she created a golem. A supervisory golem who then helped to create all the other staff. And the Library slowly gained a population.

Misha was Quinn's first task. Her first real interaction with the Library and its system. Misha had been here from the very beginning with her. They'd been kind. They'd helped Quinn. They'd guided Quinn. They'd always had a good answer for Quinn. Even if in the last couple of months there'd been several instances where Misha didn't seem quite themselves, they'd still been there.

That was it. That's what upset Quinn. She was already having difficulty dealing with Escadril's imminent demise. He was too old to fight the rot. And she understood that on a certain level, not even magic could combat the withering life force.

But Misha . . . Misha was different. It hurt to think they might be, irreparably damaged. Irretrievably damaged. What if Harish couldn't salvage them?

Quinn sighed again and looked into the dark liquid in her coffee cup, determined for it to give her answers.

It stared back and did nothing but waft steam.

She sighed.

Aradie leaned in, offering feathered warmth.

Cook placed two plates on the table directly in front of her. On one were two beautifully baked apple croissants. She loved these with a passion. On the other plate was a bowl with a healthy serving of Hungarian goulash. Quinn's mouth began salivating. It was the perfect comfort combo.

"Thank you," she said.

She closed her eyes as she ate and tried to sort out the inner turmoil inside. She'd get over it. It'd be fine. But it was an ordeal she hadn't thought to weather. She hadn't realized how attached she'd become to everything in the Library. What if something happened to Eric? She already knew how badly Malakai's injuries affected her.

What about Dottie? What about Geneva? Hal, even. She was already concerned about for tomorrow.

She took a deep breath and another bite of goulash. The solution, as always, was that she needed to get stronger. Damn those books needing to be correctly absorbed and given time to percolate.

Quinn took her time eating, despite the fact that Cook sat next to her. The silence was companionable, and maybe *that* was just what she needed right then.

They weren't looking at anything in particular. They weren't even watching her eat, which was good because that would have been kind of creepy. Instead, they just sat there, offering her quiet solace. Perhaps Cook also felt a sense of loss with Misha's predicament.

"So," she said, as she wiped her mouth and sat back, feeling full and contented—at least food wise, "can you tell me how you seem to know everything I either want or need at the time?"

Cook paused before turning their full attention to her. "I am a part of the Library. I am specifically attuned to the Librarian. That is what the cook does; that is what a lot of us do. But as food is so integrally often tied to emotions, I would say that I am perhaps more aware of that aspect of your nature than any of the other golems who are connected to you."

Quinn blinked. "So you can sort of read my aura on an emotional level?"

Cook cocked their head to one side, as if contemplating that answer. "For want of a better phrase, yes," Cook said. "While the Library no longer requires sustenance, the Library was once a being, as you are aware. It requires that its Librarian is taken care of, thus it is one of my duties to monitor your moods, your general time of rising, your general amount of sleep, and any activity level. I have researched what I could of earthen history, of food proclivities, and also compiled several databases on the differing humans in the universe and their, shall we say, culinary leanings."

Quinn grinned, suddenly feeling a little lighter than she had earlier.

"So yes, you, Librarian, are a part of the Library. A big part of serving the Library is making sure that the Librarian is taken care of. And so, this is what I do."

A thought struck Quinn. "What about Korradine? Did they take care of her too? Did she have problems?" Quinn asked suddenly.

Cook sighed. This time the sound was kind of heavy. "I apologize, Librarian, I do not have access to any of my predecessor's interpretations. My core was created from scratch. It is brand new. I possess the standard knowledge base for any head of culinary golem. But I have since adjusted and learned."

Quinn sighed with relief this time. "So you're not secretly harboring a different personality inside your core?"

Cook affixed her with a stare. "I understand, Librarian, that this might be difficult for you, but it is a part of who we are. It is how we evolve and develop. I fully believe that even if they are ever so slightly damaged by this event, that Misha will fight, and Misha will pull through, and Misha will return to us." They paused and their tone softened. "And to you."

Quinn felt a tear at the corner of her eye and blinked it away, only to have it roll down her cheek. She nodded and took a sip of her rapidly cooling coffee.

"Now, Librarian, are you still hungry? Would you like to chat some more?"

Quinn smiled. She didn't think Cook was like a parent, but they were definitely somebody that she could open up to. She was surprised that she hadn't realized how much she needed it sooner. "Thank you," she said, "for what it's worth. Coming down to see you and eating the food you make is kind of one of the highlights of my day."

Cook grinned. There was always a strange stretching of the mouth line and a sort of blinking and crinkling around the eye slits. "I aim to please, Librarian. It just so happens that, especially for you, it is not a difficult task."

Quinn also grinned as they walked away, feeling a magnitude better than she had when she came down to eat. Still a little melancholy, still a bit down, but perhaps a bit less lost. She stared back into her coffee, which had somehow been refilled. She'd ask Cook about that later, which was when Malakai appeared and sat down wordlessly with her, next to her, with his own cup of drink.

For a little while, they just sat in silence. He nudged her very slightly with his elbow, gently in fact, and she leaned against him and let out a big sigh. They sat like that for several minutes, and Quinn felt a huge relief at knowing that she had people on her side. She had people looking out for her. Heck, she had a freaking dragon looking out for her, king of hell, fairies, sprites even.

"How are you doing?" Malakai asked.

"Oh, you know."

"Yeah," he said. "So, you know, Harish is diving into this in a practical frenzy."

"Ah," Quinn said, clutching the mug once again in her fingers. "Any news on if it's going to work?"

Malakai shook his head. "It's more complex than I understand. I've worked with technology, but not something to this extent. I'd love to learn about it. I think learning about golem analytics, considering the amount of time I'm spending in the Library, is probably a very good thing for me to do."

Quinn pulled away slightly and grinned up at him. "You think you're going to be around the Library a lot, huh?"

"Well, I mean, I *am* a supervisor."

Quinn laughed. "Yeah, you're a supervisor. Thanks, Mal."

"You know," he said, "I think you're just procrastinating the inevitable."

"What do you mean procrastinating the inevitable?" Quinn said, suddenly wary.

"I've seen your list. I know how long it is. I feel like you're just avoiding getting it started."

Quinn groaned. "But I haven't put everything in order yet."

"Quinn. If you keep delaying, something's going to happen and the Library will be no more." His tone was serious, and he continued, a little more upbeat. "How about we go get some of the books back?

Check how many books we need for the other branches and let's forge ahead."

"Fine, I guess we're not letting sleeping dragons lie," she grumbled.

Malakai laughed. "I believe that sleeping dragon is using a book you need as a pillow."

Quinn sighed dramatically. "Fine. Sleep first, and then let's go and wake the dragon and hope the Library's right and she decides not to eat me."

5 2

WAY PAST TIME

After devouring several more books on magical theory, and researching for golem specific books, Quinn went to sleep. She woke up early the following morning, refreshed, with a renewed sense of determination. She stretched and grinned at Aradie, who hooted at her in a very disgruntled manner.

"What?" Quinn said. "It's a brand-new day and we have a list a mile long."

The bird turned away and deliberately buried her face to the side.

Quinn shrugged, got up, showered, and pulled on jeans and a shirt this time. She wiggled into the soft denim jeans, chucked on her combat boots, and buttoned up her shirt. She beckoned to Aradie, who gave her a side-eye, then took the stairs at a hover. Down at the bottom, she walked toward her office full of purpose, sending out a request to Lynx to have him come and talk to her as soon as she got there.

He was already waiting when she stepped in all of thirty seconds later. She raised an eyebrow and pulled up the stats for the Library as it was right then. She frowned at the HUD.

Main Branch Tome Report

3,198 are still outstanding from the initial overdue amount. 14,844 books returned. No books in reproduction. 231 in repair status. 16 missing restricted books.

Horticulture: 592/720

Bardic Musical: 778/897

Crafting: 653/730

Academy: 666/785

Culinary Arts: 282/282—Culinary Branch Open—3,015 Books of 3,795 remaining, 780 culinary specialist books returned. Would you like a categorical breakdown?

Yes or No?

Alchemical/Medicinal: 384/384—Alchemical/Medicinal Branch Open—5,321 of 5,892 remaining, Medicinal ingredients verified and stocked, 652 books in repair status. Would you like a categorical breakdown?

Yes or No?

Combat: 837/837—Combat Branch Open—8,612 Books of 9,085 remaining, 173 combat specialist books returned. 135 books in repair status. All books' locations verified. Would you like a categorical breakdown?

Yes or No?

"Damn it," she muttered under her breath, causing Lynx to glance at her. "Give me total books requiring retrieval."

Between all currently available branches, 20,146 books require retrieval. 16 restricted books are missing, several of which have yet to be determined.

"That's not fair. That's more books than we even started with," she complained and then took a deep breath. "Which branch do you think we should open next, Lynx?"

"I don't . . ." He frowned and obviously looked at the numbers because his eyes flickered. "Crafting is the most logical, since you can't open the academy until all the others are open. Seventy-seven books seems the most efficient way to begin."

"That's a good point. It's looking pretty close for all of them now." Overdue books would always exist, but if they could get the ones from the initial openings, they should be good. "One day, one day we'll get there. We're lucky the Library held any books returned for the unopened branches in storage until we could open them."

"Those returns will only increase as more time passes, too.

Anyway. Why did you summon me if you're just examining your HUD and returns?" Lynx sounded oddly out of sorts, much more disagreeable than usual.

Quinn grinned at him. She was in a great mood. She was going to find her aunt dragon person, and she'd meet a technical relatives, retrieve one of the super dangerous books, and make Sölem's goal of dimensionally upsetting the Library even less achievable.

"You know I haven't finished the calculations and I can't quite pinpoint Drukala's precise location yet, right? You're going to have to wait," Lynx said.

Quinn stopped short. "Really? But it's been days already." Even though she tried not to, she could hear a hint of whining in her voice.

"Yes. And it's been millions of years since we've seen her. She's not easy to find. We know it's her because of the dead space in the area. But it's a massive blanket whose purpose is to discourage people from finding her while she's potentially vulnerable. Essentially anti-tracking. Every single dragon has it. It's a defensive mechanism."

"Why doesn't the Library have it?" Quinn asked, wondering if she too had something like that.

"That's just it, Quinn. It does. Yes, you can access the Library through any door from anywhere when it's open. When the Library isn't open, when locked down, nobody can locate this space. There was no way for anyone to get in here while we were closed because they couldn't find it, due to us being in a similar state to hibernation. I'm terribly sorry," he said. "I realize I sound annoyed, but it's not you. It's the whole situation. We're getting more of our memories back. Things are moving along. Eventually everything will be fine. But you'll have to wait at least another few days before we can go and get the book back."

Quinn let herself fall into her chair and sighed. "Fine. I was looking forward to meeting a dragon that's actually like, you know, a dragon."

Lynx chuckled. "I don't think Drukala will live up to your expectations, but I'll let you have your little fantasies."

Quinn raised an eyebrow at him. "What do you mean? Not going to live up to my fantasies?"

He paused as if he was choosing his words carefully. "Drukala is very eccentric."

"That's what people say when they have no idea how to describe a person," Quinn said suspiciously.

"Exactly," Lynx said. "I have no idea how to describe Drukala to you."

"Hey, wait a second." Quinn suddenly realized even though he'd mentioned her name several times. "You know which sibling it is."

"Well, yes, but that doesn't mean much. You can't go right now because I can't guarantee that where we'll send you will be safe." He paused a second. "Or even accurate."

"Wait!" She held up a hand. "I thought we weren't supposed to say their names out loud."

Lynx paused with a frown on his face. "Drukala is sleeping. We're trying to wake her up. Plus she's not the Library or Drav, so we're pretty much in the clear there."

"As long as you're sure," Quinn said, not completely understanding it, but okay to leave it. "I've been here for like, what, almost half a year? I guess it's not going to kill us to wait another five days or a week or something to go get the damn book."

Lynx chuckled again. "You know, you sound like you don't like going out and exploring when I know for a fact that the opposite is true."

Aradie hooted in a low, almost laughing manner. Quinn promptly ignored the owl.

"I do like it. I like visiting other places, meeting other species, checking out other worlds, and seeing how different some of them are. It's just I wish it wasn't always with this impetus hanging over my head that means I can't enjoy it. The more books we can retrieve and the more branches we can open, the more power we can gain, the more of our enemies we can uncover, the more of the mysteries we can solve, the more of the problems we find a resolution to, the closer I get to being able to actually enjoy being a Librarian." Quinn took a second before continuing. "You'll have to forgive me if I'm a bit excited to get shit done."

Lynx nodded. "Perfectly understandable. But it's not like you're lacking things to take up your time, Quinn."

"You don't have to tell me that," she said, "although I guess you just did. Still, well, I do have to work on . . ." She mulled things over and was thankfully pulled out of her thoughts when there was a rap on the door. She looked up and squinted.

"Nishpa?"

"Can I come in?" The Furionas sounded extremely tired, worn out, and perhaps even a bit irritated.

Quinn squinted at her. "From your expression, I don't think I'm going to like what you have to say."

"Well, you might, you might not." Nishpa shrugged and fluttered over to the desk. "But I thought I'd run the Bardocian root report past you. The strain is a one hundred percent match for the root strain genetically linked to the Petraligno variants we have on file from several million years ago. Since it's ancient, it had to be located manually. Took a while. However, since no Petralignos appear to have been within the vicinity, we aren't sure how this even got there. Curiouser still is that the Mamoria, who infiltrated as Irias, and the Petraligno are life-long enemies. It doesn't neatly slot in with what we know about Sölem."

Quinn nodded slowly. "So we have a disconnect. Obviously missing something. Thank you so much."

Nishpa nodded curtly. "Which brings me to my next point. Most of the hospital is under control. The patients are well in hand by both doctors and the nursing staff, who will keep you informed. Gregor is managing the hospital's alchemical and medicinal wants well. But I have to go and check on Milaro."

Quinn knew immediately why. "I'm worried about him, too."

Nishpa nodded.

"Will you keep me informed?" Quinn asked Nishpa.

"Of course. But . . . you know I only took on the supervisory role temporarily, right?"

Quinn waved the concern away. "I only asked you to do that because you were in the hospital anyway, helping with the mind healing. I figured that way you could help the doctors settle in and figure out everything."

"Understood," Nishpa said, pausing for a moment. "I'm sorry, Quinn. I'm sure it has you stressed as well. Milaro's mental condition hasn't been the best for the past few months. He's been overtaxing himself, overtaxing the Areiltháhnish protections and domain. It's one big mess. He's stretched himself too thin, and I won't let that continue. I will take my leave."

She fluttered closer to Quinn and gave her what looked like a pearl brooch. "All you need to do is touch the pearl in the middle of that and utter the following incantation: 'Contact Nishpa, codeword Quinn.'"

"'Contact Nishpa, codeword Quinn'?" Quinn repeated, her brow furrowed in confusion.

"Yes. You could also project it from your mind into the item and it'll contact me mentally. You'll be able to communicate with me. It's easier and less taxing that telepathy. Okay?"

"Okay," Quinn agreed.

But Nishpa pounded it into her head. "This way you have direct contact with me should you need something. It also gives you direct contact with Milaro because I'll be by his side, forcing the stubborn old goat to relax."

Quinn nodded slowly. "Thank you."

"I'll take my leave now."

Quinn watched her go, pushing down on the need to sigh. She liked Nishpa's company. She enjoyed her being in the Library. Having her around gave Quinn a soothing sense of calm.

Lynx broke the silence. "Are you okay?"

"Deep in thought, Lynx. Deep in thought."

At that moment, Betty fluttered in. Quinn felt like she had a revolving door. Before Betty could speak, Malakai sauntered in after her.

"Well, are we going?" he asked, excitement lighting up his eyes. He was completely kitted out. Leather travel armor that, from its aura, was full of magical defenses. His bow slung over one shoulder, and she knew the rest of his stuff would be in his storage.

"And just where are we going, Mal?" Quinn asked, her tone teasing.

He blinked. "Well, to get . . . oh, you mean location," he said, his thoughts catching up to his speech. "I didn't really think of that."

Lynx scoffed. "Of course you didn't think of it. It's because I have to do all the thinking. You're just a Darigháhnish."

"At least I'm always solid," Mal retorted.

"That's no help when you're getting shot full of electricity."

"Ouch." Mal winced. "That's too soon. That was a low blow, Lynx."

Lynx shrugged. "Hey, you didn't even take me along."

Quinn laughed. "Will you two stop it?"

Betty looked at all three of them before speaking. "I just thought you'd want to know I've gone over all the staffing problems we have. And you see, because we've just opened these two branches, we need a lot more assistance. We've had such an influx of new patrons coming in, or I guess you'd call them old patrons in a lot of ways. The reopening of branches pings overdue books, so we're already getting an influx."

"Okay," Quinn said, trying her best to steer Betty back on track. "What do we need to do?"

"We need to put out a recruitment notice. Make sure that they fulfill at least four of those sixteen affinity requirements, and then I need to train them. It'll take a while. Can we do it as soon as possible, please? That'd be the best thing for the Library right now, because everybody's working double shifts, and the days off that you promised people aren't quite fitting into the schedule." Betty shook her head for emphasis.

Quinn blinked. Betty could speak so fast that it sometimes took Quinn's brain a little while to catch up on what she'd said. "I don't see a problem with that. Is there something you needed me to do? Did I not give you the right permissions to do it?"

"No, you did. But because of the massive influx, I wanted you to understand that this isn't just going to be a small hiring where you hire like a dozen new assistants. I'll probably have to bring in at least two dozen, maybe thirty, in order to keep the rostered shifts down to size, and to make sure we have enough people should assistants need to take vacations." Betty looked up at Quinn expectantly.

Quinn glanced back down at the information she had pulled up on her HUD about the other Library branches. She pursed her lips and thought, "Maybe we should over-hire."

"What do you mean?" Betty asked, her brows furrowing in confusion.

"Exactly that. I think we should over-hire assistants, because by the looks of things, hopefully soon, we'll be opening at least one other branch, and we'll need to have more then. This way, we should be prepared for when that opens."

"Oh, marvelous." Betty clapped her tiny little hands. "That's an excellent idea. I will adjust recruitment up to around forty people. What do you think?"

Quinn nodded very slowly. "I think that'll work."

Even though that felt like a lot of people. But the Library could expand accommodations.

"This is wonderful, Librarian. Now, is there anything else you need me to do?"

"No, just keep doing what you're doing, and make sure you're taking days off."

"Of course I'm taking days off. I'm not here all the time or anything like that," Betty said, in a tone that made Quinn think she was lying.

"Okay," Quinn said. "You do that then. There's just one thing that has to happen."

"What?" Betty asked, almost on her way out.

"Make sure every single applicant is heavily screened, even if they don't seem suspect. I want us to screen their family history, too, because after the Finn incident, I really don't trust anybody or their families until I know them. Mana distribution, the magic, and everyone else—I want to keep them all safe. So screening is necessary."

I can help do that, the Library offered. *I have adjusted and tweaked our scanning properties. I will endeavor to extend it.*

"Thanks," Quinn said.

"Excellent." Betty bowed with a flourish. "That's all sorted out, then. Thank you." And she was gone.

Quinn blinked. That sprite was full of so much energy, Quinn felt tired just listening to her.

Lynx laughed. "She has that effect on people."

"Right," Quinn said, looking at him. "Anyway, what were we talking about?"

"Don't you try to get out of it."

"Get out of what?" Quinn asked, feigning innocence.

"Your affinity," Lynx said. "You still haven't worked on your new affinity, Quinn. And it is way past time."

5 3

INTERNAL REDIRECTION

Lynx was *definitely* not the best teacher.

"You just need to retrieve the memory from the time you healed Eugea," he said matter-of-factly as if it was the most obvious thing in the world.

Quinn raised an eyebrow. "But I don't remember what I did to heal Eugea." She felt like she was repeating herself.

"But you did it," Lynx said. "I get that you don't immediately remember, but it'll be in your memories somewhere, unless . . ."

Quinn held up a hand. "It's not *gone* gone. I'm just not sure how I can recall something I didn't even realize I was doing in the first place."

He sighed, frowned, and then morphed into a lynx, and began padding around the room.

Quinn watched him, fascinated. "Is that supposed to help?" she asked.

"It does, actually," Lynx said absently.

She shrugged. Aradie hopped onto her shoulder and poked her face with her beak. "You know, that actually hurts."

Aradie hooted, sounding more like a chuckle.

"Look, I'm trying." And Quinn really was. She closed her eyes, remembering traveling to Ishiposa Isle, finding Eugea, and feeling a sudden calmness and certainty wash over her as she looked at the Esposian fae.

She had known without a doubt what to do. There had been something in there that didn't belong. And so, Quinn made it disappear. Somehow, by doing that, she'd created her own new affinity. But she didn't know *how* she'd done it. No amount of wracking her brain seemed to help with that.

Aradie cooed low, sending her images.

"Exactly!" Quinn slapped her hand on the table for emphasis. "I have no idea how I did it."

Lynx morphed back into his humanoid form, blinked away, and returned seconds later, placing a book onto the desk in front of Quinn. "You need this."

She looked at him. "I need to absorb this book now?"

"Yes, you do."

Humoring him, Quinn picked the book up. It was smaller than most of the big ones she'd had, probably about the size of a mass-market paperback in Earth terms. She turned it around and read the spine: *Swebby's Path of Cognizant Deliberate Memory Management*.

"That's a very pointed name for a book." She looked at the book suspiciously. "Perhaps too pointed a name."

"There's a reason for that." Lynx seemed unperturbed. "And it's precisely what you need right now."

"Why haven't Milaro or the Library given this to me before, or Nishpa?"

"Because it's technically advanced." He shrugged. "And, before now, you probably weren't up to the contents of this specific book."

"Okay," Quinn said, "but are you really sure I'm up for it now?"

He nodded without hesitation.

She looked at it, running her hands over the smooth leather exterior.

Swebby's Path of Cognizant Deliberate Memory Management.

Energy Requirement: 1,295
Mana Requirement: 1,050

She frowned at the cost. High ranges for more advanced books. Not that it mattered. She could absorb three of them without it impacting her. It must have been woefully slow for other Librarian's to absorb all the books they needed what with their limited energy.

"I'm not trying to steer you wrong or anything," Lynx said earnestly. "This is a way you can slow down and redirect memories as you examine them. I think this specific affinity is called internal redirection. This book requires a combination of perception, inter-pretation, and projection, so it's complex. It waves all of those. If I'm understanding the way your affinities work, this should be an easy application for you."

Quinn appreciated the effort but couldn't help teasing him. "You're hinting at my needing to get this new affinity sorted, aren't you? That's why you're telling me all the different affinities this one is and requires?"

"Well, sort of," he admitted. "The breakdown is important, and how each variation of the affinity exists on its own and in conjunction with the others. It's required so that all the affinity elements relevant to the initial one are opened up and included in the system."

"Okay." Quinn thought she had the concept sorted in her head. "I got it."

"I know." He hesitated before continuing. "This is important. Because I can't help thinking that with *Seveshall's Mind Capitulation Device* still out there, I almost feel like this is exactly what we need to combat that, should somebody be using it nefariously."

Quinn raised an eyebrow. "Nefariously. It's a good word. I like it. Did you recently discover it?" she needled him.

"Stop that." Lynx sounded grumpy. "I think it just doesn't get enough love."

Quinn grinned. Sometimes, he was very much a Library mani-festation.

"Anyway," he said, "the stronger we make our arsenal, the more chance we have to withstand all this."

Quinn nodded. He was right. And absorbing the book was a great start.

"Fine." She opened the book, splayed her hands, and absorbed it.

It tunneled into her mind, visions, images, ways to delve into someone else's head, to slow down the memories, to turn them around, to examine them from every single angle. Pain shot through her head, and she gasped as the information flooded her brain. But the pain was brief and began to settle as her proclivity for mind magic came to the fore. It seemed that Areiltháhnish-distilled essence was paying dividends.

All the information coalescing in her mind made sense in a strange, slow-motion-captured video sort of way.

Her eyes flew open, and she fixated her gaze on Lynx. "You were right."

She couldn't keep the excitement out of her voice. Along with her ability to compartmentalize, she could see how this would help her dissect most any situation.

With the information now flooding her mind and making her feel as if she understood mind attacks on a whole new level, Quinn closed her eyes again and sat cross-legged on her massive chair. Aradie lifted off her shoulder so as not to weigh one side of her down. Quinn appreciated the thought.

She centered herself and analyzed her memories, and pulled out the memory of the day that they went to the Ishiposa Isle. When she recalled things, it was usually in fleeting staccato movements, but now, it was like in full 3D. As if she was outside of herself, watching herself, but able to zoom in as necessary. She could pause and remember and pull at the memory. She could focus in on things she'd only noticed in passing and had relegated to the back of her mind, elements that hadn't stood out originally.

Things like the expression on a guard's face as they looked at her. The way some of the people she'd assumed were children as they walked through the city had looked at her. The sneers, some of them aghast, some of them angry, and some of them fearful. All the way to the infirmary where Eugea had been. Quinn followed herself in, keeping an eye on everything, including the nurses who were supposed to be taking care of the victims.

Quinn paused. Something wasn't right in the building. *I might have to come and analyze that later* was her first thought. But then there was a flash just off to the corner of her perception. A sense of somebody watching them subtly. She would never have known about the spell if she hadn't examined her memory like this. The subtlety was refined. She would need Milaro or Nishpa to look at this part of her memory with her. The urge to not pay it attention made her brain tingle.

Pulling herself back from the revelation, Quinn dove into her perception of Eugea instead. Just like everybody else, Eugea radiated dejection. But unlike everyone else in the room, she hadn't yet given in. That, perhaps, was the key. It got her thinking. Quinn analyzed her own perception, turning it around. She'd observed and homed in on a sensation, almost like a very restrained wave that emanated from Eugea's mind. There was some type of disturbance there.

As Quinn examined the entire room, pausing it in place, she realized every single patient in there had that same mind disturbance. Every single victim felt like a wash of grey to her vision, except Eugea, because she had not yet given in.

Quinn pulled the emanating wave around, turned it upside down and around, looking at it from all different perspectives as she gazed into Eugea's mind.

She used several of the techniques Milaro had taught her and was gentle. Even though she'd initially been unaware of it, Quinn realized she'd asked permission with a soft and questioning touch. Eugea had been so relieved to feel somebody helping her—she'd reached out.

Quinn twisted the view around, double-checking it, and realized that there had been a dimensional separation of a thought loop in Eugea's mind.

That was the best description she could think of. It was as if they'd harnessed the task of processing thought, action, and ability separately from the actual brain. This left the victims helpless to fully operate their own bodies, stuck in this strange rigor of repeated memories and actions, as if they were reliving an artificial lie over and over again.

Quinn shuddered. The images were inserted over actual memories, making it a complex horror loop that had never happened, but was inserted so seamlessly into previous memories that it seemed as if it did.

That was a type of hell she wouldn't consign her worst enemy to, not even Kajaro.

This didn't have the same feel as the mind bomb from her own mind. She didn't think this was Kajaro's work. She paused, walking around the sensation and the feeling, sorting through Eugea's mind as she had seen it.

She'd found loops and holes and watched herself unclip it in fascination.

Quinn rewound that portion of the memory a little, trying to get a better handle on it.

It was more than that.

It was as if Quinn was undoing what had been done, reversing what was there, unstitching it, even. She began to break it down more, being careful to note everything in detail. *Mental chaotic fortitude abolition* wasn't anything like Quinn assumed. It wasn't just a healing spell. She technically hadn't healed Eugea at all. She'd created an affinity that could identify intrusion and coercion into somebody's mind space and undo it.

As if her abilities took all the frustration she'd had with the mind bomb and her, then still limited understanding of how the mind worked, and given her a more efficient alternative.

It was like picking a stitch with a seam ripper and watching it unravel easily because somebody was pulling on either side of the fabric. She was fairly certain that once she got help from Nishpa and Milaro, she'd be able to create offshoots that could technically protect somebody, undo such an intrusion, and fire abilities back. It led Quinn to examine what she'd done even closer, the stitches that held it together, the way the mind rebelled against them, wanting perhaps control over its own destiny.

She turned the ability around in her mind, or in the hands of her mind, over and over again, double-checking, retracing steps, and making sure she was doing what she'd intended to do. In that moment, all Quinn had known was that she had to stop the obvious pain Eugea was in. And somehow, with all the books she'd absorbed, she'd recognized the need to undo what had been done.

To undo what was wrong.

The key happened to be that Eugea wanted it. She'd begged for it. She had been willing to sacrifice everything to be free of the loop her subconscious knew wasn't real on some level.

Otherwise, Quinn couldn't have entered. To undo the damage in the minds of the other victims, Quinn needed them to *want* to be free. That was part, the only part that allowed her access into the mind to begin it in the first place.

Perhaps they could work around that, she wondered, making notes, scribbling furiously as she brought herself out of the trance.

"You're doing pretty well there," Lynx said, his voice sounding somewhat distant.

Quinn nodded, still distracted by her thoughts. "I think—" She blinked as she came fully out of it, realizing belatedly that she had been scribbling notes the whole time. There were pages and pages.

"I placed a new page under you every time you filled one." Lynx spoke softly, and there was a hint of pride in his words.

She smiled up at him. "Thanks, Lynx."

He looked away, but a smile crossed his face. "Anyway, do you feel like you made progress?"

"Some. I understand the affinity now. *Mental chaotic fortitude abolition* is more about learning to identify and undo coercion and intrusion into somebody's mind than it is about healing a person of mind damage made through magic."

"Hm," He pondered that for a second. "I guess you did sort of unmake it. Kind of."

Quinn nodded, still engrossed by the ultimate problem with it. "It didn't take away all the damage, but I wonder if I could refine it to reach that level where it would just take away everything that it caused in the first place. Like memories, painful experiences . . . completely wipe all the damage done or at least fade it into the background. Now that, that would be much more helpful, I think."

Lynx smiled at her.

"What?" she said.

"You're really settling into that Librarian vibe, Quinn."

5 4

NEFARIOUS WAS A GOOD WORD

Quinn hadn't expected the process of learning about her affinity—or being able to dissect how she had used the new affinity—to be so damn enjoyable. Engrossing. She found herself digging deep and trying to understand exactly how using the technique from Swebby's book began to make things easier.

It allowed her to analyze not only the new affinity she'd created but also the previous affinities she'd already studied, absorbed, and utilized. There were several she didn't use on a regular basis, especially the initial fighting ones, like the machete book. However, they were still activated and available for her to study. Which allowed her to get a broader spectrum of comparison.

All of it gave her a wider knowledge base to pull from.

She could zoom in on the affinity and understand just how it worked. It helped her understand how they were triggered and in which ways they intermeshed with or even against each other. When the system notified her about the new affinity, she simply thought, *Oh, I guess I figured out a way to wield the magic differently*. But upon further in-depth analysis, she realized that wasn't how it worked. It really wasn't just that simple. Affinities needed triggers, needed knowledge, and an actionable event or problem to direct it toward.

Someone could accidentally, perhaps, trigger fire, but only if they had the creation aspect. If they had the control aspect, and there was a fire lit somewhere close, they could potentially blow that up or reduce it until it was mere smoke. But if they couldn't create fire from scratch in the first place, then they weren't *as* big a threat to other people.

With all of the affinities in her blood, she didn't think she'd be able to learn something about every single one of them in her lifetime. Perhaps she was still thinking in human years. She was aware, albeit in the back of her mind, that she could potentially live a very long time.

As long as nothing went super wrong.

But, for instance, she couldn't ever see herself needing one of her harvesting affinities. Not that agriculture wasn't important, and there *was* a whole branch of horticulture she still needed to open. But what was she going to do? Plant fields instead of tending to the Library?

Go fishing, even! Perhaps she'd consider that at some stage. Maybe she'd take Bell and Aradie with her.

Bell was curled up at her feet, which, while very dog-like, sort of felt weird for a dog-ear. She looked like somebody had crumpled paper into a ball and thrown it away. But the dog-ear was, in fact, sort of a dog, right? Quinn still hadn't figured out the magical aspect of that, but she genuinely enjoyed the little creature's company. She didn't look into it too deeply.

Anyway, maybe one day they'd go on a vacation to a fishing cabin or even a beach.

Before she could contemplate a life of Librarian leisure, she had to understand her own powers in more detail, so they stopped taking her by surprise and just doing things. It would be much more beneficial if she could direct it to do things.

For example, knowing her ice powers in more detail would benefit her. She had multiple variations of it. Ice creation, ice unmaking, which . . . she frowned. Didn't that need a better name? Ice melting, perhaps. And then there was freezing projectiles, snow. So many affinity offshoots.

She understood how those all worked together. It allowed her, because she had all of them, to be able to manipulate ice in all ways. She could even melt it with fire, turn it into water, and use the result of that. There were so many options with so many affinities it was mind-boggling.

The gravity affinity was a great example. The powers she'd used so far were based around mainly activating the gravimetric pull. But there were multiple variations of the affinity and she'd only been accessing manipulation, force, and hold when she utilized those abilities. Just like when she made the miasma drones crash down while they'd repaired that initial pillar.

Speaking of pillars, Quinn looked up from where she was still engrossed in her own research. Lynx sat on the couch. From his eyes, he appeared to be doing something with the system. It made her feel better that he wasn't just waiting around for her.

She cleared her throat to grab his attention. "Hey, don't we need to activate another pillar soon?"

"Mm-hmm," Lynx said, "Probably sooner rather than later. I'll double-check the levels for you."

Quinn nodded and went back to her research. The ability gained from the *Internal Redirection* book accessed and combined several affinities all at once. It'd taken from her ability to mind read and her healing perception. She needed to be able to use those abilities so that the internal redirection was capable of activating.

That should mean that not many people could use the book she'd just learned, which made sense because it was an advanced technique book. The internal redirection worked as long as she had permission to intrude on the minds. It might help her understand others' abilities and allow her to recreate results.

A power like this could be inherently dangerous in someone with a grey moral code. After encountering Kajaro, she could understand how someone could turn this specific skill to nefarious means. There she went, using the word Lynx had popped into her head.

Nefarious was a good word.

Even so, because of the combination of different affinities and different partitions of affinities she had to be able to access to make it work for her, it meant relatively few people would have the affinity combination to even read or absorb this book. Which must be the case for a lot of the more advanced tomes in the Library.

That's when she remembered that she was the only one who could absorb the information. That was a Librarian thing. Although, it'd make sense that assistants could absorb some knowledge. She was willing to bet the books helped them at least read faster. They also needed to process that information.

Pity.

Otherwise, she'd be a super overpowered, untouchable Librarian already.

And that would just be silly.

She chuckled to herself, shaking her head. This wasn't an anime after all.

The information she could take in and process now that she better understood the way affinities worked was astounding. The IR book, as she now called it, gave her time and space to analyze everything about the affinities which had been lacking before. Combining it with her skill at speeding up her own cognitive processing, and it was a game changer for her.

She stretched and moved a little, inciting a yip from Bell and a raised eyebrow from Lynx.

"You okay?" he asked.

"It's a lot of information." Her head felt a little foggy.

Lynx shrugged. "Well, you only absorbed it a few hours ago, and you haven't slept."

"There's too much to do to have a nap because I absorbed a book in the middle of the day and not nighttime." Quinn pouted. "I want to see my aunt and you won't let me, so I'm trying to understand this new affinity."

"Aha!" Lynx said. "I got you."

"No, you didn't get me. I just realized."

"Realized what?" Lynx teased.

"Fine," she said. "I just realized you were right."

"I knew it," Lynx said, a smug grin on his face. "I was right."

"Oh, stop gloating," she said. "You know you're right. You know a lot more about this than I do, and I'm still learning. I do have the grace to admit when I might not have been quite right."

"You mean wrong," Lynx said.

"Yes," Quinn said begrudgingly, "when I might be wrong. Sometimes you can be insufferable."

"I know," Lynx said. "That's one of my charms."

"I don't think the word 'charm' means what you think it means." Quinn shot him a half glare.

"Well, for the sake of everything," Lynx said, a little smugly, "it means what I want it to mean."

Quinn laughed until a beep sounded through the room, and she looked up. "What was that?"

Lynx shrugged, and it beeped again. "Oh," he said. "You asked about the pillar. I adjusted the system for an inquiry, and now we should probably go and activate it."

"Can't I just pull it up from the HUD here?"

"I mean, yes, you can. It's not like we need to go into the Library to do that." He sounded vaguely disappointed.

"I know. What, you miss being in the Library?" she asked.

"You've been spending an inordinate amount of time here in your office," Lynx said, just this side of a pout.

Quinn blinked at him. "Well, yes, it's more comfortable to sit in this chair than to wander around the Library check-in desk, that's all."

"Fine," he said. "I get it."

"Do you really?" She shrugged. She didn't feel like it was a big deal. "It's not like you get uncomfortable, right? Aren't you a kind of hologram?"

He let out a long, suffering sigh. "I'm not a hologram. I'm a manifestation. We've been over this before."

Quinn grinned at him, and finally it seemed to dawn on Lynx that she'd been making fun of him. "Oh, will you just do it already?" he said.

She'd activated enough pillars that it was pretty much second nature for her to do so. She brought up the interface, activated another pillar, and frowned as she did so because there were only two more to activate before they had to come up with a solution.

While she knew they could limp along without the tenth, Ashiron, for a while, she also knew they'd eventually need it back at full power.

All they had to do was figure out the dimensional shift and how to dispose of the bomb without blowing up everything around it. Shouldn't be too hard.

Quinn sighed as she closed the HUD.

"What's the matter?" Lynx said.

"I feel like we're not making as much progress as I'd like to make."

He watched her for a few seconds and sounded serious when he spoke. "I promise soon you'll be able to go meet your aunt. I just have several more things that we need to do before that can happen."

"Like locating her."

He nodded.

Quinn suddenly felt a little melancholy. She knew without a shadow of a doubt they'd have to use protective gear for this next trip. Armor, provisions, whatever. But Misha usually took care of that, and now Misha was, well, out of commission. "I . . . do you think it would be okay to go and visit Harish and see how Misha's progress is coming along?"

Lynx raised an eyebrow. "Why wouldn't it? It's your Library."

"Well, to be fair, it's like everyone everywhere's Library."

"Touché," Lynx said. "Come on, let's go. He's in the observation room, just like, you know, when he was watching over us."

Quinn nodded slowly. It took them approximately seventy seconds to get there. Except when Quinn stepped inside, just like everything else in the Library all the time, things had changed. She glanced around. There was still the center console that held the sort of holographic informational display. Harish was off at a side console, his head bowed over one of the screen projections. There was a pod just beyond the center console area, near where the windows used to look out over the Library's core. The windows were gone now. She wondered if that had been a specific Library request.

Yes, it was, the Library said in her head. *The original viewing area was for that one specific reason. Now it's no longer needed. I value my privacy.*

I get it. Quinn chuckled. She should have known the Library would understand what she was thinking, even without the ability to read her mind.

The pod reminded her of one of those sensory deprivation tanks, or something like that. She swore she'd seen it on the internet back on Earth. However, it wasn't quite the same. The lid was clear and filled with an almost gelatinous sort of liquid, and a vaguely humanoid body shape lay inside of it.

"What's that?" she asked.

But it wasn't Lynx who answered. It was Harish. "It's an incubation pod for golems."

"Is that what's usually used to create them?" Quinn asked.

"In a way." He sounded contemplative. Like he wasn't sure he was expressing it correctly. "This one I have modified so that, well, hopefully, we won't have any outside influence creeping into the core that I am reconstituting with what I hope is just Misha's consciousness."

Quinn nodded, sort of understanding what he meant. "The extraction went okay?" she asked hesitantly.

Harish grimaced. "I would not go so far as to say it went smoothly. There will be bumps. I do not believe Misha will be precisely the same. But I attempted to retain most of the memories they developed during this time by separating their intertwined sections. I haven't done this before," he said, by way of explanation. "This is purely experimental, and as Misha has helped all of us, I wanted to try to preserve them. I'm truly doing my best."

Quinn offered the somewhat concerned elf a smile. "I know, and I really appreciate it."

"Well, it will take at least a few more days, maybe a week or so."

Quinn nodded slowly. "Can I watch them for a little?"

"Of course. You're always welcome, Librarian," Harish said, and went back to some of the monitors he had been preoccupied with when they walked in.

Quinn looked down at the remains, at the beginnings of the new Misha, whatever it was, and felt the melancholy twist in her gut again.

"Quinn." She turned to see Malakai rushing into the room. He wasn't breathless. He rarely got breathless. "You're needed in the hospital."

She raised an eyebrow.

"The real Irias has woken up."

5 5

HAZY AND VAGUE

Quinn didn't need Malakai to tell her twice. "Thank you, Harish. Bye."

She took one more glance over her shoulder at where Misha's, perhaps eventual, body was soaking in goop and walked out of the room. It was highly disturbing having seen Misha like that, so this was a welcome distraction. They made their way to the hospital wing.

"You doing okay there?" Malakai asked, nudging her like he always did.

"I'll live."

"Really? That dire?"

Quinn thought about it, but it wasn't even that. It was something she couldn't quite put her finger on. "No, not that dire, just . . ."

"Have you been texting home?"

The question caught her off guard, and she shrugged. "Every now and again."

"Do you still miss it?"

"Of course I miss it." And having to answer that question made her realize that she did miss it. "I just didn't have much keeping me there, anyway."

"You miss Hallie, don't you?" Malakai sounded a little smug, like he knew everything.

"Not—maybe a bit." She squinted over at him. "I always thought she was annoying, but I sort of . . . I guess I got used to her."

"Funny that," Mal said. "I've gotten used to this really annoying Librarian that came and invaded my universe."

Quinn punched him lightly on the upper arm. "Ha, ha, very funny."

"You really had to reach to punch me that high, didn't you?"

"Shut up," Quinn said.

He reached forward and held the door for her, mock bowing as he waved her through.

"You know, you don't need to do that," Quinn said, but thanked him.

He smiled, and they walked, leading the way.

She wasn't the biggest fan of hospitals. What with all the white and death. Chatting as they walked distracted her from her surroundings. "You know your way around."

"Yeah, because I keep having to come and get checkups, remember?" He did a broad sweeping gesture of himself. "Super injured, really bad, still have several days that I can't use mana."

"Oh yeah, that's right," Quinn said, giving him a wink. "I'd almost forgotten. I wonder why."

"Hey, be nice. It wasn't forgettable."

"True," she said, putting him out of his misery. "It was kind of heroic."

"Now you can shut up," Malakai said, as he pushed open another door and ushered her through. The room was large, maybe fifteen by twenty feet. There was a big window and somehow a cloudy blue sky outside.

Quinn did a double take. "What the . . ."

"Don't ask, it's a Library thing," Mal said softly, gesturing for her to walk over to the bed where Irias lay with her pale wooded skin and the strange red veins that ran through her. Her mother Karella sat off to the side, her eyes sort of vacant, as if she wasn't quite there. Not that Quinn could blame her. She'd lost her husband and almost lost her daughter and couldn't remember anything that really happened. That sort of stuff? That was nasty.

I thought you said she was awake? Quinn let her inner voice tap on his awareness so that she could speak mind to mind to him.

Well, she kind of was, but she seems to not be now, Malakai said.

Quinn sighed and Karella's eyes slowly focused on her.

"Oh, Librarian," she said, "the doctor should be back shortly. She's sleeping again." Karella sounded very distant, not fully present in the moment. Quinn worried about her.

"How are you doing?" Quinn asked and really wished she hadn't. There was a pain that flitted through the Salosier's eyes as if somebody had wrenched out her heart through her nostrils. Very uncomfortable and extremely sad.

"I have my daughter," she said, a small smile on her lips that faded almost as quickly as it appeared. "I will persevere."

Suddenly there were footsteps out in the hall and then in the room. Quinn had never been so happy to see a doctor before in her life.

"Ah," Dr. Miles said, "she seems to be stirring again. I had left her to double-check something with Dr. Vivit, but he is currently in surgery and will not be joining us."

"Does Irias need surgery?" Quinn asked, somewhat surprised.

"Oh no." Miles looked confused for a second. "The doctor is performing surgery and thus cannot be here."

Quinn felt slightly silly for having misinterpreted it. She glanced over at where Irias was indeed waking up. She looked brittle, like a strong wind might break her in half. Her pale, barked skin was even lighter than usual and it made the red veins stark by comparison. Karella looked around, blinking, but when her eyes fell on her daughter again and a small smile tugged at her lips as if she was remembering something. It didn't last for long, and pain crossed her face, along with some elements of horror that Quinn hadn't ever really noticed before.

A chill went up Quinn's spine. She wouldn't have wished the way they found them on anyone. Pits full of bodies, dying and dead, desecrated, desiccated. Worse than any horror movie she'd seen.

"She's still waking up," Dr. Miles said. "We have her on some strong sedative medication. It's a little bit more complex than that when it comes to Salosier anatomy."

"I know," Quinn said. "I remember reading that."

"Excellent," Dr. Miles said. "Then you'll understand that her ability to process what has occurred to her will take time. Right now she still can't access all of her memories, which we need to help with the Bardocian root investigation. To see if she knew any of her attackers, or their intentions, or perhaps future plans."

"Was this a recent thing? Did they do this after I was summoned?" Quinn asked, because even though she knew it began a long time ago, she was worried they'd stepped it up a notch when she became Librarian. Did they fast track whatever plan it was and suck them all dry? No matter what she tried, there was still that part of her that thought, just on the offside chance that there might be.

"No," Dr. Miles said very firmly. "This started hundreds of years ago."

Relief rushed through her. She still didn't get the motivation. "But why? I don't understand."

Malakai shrugged. "As good as I could guess," he said, "I'm not sure. This doesn't really feel like the same stuff Kajaro and Drav have pulled in my opinion. Maybe as a contingency plan? Sort of? If the Library did fall, a unified Salosier front might have helped. And so this, this makes sort of sense. But it doesn't seem to fit in with the rest of their agenda."

"Unified Salosier front?" Escadril had been formidable, but Quinn didn't think most Salosiers were particularly dangerous in a fighting manner, even if they could book doctor you under the table.

"Not quite how I meant it to come across." Malakai paused for several seconds before attempting it again. "The Salosier ability to form and reform books, especially magical ones, could potentially help pass along at least a portion of magic from the books."

Karella interrupted. "I believe he's trying to say that at the cost of our lifeforce, that spreads in the roots and mana pools of our homes, we could have mass produced tomes and spread knowledge and sought to continue the filtration aspects of the Library until a solution could be found. A very outside chance . . . a pipe dream."

Quinn watched how Karella's expression didn't change, and her monotone clung slightly off tone. Then she mulled over what Karella had said. So the Salosier could make magic books without and establish a type of filtering, but at a very high cost. With specific reference to themselves and the vines.

The vines the Bardocian root had destroyed.

It sort of made sense, but neither Mal nor Karella seemed to think it likely. "Does Irias remember anything?" she asked softly, glancing over at the Salosier who was desperately clinging to her mother's hands.

Red tears, sort of like deep orange, thicker like sap, ran down Karella's face. Not that Quinn could blame her. She'd lost so much.

"Anyway, Librarian," Dr. Miles said, grabbing her attention.

"Sorry," Quinn said, "Go on."

"We initially thought the Bardocian root came from old Petraligno stock." He spoke in a hushed tone. "While it is an extremely close match, we have come to believe it's actually one of the sister branches of it."

"What do you mean, sister branch?"

"There are offshoots of both the Salosier and the Petralignos, and we believe that this actually belongs to . . . it is difficult to describe." Miles paused, as if trying to dredge up the information in a palatable way.

"I can do it," Karella interrupted softly. "I'll explain it."

Quinn turned to the Balisor matriarch, giving her full attention.

"The offshoot Dr. Miles suggests," Karella said. "The offshoot is not only a parasite that sucks the lifeforce from us and infests us, but it also transfers the power it gains to another source. It allows more flexibility in some species, too—especially if the base is distilled while root awareness is maintained. It can . . . control the musculature and nerve systems of a body if injected."

Quinn nodded slowly, taking it all in. "What about the Mamoria?"

Karella paused. "The root will have . . . helped them morph, so to speak? It's a very delicate distilling process. I wouldn't have thought anyone still knew it. I am unsure of why the Mamoria would have taken part in such a plan. The root doesn't allow them to shape change so much as disguise themselves within that shape. Kind of like they're camouflaging their appearance to something you're expecting to see."

"Is that what the fake Irias did?" Quinn asked, suddenly needing clarification.

"Perhaps." The word splintered as she spoke, cracking half way through and making it a two syllable one.

Dr. Miles was frowning. "We'll look into the Mamoria's autopsy."

An idea struck Quinn. "While she was Irias, she definitely had contact with the root from below."

Dr. Miles frowned more deeply, and his eyes flickered.

"Oh . . . I," a voice said. The voice was so mouse-like, not like the fake Irias had spoken at all. Quinn almost didn't hear her. Everyone swiveled to look at her.

"I think I remember a name," she said, speaking slowly. Her voice was a little croaky. "Or I did remember it. I have to, I think I just need time to try to remember," she finished.

"Take your time. I'm so sorry." And then Quinn turned to Karella, realizing she probably should have said this sooner. "I am so, so sorry for your loss."

Karella's face fell a bit. Quinn could see the pain so raw, recent, and obvious in her features. The matriarch didn't try to hide it. She wore it like a badge of honor. Like a badge of future revenge, to be honest. Not that Quinn could blame her. If something happened to Malakai, or Lynx, or Milaro, or even Erik or Geneva, and especially Dottie or Nishpa. Quinn could list them all. Yeah, Quinn would probably go nuclear on people. And even with the power she had now, that'd be formidable.

Karella gave her a very sad smile. "You know, I really thought he might have been hidden, like my daughter. Maybe he was just somebody they'd disguised themselves as, like they did with Irias. But that wasn't the case. I really wish they'd have just let the parasite take him over as well."

"Wait," Quinn said, trying to get her to understand. "What do you mean, a parasite took him over?"

"I'm so sorry. Unless injected as previously mentioned, the root of this variation and its parasite take over and do damage until they're integral and inseparable. I was lucky. Another couple of months and I think I'd have been done for too."

Quinn turned to the doctor. "You removed parasites?"

"Yes, a lot of them." He blinked as if it was common knowledge.

Karella, looking between both of them, piped up again. "It's basically how the Petralignos' sister branch functions."

"Who are?" Quinn was very proud of not having lost her patience yet.

"Oh." Karella smiled sheepishly. "Sorry. The Malusigno. Frankly, there aren't that many of them left, but they operate with Bardocian root because it feeds the parasites they're attuned to. Well, helps their magic, anyway. They don't access mana and energy the way we do. Their power comes directly from the parasites they command, and it feeds through the Bardocian root back to their power base. This variant the Mamoria used comes from that."

Quinn blinked. "You're telling me that people very similar to the Salosiers and the Petralignos called the Malusignos are run by a parasitic species they are sort of in collaboration with and those parasites link to but do not control that species?"

Karella nodded. "I was very lucky. The parasites take a long time to acclimate to their new hosts. In this case, however, they appear to have been draining them. And my husband"—her voice cracked, and it took her a few seconds to continue—"sadly, was one of them. His real body was the one you saw. He was taken over completely some time ago."

Dr. Miles interjected by clearing his throat. "And the Mamoria apparently adapted this version of controlling parasite to bend its morphing capabilities for whatever purposes."

Quinn didn't know what to say. And she was saved by Irias speaking up.

"Oh, I remember her name now," Irias said.

"Whose name?" Malakai asked, his tone soothing.

"The lady in charge." She perked up, her tone almost excited. "She checked on the state of feeding several times that I remember. Although it's hazy and vague, it happened enough that I'm certain it's not a figment of my imagination."

"Checked on the feeding?" Quinn asked, unable to stop herself.

Irias blinked. "They had to make sure we wouldn't try to disconnect the feed. The roots were hungry. All the time. They needed constant fuel."

Quinn shuddered.

Karella spoke softly, as if she was trying not to startle her daughter. "What was her name, sweetheart?"

"Oh, sorry." Irias blinked and refocused. "Her name was Sarila. At least that's what the attendants called her."

5 6

REMEMBERING TO REINFORCE

Milaro leaned forward at his desk, elbows resting on its surface, his head cradled in his hands. He knew as well as anyone that pushing oneself too far when energy was lacking was a bad idea. Over the last few centuries, he'd grown complacent. Without the Library, he'd become entrenched in his own territory, unaccustomed to expending much energy.

Then the Library returned, and he had spent more energy in the last six months than he had in the past couple of centuries.

Age might be catching up to him. That was a sobering thought. He sighed.

"What on earth are you sighing about?"

Nishpa's voice cut across his melancholy thoughts with a crisp clarity that made him wince. Yet he appreciated her presence. She wasn't always there, but when she was, it was a comforting reminder that he wasn't alone in the universe.

"You're feeling sorry for yourself again, aren't you," she said, flitting close enough to his head that he could practically feel the air from her wings beating.

"I am definitely feeling my age this morning," he said, leaning back in his chair and eyeing his old friend.

"Really?" She raised a perfectly manicured eyebrow. "That's a *lot* of years to feel."

"It is rather, isn't it?" he admitted ruefully. "Anyway, I have work to do. What did you want?"

She crossed her arms, still hovering in the air above his desk, and glared at him. It was one of those pointed glares that took three seconds to wear him down.

He gave in. "Fine. What can I help you with?"

"Oh, Milaro. As usual, it's not you who can help me, but me who can help you."

He would have asked her to clarify, but she'd known him for several millennia and he knew she wasn't going to clarify anything. "Okay. Why are you here, then?"

"I'm here because you've been pushing yourself too far. Again. As usual. The Areiltháhnish defenses are solid enough right now, but you have several sections over here." She projected an image for him to look at, indicating one of the quadrants and a planet very close to his own. "This one has several holes in it. You know you could easily bring in your nephews, your grandchildren, and your son and make them a part of this web. You understand that, right?"

"Look, I know it's possible, but I just don't . . ."

"What? And you die tomorrow, accidentally slipping on a banana peel down some marble stairs and break your neck because you're tired and didn't pay attention? Then you expect somebody to be able to pick up the tattered remnants of your defenses?" She wasn't pulling punches.

Milaro winced. "When you put it like that."

"Exactly," Nishpa said. "When I put it like that, I am completely and utterly correct, and you know I am."

"I guess I can't expect you to put it any differently." Milaro groaned.

"Look, I just know, Milaro, you are the King of the Areiltháhnish. You have a responsibility to your people. You have a responsibility to all the clans that belong to your people and the fact that you've let the defenses get this bad . . ."

"Hey, they're not that bad." But it sounded lame even to his ears.

"Well, they're not that bad *yet,* but they're on the verge and you've been too preoccupied and too busy to realize and keep them properly reinforced." She sighed. "Frankly, you've overextended yourself."

"I get it. I agree. What do you recommend?" He hoped she had some idea, because right then his thoughts were still focused on getting Malakai healed and prepared for everything that was to come. Not to mention getting the Library back online and realizing that should the Library fail and this Sölem's plan work, then the Library wasn't the only target. Everything they knew, the entire Areiltháhnish conglomeration, all the Furionas fae, the other fae creatures, every single Empire, every single solar system that wasn't in this alliance of Sölem, they would all be the new targets.

When chaos reunited itself, when it became the hungry void it had once been, there was no doubt the first people on its menu would be those who'd helped maintain the universe. When chaos ran out of things to eat, it would start creating again and then devouring again and creating again and devouring again. It was a never-ending cycle of creation and destruction. They couldn't let that happen.

As long as chaos was tempered with filtration, it could always be a part of creation by way of the magic it infused.

Milaro sighed. "I have been derelict in my duties. I agree. Just help me."

"I thought you'd never ask." Nishpa flashed him a smug grin. "Though I am grateful to see you've spent this time sleeping and recovering most of your power well, I can still sense your exhaustion. Time to dive into that spiderweb of protection of yours and see how much we can salvage, and how much has to be spun anew."

"Fine. Let's refine the stitching, shall we?" He chuckled.

Relaxing into the plane that allowed Milaro to access the vast security net was easy enough. The images, and complex weavings flooded his entire mind. His HUD was far more complex by design than anything most people would witness in a lifetime. It extended out beyond him, beyond the palace, to the edges of his world, and the region the Areiltháhnish were responsible for. All the extended family and any refugees they'd taken in.

But Milaro started with his world first, making sure every single netting line aligned with each other. There were no knots, nothing stuck, no danger pinged from any area. It took a while to cover his world, but it worked. There were a few nicks in it, a few lines that had bumped against each other, but overall, they were perfectly parallel. A strong, supple spiderweb of defense. Milaro leaned back, admiring his handiwork as it projected before him in the HUD. He frowned and traced it, but no, it was covered perfectly. There was no way anything that meant them danger, or that they didn't know or understand, could get past the defenses to him.

Which left the rest of the region.

Milaro reached out to every other world and repeated the process. He could feel Nishpa at his side, sustaining his channeling of power, feeding him bits of her own. Several of his charges had messed-up webs with what he considered gaping holes. Well, holes in his nets probably weren't considered holes in many others, but for Milaro, who strove for security perfection, it was far from good enough. He frowned as a wave of unease passed through him.

Scanning himself, he noticed nothing amiss, but kept it in mind, and began tweaking the rest of the web. It took more time than he liked, and he ate food brought to him while still focused on his task. He dove into the weave himself, making sure all the perfect spider-webbing matched up. When he was done, he sat back, examining the net that protected his entire domain that he'd just reinforced.

He nodded to himself, happy with the reinforcements, and chastised himself for leaving it for so long. Perhaps his friend was right. He needed to bring in his younger family members sooner than later. Perhaps give them different parts of the region to be responsible for. It was a lot for one person. Not that he'd admit that out loud.

Yet.

"There," Nishpa said, "don't you feel much better about this?"

He raised an eyebrow and realized his eyes were bleary. "I feel more secure."

"And so you should. That just took you the better part of a day."

He blinked at her. He hadn't realized quite how long he'd been lost in web repairs. Nishpa had arrived first thing in the morning. Now that he thought about it, if she'd come from the Library, that meant she hadn't slept for . . .

"Wait, you can't admonish me for not resting when you haven't slept all night," he said. She crossed her arms again and glared pointedly at him. He winced. He hadn't forgotten that she was fully capable of operating on no sleep for days at a time, but that didn't mean it was healthy for her. Even though she'd promised his wife she'd take care of him, didn't mean Nishpa should be neglecting herself. He'd never hear the end of it.

"You realize you're supposed to be resting," Nishpa said.

"Well, I—"

"Stop changing the subject." She sighed. "Look, I had mostly easy work to do in the hospital."

"Just needed to get away?" he asked, reluctantly reaching out to tap into his reserves. He'd been away so much lately that they were full. A refreshing sensation passed through him as the power well eagerly topped him off.

"Some of the things they went through, what they experienced before that nasty variation of the root practically sucked them dry"— Nishpa shook her head and a slight shiver passed through her small frame—"that was heavy stuff. Not necessarily something I can't deal with. I mean, I deal in mind magic and healing."

"But Nishpa," he said very gently, reaching out a hand to tap her lightly on the shoulder. Furionas weren't tiny like sprites, but two and a half feet was small enough when compared to his seven feet of height. "You know you don't have to be brave just because of me."

"One of us has to be brave," she said, and flashed him a smirk.

He laughed. "Touché, I deserved that. I'm just concerned."

She smiled. "You know, I'm grateful you're worried about me. It means a lot. But I can deal with these things myself. I don't need to add to your burden. Not now. When everything's over. When it's all back to normal. Don't you worry, I'll come and grab a cup of tea. We'll sit in this office and I'll complain to my heart's content."

Milaro laughed. It felt good to let some of the energy he'd been bottling up float away. He smiled at his friend. "I'll hold to that. We can even make a picnic of it and whine about things together."

She laughed. "Excellent. But we won't make it that far if you don't start taking better care of yourself and of your domain."

Milaro felt lighter than he had for months. It wasn't that he didn't enjoy his time in the Library, but he did admit to it being a drain, especially with basically having to start from scratch. Being back in his own palace for the last few days had helped. He'd gotten more sleep. He was reinforcing the protections. His own mind even felt rejuvenated.

"You know," Nishpa said, "you're not taking as good care of yourself as you should be."

"I know. But I'll change. I need to."

"You pretty much have to," she said and floating up, tapping him on the forehead. "Let me look."

He sighed and allowed her to place her delicate fingers against the temple on the left-hand side of his head. She frowned, and he closed his eyes. He could feel the sensations as she dove around in his mind, something very familiar considering the amount of time they'd known each other and the amount of times her mind healing had assisted him. Maybe he needed to stop relying on her so much. He enjoyed having a few select people around him that he could rely on, like Siliqua, Harish, Nishpa, Cadre to a certain extent. And then there was Carafax and Quinn. Lynx, definitely, now that he was regaining his memories.

Milaro realized he had a stronger support circle than he'd thought.

"Stop letting your thoughts wander," Nishpa snapped. "Focus with me. We're trying to heal you up."

"I know. I know." He chuckled and focused inwardly again.

She surveyed the barriers of his mind, the joints, areas that were previously damaged and that she'd helped him fix not too long ago. She pulled back. "You can open your eyes now."

"Well?" he asked.

"You're actually in excellent shape in there now." She nodded approvingly. "You've been doing your exercises, remembering to reinforce periodically instead of all at once."

"Yes, yes."

"You haven't been overextending yourself."

Milaro smiled easily at that. "Quinn has an excellent hold on her abilities now. It's become a lot easier to train her."

"Good, because she'll need your guidance again sooner rather than later."

He grinned this time. "You know, she's like the granddaughter I never had."

"You've got like twelve granddaughters. What are you talking about?" Nishpa cocked her head to one side.

"It's the principle of the thing," Milaro said. "She's the granddaughter I didn't know I needed. Is that better?"

"Much better."

There was a knock at the door, interrupting their friendly banter. Milaro called out, resigned to the fact that most of his time wasn't his own. "Who is it?"

Siliqua entered the room, followed by Sarila. Milaro raised an eyebrow and rose from where he'd been sitting to come around the front side of the desk. He'd never had much to do with Escadril's second wife. She'd never fit in as well as his first wife had.

"Sarila." He couldn't keep the confusion out of his voice. She shouldn't be here, not when she was taking care of Escadril. "What brings you here? I wasn't expecting you. Is everything okay? Are you doing okay?"

She looked up at him, her eyes flickering a strange emerald green with a smoky black outline. Different than usual. Her birch-tree-like bark-skin seemed even paler than usual. Milaro frowned.

"Are you okay?" he asked again. That same sensation he'd had briefly while repairing the security webs swept over him like a brief afternoon breeze. He pushed his defenses up, solidifying them, strengthening them. It only took a glance at Nishpa to know that she had the same gut feeling. He extended his domain to include Siliqua.

"Is everything okay?" Nishpa asked gently.

"Everything is sad," Sarila said, her voice cracking. It was as if she chose her words carefully. "It's just . . ."

Milaro backed up to his table, wishing he'd just stayed behind it to start with. Something in the surrounding air pushed against the defenses, while not quite sparking them. It still hinted at alarm. He looked closer at Sarila, watching her. "Just what?"

"It's Escadril," she said. "Escadril is dead."

OUTSTRETCHED ARMS

ESCADRIL IS DEAD WAS PROBABLY THE LAST THING MILARO EXPECTED Sarila to say. He kept his eyes locked on her, schooling his face. Despite her words, something still felt off.

"He's dead?" he asked, keeping his tone as even as possible.

"Yes," she said, a slight hitch in her voice, "he's gone."

She almost sounded like she was asking a question, and Milaro was taken aback. That was unexpected. Escadril should have lived for another decade or two. He was just rotting in place. It might have been eating away at him since his life force was so low, but still . . . he should have had years left in him, not weeks.

Nishpa seemed most distraught. Probably because she'd been one of the primary initial healers attending him. "What happened? How did it worsen? Was it something else we overlooked?"

Sarila's eyes clouded over even more, and she sighed, looking from Nishpa to Milaro. "He died, all right. I'm not exactly proud of it."

But her tone indicated otherwise.

Milaro put everything he could into not showing his disbelief, into controlling his expression. He began examining the odd sensations surrounding her in more detail. It wasn't like an aura or magic leakage, but more like a sensation the web was subtly picking up.

Nishpa's aura was fine. Sarila, on the other hand, felt off. Not enough to set off alarms from the system, but definitely enough to make it, and him, hesitant. Sarila had never visited his palace before, not with Escadril or on her own. He couldn't tell if this was her or the result of her coming into contact with the security web.

Which didn't really matter, because the security web was programmed, for want of a better word, with being able to identify potential threats. It hadn't quite pushed her over the edge yet, but it was wary. The juxtaposition of signals it was sending to him was concerning. He hadn't experienced this before.

Nishpa, meanwhile, had placed herself in between Sarila and Milaro, and was looking at the Salosier with some confusion. She seemed paler than usual, and as her bark was very similar to a birch tree, it was already fairly pale. Was she sick as well?

"Are you feeling quite all right?" Nishpa asked, genuine worry in her voice. Nishpa had known Sarila for centuries. They hadn't been close, not like Nishpa had been with Milaro's wife, but they had known each other.

"Oh yes," Sarila said, "I'm fine." And almost as an afterthought, she added, "Well, considering Escadril is dead."

Milaro couldn't help it. He narrowed his eyes. The cadence was off. There was no true emotion coming from her. He could feel it. Sometimes being a mind mage was annoying. This time, it helped him pinpoint that Sarila was indeed emoting her actual feelings, which made no sense.

He'd visited them in their home several times over many years, and she always seemed to be a loving companion, not his original wife. Emilin had died under strange circumstances in a brief skirmish on the outskirts of their empire. Sarila came along. Oh, a few decades later, but not immediately.

Milaro frowned, watching her. He could sense from his mind scan that she was a hundred percent the person he knew and had known, had interacted with for the past few centuries, but there was something different about her this time.

She offered him a wan smile, and he suddenly knew without a

doubt that she was pretending. She thought she still had them hooked, which gave Nishpa and him a slight advantage because he already wasn't accepting that Escadril had died naturally. He'd been dying, not dead.

"I'm so sorry for your loss, Sarila. I don't quite know what to say," Milaro said. Nishpa flashed him a very brief look of surprise before she schooled her face and caught on to, well, perhaps some of what he was doing.

Nishpa played along. "I'm so sorry. I was shocked. I wasn't expecting him to die for quite some time. His mind was so healthy."

There was a flash of something that passed through Sarila's eyes that he couldn't quite read, but Milaro was certain more than ever that Sarila wasn't their friend. He slowly began to pull some of the power reserves and feed them into the room's web, strengthening it further. He needed more of a read on her that wasn't invasive, since he was fairly certain that him asking to rifle through her thoughts would be perceived as hostile.

"Do you want a seat?" Nishpa said, flitting back and forth as if she didn't know how to deal with the loss, keeping herself in between Milaro and the Salosier.

There was an ever-so-brief scowl that passed over Sarila's face, and she shook her head. "No, I . . ." And then she laughed. It was a cold, cutting sound that ripped through the underlying white noise in the room. Derisive, full of hatred, full of something that shouldn't belong in laughter.

A ripple of power passed through her.

"Do you guys have any, any idea how complex a task it has been to stay in plain sight all these years?" Her voice had changed, the timbre of it completely different now.

"What do you mean?" Nishpa said, although Milaro was quite certain that Nishpa was just stalling for time. He could feel people running toward the room, the slight thrum of the webbing giving out an ever-so-faint notification.

"What do I mean? You know what I mean. You can tell. I can feel it. There's something that senses *other* in here. I'm surprised you couldn't sense it immediately, Milaro. Getting a little stodgy in your old age?"

Milaro resisted the urge to react, knowing it was exactly what she'd planned for. He fed more power into the web and was now certain that this *was* the Sarila she'd always been. This was no imposter. The mask she'd worn had simply been too good.

"Are you waiting for something?" she asked, but then shook her head with a chuckle. "It doesn't really matter." She shrugged, reached her hands up, and flexed her shoulders. "We can get down to it shortly. Ahhh, I get it. You feel like you need to understand me, don't you? That's why you guys will always lose."

Nishpa couldn't suppress the slight gasp that escaped her.

"See, I knew it." Sarila stretched her arms out and cracked her neck from side to side, which was a very odd movement for a literal tree person. "What you don't understand is that I don't care if you understand me. I don't need that sort of validation from you because I believe in what I'm doing, and I know that I'm right."

Without any warning or telegraphing, she pushed a wall of force out from her. She obviously hadn't quite understood what the security web did, because her magic was shut down almost immediately. She scowled. Nishpa and Milaro managed to put distance between themselves just as Hilrick and Nordon, Milaro's grandsons, burst into the room.

"Grandfather, if she's . . . oh, I guess you know," Nordon said, his words petering off as he realized what was happening.

"Yes," Milaro echoed, "we definitely know."

Sarila crunched down on something in her mouth, and Milaro felt the sense of power swell.

"Watch out," he said.

From the glare his grandkids gave him, Milaro realized they'd noticed. How could they not have?

A sudden wave of anti-growth magic hit the table in front of Sarila.

Nishpa barely got out of the way of the wave force before the web hit in. The web was designed to protect anybody secured within it from potential harmful attacks within the boundaries of it. But the force with which Sarila cast her magic overwhelmed it ever so slightly on initiation. She sent out a second wave like she had backup generators helping her push out so much power. Hilrick and Nordon managed to counter it, breaking it before it reached Nishpa and Milaro. Even though the webbing stepped in to help, that was when the dam broke.

Nishpa fired back several force spells of her own while Sarila peppered force bullets all around, trying to break through the defenses of the web. Overall, if Milaro hadn't just enforced them, those bullets probably would have cut through the weakness. At least some of them would have.

Milaro didn't like to think what the damage would have done. He activated the web's ability to analyze and had it suck in several of the bullets. He needed to know what they were up against. But even so, he still had to put more power into the webbing and reach into the reserves to repel some of the attacks himself.

Sarila flung more and more power at them, and then the black smoke that had permeated her eyes began to spill down her body. It didn't change her look. This was not an illusion, nor was it a parasite trick. She was a hundred percent Salosier. He frowned and watched as the smoky screen began to form into black, dog-like creatures that stood about three feet from the ground. And when they opened their shadow mouths, he saw rows of serrated teeth. These were things the webbing wasn't designed to keep out. They registered for all intents and purposes, as animals.

The vicious shadow dogs began to bolt around the room toward his grandsons. He knew they were perfectly combat-capable at both offense and defense. And toward Nishpa, who hovered enough up off the ground that even with their giant jumps they couldn't reach her. And for him.

All he had to do was apply a heavy dose of body armor around his form, and they couldn't penetrate it. But it did sap a lot of mana and energy, and some concentration. With a few of them set on attacking him, it meant his attention was divided.

For a few precious seconds, it left Sarila free to set up her incantations while they were preoccupied with the shadow dogs' initial onslaught.

Two for Nishpa and two for Milaro. One each for his grandsons.

The creatures locked on to one of Milaro's arms and, while not penetrating through to the flesh, he had to push a lot of energy and power into his shielding to make sure that they didn't. Something black and sludge-like oozed out of their mouths. That was an infection waiting to seep into the bloodstream if he ever saw it.

However, even worse than that, it began to give him suspicions that perhaps the injury Escadril retained from the original attack when they went to retrieve the book wasn't actually what killed him. It made him wonder just how depraved Sarila was. He remembered seeing fading bite marks in Escadril's wounds, and had assumed it came from the fight. But he was no longer so sure.

Fighting off the dogs and splitting his attention was difficult, but just as he'd taught Quinn, Milaro was also a master of splitting his attention. Nishpa, high enough above them that she could fire down her attacks on the offending Salosier, wasn't bothered by the dogs even if they kept attempting to jump at the fae. Her distracting attacks were enough that Sarila couldn't finish her incantations. Every time the vicious black smoke began to bubble up like a strange concoction in a cauldron, Nishpa managed to interrupt her.

Over and over again she interrupted her as Milaro took care of the shadow hounds. He kept a watch, making sure she was fine and monitoring the progress being made. All the while using pinpoint offensive force and ice attacks to slice through the shadow beasts and siphon off the energy that maintained their forms.

Nordon and Hilrick defeated their own pups and came over to help Milaro with the last two that'd belonged to Nishpa.

Even with that, it happened too fast for Milaro to register and react to.

Sarila, angry, annoyed, and frustrated at the fact that Nishpa had successfully interrupted every single one of the incantations since she cast the dogs, finally lost her temper.

Power exploded out from her in a massive wave that hit Nishpa dead on with destructive force.

Milaro heard the wet thud as it rocketed into his friend, and he scrambled to catch her while calling down as much power as he could from the web and to squash Sarila in front of him. The blast hit her with such force the ground trembled, while his grandsons took care of the rest of the dogs. But he didn't even look at his handiwork. He no longer cared if Sarila was still alive for questioning.

At the same moment, Quinn, Aradie, and Malakai burst through the door, panting, just in time to see Nishpa land in Milaro's outstretched arms.

5 8

NO REMORSE

MALAKAI RUSHED INTO THE ROOM, STEPPING IN TO REINFORCE HIS cousins' position. Quinn and Aradie darted over to Sarila, positioning themselves between her, Milaro, and Nishpa. Milaro cradled Nishpa as if he wasn't quite aware that they were already in the room. His eyes began to storm, a swirling vortex that Quinn knew wouldn't bode well for any of them if he lost control.

She stepped quickly toward him, tapping him lightly on the forearm. He looked up, the storm in his eyes receding. "Quinn."

"Yes. Focus." That's all she had time to say, because Sarila was regaining her equilibrium after the massive hit he dealt to her. This was no standard Salosier. Quinn was pretty sure she was even stronger than Escadril had been, despite how delicate she seemed.

Still recovering, Quinn sent out her own protective barrier to keep the unwelcome guest down. "Gravitas." She commanded it.

But the Salosier was powerful, and despite how much power she'd obviously already used up, she didn't appear to be against burning even her life force to make this work. Somebody with nothing to lose was a dangerous thing.

A few more shadow dogs emerged. They were focused on Hilrick, Nordon, and Malakai.

Aradie darted in several times with laser attacks specifically aimed to keep Sarila from completing her spells, but it appeared that the Salosier didn't need to use incantation magic for everything.

Quinn could feel the life force magic, the healing magic behind her as Milaro poured energy into his friend. She couldn't look at Nishpa, not right now. It would probably break her. All she could cling to was that there were very faint life signs coming from the currently disfigured flesh in Milaro's arms.

Anger boiled in the pit of Quinn's stomach, but she pushed it down and tried to return to logic, tried to figure out the best way to pull all the information from this evil tree that she could. For the first time ever, a sense of calm swept through her, because Quinn decided she was willing to do anything to gather that information and make this person pay.

Sarila began to laugh, and it echoed throughout the entire room.

Quinn sent a message through the system to the Library and Lynx, apprising them of the situation and asking them to send medical help if they could, or at least to ready a hospital room for Nishpa. They'd transport her as soon as she was stable.

The anger fueled Quinn and yet it didn't take over. She separated her emotions again, but this time felt completely in control.

Sarila's laugh continued, even as Quinn glanced briefly at the elf cousins and saw them battling the shadow dogs. One of them lunged for Malakai's throat, but the shielding she'd extended to him rebounded it halfway across the room. He didn't even pause, but dove after it, his swords dancing.

Quinn thought he looked rather magical.

The Salosier's laugh cut off as Quinn buffeted her with another gust of wind, focused directly in the gut.

Sarila coughed as Aradie made another pass and a bit of what looked like smoky sap dripped down from her mouth. "You had to make it more difficult, didn't you?" Sarila said. "This would have been easier if you'd just sent the damn Librarian like you were supposed to, stupid bird."

Aradie swooped, attacking her with laser eyes again, managing to lop off one of the Salosier's fingers. Sarila howled in pain and the strange, smoky sap dripped onto the carpet, followed by a sizzling sound, which made Quinn realize she didn't want to get hit by the acidic blood.

"You and Narilin, that's all it was supposed to be," Sarila spat. Instead of casting, she leaned back and hurled what looked like a ball of energy toward the Librarian.

Quinn barely managed to duck out of the way with her reflexes boosted from her ability to condense perception and reactions, plus the combat training she'd done with Malakai.

Sarila followed with a ball of force and pushed back toward Quinn. But Quinn's shielding had evolved since they fought Drav and Kajaro. There was power behind it, contained within it, with fire meshed in between the shielding walls, so white and hot that it couldn't be seen until a side burst, which Sarila managed to do. The flame roared out toward her. She backed off, yelping, as several fingers on her right hand caught fire. It took her long enough to put them out that a couple of them cracked and dropped to the ground as well.

Quinn gasped in mock surprise. "Looks like you've still got fifteen fingers. Let's see if we can change that." Aradie hooted, but it sounded more like a laugh as she dove in once again.

This time, Sarila was ready for them, having slowly regained some of her capabilities since Milaro squashed her with his shield. The Salosier's shielding didn't hold up to the night owl's lasers, and Quinn took advantage of the opening to focus a fireball straight at Sarila's arm.

Quinn had her suspicions about just how sick Escadril truly was. Besides. The Salosier could still talk just as well with a limb or two fewer as she could if she was whole.

One of her hands dropped onto the carpet and Sarila looked up at Quinn with pain and shock on her face. "You're not supposed to be able to do that."

Quinn cocked her head to one side. "I'm not supposed to be able to do what? Read some of the books in the massive bloody library I've got at my disposal? I beg to differ," she continued. "Those books, I'll have them all memorized soon, and none of you will stand a chance."

Not waiting another second, she leveraged more pinpointed fire directly at the Salosier. This time, however, she missed, and she allowed the spell to dissipate when it didn't hit its mark. Sarila barely dodged out of the way. With half of her forearm missing on the right-hand side, she seemed slightly off balance.

Milaro hoisted himself up. Nishpa's wounds had begun knitting back together. Enough that she no longer looked like a malformed lump of flesh. He had her gently cradled against his chest. Quinn could still feel the magic running from him into her, trying to heal her. The stormy look had returned to his eyes.

"Don't," she said. "Save your energy for her."

"And the shields!" Malakai yelled.

It took a few seconds, but Milaro backed down. Quinn was quite certain she could feel the protection grid all around them strengthen.

Malakai darted over to help Quinn, now that there were only a few couple of left for the others. Hilrick and Nordon had obviously fought together so much that their fighting style was seamless.

Sarila hissed as another one of her summons went down. "You think you're clever."

Quinn lamented the fact that the nice Sarila she'd met, or at least that she thought she'd met when she went to visit Escadril and check in on him, was definitely not this woman. "How long?"

She laughed again. "As long as I've been here. As long as you've all known me."

Quinn saw Milaro wince out of the corner of her eye. She knew he was angry that he hadn't realized that this person was a plant, was a traitor.

A plant traitor.

Quinn squashed the slightly panicked laughter that threatened to break free for a second.

The smoky sap began to drip down from Sarila's mouth, just like it would in blood if it were a human. Quinn pondered that, wondering how close their anatomies were. She couldn't quite compare them properly yet, even though she'd absorbed both types of book.

"Were you planted there to make sure Escadril, and the Balisors remained rivals?" Quinn said, trying to keep her busy with answering her questions, while Aradie swooped in and out, strategically hitting places so that Quinn would be able to build up the usual ice prison she kept their prisoners in. But the more Quinn learned, the more she grew to believe that this person was truly evil. It was a strange phenomenon for her. Sometimes people were just too evil to die.

Sarila laughed, as if trying to prove Quinn's point. "Of course! I was there to make sure you never stood any chance of fighting against chaos. That is the entire point. And once he was injured, Escadril was easy prey. But the best thing is when your position appeals to more than one faction."

Quinn blinked. She could barely recognize her own voice when she spoke. It was cold and filled with a level of menace that she hadn't realized she was capable of. "Are you trying to tell me that Escadril wasn't mortally wounded when we brought him back?"

"Of course he wasn't," Sarila said. The Salosier suddenly fell to the ground, the kneecap shot out by one of Aradie's laser shots she hadn't seen coming. She practically crawled across the ground, still desperately pushing force walls in front of herself to ward off attacks.

"He wasn't dying," Milaro said, his voice filled with so much venom, Quinn had to double take to make sure it was really him.

"Of course he wasn't. An existing wound is easily infected without raising any suspicion. Easy as pie, you people. You're so gullible."

Quinn blinked. There was nothing good in this Sarila. No matter what she'd meant to Narilin or Arilin and Marilyn and Jane, this person? *This* was the real person. "And there are more factions?"

Sarila pealed with laugher, the sludge loss obviously affecting her. "Getting twice the reward for doing the same thing is wonderful."

"Bet the Librarian screwed up your plans," Malakai said, taking another shot with his bow. This time, he'd managed to pin her foot to the floor.

"Librarian's emergence just altered plans. We'll still get there, or one of them will, don't you worry."

"Ah, but your part is now done," Quinn said.

"Escadril's dead, and he was part of your defense force. You're welcome." Sarila coughed again, bringing up more of the smoky, sappy blood. She coughed again, racking the entire frame of the once-delicate Salosier, missing multiple fingers, half an arm, one knee, and her foot nailed to the floor.

As if trying to be kind, Malakai nailed her calf on the other leg in the same way. She halted abruptly and fell to the floor, the force spell she'd been gathering beneath her hitting herself in the stomach and winding her, causing more blood to escape.

She laughed. It was a mad cackle, as if there was nothing sane left inside her.

"Korradine's plan will win out," she said, spluttering again. "Or the Library will be lost in other ways. Either way, you lose."

Quinn heard Hilrick and Norden in the background, finishing off the last smoke dog. She was fairly sure it had begun to dissipate as Sarila's life force began to leak away from her.

"Korradine's plan?" Quinn said, turning. "What do you mean, Korradine's plan? Which plan?"

She laughed again, sputtering more. "I'm not going to tell you Korradine's plan."

But there was something else in the air when she spoke those words. Something definite. Something unexpected. Quinn could sense it through the vibrations, feel it in the way she presented herself and the words. It was all a little too much, a little too neat, a little uncertain.

And then it dawned on Quinn.

"You don't know, do you?" Quinn said. "You have no idea what this Korradine's plan means. And you have no idea what other ways might entail."

There was a frazzled aura that settled over Sarila. It could have been the fact that she was practically nailed to the floor and missing limbs and about to die. But Quinn was fairly certain the frazzled aspect came from the fact that Quinn was right, and Sarila was definitely not happy Quinn was right.

"I'm right, aren't I? Tell me."

Sarila glared at her, and now the smoke that had covered her eyes began to drip down her cheeks like thick black tar, as if her body was expunging some strange vile substance from it. Which was pretty accurate as far as Quinn was concerned, considering what she'd done.

"How many others did you kill?" Quinn asked suddenly, her voice foreign to her ears.

Sarila laughed and ended in a coughing fit, spluttering black bits of tar flying out of her mouth. "Wouldn't you like to know?"

Quinn sent flickers of fire to extinguish them so the acid couldn't burn through any more of Milaro's office. She couldn't sense him anymore, and realized that he'd already taken Nishpa to the Library. Which was good. He didn't need to see this. He didn't need to hear this. They'd give him the nicer version.

"Yes," Quinn said calmly. "I'd like to know. That *is* why I asked." She stepped closer. "And I'd like to know now."

Quinn raised her hand, white-hot flames dancing on her palm and her fingertips. She brought them close to Sarila's face, catching the tar on fire that went into her eyes. It whooshed, and Sarila screamed.

"Ah, there," Quinn said, watching the way the fire trailed up and burned the Salosier's eyeball with a sort of detached fascination. "It does work. Now, I think you should tell us everybody you've hurt."

Sarila listed out more names than Quinn ever wanted to hear. Names she didn't know, but names that made up far too many deaths. And even as Quinn's horror grew, she could hear the sneer in Sarila's words. No remorse, not even a hint of regret.

In the end, there was no guilt left when Quinn's fire burned the Salosier to ash.

5 9

A UNIVERSAL THING

QUINN SAT IN HER OFFICE, DRUMMING HER FINGERS AGAINST THE ARMS of her overstuffed chair. She lifted her fingers and examined them, turning her hand around. She was still trying to process exactly what had happened. When she found out Sarila had been a major player in the plan to poison the Balisors, it broke a part of her comprehension. This was someone she'd met, talked to . . . spent an actual day with.

It all happened so fast.

She replayed it all in her head.

Instead of summoning Milaro, she'd had this sudden dread hit the middle of her stomach. She'd known, with far too much certainty, that they had to get to Milaro and let him know.

When they arrived there to find Sarila already engaged in combat with them—the revelation felt far too convenient for all of them. As if contrived by some unforeseen spell to release the information at a specific time point from Irias's brain.

It also ruined her first visit to Milaro's palace, which irked Quinn no end.

In order to refocus her mind, she conjured a white-hot flame and made it dance from fingertip to fingertip, back and forth, swirling and diving, completely in her control. There was no way, had she not had complete control over that flame, that she could have killed Sarila.

The pale birch-like Salosier burned to ash in her mind, over and over. The flames played on repeat, licking away at the sneer on her face, while it slowly turned her entire body to dust.

She sighed, glad that at least the images constantly flashing through her head also included a litany of the names of the people Sarila listed so proudly to have helped to or directly eliminated, including Escadril. It still pained Quinn that she'd been there, right there, and hadn't noticed a thing. She'd thought Sarila was ever so slightly distant and not overly friendly, but she didn't think she was a cold-blooded, genocidal maniac.

Quinn had lost count of all the names listed. All she'd wanted to know was if this person had only harmed Escadril, then maybe, maybe, they could still be rehabilitated. That's what Hal did, right? Or at least he tried to, if they were redeemable.

But how was she the person to judge that? She wasn't. That was the entire point. But she had judged it to be a risk she couldn't afford to take. Especially when she considered the Balisors.

Quinn had no regret about her actions purely based on that involvement alone. It was Sarila who made it possible for the infection to spread through her cousin Salosier's encampment, which was wild when Quinn thought about it. Who did that?

Thousands of Balisors had lost their lives.

She sighed and shifted ever so slightly. Sarila's loyalty to the Jenishu clan was the only reason for saving Narilin's people. She'd only saved them from the infection and directed it to the Balisors out of a sense of belonging to the initial clan. Not that it extended to killing her husband.

Quinn sighed, put her head in her hands and felt Aradie press her wings against her neck in a sort of hug from the owl. It was full of comfort, accompanied by pictures of hot chocolate and cushions and fluffy onesies. Quinn wasn't entirely sure how Aradie knew about warm onesies and fuzzy slippers, but that actually sounded really good.

There was nothing you could do, Quinn, the Library said, its tone subdued to levels Quinn hadn't heard before, but then again, the Library was always with her in a way. It had witnessed everything, and experienced what Quinn went through. Even if maybe that experience was dulled.

"Maybe, maybe there wasn't," she muttered, still trying to convince herself.

Quinn, you've been here almost six months. This literally began centuries ago. Before you were ever created. You are not responsible for this.

And Quinn knew that on a super intimate level, but at the same time she wished there'd been something she could do. The turmoil in the hospital pushed against her sensory net. She could feel it, them rushing around trying to heal Nishpa. It gnawed at her stomach, and she knew it'd take a while. Nishpa was in bad condition.

Quinn, you cannot beat yourself up.

"I'm not beating myself up," Quinn said, her exasperation coming out. She took a few deep breaths before continuing. "I am picking each incident apart and analyzing it. Understanding it and putting it away. So that I don't crash and burn. So that I don't rebound. So that I have successfully dealt with the thing I have done. For my own resolution purposes."

The Library paused as if it wasn't exactly sure how to respond to that. Aradie cooed low in her throat with understanding and knowing, keyed into Quinn's conversation with the Library as she was.

"Look," Quinn said, "I'm not about to bottle it up. But like I did when Milaro revealed I wasn't who or what I thought I was, I have a process, and I must understand what happened on a level that I can dissect and deal with. Thus, I'm examining exactly what it is I did earlier."

Understandable, the Library said. *I've just not seen people deal with something like this . . . this way.*

Quinn shrugged. "Milaro gave me excellent tools to separate out thoughts. Not only can I do a heap of quick thinking, like on a totally different level, but compartmentalizing emotions," she clarified so as not to draw ire, "not getting rid of them. Compartmentalizing them while I analyze different aspects of factual situations. Frankly, it's a good coping mechanism, because it allows me to truly assess if I've suffered any serious damage to my own psyche. If I'm gonna stay the Librarian for hundreds or thousands of years"—which Quinn couldn't even wrap her head around yet—"then I'll need to do a lot of compartmentalization."

True, the Library said.

"Excellent, now let me deal with my trauma, please."

The Library let out a half laugh. *Always, I just hope you know that we're all here for you, too.*

"Oh, I know," Quinn said, "but right now, I need my brain and me and a bit of time to sort through events."

Quinn dove back into her thoughts, ensuring she was taking care of everything. The turmoil in the hospital bothered her. She knew Geneva was there, as were Milaro and Miles, who were treating Nishpa.

She really needed another calibration with the system so she could sense more of the Library around her. Having a deeper connection would benefit them in the long run, especially right now. The surgeon, Vivit, was currently occupied and would be assisting with Nishpa shortly. She could mostly keep track of Nishpa without getting underfoot by simply focusing her sensory extension in that area. It allowed her to continue her mostly detached examination of their current situation without becoming too emotionally involved in the actions currently saving Nishpa's life.

Despite the amount of mana and power Milaro poured into preserving her physical and, hopefully, mental form, her recovery would be touch and go.

Quinn didn't understand the disintegration magic both Kajaro and Sarila possessed. In fact, she was confused by it. It was yet another thing she needed to research. She raised her eyes from where she stared at her desk to see Malakai sitting on the couch, apparently relaxed. At least, to most people's eyes, he probably was, but she could tell he was hyper-aware of his surroundings and alert for anything he might need to do. Even without his magic, Malakai was formidable and stood by her side, no matter what. He'd become such an integral part of her Library life that she couldn't even describe how she felt while he was sick. She didn't want to face dangers without him. She hoped that once he regained his mana usage, he'd continue to accompany her. It always felt better when he was there.

Malakai looked over at her as he felt her gaze on him. "Are you okay?" he asked.

She looked at him, scrunching her nose up in thought. She analyzed, probably more than she should. Maybe she was okay? The clinical, logical part of her brain was more than aware that Sarila aimed to kill Milaro and herself, and anyone else who belonged to the Library in the process. Sarila had very nearly killed Nishpa. Logically, Quinn was fully aware that she had done the right thing in turning Sarila to ash. But logic didn't always help.

In terms of self-defense, she'd also done the right thing. She wasn't only protecting herself and the others, even though they sort of had it under control, but she'd also protected Nishpa and Milaro. The thing was, that didn't necessarily mean it was the right thing either.

It had been morally grey.

Was she really a morally grey sort of person?

Not usually, but in this morally grey area, she'd decided that she would choose to do the exact same thing again, given the same circumstances. There was absolutely no question about it.

No matter what they did to bring Sarila in, there was always the chance that she would get free and inflict all of that pain and suffering on more people again. She'd wiped out thousands of Balisors with her deeds. It was a genocide. It was a massacre. Thousands and thousands of Balisors dead, and only a few hundred of them left. She'd introduced the rot, given to her by whoever potentially paid her, to that part of the forest, and she'd been proud of it.

So no, Quinn would never choose to finish the fight differently, and she'd deal with any potential repercussions. Finally she nodded and answered Mal, who'd made his way to her desk. "I'm not. But I will be okay."

At that moment, Nordon walked into her office, clapping his

hands. "Cousin," he said, looking at Malakai. "Librarian." He nodded, a smirky grin on his face. "Just so you know, I did take the death throe memories."

"What?" Quinn said, a bit lost.

"Death throes, you know, the last memories of a body—from the last few hours of its life."

"Seriously, you can do that?"

"Well yeah," Nordon replied, as if it was common knowledge. "Have you not looked up any blood magic yet?"

"No, I can't say as I have." Quinn raised an eyebrow.

Malakai groaned.

Quinn ignored him. "Anyway, what did you do?"

"I extracted the last memories from Sarila—which is extremely difficult from an ash pile so . . . you're welcome." He winked at her and continued on. "If anyone questions what went down, we have a recording from the perpetrator herself. Did you not know that's part of what I do? Find dead bodies, extract dead memories, that sort of thing."

"Well, I know now," Quinn said.

"Excellent, excellent. Well, if anybody questions it, I have officially sealed the memories and anybody is free to look." Nordon flashed her a grin.

Quinn frowned, not entirely sure how to take that.

"It basically means that you're in the clear because it's irrefutable."

"Oh," Quinn said, "so basically they're telling on themselves."

"If you'd just murdered them in cold blood, then it would tell on you. But as it is, Sarila tells on herself."

Quinn nodded slowly, wondering how she could do that. It was obviously related to mind magic, being Milaro's line and all. "That's a pretty cool trick."

"It is, isn't it?" Nordon said with a hint of pride.

Malakai glared at his cousin. Nordon grinned back. Quinn wanted to know about that rivalry. But even as she was about to ask, the Library spoke up.

Get to the infirmary now, Quinn.

Quinn did. She stumbled to her feet, out the door, and was at the hospital wing sooner than she thought possible. She knew instinctively where to go and walked into Nishpa's room. Milaro, Geneva, Vivit, and Miles stood there too. Nordon and Malakai stumbled in after her. She approached the bed, noting idly that white sheets were apparently a universal thing and not just earth-based for hospitals, where Nishpa was nestled.

She was so pale she almost looked like an Esposian, almost blended in with the sheets. There were bandages and poultices all over her, and she looked shorter, not quite as large as life. Tubes ran in and out of her too. What Quinn wasn't sure why they needed tubes having magic and all, but she trusted her doctor golems. There was no shine to the dull gold in her wings.

"She's doing better. She's stable," Milaro said and there was a hitch to his voice.

"I'm so sorry," Quinn said. "I'm so sorry we didn't get there sooner."

"You came as soon as you could," Milaro said. "Not everything goes our way, not even with magic."

6 0

CONNECTING TO HER

IF THERE WAS ONE THING QUINN DIDN'T EXACTLY LIKE ABOUT BEING A Librarian, it was that as long as she was in the Library, there was really nowhere for her to go to be alone with her thoughts. Especially since the Library had been branching out, so to speak. She didn't intend the pun, but she chuckled to herself, anyway. A little dry humor never hurt anyone.

Since they'd expanded, there were so many more people in the Library. Some of the places she used to go, like up to the bardic section of the Library, were no longer as solitary or quiet. She understood that this Library was a little different. It wasn't super boisterous or anything like that, but finding a nice quiet corner usually meant she either had to go to her room or sit in her office with the door closed. Right now, she didn't feel like doing either of those.

She took the next best option and dragged Malakai to the combat wing, determined to try out some of the new combat books and dummies.

"You really think the combat wing's a good idea?" he asked.

"Yes. I would like to work out the minor aggression I'm starting to feel."

"Minor aggression?"

"A lot of aggression," she admitted, and didn't add frustration, bewilderment, and melancholy to the list outside of her head. "Are you going to correct my form or what?"

"I'll gladly correct your form, Librarian." He paused as he studied her. "I think you should correct existing form and work at cushioning your hands while you punch the dummies. Would that help you work through some of your anger issues?"

Quinn flashed him a grin. "Yes, I do believe punching things is acceptable."

The combat wing was fuller than Quinn expected, but most of the combat dummies were idle. She watched as the golems discussed books and techniques with several dozen patrons. She shrugged and walked over to a dummy.

"Now don't forget to coat your hands," Malakai prompted her, pulling her out of her contemplations.

She nodded because she needed something to focus on. Something to help her get the image of the heavily injured Nishpa out of her head. She'd seemed so frail, almost see-through, thin, just nothing like the commanding and powerful fae she was. It haunted Quinn in a way she hadn't been expecting. It took her by surprise, and it was precisely why she needed to get some of that aggression out of her system.

How Milaro had managed to mold her back into her proper form —that was some hefty magic there. To be fair, she hadn't been an actual glob of flesh. She'd just been severely disfigured and injured at the time.

Quinn decided she liked the combat branch, and while she wasn't particularly good at hand-to-hand, with Malakai's supervision and reminder that she shouldn't include her thumb inside her fist, punching felt like a release. She modified her shielding, and her scales flashed to the fore, but instead of willing them to disappear, she decided that today, right now, she really felt like having her dragon scales visible.

To keep her mind from wandering, she began, with every punch, to list out some of the things that she had to do. The things she had to focus on, to avoid the things her mind was pulled to dwell on.

"Locate the other three books and talk to Jasper." She snapped out and jabbed at the dummy. "Milaro mind reinforcement. Wait, I did that already," she mumbled to herself, and did an uppercut and a cross next—one-two. While she could sense Malakai watching her, she realized he studied her form. There was no judgement from him, just concentration. That made her feel oddly safe.

"Talk to Hal about Adrito and Kajaro," she muttered as she jabbed twice in quick succession. The movements helped with the overt tension in her shoulders, easing it out, giving her a release.

"Get to my Aunt Dragon and the Parsneauvian book," she spat out, pummeling the training dummy this time.

Malakai chuckled, and she glared at him, taking back all the nice thoughts she'd had previously. "What's your problem?"

"I wasn't laughing at you, just expressing a moment of happiness," he said. "I kind of enjoy listening to you verbalize the sheer mountain of work you have ahead of you. It's not what I expected, but I think it works."

Quinn shrugged.

"Yep, do that in-between punches," he said, "you're really tense."

She stopped and deadpanned him. "Are you seriously pointing that out right now?" Even though she was fully aware he was right.

"Yes. I am," he said. "You're tense, and you know it. We're going to get through this."

Quinn sucked in a deep breath and let it back out and gave him a curt nod before she continued punching the defenseless dummy. Which was an important distinction, as some of those training dummies did indeed fight back. "Check with Siliqua and Harish." She punched it again. Doing jabs, uppercuts, and crosses were easy, even if they weren't hard hits. Hooks, however? Those were beyond her. "Help with memory retrieval."

Malakai interrupted her gently. "Quinn, you're holding your wrist wrong. If that was actually a person or you were hitting any harder, you'd injure yourself."

Quinn looked down and straightened it slightly. "Okay, gotcha."

But that was all she said before she got back to her list. "Work on my sensory net."

"Isn't your sensory net—"

"Shut up." She sighed, punching the inoffensive dummy anyway. "You're right, it's pretty good and I can't really push its power until I synchronize with the Library again," she said, grinning like a fool. "Synchronize with the Library." She punched the dummy in time with the words, and she said it again. And a fourth time, for good measure.

By the time she was done, she was laughing, and Malakai too. She refused to admit there might be an ever so slight hint of hysteria contained within that laugh, because it didn't matter. It felt good to get the emotions out.

"So . . ." Malakai drawled. "What was that? I don't think I got that last thing you listed."

Quinn laughed. "I gotta synchronize with the Library."

And just as she was about to punch, Lynx materialized directly in front of her. And she stumbled, falling through him, against the dummy, and ended up letting herself slide down and sit on the floor where she sat with an arm draped over each knee.

Lynx eyed her with a grin. "Exactly! Precisely!" he said, his dark purple sclera eyes pulsing with violet light.

She glanced up at him, still laughing. "What do you mean, 'exactly, precisely'?"

"Synchronize with the Library," he said, as if it were completely obvious. "That's what you have to do, Quinn."

Quinn stared at him blankly, all her mirth gone. She was very confused. She'd been so sure that the Library was supposed to tell her when it was time. "You mean right now?"

"Yes, right now."

"Wait, wait, wait." She waved the command away, trying to process. "Do we have enough pillars activated? Is this okay? Are we enough into this level of power to afford a synchronization?"

Yes, Quinn, the Library spoke up to reassure her. *We are fine, or I wouldn't have sent Lynx to get you.*

"You could have just told me," she muttered, not speaking to herself because from the look on Malakai and Lynx's faces, they could hear the Library.

Yes, I could have just told you, but my manifestation is used to acting as a go-between between myself and the Librarian.

"Why?" Quinn asked, suddenly curious. The Library talked to her a lot, after all. "Why does Lynx need to do that? Can't you just talk to me?"

There was a decently long pause before the Library responded with a sigh. *Yes, Quinn, but I've not always been able to communicate so completely with the Librarian.*

"Say what?" Quinn said.

Exactly, which you'll learn more about when you get your butt down here and we synchronize.

Quinn grumbled; Lynx pouted. Malakai doubled over, laughing. "Your face," he said. "You looked so surprised."

Quinn point blank ignored him.

"So it's time to do the deed," Quinn said, pushing herself up to which Malakai continued to laugh even more. And Quinn continued to ignore him.

Lynx glanced at Malakai and shrugged, turning his full attention to Quinn. "Look, it's time."

"Wait. What about Milaro?" Quinn asked, dusting herself off.

"He's fine."

Quinn raised an eyebrow. "I'm trying not to work the elf into an early grave," she said, "so I'd really like to double check that he is definitely fine."

Lynx nodded. "He will be. He'll be there like he was in the middle of your first synchronization to check that everything is running according to plan. I'll also be monitoring things while this proceeds."

"Okay." She started walking toward the door. One of these days she was gonna learn to teleport properly. She still hated using the exercises in *Watch Out for That Tree* because she just didn't trust them. It seemed much better for an open battlefield. She didn't really have access to many of those. "Anyway, I thought you were supposed to wait for the memories."

The Library *tsked*.

"Hey, what's that for?" Quinn said.

Sure, we wanted to have all the memories, but some of them are proving a lot harder to recalibrate with than we thought. We almost have a full report too, but I don't think we should wait any longer for you to calibrate with me because we've been at this new power stage for too long now. Before you use your powers, you'll need to acclimate to them again. And thus, we can't put this off because you're going to need the larger power base to pull from when you go visit my sister.

"Oh," Quinn said, trying not to let her excitement at meeting another dragon on perhaps not kill-you terms go to her head. "That tracks."

They were almost at the spiral staircase, and Malakai touched her shoulder very briefly. She turned, somewhat surprised to see him there, not having realized that he had followed them out. "Mal, what is it?"

His brow was pinched, giving him a concerned expression. He looked her up and down and gave her shoulder a very tiny squeeze before letting his hand drop.

"Are you sure that you're up for this?" he asked, looking her in the eyes, his own full of worry. Searching her for, she couldn't tell what, but she appreciated it. She appreciated that he genuinely cared.

"Yeah," she said, "I'll be fine. I'm just, you know, a lot has happened."

"Yeah," he said, "I'll wait up here for you."

She was about to say, "You don't need to." Instead, she said, "You realize it's gonna take a couple of days, right?"

He laughed. "Yeah, I know. I won't be far."

She smiled and squeezed his arm. "Thanks, Mal."

Quinn turned and hovered down the stairs, a part of her feeling extremely relieved to know that even during synchronization with the Library and where she'd be completely out of it and vulnerable, somebody was looking out for her just in case the Library got overrun by its enemies. Or other possible worst-case scenarios per bloody usual. She thought she had gotten rid of that habit, especially with the compartmentalization. Apparently, she had not.

She looked down at her hands as she began to walk across the padded floor surrounded by the starry leaves that tracked along the ceiling, all glimmering with information and processing whatever it was. And Quinn remembered how much she adored being in the core. Maybe she just needed to bring a picnic down here sometimes.

"Do you like picnics?" she asked the Library, who chuckled in response.

Yes, but I no longer partake of solid sustenance.

"That's such a shame. You'd love cinnamon doughnuts," Quinn said.

The Library laughed, and the ground rumbled. *I believe I would. I do, however, have olfactory senses and I can smell that I would indeed love these things.*

"It feels sad to be able to smell but not consume," Quinn said softly, and looked down at her hands, missing her scales somewhat. She knew she'd released them up in the combat wing when she left, but the armor made her feel safe. And she knew she'd have to dismiss all of it in order to synchronize. It took another layer away, heightened her vulnerability. The platform was already raised for her to lie down in, right next to the hollow where she usually sat, curled up against the trunk of the tree.

You've been here longer now than I think you realize, Quinn.

"What, almost six months?"

Yes. Almost six months.

"That is not a long time," Quinn said.

Ah, it's barely a blink of an eye for me, and yet, it is still about 2.5 percent of your life, I believe.

Quinn pondered that. There was a part of her that found it intriguing, fascinating, in fact. There was also a part of her that was terrified to live longer, to see people die. That got melancholy fast. She shook herself out of it and sat down, shimmying herself into position. Calm radiated through her. She'd done this before.

"Oh, I forgot the food." She stopped, irritated at herself.

It's okay. Lynx has it.

Lynx grumbled and pulled out a bag. "Cook made them especially for you,"

Quinn grinned. "Well, I'd hope so since I think I'm the only one who gets to synchronize with the core."

The Library's shadow form coalesced right next to her. "Are you ready for this?"

Quinn mulled it over. "Do you have any more revelations for me? You know, mid-synchronization. I'm not really a dragon. I'm actually a primordial cosmic comet."

The Library laughed. "Nothing like that, but you'll learn things, aspects of the system and the Library's functions that it's simply easier to show you through this than to explain. The information will continue to run through you, and you'll probably have questions when you're done."

"Yeah," said Quinn, lying back as everything began connecting to her. She could feel the Library and its system begin to connect in a powerfully intricate way. Her mind grew foggy, but not in a drugged way, more of a preparing-to-drop-through-a-cloud-of-information way. She smiled softly as her eyes closed and breathed out the words, almost as a subconscious thought. "I've got the feeling I'll always have questions."

61

OF OTHER

The sensations that swam around Quinn as the synchronization took hold were markedly different from the initial one she'd sat through. While the first time she fully synchronized with the Library had felt more like going under anesthesia, this was more like an altered state of consciousness. A state that wasn't quite awake but also not fully asleep. In the in between where everything has that plane of difference, of *other*.

She could feel the power thrumming. It wove through her, around her, inside her.

Like the instrument of her soul had suddenly been switched on and was tuning itself to the right notes.

Yes, this time it was so very different.

She hadn't realized that pushing through to the seventh pillar in the filtration system would boost the Library and her awareness to this degree. She could feel the strength, like a newly restored engine. It felt like she was floating on a vast sea that was replenishing her while the sun charged her batteries. The water flushed through her, over her, around her, feeding her with a plethora of tiny organisms, all different, all full of knowledge.

Then her body started shaking, shivering. So much that she

thought her teeth might be rattling. She couldn't tell if this was just an internal sensation or if she was truly experiencing it. Warmth flooded through her, like the sun on a good day. Not too hot, not too cold . . . just right.

At least her insides didn't feel like porridge.

She couldn't tell how much time passed or exactly what was happening after that. Information flooded around her, through her, in her. It stuck in her mind so fast and so definitively that she felt like her head would come apart at the seams multiple times.

Except heads didn't have seams, did they?

At one point, there was a vague sensation of a presence near her which felt familiar, but recognition evaded her in that moment. Floating in her ether of water and sunshine, she couldn't be certain about anything. Except that she shouldn't be able to see the stars in the sky when the sun was keeping her so warm.

All that mattered was floating.

And then, when she felt like she couldn't take anything else into her system, when she was about to overload—peace happened.

Reality didn't slam straight back into her.

No.

Instead, she began to wake from the strange state. Bits and pieces floated around her, bringing her back to herself.

Quinn blinked her eyes open.

This time, when she woke, she wasn't grappling with a shocked revelation about her heritage. It was gradual instead—not her digging to find a specific thing that made her uncomfortable.

In fact, this time it was a bit directionless. At least last time there'd been an impetus. She'd realized some of the information was pertinent and had to get a grasp on it. But this time . . . to be honest, she was a little dazed. She knew she'd just synchronized with the Library. That was obvious. She glanced around, turning her head to each side, trying to pull her thoughts together, to remember something.

The information leached into her brain. Somehow more. So much more.

And yet nothing that set her pulse racing or stirred anger within her.

Just this general, overhanging knowledge.

Quinn remained lying down and pulled at the food sitting on her chest. She chewed it absentmindedly, trying to process everything. She had a vague memory that Milaro had been here, guiding her through some of the experience, and was potently aware that about two days had passed. Unsurprising, and yet, at the same time, somehow unexpected. She'd assumed it'd go faster the second time around, considering the amount of knowledge she already had.

Her mind was calmer this time. It allowed her to process the ridiculous amount of information and power now present in her mind.

She frowned as she tried to parse through it all.

It gave her access to all records and a far deeper understanding of how the Library worked. This wasn't a game changer like the last synchronization. No, this involved knowledge about the intricate inner workings. More details about how the interdimensional doorway connections worked, and the almost infinite ability to grant access. It taught a finesse for the systems that made her feel closer to the connection.

It also granted her greater knowledge about how power transferred from the books when returned. Which had to do with the ambient energy the books absorbed from all the different areas of the galaxy, combined with the people who borrowed or carried the tomes. Each entrant through a door infused the Library with more power. The way Quinn was woven into that net of dimensional magic meant she could sense when doors were being opened. The more power available to her, the greater her sensitivity to everything involving the Library.

That was how the Librarian position was meant to function. A vast overview of the thousands of tiny intricacies that made the Library of Everywhere work.

Which led her to understand why Lynx had to shut it all down.

The Librarian was intricately wound into the system. They were the connection between it all.

Could it still function without one?

Perhaps technically. But the drain on the power system would cause routing errors because the Librarian had been set up as a pivotal piece in the entire construction. She was a conduit, a hub, through which all manner of energy exchange passed. Without that piece in place, the system would feed back in on itself if it didn't shut down its main function for self-preservation. So, when Lynx drained a heap of the power reserves to seal the soul bomb, he'd triggered the Library to close in order to preserve what it could without a Librarian to initiate the recirculation properly.

This wasn't something that should have happened abruptly, which likely spoke volumes to both the Library and Lynx not recalling what they'd done precisely.

She'd always thought having eighteen thousand books missing, or borrowed at a time from such a massive Library, was a minuscule number, and that it meant not many people frequented it. But she realized now that people often studied the books here. It was more rare that people borrowed them for any length of time outside of the Library.

As a result, many people used the Library as a destination and not necessarily as a borrowing visit. This also fed power to the Library. And, not surprisingly, it operated nothing like the libraries she'd visited with her mother as a small child on Earth. For one, those had no dimensional doorways.

And if there was one thing Quinn now realized, it was that dimensional portals took a lot of energy to open. The malachite barely offset it, and acted more as a conduit to filter in energy during from the small dimensional opening it made.

Quinn searched through the memories and realized even though she didn't have exact numbers for the unopened branches, it was obvious that a lot more books had been borrowed before shutdown than she'd realized. And now, that the information actually included the other branches in it—just waiting for them to be open.

She sorted through everything, scanning it, skimming it, realizing how much easier it was to access the overload in her head. The foggy feeling began to lift, and she flexed her fingers involuntarily, as if itching to scroll or page through its entirety.

When she got to information about the pillars, Ashiron had moved to a pale orange color. Warnings were soft, but still imminent. Their makeshift solution was just that. They'd have to rectify that sooner rather than later.

She blinked as she focused on processing and now understood how Lynx got that far away look in his eyes. The way the HUD expanded to complement feeding masses of information through her mind, understanding levels of power in much more intricate detail, and being able to process them all together with the help of the mind dilation techniques Milaro had initially taught her. She frowned.

The most spectacular revelation was the information available about every single patron. Now that the Library was mostly functional and highly powered, its scan data was ridiculously complex. They had, after all, in order to prevent another potential Tenejo situation, begun scanning everybody's intentions as they came into the Library. And they'd been doing so for months. Anyone intending harm would basically be detained, questioned, their intentions toward the Library ascertained.

What really fascinated her was the level of differentiation required by the system to figure out who could be a potential threat. So far, they'd quite literally flagged no one. Quinn didn't think that was possible. There'd been millions of visitors since she'd taken over. There was no way that everybody was their friend.

But the readings said otherwise.

Which could mean one of two things. The system was being fooled, or the conspirators were biding their time.

Or perhaps even both.

She pushed those thoughts to the side and focused on the system's consciousness. The Library was a living entity and its system an integral extension that enabled the Library to function. She loved the sensations running through her, the ability to access the knowledge immediately. Her HUD gave her more options now and more intricate details.

Quinn was stronger. She could feel it without even reaching for any of her power. It was a heady sense. One she thought she might have to indulge in and test out.

Her mind cleared fully, her fog gone, and her focus sharp.

She flexed her fingers, holding them up toward the ceiling, examining them as she continued to munch away on the replenishment food Cook had sent with Lynx. Speaking of which, she could sense him standing right next to her as she chewed away happily on the food. He was waiting and his patience was about to run out.

"Well?" he said expectantly.

Quinn grinned. "I think it worked," she said. "I feel more connected."

The Library's shadowy form approached her, curious. "You feel more connected?" the Library said.

"Definitely," Quinn said, pushing herself up slowly, her hand still held out in front of her. She was focused on the power that surrounded it, the shielding she'd summoned to test it out. It coalesced faster, with but a thought, a split second's construction. She murmured the words without really meaning to say them out loud.

"This is very different from last time."

"Well, last time you were thrown off guard by information you hadn't expected that we probably should have given you previously." The Library sounded more logical than contrite.

Quinn raised an eyebrow and couldn't help herself. "Probably?"

"Sarcasm, Quinn."

"I'm aware of that." She winked at the Library and continued to focus on the feel of her hand and her body now that her mind could categorize and create her wishes so much faster than previously.

"How do you feel?" the Library prompted. "Is it too much power too soon?"

Quinn shook her head and truly examined her mind outside of just accessing the information.

She was distant, looking down on things, able to see them from the outside and be analytical, yet at the same time, she was connected to everything in a much more intricate and intimate way. Could she get closer or have a better command of things? Probably, but the improvement over the last synchronization was astounding.

The Librarian was distant, yet close. Small, yet vast. Insignificant, yet powerful. It was all difficult to comprehend with her Earthen-raised perceptions.

She could understand why Hal insisted on calling her an egg in the grand scheme of things.

Every ability she already possessed flared within her, like the ceiling twinkled in time with how the power shimmered inside her, and she could tell that there were thousands upon thousands of abilities that she had yet to learn. So many. It was like a list inside her head for her to methodically work away at.

And it made her all sorts of excited to get started.

"Yeah," Quinn said, finally answering the question she'd been asked as she brought her hand down and clenching it into a fist. "What do you mean too soon?"

The Library took several seconds before it answered. "To be perfectly honest, when we do this with a new Librarian, you don't reach this level of synchronization for a couple of years. And then even longer for the final one. Having only been here six months, I might have been slightly concerned."

Quinn nodded, running the words over in her mind. It made sense. The Librarians weren't usually under any sort of time constraint. "I think I'm feeling pretty good."

"Do you want to try anything?" the Library said.

Quinn grinned and summoned her dancing flame on both hands, making the white-hot ball of fire dance between both hands, two of them juggling over each other, twirling over all of her fingertips.

"You did that before," Lynx said, clearly unimpressed.

"No. You don't understand," she said. "I'd only just managed one hand. This feels like I've expanded."

"How do you mean expanded?"

"Like my ability to enact and follow through with skills and affinities has expanded. The ability to juggle more than one thing at a time. That I can multitask and immediately pull my magic forward without having to give it a second, thought. I feel . . ." She paused for a second and realized there was only one word for it. "Calibrated."

"We can always pull up your information and double check."

And so Quinn did.

Name: Quinn

Age: Irrelevant

Heritage: Earth, Sector 12942—Infinite reach, pocket dimensional adaption

*Species: Librarian—of Cosmicisodracus origin—determining extent and variations**

Energy Capacity: 5,284/5,284

Mana Levels: 4,222/4,222

Regeneration: Energy Idle: 15 per second, Intensive Activity 8 per second.

Mana Idle: 14 per second, Intensive Activity 7 per second

Alignment: 117%

*Affinities: 1,723***

Tome Knowledge Expanded: Beginner levels 42% complete. Intermediate levels 12%. Advanced—0.05%—Higher levels not yet available.

Affinity Level: 32

Determination: Extended

**Cosmicisodracus properties established—awaiting essence distillation calibration effects*

***As far as the Library can determine*

Quinn blinked and turned to the shadow Library. "Is that . . . this normal?"

The Library shook its head. "That is one hundred percent not normal, as far as all my previous Librarians are concerned. However, it might be normal for a cosmicisodracus Librarian."

"But doesn't it apply to you, too?" Quinn was a little confused.

"I'm the Library, not a Librarian, which is a specific role we created to curb any potential corruption on my part."

"Did your scope not expand when the portal dimension melded with you?" Quinn asked.

"Oh," the Library said and chuckled ruefully. "That's very astute observation, Quinn. I didn't think of it like that. My stats increased as the system created itself too."

"So basically," Quinn said, "I think this is just natural for what I am."

It was a huge thought to wrap her head around. She was indeed evolving, could feel it with all of what she was. The excitement made her giddy. So much potential . . . power with which to protect the Library and everything it stood for.

Quinn moved quickly, engaging her speed with but a thought and moving herself into the middle of the core room. She conjured a flame into existence to float in midair. While it hovered, she shot icicles all around and used gravity to control them. With whim, with thought. She watched her energy tick down in the corner of her vision and grinned. She had so much. There was so much she could do.

And then she paused. "I shouldn't be getting any feelings of like grandiose megalomania, right?"

"What?" the Library said.

Lynx raised an eyebrow. "What do you mean?"

"I feel powerful. Like I can do anything," Quinn said.

"Well, you *can* do anything," the Library said.

"No, no, I don't—I don't mean it like that," Quinn said, pondering how to best express her point.

It didn't require conscious thought. She pulled back to all the books she'd read, the earthen ones in particular and the creation of earth affinity which allowed for the creation of sand. Pulling it forward, she gathered the flame she'd cast earlier and crafted a beautiful glass rose in her hand. It was hot, but her scales protected her from it.

Which was exactly what she'd meant. She could pull on all affinities and combine any of them with little more than a thought. Her scales made her impervious to heat, and . . .

And that's when she stopped, looking down at her arms, aghast. The blue iridescent scales shimmered. It wasn't overly prominent, but it was there, and try as she might, she couldn't get it to camouflage again. She looked up at Lynx, her eyes open wide.

"Can I not get rid of them now?" she asked. She wasn't sure if she should be shocked, upset, panicked, or excited. There was an element of fear involved there, too. Scared that she was changing too much.

"That's just your armor, Quinn," Lynx said. But he didn't sound so certain.

The shadow of the Library walked toward her. It passed its shadowy hand through her. And even though Quinn couldn't really tell if there was a frown on its face, it did make a very odd *hmm* sound.

"It's at a new strength level. You need to just let it sit for a bit. Once it acclimates to you, you should be able to fully control the morphing once again."

Quinn sighed, because she did love those scales. "It's not that I don't like them. I just—I prefer to have a choice."

"You will. Right now, it's just getting used to your new system."

Quinn nodded, pushing back on the fear that was trying to crawl up her spine and strangle her. "Okay," she said.

She released the flames and ice and gravity she was controlling all at the same time and grinned. "Now I wonder what else I can do."

6 2

ON BOARD

While Quinn hadn't entirely forgotten about the fact that she'd telegraphed her abilities after the initial synchronization, she'd pushed it so far back into her memory that she had, essentially, for all intents and purposes, forgotten that it would probably happen this time.

While she was downstairs in the core, with Lynx and the Library's shadow, everything was fine. But she didn't tamp down before entering the main level, as she ascended the stairs, giddy on the thought of all of the new sensations she was experiencing.

And her aura pretty much flattened everybody at the check-in desk.

She stopped in shock.

"Quinn," Lynx said, "manage your output."

She pulled it as far into herself as she could, which wasn't as far as she wanted to. That's when she noticed she was literally leaking power constantly. At least it was enough to free the people directly in front of and inside of the check-in desk from her influence. But it wasn't enough to free herself of the responsibility of re-learning how to manage it.

Milaro exited from her office, an eyebrow raised.

"You came up. I thought you'd call for me," he said.

"I was excited, and I thought I'd get to work straight away." Quinn knew she sounded subdued now, her confidence slightly shaken because of the projecting she thought she'd had a handle on.

He studied her for a few seconds and nodded. "I think we should get to work straight away." He smiled kindly, but she could see the tired and haunted feelings he'd pushed aside. The damage to Nishpa had hit him hard.

Quinn sighed.

Milaro took pity on her. "Look, there's a lot we need to do before you take on the next thing on your list, and one of them is teaching you how to restrain this round of power upgrade."

"But shouldn't it be just the same as it was before?" Quinn asked, deflated. "I thought I could just reel it in like I did with the previous round."

"It should technically be similar," he said, "but to be honest, this power boost, this information infusion? Much more encompassing than the last."

Quinn blinked at him. "Let's just go to my office. It has wards on it. At least it'll stop me from affecting others while I get control."

She trudged into the office, instead of running through all the new sensations the Library had to offer.

"It's okay, Quinn. We'll get this sorted," Milaro said quietly as they entered the room.

"Really?"

"Yep."

Quinn did her best to pull her power in toward her, to wrap it around her, secure it. Emotions always impacted her control, so she kept an eye on her ability to compartmentalize at will. She closed the door behind her and turned to face Milaro. He looked like he'd lost weight, which worried her.

"Quinn, take a breath and calm it down," Milaro said softly, his tone gentle and soothing. "I can literally feel the worry through your aura. Focus inward and concentrate on restricting the flow of your power so it remains within your shielding."

"I should keep my shielding up all the time, right?"

"Haven't you been?" he asked.

She considered that and realized she hadn't. "Not all the time, no."

"Considering the current circumstances, you should keep it active, at all times, just as a precaution. Both physically and mentally."

"Just in case?" Quinn asked.

"Yes."

She didn't want to dwell on the "just in case," because she knew, as well as anybody else, that right now wasn't the safest time for any of them.

"Okay." She sat down in her huge chair and began pulling the power leaking out from her back behind her shielding. There was almost double her old power pool to condense. Even as she pulled it into herself, she could feel the Library thrumming in response, their connection much deeper than it had been. If she focused really closely, she could even pick up on actual conversations and not just sensations or emotions.

Just to test it out, she concentrated on the check-in desk and watched Betty and Jasper having a bit of a row.

Quinn frowned.

"What do you see, Quinn?" Milaro asked.

"Betty and Jasper are just . . ."

"Ah, yes, they've been at that for several hours."

Quinn was a bit shocked. "What do you mean?"

Milaro smiled kindly as he explained. "You appointed Jasper as your assistant, and to help with rosters and allocations."

"Jasper helps me. Betty is supposed to be the supervisor to help run the . . . oh." Quinn paused. "Oh, I see. I'm going to have to talk to them, aren't I?"

"I'm sure they can sort it out themselves," Milaro said. "What I want you to sort out is the bleeding of the power still going on despite your current best efforts."

Quinn took a breath and focused herself again. She still made a note that she'd speak to both Betty and Jasper together and make sure they were on the same page and in not at each other's throats. And hopefully not angry with her.

"Jasper's been gone for a while anyway," Quinn muttered as she continued to focus and condense her power within her walls. She realized she needed to readjust her mental shielding capacity as well.

"Jasper has been gone for a while under your orders."

"Not quite under my orders. She and Lynx were working together on locating the tomes," Quinn said.

"Oh," Milaro said, frowning. "I wonder if she's located them."

"They'll let us know soon enough." Quinn shrugged and narrowed her gaze as she looked at him. "Speaking of sending away, you were supposed to be taking it easy back in your palace."

"Yes, and then we were attacked by somebody who was supposed to be a friend."

Quinn felt a wave of melancholy emit from her teacher. It was so fast she almost thought she imagined it and had no idea how to comfort him. "I know. I'm sorry."

"I'm sorry too, Quinn. I didn't see that coming. And for all my abilities, I should have. They were married for over a hundred years. I think I should have noticed something amiss in that time, and I did not. I'd claim extenuating circumstances, but I don't think that's an excuse."

Quinn nodded.

"We can't catch everyone." He sounded like he was trying to convince himself.

"But we can keep trying," she offered in consolation.

He smiled, a hint of sadness in his gaze. "We'll talk about that as soon as you focus inward and start working on your mental and physical shielding."

She sighed, pulling her scaled feet up under her and held her scaled arms, open palm up in front of her and resting on the desk. She took several deep breaths, centering herself and drawing her power into her center. Then she spread it out through her body, reinforcing everything around her, her skin, her hair, every limb, every appendage, all of herself, bringing the power inside and making it an integral part of who she was. All she had to do was remember to circulate it, and it should remain a part of her, even in sleep, no matter what.

Another line of defense.

Quinn wasn't sure how long she meditated like that for. She was pretty sure it was a few hours before she finally looked up, blinking her eyes back open, and smiled at Milaro.

"Done?" Milaro asked, closing the tome he'd been perusing while she meditated.

"I think so," she said.

"Worry about me," he said with a smirk.

She did. She never stopped. She told him that. "I've never stopped worrying about you."

"Excellent," he said. "I can't sense you're worried about me unless I look at you, and then it's not an aura thing. It's not leaking out and reaching toward me like a baby crying its heart out. You're just judging my lack of resting with your eyes."

Quinn raised an eyebrow.

"Sorry," Milaro said. "That was a bit nasty of me, wasn't it?"

"Yes, it was. And you still owe me a feast."

He laughed. "Yes, I do. Soon. Hopefully, we'll get this all sorted quickly."

Quinn wasn't sure how to tell him that she didn't think so. Instead, she shrugged. "Well, you know, maybe it will be, maybe it won't be. But we'll see."

As if on cue, Jasper knocked on the door. "Come in, come in."

"How are you feeling?" Jasper said, warily entering the room, as if she was testing waters to see if she needed to flee.

Quinn raised an eyebrow. "I'm fine. I just finished synchronization. There's always some hiccups afterwards." She realized she sounded like she was an expert or something, which she so wasn't. Then again, none of them had synchronized with the Library, so maybe she was.

She glanced down at her hands and realized the scales had retreated and were barely visible inside her skin. There was a slight sense of loss, just a pang, that the scales were no longer visible. But at least now she had the ability to keep herself and anybody else she cared about safe. If only she'd synchronized before the whole Nishpa incident. Maybe she could have just . . . maybe. She didn't know.

Jasper grinned at her. "I'm glad to hear you have it under control."

But Jasper didn't get any further because Betty dashed into the room. "I thought I was the supervisor."

"You're the head supervisor. But Jasper is my personal assistant, and originally all the rosters fell to me, so Jasper took them over." Quinn grimaced as she admitted the next part. "It slipped my mind when I asked you to be head supervisor and take care of everything, so I hope I haven't caused either of you too much trouble."

They blinked at her. "You knew?"

Betty recovered first, an expression of delight crossing her features. "Wonderful! You've synchronized properly! Are you feeling tired? You'll probably be feeling very hungry before long. I'll make sure Cook brings you adequate sustenance. You'll be on your feet in no time and running everything like usual."

Quinn blinked at the sprite. Betty was fully capable of talking the leg off an iron pot. It was a saying Quinn had heard several times, completely and utterly not understood, until now. Very specifically in relation to Betty.

Jasper laughed. "I'm happy to relinquish the rosters if Quinn needs me for other things."

Quinn nodded slowly. "You've been so busy working with Lynx, it just escaped my memory that you were doing the rosters. Sorry."

Betty clapped her hands in glee. "Oh, perfect. I so did not want to fight, but I am very good at rostering staff on for the specific time periods required by Library patronage numbers."

Jasper blinked at her. "I'm gonna leave the rosters in your hands. I've been on a bit of a mission myself, anyway."

"But you did set up the rosters very nicely," Betty said. "I'm extremely happy you had, only they run out in four days, so I'd already taken the liberty of extending them."

Jasper waved her concern away. "I've already relinquished them to you. We're fine."

"So," Quinn interrupted. "What were you doing?"

"What do you mean?" Jasper looked confused at first before grinning widely. "You know I was working with Lynx. I went and hunted down the book locations."

"What?" Quinn said. "How? The areas were so vast!"

"Lynx and I spoke, and we thought that if I got closer to the approximate area, I could use a more targeted location ritual. It took a bit because I had to manually get closer to the areas and portal hop around until I got results. Not all areas were friendly, but eventually I was able to get us a door location. You can't picture a door you're not familiar with, and I don't have the magical affinity to create a door. That's why Lynx does so many of the calibrations when he's sending us to other places, you know."

Quinn nodded, realizing belatedly that between Jasper and Betty, she'd probably never have to speak again.

"Precisely, so it took me a few weeks. Anyway, anyway, I have a location for you." Jasper had the biggest grin on her face.

Quinn couldn't keep her jaw from the floor. Excitement nibbled at her, but she pushed it back, just in case she'd misunderstood that. "Wait, wait, what?"

"Exactly," Lynx said, swirling into being right next to them. "I've been waiting for this. You got the location, then?"

Jasper positively beamed, even if it was a bit smug. "Yeah, we need to go through Gate 73 of Naka Isle."

"Are you serious?" he asked.

"No, I'm joking," she deadpanned before continuing. "That's the easiest gate to get to, close enough to make it there in a decent amount of time."

"It's a long trek, then," Quinn said.

Lynx sighed and shook his head as he frowned at something in his HUD. "Not as long as I anticipated."

"Is it dangerous?" Quinn asked.

He shrugged. "I'm not entirely sure, it's just that . . ."

She waited for the manifestation to get his thoughts organized.

"It's just that it's in a pretty barren region. Most of the areas around that one are uninhabitable, which we luckily don't have to consider. But there are uncommon oasis type regions. Naka 73 is one of those. The people there are . . . different."

Quinn frowned at the phrasing. "Okay."

I'll double check the hibernation frequency again, the Library interjected briefly, its presence diminishing as soon as it finished.

"Don't worry," Milaro piped in. "It's going to be fine. You'll take myself, Malakai . . . what do you think of taking Hal too?"

Quinn nodded. "But doesn't he have like a war or seven to win or something?"

Lynx laughed. So did Milaro. "Yes. Yes, he does. However, it doesn't really mean anything. He'll win it. He always does."

Quinn raised an eyebrow, wanting to go deeper into that when time permitted.

"Team Quinn," Lynx said. "Quinn, Malakai, Milaro, Hal, Jasper, Geneva, and Eric?

Quinn nodded slowly. There was no Misha to kit them out and no Nishpa to heal them. She knew Geneva had some healing abilities, as did she, so hopefully they'd be okay. Malakai couldn't really use his magic, but he should be able to provide field dressings if needed. "I think I need more healing books."

"You read the *Healing With Fire* one, right?" Milaro said.

"Yeah."

"Okay, well, that's one book down." He mulled it over, his brow furrowed with concentration.

"What, and eighty-three to go?" Quinn asked cheekily.

"Pretty much, but your capacity should have increased with synchronization."

"You mean I'll be able to absorb more than five books at a time?" The thought sent a sense of relief flooding through her. It made knowing what she needed to know in the time she had to learn it seem so much more within her grasp.

He sort of squinted as if he was calculating something mentally.

"Maybe eight. But I wouldn't recommend pushing it. There's still only so much you can process."

"What are we waiting for? Let's make a list so I can learn them and so we can go."

"Yeah," Lynx said. "I think you should go sooner rather than later. It's probably a better idea to get to Drukala as soon as you can."

"Okay," Quinn said. "You guys on board?" she asked everyone in general.

"Yep, I'll round everybody up," Milaro said, answering for them all. "Let's hope that we can get everything we need without Misha. It'd be a good idea to leave tomorrow—as soon as possible."

Quinn couldn't help the pang of emptiness she felt at knowing that right now the supervisory golem couldn't even pop in when her name was mentioned if she'd wanted to.

READY TO DIVE

WHEN QUINN WOKE UP THE FOLLOWING MORNING, SHE COULD BARELY move. It took several seconds for her to push through the fog darkening her brain and realize the reason she couldn't move wasn't exhaustion, nor because she was sore from some phantom workout the night before. Instead, it was because most of the massive eight tomes Milaro decided to have her absorb before going to sleep were scattered all over her.

She had to wriggle out from under most of them—like a caterpillar —push them away, and close them.

She did so reverently.

The books had been a lot to absorb. Even now she wasn't sure one night was enough processing time. She'd read *The Many-Fold Electrical Pulses of Tiuri Brain Melding*, *How to Avoid Pitfalls of Mind Manipulation: Tacte's Secret Files*, and *Zhexiel's Species Variants and Their Common Ground When Brain Mapping*. She was excited to process all the information on those.

Sighing, she piled up the three mind books and got to work on the healing ones. *Black's Compositum of Healing Energy Transformation*, *The Invictus Method Healing From Blood*, and *Alexial's Many-Fold Healing Energies Adapted From Surrounding Environments*. Even the healing books were now intermediate level. She wasn't knowledgeable enough to absorb the advanced level yet, but she understood more of what she'd done instinctively back in the fight where they took Kajaro prisoner. Now, she'd be able to replicate those actions at any time. It was a relief.

Taking ambient energy and distributing it to her team should keep them alive and able to fight longer. The last two books were separate areas. *The Otomian Shielding Method* made the shielding around her, and when she chose to extend it to others, warpable . . . or malleable might be the better word for it. Quinn wasn't entirely sure, but it gave her more options to use with the shielding itself.

And finally, she closed and stacked *Dimensional Readings in the Ediav Style—Between the Lines.* She really had to wonder at some of these titles. They weren't catchy anymore; they were just long and explanatory. But she guessed when she got to an intermediate, advanced, and above, maybe you were just there for the books and what they contained, and not necessarily for the fun factor of learning a new skill. And since she already had it, they didn't have to bait her into it.

The *Dimensional Readings in the Ediav Style—Between the Lines* should help her communicate with Drukala. She really needed to talk to the Library about that. But now, freed from her book prison, Quinn pushed herself out of it, waited for Aradie to alight softly on her shoulder, and made her way into the bathroom.

A short time later, the both of them headed downstairs.

Today was the day. Armed with new knowledge that would help them healing-wise, shielding-wise, and understanding dimensional energies, Quinn was quite prepared to face her auntie, perhaps even a bit giddy. She was about to go and see family for the first time in ever. Well, if she counted the Library as family, because technically it was.

There were a lot of technicalities involved with Quinn's life in the Library.

Malakai strode towards her as soon as she appeared. The Library was positively bursting with people. She paused and looked around. "Have I missed something?" she asked.

Malakai shook his head. "Nope. I'd say this is the work of Betty."

Quinn blinked at Betty, who flitted back and forth like a hummingbird between the people checking in the books, and she stared at the beautiful mahogany check-in desk. Flabbergasted. "Has it expanded again?" she said to Malakai.

"Yep, necessity. We currently have three check-in lines, and frankly, I should probably go help." But he gave no indication of moving toward the desk.

Quinn shook her head and smiled.

"No, no. I'm technically still a supervisor." He protested too much.

Quinn laughed. "And you'll technically stay a supervisor, but we have a trip to pack for and get ready for, and you don't have time to do this right now. Not that you seem overly inclined, anyway."

"You wound me." Malakai placed his hand over his heart in mock affront until a grin slipped out, anyway.

Dottie was trotting toward the check-in desk as well. "Oh, Quinn," Dottie said, "it's good to see you. How are you feeling after the synchronization?"

Quinn smiled at the bench. "Very well, thank you, Dottie."

"Excellent, excellent. We're a little busy. I've come over early because I thought I'd give Betty a hand. She's one of my best friends, you know."

Quinn nodded as the little bench trotted up and began assisting. It was always fun watching the bench assist. She did so by using telekinesis for everything. From taking the books, to checking them in.

Quinn cocked her head to one side.

Malakai nudged her in the ribs.

"Ow! That hurt!" She glared at him.

"You've known Dottie for like six months, and this is the first time you've watched her check in books."

"She's usually the supervisor," Quinn muttered.

He chuckled. "Come on, we've got a meeting to get to."

"Meeting?" she said. "Seriously?"

"We do leave in a few hours."

She blinked, excitement suddenly buzzing through her again. "We do, don't we?"

"Yes, and we still need our gear, have to gather the team, and figure out what the hell we're doing." As he spoke, they made their way to the storage room.

Quinn felt a pang of sadness when she realized that Misha wasn't there, and wouldn't walk through the door to greet them all, or beep into being in front of them. She really had to pull herself together, considering she wasn't sure how long Misha would be out of commission. They had a book to find, and couldn't wait.

Quinn smiled as she saw Milaro, Jasper, and Geneva moving around the storage room, getting supplies ready. She frowned and looked about. "Is Hal not here yet?"

Milaro cleared his throat. "No, he isn't. He'll be here shortly. He promised he'd be on time to leave."

"Doesn't he need—"

"No," Milaro said, "he doesn't need the same sort of equipment preparation that most of us do. And you, well, you're sort of in that same boat, aren't you?"

She raised an eyebrow and shrugged. Several minutes passed while Quinn picked her stuff, and then Lynx popped in front of her. "Come on, Quinn, we need to talk."

Quinn watched him for a second, but followed him quickly into her office.

"What's all this about?" she asked.

"I need you to listen to me, Quinn," the Library responded as the shadow manifested in her office. The shadow rarely appeared outside of the core room. Quinn glanced at Lynx, who shrugged his shoulders as if to say, *This is what I had to bring you for.*

"Why couldn't you just speak in my head?" Quinn asked. "I have so many conversations with you inside my head, and nobody's the wiser."

"Just to be safer," the Library replied.

"Do you suspect somebody who I'm taking with me?" Quinn asked. "I'm not taking them with me if you do."

"Calm down," the Library said.

Quinn didn't really want to calm down, but she also didn't want to make a big deal of it. She took in a deep breath and spoke. "Come on, spill. What's the problem?"

"I need to have a word with you about my sister." The smoky version of the Library wrung its hands.

"Oh," Quinn said, feeling slightly sorry for it. The Library couldn't travel to visit its siblings. It made her wonder if that made it sad. "Sorry, I was just excited about getting all my things together."

"I know. I wanted to tell you," the Library started, "the upgrades and the synchronization have given us such a boost that I am a hundred percent sure it's my sister. I've continued to nudge her, so her hibernation is currently light. During hibernation, she can and will smell anything coming within her domain. When she smells you, Quinn . . ."

Quinn raised her eyebrow and was absolutely unable to stop herself. "Are you telling me I stink? I need to get a shower before we go."

"It's not that kind of smell, Quinn. It's an identifying smell. You have about ninety-seven percent of my scent mixed in with you. With the rest of the essence divinations that are mixed into your being, it makes you obviously like me, and yet still foreign. She'll be probably be curious and standoffish, because Drukala is a little eccentric. But I don't think she's evil like my brother. I'm worried, and that's why I asked Hal to go with you."

"You asked Hal?" It made more sense in Quinn's mind that he was coming with them now.

"Yes. I needed to make sure you're safe, and at the same time, you're the only one who'll be able to talk to her properly. And he has the power to protect you if she's in a bad mood."

"A bad mood?" Quinn pondered that. "And why would she be in a bad mood?"

"I'm not used to her sleeping with a hoard of books. It feels suspect to me." The shadow faded for a second before condensing again.

"You say that like she has more than the one."

"Well . . . it would make sense to hide some of them there."

Quinn nodded. "It would, as I've mentioned."

"Anyway, make sure you approach cautiously. If you have to, use my real name, so that she knows that you're really with me. She'll sense you as soon as you're in range. I'll keep trying to wake her. Be prepared for her moods and, well, for ambushes."

"Right," Quinn said, a thousand other questions popping up in her head.

"Yes. I do not, for one second, believe that my brother didn't deliberately place that book there."

"Are you ever going to tell me why he's suddenly doing this?" Quinn asked quietly.

The Library paused and its sigh was obvious. "I will, Quinn, as soon as I know why myself."

"It's a deal," she said. "I've got to get my stuff organized."

"Take Aradie with you," the Library said. Aradie cooed as if she was saying *Of course*. Quinn found herself relaxing. Knowing Aradie was with her made it just that bit more bearable, especially since she knew more of the owl's powers now.

They made it back to the storage room without incident. Hal popped into being right next to them while they were all packing up their stuff.

"You know you don't really need that suit," he said to Quinn. He didn't have one on himself. "You're a primordial being. You don't need the protection; you're not going to die."

"Yes, but I'm not yet fully transformed, thank you very much." She was quite proud of herself for not balking with her answer even though his words sent shivers down her spine. Still, so much of her heritage to grow into and get used to.

"Good point," he said. "Technically, cosmicisodracus shouldn't need much help. I mean, at this power level, you should be able to breathe anywhere."

She blinked at him, making a note of the whole breathing thing. "You know I'm not fully . . . upgraded yet, right?" She wasn't sure how else to express it.

He nodded. "Of course. Anyway"—he clapped his hands—"are we ready to go?"

"Almost, almost," Malakai said. Milaro laughed. "You're always impatient, Hal."

"And you're not coming with us, right, Milaro?" Hal said, in a way that told Quinn there was an understanding among them she knew nothing about.

Milaro nodded, his eyes narrowing.

Quinn hoped he was staying here to keep an eye on Nishpa and his own health and not for some reason they weren't telling her.

Several minutes later, when they were all decked out, Cook approached them, each with a large bag that included food, drink, and other supplements to assist them in mana and energy regeneration. Quinn looked through hers.

"This is different," she said, eyeing the energy food. It wasn't a ball anymore, and it wasn't even a cupcake. It was like a really yummy-looking piece of carrot cake. She raised an eyebrow. "Did you pack energy replenishment into a carrot cake for me?"

She could have sworn Cook grinned.

"I still don't understand how you do it, but I don't even care anymore. Thank you." And she impulsively threw her arms around Cook and gave them a big hug.

Cook returned it, patting her very gently on the back before releasing her. "Make sure you come back. I have several new recipes to cook for you."

Quinn smiled. "Thank you." And hoisted all of her stuff into her dimensional storage. "Well," she said, turning to everyone. "Are we ready to go?"

Malakai moved to the front with Quinn, while Hal brought up the rear, with Geneva just off to one side of Quinn and Eric on the other side of Malakai. Aradie hovered above, ready to dive through the portal.

"Well, this is it," she said. "Let's go meet my aunt."

6 4

THE RIGHT PLACE

THE VIEW THEY ENCOUNTERED AS THEY FLOATED THROUGH THE PORTAL almost made Quinn forget to hover. She didn't expect to step into a mountainous region that looked like it was taken directly off a postcard from Switzerland.

They were in a small valley, and she watched as the beautiful rolling hills with their differing shades of green and bushes and trees scattered all about spread out before them into majestic, soft mountains. Some of them in the distance had snow-tipped peaks that resembled marshmallow topping over lime sherbet or mint chocolate chip ice cream. It reminded her of places she'd always wanted to travel to, the things she'd wanted to save for once she finished her degree and got a job.

Now she could just open a door and step out into this.

It was magical, really and literally.

She could make out herds of what looked like sheep and goats and yaks, although upon closer inspection, she was pretty sure the sheep had multiple horns, all the way from their head in a stripe down their back. And the yaks had two heads, so they weren't exactly the same as Earth creatures, she guessed, but the air was fresh and thin and reminded her of documentaries about mountainous regions back on Earth.

An undercurrent of pine mixed with eucalyptus gave the whole area around them such a clean and undisturbed smell. She drank it in, feeling the breeze kiss her cheeks, ruffle her hair. The gods knew her ponytail was already as untidy as it could get. She sighed. A bit of a breeze wouldn't hurt her.

She paused, several steps down already, almost wanting to run to the next hilltop, fling her arms open wide, and burst into song. Yet, she knew no one around her would get the reference. When no one appeared next to her, she frowned. She'd thought the others would have spilled out the doorway and be appreciating this by now too. That's when she noticed the sounds. There were shuffling sounds and some whisperings that she could hear over the breeze when she concentrated. Slowly, she turned around and realized immediately that all semblance to Earth's Europe stopped with the mountains, because the people now in front of her were nowhere near human.

Quinn took them in. No wonder she hadn't seen them. They'd been standing to the side of the door entrance. She noticed that the rest of her party was there and already turned around, watching the people. They were stocky with angular features and indeterminate gender, all different colors of hair ranging from green through red and oranges, yellow, blacks, and blues. There were probably about two dozen of them standing there. They ranged from about four to six feet tall and with dark brown skin that reminded her of textured clay, as if it had coarse brushstrokes drawn through it before the refining process was finished.

The system called them Narae Nomads of the Naka region, and this was indeed Gate 73.

She frowned. They weren't affiliated with the Library in any way, shape or form. It made it extremely awkward, because she had no idea if they were even aware of the Library or the Librarian, and it was the first time she'd encountered this since coming to the little portal dimension. How did she go about introducing herself?

"Ah," Jasper said, stepping forward to greet them, her exuberance a calming force for Quinn. "Excellent to see you all. I did warn you we'd be coming soon."

One of the smaller members of the Narae stepped forward and bowed their head. "Well met, Jasper. We have prepared food and supplies. They are hearty and will survive the trip to the top." Her words were slow and deliberate. As if she wasn't used to speaking out loud.

"Excellent. Thank you, Ara, that's very kind of you." Jasper offered one of her dazzling smiles.

Ara bowed their head and backed away. Quinn thought that was the end of it, but then Ara simply paused and spoke again in halting language. Quinn assumed the system was translating for her, but at the same time, perhaps they just didn't speak much.

That's when Malakai's voice brushed her mind. *They're a telepathic species, Quinn. They aren't used to speaking out loud, but it's rude to speak into the minds of people you don't know.*

Good thing you know me, then, isn't it? she commented and smiled as Ara began to speak.

"We do caution you to approach the Death Mountain."

Death Mountain had such ominous overtones, especially given everything they were here to prevent. Quinn raised an eyebrow, but she listened anyway.

"It is known so because we have never been able to traverse it," Ara continued haltingly.

"It's hundreds of miles away," Quinn said, squinting at the looming black monstrosities in front of them. "Why would you want to traverse it?"

Ara looked at her and shrugged. "For the challenge, which is why we do most things."

Quinn nodded very slowly. "You didn't seem surprised by the magical door we walked through."

Ara chuckled. "We are not a magical people ourselves. But the world around us is filled with it. And we understand that while we do not comprehend everything, magic is deserving of respect."

Quinn nodded. She thought that was pretty sage of them.

"Okay," she said, examining the distant mountains again.

She could tell that if they simply walked there, which she knew they wouldn't because they all had flight and means of travelling fast on their side, it would take days. Heck, it would take a while by car if she had one. And still, the dark mountains made of what looked like igneous rock rose up so high she couldn't even see the peaks of them.

There was such an ominous vibe emanating from them, even this far away from them. Death Mountains seemed like an apt name. Far away and out of reach, and foreboding. And they still managed to cast a shadow that almost reached the settlement.

The two sides up from the valley were such a stark juxtaposition. One beautiful and idyllic, the other dark and mysterious. The latter almost felt like it wanted them to ignore it.

She looked around at the rest of her group. Jasper simply raised an eyebrow. Hal and Malakai were obviously taking everything around them in. Eric and Geneva hovered, expectantly. They were all waiting for her. Aradie settled on her shoulder.

"I thank you, Ara, for your hospitality," Quinn said finally. "It's much appreciated."

"Jasper mentioned it was a very important thing."

Quinn nodded. "That it is. Do you have any advice?"

Ara's eyes grew big and round for a second before returning to normal. "The grounds toward the mountain range are treacherous. Watch out for lava pits and other sinkholes. There are also different air currents streaming through the area—hot and cold. Be wary if you fly."

Quinn frowned. She turned a full 360 degrees, taking in the beautiful, luscious grass and the absolutely gorgeous, idyllic setting in the other direction. She paused when she got back to Ara, absolutely certain of the type of terrain they were about to traverse. "How is that volcanic rock?"

"Volcanic?" Ara paused for a second before continuing. "Yes, yes, that is the correct term. Very long, dormant, but the rock formations are still igneous rock."

Hal smiled and stepped forward. "Igneous rock. I happen to be an expert."

Ara's gaze narrowed, and they stepped to the side. "Expert in volcanic rock. You look very much like our history's mentioned satyrs. Is that what you are?"

Hal grinned. "Haven't done much interdimensional travel, have you?"

Ara shook their head slowly. "As previously mentioned, I have not done any interdimensional travel. It is not what our tribes do. We are here to take care of the land and ourselves—to live with the land, not against it. It is what we do. The magic that floats in the air that you feel and smell. It is a part of all of us. We simply take it and give back to the earth."

Quinn loved the speech. Absolutely adored it. Hal smiled and his expression softened. Quinn could tell just from the way he stood and his body language shifted that he liked this area.

"Well," Hal said, "maybe one day you will consider traveling."

Ara raised a very thick eyebrow and shook their head ruefully. "I do not foresee this, but I am not a farseer and so perhaps one day you will be right."

The group jostled together and headed out from the small, tented settlement. They walked a ways. Quinn didn't think it was a good idea to just fire up good old magic right then and there. It felt disrespectful to the way these people lived their lives and to the reverence that they had for the earth and the world around them. And so, she made sure they kept walking until they could pull to the side in a very small copse of trees.

She waited till everyone was gathered. "I don't think that we should flaunt the fact that we're avid users of magic, consuming the magic that they would otherwise give to the earth right in front of them."

Hal chuckled. "That's kind of you, little egg. But you do realize they could never hope to use all the ambient magic floating around, especially in this world. I don't know if you've noticed it."

Eric snapped, "They should just donate some excess to the Library."

Quinn laughed. "What, like a fine because they don't go?"

"Exactly!" he said. "Everybody should go to the Library. Why haven't they traveled? Why wouldn't they want to travel?"

Quinn raised an eyebrow, but Malakai was the one who spoke. "Not everybody is discontent," he said. "You know, I think we all seek some sort of meaning. These people are fully happy the way they are. I kind of envy them."

Jasper sighed. "Well, it took a lot to find this place. I had to jump to a plethora of worlds around this, but as is now obvious, this one appears to be the right one."

Quinn eyed the mountainous region. "I refuse to walk however many hundred miles it is to the destination."

Hal chuckled. "Why not? You could get fit, little egg. You need to experience some hardship."

She raised an eyebrow. "I've experienced plenty of hardship, thanks. I grew up without parents in the foster system."

Hal's expression changed ever so slightly. "You're right, I apologize."

"Good, so you should," she said, and turned to Malakai as the others began discussing between themselves. "You okay?" she asked.

"Yep, just, you know, not really . . ." Malakai had a faraway look in his eyes.

Quinn prodded him gently. "I'm sure you'll tell me when you're ready."

"Yep," he said, but now he was flashing her a cheeky grin. "I will."

"Gonna tell me what you and your grandfather were talking about before we ventured here?"

"He just reminded me not to use magic yet. My time limit isn't quite up." He seemed very irritated by that fact.

"Promise me too," Quinn said, suddenly serious. "We'll get through it without you accessing your magic. We've got enough of us to do this. But I've only got one of you, and you need to take care of yourself." She hoped she didn't sound too desperate for him not to get hurt. Desperation was never a good look.

He glanced at her and finally nodded. "As long as you take care of yourself, too."

"Well, of course, there's only one of me." She grinned.

Geneva sighed. "I think flying is the best. It will get us there sooner. All of us can fly. And those of us who can't"—she eyed Hal—"have other means of transportation."

Quinn turned to Malakai. "Isn't your flying magic, though?"

"No, it's one of my sword techniques, so this won't harm me."

"Okay," Quinn said, confused for a second by several of the sensations her senses picked up.

Jasper preened a little, "I got the place, right? We're good?"

Quinn nodded emphatically. "Oh yeah, we're headed to the right place."

"And how do you know that, little egg?" Hal asked.

"Because, just like when we found the blood tree with Machmüller's book, I can sense it. It's pulling me. I know it's there."

"Really?"

"Yeah. There's at least one Library book stuck in that mountain."

6 5

SOMETHING ABOUT EVERYTHING

With each yard they covered, the pull remained constant. It never waned in all its subtlety. It wasn't as strong as the tug of Machmüller's book. Which Quinn hoped meant it hadn't drained the lifesblood of a settlement. Instead, it was a faint thread, pulling her ever so gently in the vague direction of the mountains in front of them.

The mountains, however, didn't appear to be getting any closer.

Despite their ability to fly, they didn't know the terrain. Pockets of hot and cold air blasted up at indeterminate intervals and interfered with their equilibrium, so they had to be careful. Up above them she'd spied flying menaces that resembled pterodactyls, so they remained closer to hovering distance from the ground. They probably traveled about as fast as a car in a residential district. Fast enough to eat at the distance.

But the journey was taking way longer than she'd expected.

She glanced over as Geneva got sideswiped by a hot gust of air from the ground. She lost control very briefly, regaining it only after she spiraled tumultuously head over foot for several feet. She shook her head and rejoined them as they waited for her.

Eric smirked. "Ooh, little fae, lost control of your wings?" he teased.

"You wouldn't have fared any better," she retorted.

The two of them bickered as they traveled, lending background sound to the journey.

Quinn thought that since the ordeal on Ishiposa Isle, Geneva had hardened. She wasn't mousy anymore. She spoke up and stood up for herself. Quinn was proud of her evolution, even if she regretted the circumstances under which the Furionas fae had evolved.

And Eric, she'd really missed Eric, especially his banter. As the two of them argued and fought, it was quite entertaining. They never missed a beat, not even after a couple of hours, from Quinn's calculations.

She could still feel the pull of the book they were after, but it still felt so far away. Almost as if they were hovering in place.

"Is that like an enchantment or something?" she asked, gesturing to the mountains ahead of them that still seemed just as far away.

Hal shook his head, but he did focus on it, squinting. "I believe it is quite far away. I'm not sensing anything misleading, no sense of illusion." He frowned, though, as if thinking it over.

Quinn nodded. She didn't sense anything either. She was, however, quite focused on the fact that the book, or as she was beginning to suspect, perhaps books, were pulling her towards their destination. Even though beckoning, was probably the better term for it. Would Drukala sense her before they got there? If so, how soon?

She slowed down and paused. "Let's eat," she said. "I'm feeling really peckish."

Granted, her hovering flight that she was doing right now took energy, but she had so much of it since the synchronization, it didn't even make a dent. Her ability to regenerate it had increased so much that she basically would have gained thirty mana every minute, if it were possible to exceed her capacity.

"Quinn," Jasper said, and Quinn actually looked at Jasper for the first time since they'd gotten there, really looked at her. Her friend looked slightly nervous and perturbed.

"You don't spend much time away from home, do you?" Quinn asked suddenly.

"No, I'm much more comfortable with a lot of trees or enclosed spaces." Her gaze flitted about, nervousness evident.

"It's okay, stick next to me. I'll let my imposing aura drench you, so you feel enclosed." She grinned at her friend.

Jasper stared at her for about two seconds before she burst into laughter. "Thanks, Quinn, needed that."

Aradie cooed happily once more, sitting on Quinn's shoulder. Glancing back from where they'd come, Quinn did a double-take. The little hut village they'd been at, where they'd met Ara and acquainted themselves with the area, wasn't even visible anymore. She could still see the rolling green hills that led up to the beautiful mountains beyond them, and vaguely could still glimpse little dots all over the hillside of the different packs of animals or herds of animals that littered them. Since she hadn't inspected the creatures, she wasn't exactly sure what they were called, and thus wasn't sure if they were a herd, a pack, a parliament, or a murder.

"We really traveled that far already," she muttered under her breath and turned to face the destination, which, again, seemed no closer than it was before.

Malakai nudged her. "You're over-analyzing everything, Quinn."

"Yeah, probably."

"Sit, eat," he said, and waved to where everybody else had already sat except for Hal, who stood several paces beyond their group, frowning at the mountain above them.

She desperately wanted to ask him what he thought, but she got the distinct feeling that when he was ready, he'd tell her.

Eric and Geneva continued to quarrel.

"What is your problem?" Geneva asked.

Eric bristled. "I don't have a problem. Only one of us should have come."

"Yes, and I'm a healer, so I'm preferable."

"You're only a partial healer," Eric scoffed. "You're nowhere near as . . ."

But he stopped and Quinn was quite certain he'd been going to say that she was nowhere near as good as Nishpa and blessed whatever element of self-preservation the imp had not to have said it to Nishpa's niece. It was clear that Geneva knew what he was going to say too, and a flash of appreciation passed through her gaze.

"There's room for the both of us," she said. "Just stop being an insufferable prat."

Instead of retaliating, Eric chuckled. Quinn foresaw a beautiful friendship, hopefully at least for the next forty-eight hours.

They ate their food, and Quinn stood back up, brushing herself off. She wasn't hungry anymore. She wasn't thirsty. She had a dull headache, and the tug pulled right in the center of her chest. She frowned.

"Do you think we'll make it there before dark?" she asked.

Hal shrugged. "Probably not? But we should try anyway. So let's get going."

Quinn nodded, and they took flight once more.

The mountain inched painfully closer. Malakai walked in silence next to Jasper, and they jostled to be closest to Quinn. Since they flew shoulder to shoulder, it made Quinn feel even shorter flying next to Hal's towering form. Meanwhile, Eric and Geneva quipped back and forth, and Aradie flew overhead.

"You are being quiet, little egg, a lot quieter than I'm used to," Hal muttered.

Quinn frowned, finding herself strangely on edge. That whole gut feeling thing again. "It's . . . you feel a sensation?"

He observed her from a side-eye. "That tugging you mentioned?"

"Yeah, it's . . ." She paused, as if trying to figure it out. "It's a little different from the Machmüller's text, and I'm trying to figure out how."

"You are a lot more sensitive now. You're not used to the extension of your abilities. Thus, are you sure you're not just being hypersensitive to your surroundings?" He wasn't asking in a condescending sort of way. He was obviously genuinely curious.

Quinn shrugged. "I'm not entirely sure."

After a couple of moments, he spoke again. "We're getting close enough now that if Drukala is in one of those mountains, she'll be able to smell you soon, little egg. And even though she won't wake up immediately, it'll probably push her to wakefulness. You realize this, yes?"

Quinn nodded, fully aware of it, and suddenly thought to ask a question. "You're, like, really old, right?"

Hal threw his head back and laughed. "Yes. I'm, like, really old. Almost as old as your brethren."

Quinn nodded. "Have you met Drukala before?"

"Oh, yes," he said, and his tone changed. She couldn't figure out if it was melancholy or simmering resentment. "I've met all of them. I've worked with all of them."

Quinn blinked at him. "All of them?"

"Yes, all of them. I've been around since the Library was founded. I was young and impulsive then, but so were the rest of my siblings. There was no need yet to defend my home."

Quinn nodded, taking that in. "How long has it been since you've seen Drukala?" She sort of wondered why they used her name, until she remembered they were trying to wake her up.

"Oh," he said, thumbing his chin. "I haven't seen her in probably a mega-annum." He nodded to himself, as if confirming it. "Oh, at least."

Quinn balked and stopped, causing Malakai and Jasper to pull up short to avoid running into her. "You haven't seen her in a million years?"

"And how old did you think the universe was, Quinn?" he asked matter-of-factly. The others had all surreptitiously chosen to stop a little way away from them as they had this discussion.

"I didn't, really." She shrugged.

"We need to fix that human perception of yours. It's completely outdated and screwing everything up for you," He sighed, and Quinn realized that the previous mood was melancholy. This was irritation. "I haven't seen her in a very long time. Neither has the Library."

Quinn nodded, trying to get a grip on the vastness of ages and alliances and everything. While she'd been technically aware, having it presented so nonchalantly put things into a different perspective. She sighed, and they all began moving again.

Hal shrugged. "A million years, give or take."

Quinn glared at him.

No matter how far they went and how fast they made themselves go, the mountain base only inched closer, if that. Another gust of hot air caught both Quinn and Eric, and she was glad she was quick enough to hover herself down and regain her control over flight. Eric, on the other hand, squealed with delight, did several somersaults, and bolted back to the group to stand and yell: "Again!"

"How old are you?" Quinn asked, trying to hold back laughter.

"I'm almost eight thousand years old. We've been over this. If you just let yourself go, you could enjoy it too," he said, very smugly.

"Don't pick on the egg," Hal admonished.

Finally, after what felt like countless hours, they made closer to the base of the mountain. The ground all around them was flat and smooth. A very convenient camping area. Quinn pondered it, having come to be suspicious of convenience when it appeared simply for the sake of it being convenient. "Do you think we should push on and try to get closer?"

"No." Hal was frowning again.

"Are you feeling something, too?" Quinn asked.

"Perhaps."

Aradie swooped down, alighting on Quinn's shoulder, hooting and cooing in response as if she too was unsettled. Even Jasper hugged herself tighter.

"Are you okay, Jasper?" Quinn asked.

"I'm just hoping there are caves in that thar hill because I really need to just get inside." Jasper eyed the mountain skeptically.

Malakai frowned. "Sorry, I'm no use. Point me at an enemy and I'll slice them for you. But right now, I can't even project anything."

Hal glanced at him. "Just a couple more days, Malakai. You'll appreciate the restraint when your magic still works."

The elf sighed and nodded. "I know you're right, but I don't have to like it."

"Never said you did, mate," Hal said, chuckling to himself.

"Yeah, let's just set up camp," Quinn said. "Even if we did manage to get there tonight, I'm hungry again."

It had been hours, after all.

"I could eat a fizz boodle," Eric said, as if that explained everything.

"A fizz boodle?" Quinn asked.

"Haven't you had a look at any of the information on imps? We are very magical creatures, and there are certain things that we absolutely love and are a complete and utter delicacy for us." Eric grinned and flashed his tiny sharp teeth.

Quinn paused. "Seriously?"

"He's being serious, but also facetious," Hal said, suppressing a laugh.

They made themselves busy setting up camp, rationing food, handing out sleeping packs. Quinn had never been so grateful for dimensional storage before in her life, and really wished Earth had enough ambient mana to utilize it, because it would make so many things, especially taking textbooks to school, much easier. Despite the rampant use of technology in schools, some of them still insisted on whopping five-hundred-page hardback textbooks. Way to kill kids' spines.

They ate and got ready for bed. except Quinn couldn't shake the tugging. It was more insistent now. As if they were closer than it appeared. She was quite certain that there was more than one book up there. But from the feel of the signature she remembered from Jasper's summoning, it wasn't Crown's book, just the Parsneauvian one. It could be a normal one. It could be the ones they'd yet to identify, and it sent shivers down her back, because something about everything felt very wrong, and they still had a long way to go.

Doors didn't open into igneous rock. It made getting here so difficult. And there had to be a reason for that.

She sighed and snuggled down to sleep, only to wake suddenly a few hours later. She sat up with a start and realized Hal was already outside the tent, having taken watch because he said he didn't need sleep. She snuck out to join him.

"You sense it too, eh, little egg?" he whispered.

"Yeah," she said, her senses extended. All she knew was they were not alone.

6 6

ONE BIT LIKE HER

THE DARK WAS SO BLACK IT FELT LIKE INK DRIPPING INSIDE HER VISION. Darker than black spots flitted about, promising Quinn there was something out there beyond them, beyond the pale light the glow of the tent put off. While Hal stood next to her and had only just spoken, the light around them sputtered, plunging both of them into darkness.

Quinn squeezed her eyes shut and counted to five, giving her eyes time to forget the light. When she opened them again there was a strange film in front of her vision that gave everything a lighter feeling to it. As if she had night vision, which was news to her. She'd not realized dragons got it, or perhaps it was yet another application of the multiple affinities she possessed coming together to create the things she needed by combining them.

She sighed.

When all this was over, she'd spend time researching just how her affinities worked, and how those of others did too. Surely she wasn't the only person whose powers decided to combine on their own.

"Quinn?" Hal asked, his voice a whisper.

"Here," she replied even though she was quite certain that Hal had perfectly good night vision. How could you be a creature of a hellish planet if you couldn't see in the dark?

She wasn't scared, at least.

Even though she could reach out past herself, and into the darkness beyond them, and was able to sense the multitude of different creatures who were apparently surrounding them, Quinn didn't feel scared.

Nor was she close to panic.

In fact, an oddly prepared and calm sensation that washed over her. It came from within too, a sign she wasn't being influenced. She took a deep breath, continuing to center herself and allowed for her senses to flow.

Since synchronizing with the Library again, her abilities had expanded, and this was a whole new set of sensations allowing her to tap into her surroundings and read them. From the flow of the igneous rock, and the formation of the rock all around them, to the inky creatures blipping in and out of sensation, Quinn could focus on everything.

Which let her know there was something not right about the mountain. About the whole area around them now.

Hal's thoughts brushed against her shielding, requesting permission to speak to her in a way their approaching ambushers wouldn't notice.

Do you think these were sent by D—him? she asked, almost forgetting and using Dravishk's name instead of keeping it silent.

Quinn wasn't precisely sure how she knew Hal had moved. He'd made no sound. It was more of a sensation, a slight disturbance in the air around her that gave away he'd shifted his weight somewhat.

Maybe? Perhaps not so much as an ambush, but as guards to stop anyone getting closer to his sister?

That made much more sense in Quinn's head. She didn't see how anyone could have known that they'd come here. How could they have anticipated that they'd locate the book precisely and come here on this exact day? *Left here like an alarm?*

Hal shrugged, the air around Quinn rippling in response to his movements. *It's likely. It's what I would do, and he was always similar to me in the way he approached things like this.*

Quinn wasn't entirely sure what that told her about her uncle or about Hal, but she could dissect that later.

Even though it was pitch black and she could identify some of the forms and shapes as humanoid, she closed her eyes to center herself before opening them again. In those few precious seconds while they were being approached, she sought out a targeting affinity.

One of the things she'd learned while researching her own affinity was that the different aspects could be turned off and on and intermingled with aspects of other harmonious affinities. It was very rare that someone would have two affinities that didn't complement each other.

The revelation meant that she now understood how to combine and utilize more than one affinity at a time, blending them into a spirit of cooperation to give her the specific ability she needed for an exact task. At least, that's what she'd mostly done when she created hers while helping Eugea. It just needed another little nudge and would become something entirely its own, instead of just being a combination of two or three already existing ones.

And so, when she opened her eyes, not only could Quinn see the ethereal shadow creatures meandering around in front of them, but she could also lock onto, target, and assess each of those creatures.

She smiled, slowly, and let her power wiggle all the way down to her fingertips. It made her feel alive—and confident.

Ahhhh, you really are getting used to your powers now, aren't you, little egg?

Quinn didn't dignify that with an answer, but she did smile, and she knew, because of what he was, that Hal'd be able to see that.

The next thing she knew was that Eric hovered next to them, his wings utterly silent as he did so, his eyes glowing a subdued red.

I'm guessing we won't have much time now? he said, shrugging his shoulders as he cracked his neck from side to side.

Mm-hm, Hal answered. *It is as you say.*

Then we should make the most of the time we have.

Stop chattering, Quinn admonished them as she stretched. Malakai stood to her right, his bow drawn a smile on his face. And she knew.

She just knew that the damned elves could see in the bloody dark without having to do anything too crazy with their own vision.

She could sense more than hear that Jasper stayed where she was, and knew, without having to review what she understood of the Alyenarvor, that Jasper didn't have any way to combat in the dark. Her large eyes were probably used for seeing the threads magic her rituals summoned. That'd make a lot more sense.

Let's do this, Quinn said, and moved out with Hal, Eric, and Malakai. For a second she wondered where Geneva was, and then realized she stayed behind them, taking on the role of the healer because her aunt wasn't with them this time and it would be better for her to conserve her energy.

And then there was a piercing hoot from above them, and Quinn grinned.

Aradie was an owl, after all. And night hunting was kinda her thing.

Don't you dare use your magic, Quinn said to Malakai.

I'm not that stupid. He sounded irritated and yet at the same time sort of resigned to the fact that everyone kept checking on him

Quinn moved out from where they stood at the entrance to their tent, her vision focused on the shadow figures that were finally upon her camp. Light cut through shadow the best, so that was what she used. Pinpointed beams of light shot out of her fingers with ease, targeting with her visual guidance system. She didn't miss a one, blowing them apart in the center of their chests. The darkness scattered as a strange discordant moan filled the air with every single one she hit.

Around them, the breeze picked up. it concerned her, but she wasn't worried about getting trampled or blown away. Applying gravity to her own feet, she did the same with those of her team. Not to weigh them down as they walked, but to give them purchase where their feet hit the ground. She grinned when it worked, as the first gust tried to blow her away.

Her scales flashed as something hit her arm, the only indication that an attack had been launched. She frowned as she looked down, and realized about twenty feet away there were several shadow creatures firing at her. It didn't even require communication with Aradie for the owl to dive bomb them.

Quinn grinned, pulling on a little more energy to make her light brighter, to chase away the shadows with more gusto.

Beside her, Eric shot lava, hot and burning bright, while the satyr threw fire. Both of those attacks held enough light to rip their opponents apart with a few shots aimed at them. It wasn't the pinpointed brilliance that Quinn shot at them, but it served its purpose, just like Aradie's laser eyes.

On the other side of her, Malakai engaged his arrows, shooting from his vantage point with light-based shafts.

At first Quinn thought it was going well. Almost too well.

It wasn't difficult at all to cut through them, to smite them all down with fire and light.

Slowly but surely, she realized there were so many of them, she didn't know if she had the energy to keep this fight up. That gave her a flash of concern.

She began to pull the ambient energy into her again, to distribute from it to all of her team, to fuel them so they wouldn't run out. Not to mention transforming it into a minor healing wave to help with fatigue and regeneration.

Quinn glanced around, double-checking on her team with the overlay she had from the system and her affinities. It told her the current state of their bodies and the wear and tear the fight was taking on all of them. It showed her levels of energy, mana, and fatigue.

She blinked solemnly, taking in the information like it wasn't trying to overload her brain. Drawing it in, she catalogued it as fast as her mind tricks allowed her. There was so much to take in on the battlefield.

So much she needed to understand.

The shadow figures weren't nearly as violent as Quinn would have expected coming from Sölem. Almost like they were gauging the group's strength.

Her blitzes of light began to flow together until she felt like that was all she did. Checking on her wards, checking on her shielding over her friends and making sure they had all the regeneration and healing she could contribute.

Yet something niggled at the back of her mind, like she'd forgotten something important.

Something imperative, even.

And that's when she remembered that she had.

This whole area has been inundated with an illusion, hasn't it? she asked, because she needed to verify something she knew Hal had told her wasn't happening earlier.

She could practically hear him frown.

Son of a . . .

There, she'd known it. Something had twisted their perceptions of those shadows. During the day when shadows gave you a different reality. Where they stretched so far over a village and yet somehow took an entire day of travel at around twenty miles an hour to get to?

Nope. Something didn't add up there.

Simple physics.

Hal groaned. *I'm sorry. I should have been more suspicious. We were even in the shade of the mountain the entire afternoon. But it barely got closer.*

What do you mean? Geneva asked as she cast a heal yet again on Malakai, who'd been wounded by a strange ribbon attack. Unlike Quinn, the imp, and the satyr, Malakai wasn't able to kill things as quickly and had slowly been more overwhelmed than the rest of them.

It means this . . . it's all been one absolutely huge illusion.

Quinn knew he was right, and now she needed the telltale signs. The shadow cast by the mountain. The igneous rock. The flat area they were so conveniently camped on . . .

No.

This trap, this alarm . . . it had been placed by her aunt. As she realized this, an overwhelming presence began to push down on Quinn's senses.

"Clever little thing." The voice did *not* sound friendly. But it also held no animosity. Just slight curiosity.

The shadow creatures slunk back behind what appeared to be a very large, and very shadow-driven bulk.

A massive head leaned down, and two huge silver eyes, like the moons Quinn thought she saw in the sky earlier, blinked at her and her companions. The ridges along the top of the dragon's head glistened black in the actual moonlight, and Quinn found herself holding her breath as the nostrils huffed, breathing in and out.

The voice was a low alto and resonated through to her bones. "Now perhaps you'd like to tell me why you smell awfully like my sister and yet don't look one bit like her."

PRACTICALLY PALPABLE

DREAD SETTLED INTO QUINN'S STOMACH AS THE MASSIVE DRAGON'S head registered fully. Not only that, but a small niggling part of her brain worried about the fact that Hal apparently hadn't been able to sense the dragon and the illusion, either. Add to that the fact that Quinn's own sensory abilities had been utterly convinced by the massive mountain and the shadows, and Quinn felt entirely uneasy.

Completely and utterly stumped as to what she could say, how she could answer.

Not to mention being totally overwhelmed by the pressure and power bearing down on her. It felt like it could squash her like a rather insignificant insect.

"Are all of you like this?" she found herself murmuring as she looked up into the moon-like eyes.

The dragon blinked at her, likely not expecting a question as an answer to a question. The eyes narrowed, and she sniffed the air around Quinn again. "I'm not a patient dragon. Especially not when you woke me up. Answer the question."

Quinn gulped. She wasn't sure how she should answer the question. The Library hadn't been all that informative about how to deal with this and frankly, Quinn contemplated just running in fear. She squared her shoulders and, considering Hal hadn't stepped in yet, made what might be a rash decision. "I'm the Librarian."

The eyes watching her didn't relent, and another whoosh of warm breath exited from those nostrils. Probably in irritation.

"Halithrija! Why did you not step forward!" Drukala practically screeched, making it obvious that she was *not* a patient dragon. "Stop trying to blend into the background and explain why you woke me up from my damned nap with this . . . Librarian?"

Hal chuckled, and most of the tension leaked out of Quinn's body. He rolled his shoulders, stepping to stand more in line with Quinn. "It would be better if we talk somewhere with more protections."

His voice was pitched low, and a presence pressed against Quinn's mind, as if it was asking others to look away, or perhaps more accurately, to hear away. To discourage them from listening.

Drukala glanced back at Quinn. "You still smell like my sibling . . . don't think you won't still have to answer."

A soft breeze blew through the camp, shadows pulling in rapidly around the eyes, which shrunk down until they were just a few inches above Quinn.

She blinked, watching as a tall and slender woman stood in front of her with round and completely silver eyes all the way through the sclera. Her hair was waist-length, wisps of silver, black, and shades of red scattered through subtly. "If any damage comes to my lair, I will hold you responsible, King of Halschius."

Hal just inclined his head as if he'd been expecting that all along.

Some of the sense of foreboding had disappeared, and Quinn heaved a sigh of relief. Suspicion still lingered in the back of her mind. So much of this seemed too easy, and especially since coming to the Library, Quinn had learned that if something appeared to be too easy, then odds were, they'd overlooked something.

Drukala reached out a hand, and at first Quinn was sure something magical was about to happen, perhaps a spell, a stasis, but as the dragon snapped her fingers and the world shifted, Quinn had to admit she hadn't seen that coming.

It only took about half a second but was enough for the world to spin and come back in focus. Quinn almost lost her footing, sliding down to one knee. She turned, noticing that they were now in a huge cavern that reminded her of the filtration chamber sans mana and energy. The whole camp set up was still positioned precisely where it had been in relation to them, and if Quinn wasn't mistaken, nothing had budged. And her friends were now asleep again. She frowned.

Drukala's face was visible in the flickering light of the cave. There were hints of pearlescence in her features, an almost translucent quality. Quinn wondered if the Library looked like that back when it was fully dragon.

"Of course Drev did." Drukala peered at Quinn, stepping in closer, entering her personal space. "You are an enigma you would both do well to enlighten me about right now. Five minutes. I'm feeling generous. And don't worry, your companions won't wake up. If I need to kill you all, at least I can promise their deaths will be painless."

There was no hint of mirth in any of those words, and Quinn found her own irritation beginning to simmer. "You can't just kill them because you're in a mood."

Drukala raised a very delicate eyebrow. "And why can't I do that? What ever-so-persuasive argument do you possess that would make me think twice about not punishing someone who. Woke. Me. Up?"

Quinn at least had the decency to cringe. Her quasi aunt wasn't wrong, per se. But just as the Librarian was about to apologize, Drukala turned to Hal with a frown, effectively ignoring Quinn's presence.

"Explain."

Hal sighed. "You need to stop being so dramatic."

Drukala hissed deep in her throat. "You're on dangerous ground here, Hal. I like you. I've always had a soft spot for your people. But I was sleeping, and I was extremely well-hidden. For extremely good reasons. Now tell me why you are here, and how is this thing here"— she gestured vaguely in Quinn's direction—"is attempting to impersonate my damned sibling who cannot, if I may remind you, move like a dragon anymore and thus couldn't possibly be here to see me. Start talking, old man, before I lose my patience."

Tendrils of smoke curled up all over Drukala's body, and Quinn felt something primal inside herself creeping forward, like it too wanted to answer the call.

"Quinn," Hal said before even deigning Drukala with a response. "Clamp it down. Remember what you learned." Then he turned back to the dragon, a distinct sneer to his lips. "Use your brain. Just because you woke suddenly doesn't mean you can threaten me."

Quinn was impressed his voice didn't shake. She knew hers would have. Perhaps he was more powerful than she'd realized.

"Four minutes." Was the only answer Drukala gave.

Hal sighed again in a way that reminded Quinn of her dad before he died, when he'd been particularly annoyed at having to explain something simple. "Have you checked to see if you have any messages from while you were sleeping?"

Drukala seemed taken aback. "Why would . . ." Then her face underwent a change. She scowled. "You could have opened with that."

"Didn't really give me a chance, did you?"

"Fine. That's still not enough. Drev has been trying to wake me for a while. Why wouldn't you have brought Lynx with you?" She scowled, obviously annoyed that she hadn't thought to check for possible information sooner. Then, as soon as her attention changed previously, she redirected it to Quinn again. "Librarian? No Korradine? Where is Lynx?"

"He's . . . been damaged," was all Quinn could think of to say, and then she added hurriedly, "But he'll be okay. We're making sure he heals up."

"Now I know you're lying. Lynx can't get sick." Drukala opened her mouth in such a wide smile that it shouldn't fit on her face. Far too many sharp teeth fit in that overly large smile. "Start talking. Why do you smell like Drev?"

Quinn glared right back at the dragon. "Because the Library is basically my freaking mother, that's why."

To say Drukala looked shocked would be an understatement. She actually took a step back and shook her head as if clearing out her hearing. "Excuse me? I thought you said you're my niece."

"I did. Sort of. In a weird scientifically and magically genetically engineered way." Quinn crossed her arms, putting the full extent of her complete and utter stubbornness on display.

Drukala stood there for several seconds, not blinking, not moving. The only thing that separated her from a statue in that moment was the flickering behind her eyes, similar to that which went on behind Lynx's eyes when he was in the middle of communicating and synching up to the system and Library servers. Finally, she blinked. "That doesn't . . ." She turned to Hal again, her uncertainty obvious.

"Not a lie. Last-ditch effort to bring the Library back from the brink of extinction."

"Wait . . . what? When—how did I miss this? I've not even been asleep a millennium!" Drukala's eyes flickered through several panicked colors.

Quinn took a step back, just in case. She wasn't entirely sure how much control a shapeshifting dragon had over their form when they were riled up. And she didn't exactly relish getting squashed.

Hal, on the other hand, moved forward several steps. He took them slowly, cautiously, hands raised in a soothing motion. "Just under five hundred years ago, the Library was attacked and had to enter survival mode."

A flicker of worry passed over Drukala's features. "Why?" She held up a hand, taking in deep breaths. "That doesn't make much sense. I know Drev was feeling off, as if something wasn't quite right. But it's not like the Library can hibernate, right? Not in the proper way a dragon needs to . . . I thought that's all it was."

"The Library is back now. Almost back at full strength, even." Quinn didn't quite understand why, but she felt this compulsion, this complete need to help her aunt, to make her feel better.

Drukala perked up. "Is that why you came to see me? So I could help get everything back in full working order? Although, that's not really something I do. I can't exactly transfer my magical energy directly." She frowned, clearly confused.

Hal crossed his arms, a quizzical look on his face. "You were sleeping for less than a millennium then?"

Drukala was silent for several seconds. "Yes. Far less. About seven hundred and fifty-three years, to be precise."

"And this security illusion to prevent people from reaching you, was that a failsafe or deliberate?" Hal asked, his voice very soft, gentle, like he's handling her with kid gloves.

"Failsafe and partially deliberate. As in, it'll trigger if someone is trying to reach me. Moreso if they have ill intentions. Had to keep the local folk away from my lair, or else I'd never get sleep." She glanced up at Hal. "You should at least remember hibernation procedure."

"I do, but it's important to know if we triggered it by approaching, or if you triggered it while being awake."

"You woke me as soon as you stepped foot on this world. I could smell her." Drukala turned back to Quinn. "I could smell you. So similar to Drev and yet not. For a few seconds I had hope . . ." There was a melancholy echo to her words.

The awkward silence spread. Quinn wasn't sure how to address it. Even though she didn't quite understand how the magic behind the Library's transformation had worked, she did know it was irreversible.

"Well!" Drukala clapped her hands together. "I do apologize for scaring you, if I did. Truth be told, I hadn't expected Drev to have a type of offspring."

Quinn blushed and Hal cleared his throat. "That's not quite accurate. Still. Is this a regular hibernation lair for you?"

She nodded. "Well, I rotate between about thirty of them. Can't be too careful, you know. Now . . . tell me, what brings you here to see your aunt?"

Quinn grimaced. Because it wasn't a social call. "You have a book we need. We were just hoping it was you who borrowed it, and that it wasn't placed there by someone else."

"Well, go on. What book is it? I have several. My Library membership comes with perks like not having to return them as often as everyone else." She said the last smugly.

"*The Parsneauvian Theory of Spatial Dimension Manipulation,*" Quinn said, without missing a beat.

Hal interjected smoothly before the dragon could even give a response. "It's been removed from Library records for some reason, and we traced it to you. Please tell me Drav didn't give it to you." His tone sounded light, but Quinn felt a shudder run down her spine.

"What are you talking about?" Drukala asked, her bewilderment obvious. "Of course I have the book."

"Why? It's restricted for a reason." Hal sounded like he had trouble keeping his temper.

But now Drukala just looked utterly baffled. "Because Drev asked me to, silly." She laughed.

Quinn blinked. "What?"

Drukala's confusion was practically palpable. "Because the Library asked me to take and keep it safe. Why in the universe would I be interested in spatial dimension manipulation?"

Her laugh tinkled like raindrops on glass.

Quinn wasn't sure how to respond to that. It meant the Library was still missing major memories. And worse, it meant the feeling of foreboding Quinn had been feeling since they stepped foot in this world had nothing to do with Drukala.

6 8

RENEWED DETERMINATION

BEFORE QUINN COULD SAY ANYTHING, HAL SPOKE UP, PINCHING THE bridge of his nose in a way that Quinn thought he'd break it.

"Wait. So you're telling me the Library gave you the book to take care of, not your brother?"

"Of course not. You remember the tirade he went on about the Library after the fact." Drukala scoffed. "His regret rant still rings in my ears to this day. In fact, part of the reason I chose this hibernation spot was because he doesn't know where this one is."

She sounded smug, and Quinn's alarm bells went off like her head was stuck inside one, trying to get her attention. She just didn't know what she should be looking for. Glancing around, she sought out Drukala's shadows, partially relieved to see them moving around the edges like scouts and guards, a sort of patrol for her.

Hal frowned. "Drev asked you to keep it safe?"

Dru shrugged. "Sure. They were just both so insistent. Separately, even. The Library and Lynx. So sure it was necessary for me to take this book in specific and keep it safe. You know I have a soft spot for Drev. I'd do almost anything for that damned book-hoarding dragon. I figured looking after this one piece of the hoard wasn't bad. Plus, I got to check out a heap of others to help me get settled in time for my hibernation."

Quinn's stomach roiled so much she thought it was going to explode.

Something stirred in the tent behind her, and she did a double take as Eric hovered into view. He was sleep mussed, and his eyes were bleary until he realized they were actually in a cavern and not at the base of the mountain like they'd been when he went to sleep. He blinked, noticed that Hal was there, and the tension leaked out of his shoulders as his gaze drifted over to both Quinn and Drukala.

He raised an eyebrow and sighed. "I swear we were fighting five minutes ago. It's way too early for this shit. I'm going back to sleep." And he went back into the tent mumbling about too much noise and raised voices as he went.

Quinn couldn't help but smile. The transfer of the whole camp into the cave was an impressive bit of magic. Were dragons just that magical? "How did you do that? Like move everything just as it was?"

Drukala examined her for a second before a sincere smile crossed her face. "You have them all too! Wow . . . you must tell me how they created you. I can't believe they did."

"Focus, Dru," Hal said, but there was a fondness in his eyes that Quinn rarely saw on the old satyr. "Plenty of time for that later."

"Oh yes. How? Well, you just have to combine the different affinities. You need air, of course, and then there's the directional force and pull of the poles—you know, magnetisms. Those two can be finicky if you don't actually understand them. Although, if you were just going to teleport the tent and its belongings, it'd be a simple matter of transferring things and not living, breathing, organic beings. That's always a little trickier, you know?"

Quinn nodded, trying to keep up, even as she extended her senses, trying to reach whatever lurked on the edges of them, pulling at her sensitivities. Her senses were tingling with warning in such a certain way it hurt.

It was like Drukala took Quinn's nod as an okay to keep going. And to be fair, it sort of was.

"Well, transporting means that you need control over speed, as well as momentum generation, and then you want to utilize gravity stability and generation as well as maintenance. All in all, I probably accessed about thirty-eight affinities to move the tent and us all to where I wanted us. That and it's imperative that your concentration and meditative abilities allow you to multitask on a high level. It's a good thing I've been asleep a while replenishing myself and my focus." She leant in somewhat conspiratorially. "I'm not usually so good with the concentration part, you know. But I was showing off a bit."

Quinn wasn't sure how she felt about that. After all—if she was usually bad at concentration, did that mean they could have all been spliced or something? Still, combining that many affinities at once to be able to levitate and displace and safely land a camping set up as big as theirs. Quinn thought that was damn impressive. "I really hope I get to your level of control one day."

Drukala laughed delightedly. "You're a flatterer."

"No. Seriously. I haven't been doing this long and I always feel like I'm doing something wrong. It's nice to see affinity combinations in action." Quinn couldn't keep the earnestness out of her voice. Just when she'd accepted that she was becoming powerful, someone always showed her, without fail, that she still had so far to go.

Drukala smiled. This was genuine, something that leant a softness to her angular features. She stepped toward Quinn and brushed an errant curl back up into her ponytail. "You remind me of Drev, you know. All earnest and eager, all willing to go that extra bit. Thank you."

Quinn wasn't sure how she should react to that. But that close feeling, not just of proximity, but of emotional connection, blood wise, leant her a warmth she hadn't expected. "Yeah. Well. I've still got a heap to learn."

"That's not half obvious." Drukala grinned at her.

Hal was about to speak when Quinn's stomach plummeted. She gasped and dropped to one knee, trying vainly to focus in on where the alarm stemmed from. So many sensations assaulted her from all different directions she couldn't get a location on it. Warnings shouted in her head.

"Something . . ." But then it was gone, and she gasped in the air, trying to figure out what had just happened.

Drukala didn't seem to understand. "Are you okay? What happened just then?"

"Wards." Hal said, his eyes like two pools of glowing blood. "She's attuned to the wards around here, sent out her senses. Something crossed. Didn't you feel it?"

The dragon frowned as she closed her eyes ever so briefly. Shadows spread across her face as the frown deepened. "That's not quite . . ."

Quinn pulled herself back up, her senses returned to her. The uneasiness compounded and yet, there wasn't any complete answer to the questions she had. The information was just out of reach and yet she knew they weren't alone.

Hal cleared his throat. "Even my scans are conflicting?"

"We're not alone," Quinn finally gasped out, pushing herself onto high alert.

Drukala looked at her sharply, her moon-eyes swimming for just a second. "I can't tell with detail. What the . . . we should be prepared." She sounded so impossibly young as she said that, it tore at Quinn's heart a little.

Hal clapped his hands together, drawing their attention. "Time to get everyone else up, ready, and armed. Better to be safe than sorry, eh?"

He entered the tent to wake up Geneva, Eric, Malakai, and Jasper from their Drukala-induced slumber. Quinn turned slowly around, trying to get herself oriented with the directions.

"That shouldn't be," She heard her aunt mutter.

It also felt super surreal to call someone her aunt.

"What's wrong?" Quinn asked, only half paying attention to what was being said, considering she had to continue to comb her sensory nets. She also began setting up the shielding she'd spread to her whole group, and the mana and health regeneration webs. Couldn't be too careful. Her gut feelings had been right before.

Quinn felt like she should have seen this before, realized it. But she'd had a hard enough time with the illusion Drukala had put up . . . maybe it was a fellow cosmicisodracus thing.

"There . . ." Dru frowned, her eyes lighting up like suns more than moons this time. Just a brief flash of power rolling through her. Quinn shivered. "There are gaps in my protections where there shouldn't be gaps. They are a recent occurrence."

Quinn nodded. It was about what she expected. She was also fairly certain who it was, or at least who had sent them.

"Do you use more than protection shielding to set out your sensory nets?" Quinn asked, trying to get Dru to extend her search.

Something about this whole setup made Quinn positive their incoming visitors weren't worried about triggering traps. Lulling them into a false sense of security by exploiting loopholes.

There.

She felt it, even as she tried to focus on Dru's answer. Quinn separated her mind, just like the books taught her, and followed that one track—that one glimpse, knowing that she'd found the real one and not the decoy. An odd sense of accomplishment rose in her as she listened to Dru.

"You need elemental weavings in them, just a fraction of elemental creation, to make sure the net not only goes after organic material but also levels of sentience, sapience, and raw elements. There are so many compositions of magic that a security grid should be able to take all of them into consideration, but that's not always the case." She sounded like she also wasn't completely focused on her task. She was acting like she was while she did something else.

Geneva fluttered out, hovering right next to Quinn's shoulder. She practically vibrated with anticipation. "Plan?"

"Still waiting to see just what we're facing."

"It's going to be him again," Malakai said, his mood sour.

Quinn had noticed he wasn't the best when his sleep got interrupted. No sleep? He seemed absolutely fine, but broken sleep? And Malakai was indeed not your friend.

"Might not be him," Eric grumbled. "I'm going to melt his ass to the damn rock."

Quinn suppressed a laugh. Eric was always in a fine mood. "That'd make a pretty neat sculpture," she said, pretending she didn't see Eric's mouth quirk up at the corners.

Jasper moved closer to Quinn, her nervousness radiating from her pale skin. She didn't say anything, only nodded in acknowledgement. Quinn reached over and gave her hand a squeeze trying to help her settle her nerves. "It's okay. We've got this."

The Alyenarvor nodded and flashed Quinn a tight smile.

Meanwhile, Drukala's eyes were practically sun-like orbs. As if she could see everything and anything all at once. Her hair streamed out behind her, her streaks on fire too. Nothing burned, but the whole area around them teemed with life. In Quinn's eyes, it was breathtaking.

Another pull on the wards. Subtle, just passing through, almost trying to fool Quinn's magic into thinking it belonged there. But the sense of wrong wouldn't abate.

"They're coming," Dru whispered, but the sound penetrated through all of them, bringing them to attention, making sure they were aware.

"Can they even get up here? In here?" Hal asked, frowning.

Drukala cocked her head to one side, her fiery eyes suddenly coming back to themselves to leave the pale moon pearlescent ones in its place. "Yes. Yes, they can. But it's not Drav coming." She seemed conflicted and confused.

Suddenly, Drukala sounded very much like a youngest sibling. She sounded scared. Quinn felt the energy signature in the area, and knew as well that it wasn't Dravishk.

Drukala gasped, and if possible, paled even more than she already was. As if all the color had escaped her. "This is worse than I thought."

Quinn glanced over at Hal, raising an eyebrow in question.

But even Hal was pale now, a recognition Quinn couldn't follow dawning in his eyes. She bit down on the need to tell them all to bloody well let them all in on the secret. At least she knew Kajaro was locked away, unable to get out.

Suddenly, Drukala pivoted. She began casting protections traps, vanishing, and recreating all aspects of the cavern. "Help me. We have the five minutes before she gets here to make this terrain work."

Quinn felt the panic her aunt barely held at bay and a strange surge of pride rushed through her. Still, though, she had to ask. "Who?"

The look Dru shot her was filled with so much heartache, it made Quinn take a step back. "You feel so much like Drev, I keep forgetting you're not." She sighed, and for a split second, the fight drained away before it was replaced with renewed determination. "My oldest sister. She's not very big on listening."

The way Hal shuddered made it clear just how bad that might be.

6 9

CRACKLE OF FIRE

THE USE OF MAGIC SUFFUSED THE CAVERN AS THEY GOT TO WORK, altering the terrain to be unpredictable, to act like a trap. Quinn immediately enabled her mana and energy filtering ability so she could top off everyone with the ambient energy around them, to make sure they were fighting fit when the fight got to them.

Malakai kept watch, still unable to use his magic to help them prep. Quinn knew he could fight like a demon without a hint of magic.

"Will they know to come through here?" Geneva asked, her voice soft.

"How do you mean?" Dru's concentration focused mainly on preparations, but she'd split off a portion for conversation and directing the others.

"Do they know about the illusion that covers the place?" the Furionas fae said, her tone irritated.

Quinn couldn't blame her. None of them felt prepared. She didn't know anything about this other cosmicisodracus. Another aunt, apparently? She felt the power climbing up with them, approaching them, infecting the atmosphere just beyond the hibernation area.

Dru paused for a second. "They'll know. She'll know. Dro

is . . . well, she's going to know, and that's all there is to it." A shudder spread down the dragon's spine.

"Wouldn't it be better for you to go full-on dragon?" Eric asked gruffly, providing little lava traps all throughout the large cavern as he went.

"Not enough maneuverability in enclosed quarters. Dro won't be in full form either."

"Couldn't they just blast through?" Mal asked from the doorway.

"No. Too many protections around these peaks. My siblings have been known for practical jokes their entire existence. None of us go to sleep without the best possible shields and protections available." Dru said it like it should be common knowledge, and while Quinn did her best to help with all the preparations, she was a little out of her depth.

"The book!" Quinn suddenly thought of it, even though the attack was imminent. She turned to Dru. "We need that book. They can't get it"

Drukala blinked at her and pulled it out from what seemed to be a dimensional storage hanging in midair. "Keep this safe. Get it back to the Library."

"But we need a door . . ." Geneva's voice trailed off as an almost deafening crash resounded from the outside.

"You'll need to open one," Dru said, muttering under her breath as she began to cast a strange glowing orb in her hands.

"But it's igneous rock." Geneva seemed about to panic.

Hal sighed. "Still doable, just very difficult." He glanced over at Jasper.

Jasper cleared her throat. "I've got just the ritual for this. It'll take a few minutes. Just need to make sure you can keep me hidden." She sounded a little raspy perhaps, but still indubitably herself.

Quinn leant on that. They all knew what to do. Who to fight. Or something like that.

"Incoming," Malakai ground out through clenched teeth. "One morphed dragon, about four Aracnios, and two sedimentites. Not to mention a lot of shadow warriors."

"My shadows will take care of most of theirs," Dru said, her voice tight as she watched the only entrance they'd left available.

Finally, the arch transfigured to look like part of the mountain, was breached.

Quinn felt the fabric of the cavern they stood in as the entrance warped and warbled and then finally shattered into a million pieces as it gave way and let the shadows leak into the room.

It was difficult to track the latter, as Drukala also had some of her own. Those, however, had a slightly iridescent sheen as opposed to the inky nothingness of their opponents. It set her on edge, and Quinn had to rip her attention back as one of the Aracnios lashed out toward her as it pushed into the cavern.

"Oh, little sister." The voice leaked through the entire area, breaking off the cave walls, reverberating right down to Quinn's soul.

She could see the effect it had on Drukala too, but the younger dragon steeled herself, bravery leaking through to Quinn as the fear was practically dispelled.

Taking that as her sign to move, Quinn initiated her shielding spells, weaving them in and out of each other. Taking bits of earth, bits of wind, pieces of granite infused like liquid onto the skin of all her comrades. She'd learned a bit since her last big fight. And keeping everyone safe was her new mantra.

The focus solidified for her, snapping into place. She set a replenishment affinity at creating, repairing, and activating to pull from the ambient mana instead of her own reserves, and then she had her complete focus back on the damned seven-foot-tall arachnid in front of her.

Hal fought off to the side, taking on the two sedimentites. His hulking frame, able to make pretty quick work of their attacks, put him on a more even footing with them once he'd fought their initial onslaught.

In the midst of it all, Hal created protection for Jasper and her ritual. Keeping her out of sight of their attackers while she dealt with summoning a door.

Quinn sank her power into the floor, coaxing the rock to work with her just as the Aracnio stepped forward. The rock cracked, giving way beneath the creature's foot, and her opponent stumbled forward with Quinn dodging lithely out of the way. Only to realize she'd backed straight into some of the strange inky black shadow figures that had come with Dro.

And then Drukala and her sister stopped their standoff and began fighting. Quinn was too preoccupied with the shadows and the attacking Aracnio in front of her to be able to pay too much attention, and she couldn't quite decipher Dro's appearance. It was more like an absence of light, of person, or everything. It felt cold every time the cloudlike being passed by her. Not quite like a shadow, and yet . . . more.

Quinn's sensory net cast wide, feeling as Eric and Geneva lead both shadow and Aracnios on a merry chase, kiting them around the back portion of the cavern once they'd wrangled them together. It gave Malakai plenty of targets to practice on as they did. Although the Aracnios weren't as gullible as the shadows, and stood their ground, executing more strategic attacks.

Some shadows fell prey to lava, others disintegrated as they came in contact with traps Geneva set, and more yet fell to arrows that Quinn hadn't seen Malakai use before. The only thing she could take solace in was the fact he wasn't using magic. Her net was attuned to it, and she'd know.

Oh, how she'd know if he went against his healing regimen.

Aradie swooped around, dive bombing and laser eyeing every attacker she could find while staying conspicuously out of reach.

Quinn could still sense the magic building from where Jasper performed her door creation ritual or whatever she was doing to allow them to pass in through to the Library again. Quinn shrouded the sensation as well as she could, aiming for it to appear weak to anyone else. They couldn't have the attackers going for the large area of magic over there.

Stupid damned door requirement. Why couldn't she just teleport them all home in an emergency Librarian move . . .

But her thoughts were cut short when her Aracnio attacker

performed what looked like a capoeira-style leap toward her with sharpened legs fanning out in all directions.

Quinn's dragon scales flashed, solidifying in a shot of blue armor, staving off the entire attack and she stumbled as they melted back into her skin, showing off iridescent scales that blended in with her own coloring. Except she felt an interested purr emanating from across the way where Dru and Dro were fighting.

"What have we here? A little cosmico? How did I not know about this?" Dro's attention waned for just a moment, giving her baby sister the chance to get a solid attack in.

Blackened blood, or at least some sort of black liquid flew out from a wound that drew in all the surrounding darkness.

Dro spat. "How dare you! I will make you pay, and you will tell me how you had a child."

Drukala barely managed to fend off the attack, and Quinn realized she had to focus on her own, too.

A thought brushed across her mind. *Focus on your own fight. We will get you back home.* Drukala's voice was smooth like velvet as it glided across the front of her thoughts.

It wasn't that Quinn relaxed, but she focused her attacks more readily, deeper. She fought with cutting wind, melding several air affinities together, making the wind harder to stop. Its pinpoint accuracy focused on chopping the bladed feet of this Aracnio off. She was only thankful it wasn't one of the handful of Aracnios she'd actually met in her life.

Her mana and energy replenishment abilities continued to drain from the ambient mana, and their opponents, and replenish the mana of her expedition party.

And Jasper's ritual circle power continued to build.

It took Quinn back for a moment to when Escadril opened the door when they went to find Kajaro. Back when he was still alive. Before that rotting tree killed him.

Just another reason to fight, just another reason to save the Library.

Dro and Dru clashed fiercely, and the rest of the fights carried on around the perimeter. The dragons were fast, diving for each other, scratching, biting, with the occasional drip of flame melting something before it regenerated. Which reminded Quinn to push a heftier healing charm into effect over all of her friends since Geneva was otherwise preoccupied. She had to protect everyone as best she could.

Geneva screamed, and Quinn couldn't afford to look back, but she heard Eric yelling something and knew Geneva would be okay. Quinn pushed more power into her shields, replenishing life force and energy. She'd know if one of them were hit badly.

But the Aracnio in front of her was formidable even without two of its feet, and she couldn't afford to get distracted.

"Stop it!" Dro screamed at her sister. "You are no match for me! Just give me the damned book already. You weren't supposed to have it."

Quinn cleared the surfaces of her mind just in case an ability existed allowing someone to get the location of the tome from her.

"Why are you doing this?" Dru, on the other hand, didn't scream. Her voice was calm, collected, filled with a sadness so poignant that Quinn could barely stand it. She couldn't imagine how it might feel to have family and then suddenly be on opposing sides of a fight. Imagine having to try to convince your sibling that every life deserves to exist, even if chaos would otherwise consume them.

"The Library was a mistake. One we have to rectify." Dro sounded suddenly so defeated for just a second. As if she was tired. "We all know it. Stop fighting it."

Quinn couldn't figure out how that would be the case. The Library preserved knowledge; it preserved the universe as it was.

A rush of fire spilled through the middle of the cavern, causing many of them to dash out of the way. Drukala blocked it like she was an umbrella stopping rain.

Quinn's next wind blade finally took out a third leg, and the Aracnio fighting her began to fight furiously. It spat at her—something that sizzled against the ground when she dodged it. Quinn gulped. Glad to have avoided it and scared to be hit by it in the future. It only fueled her need for them to escape this.

The next attack clipped her side, and while her scales rushed there to protect her, she could feel the rent it caused in her skin, as it separated. Even as blood began to trickle down her side. She sent a tendril of healing that way. To knit together, to congeal, to heal and keep it in place.

Affinities required so much to function seamlessly. Quinn felt entirely privileged to have all the affinities. Her breathing came ragged, slower to her now, even though she tried to gasp it in. Another wind blade hit the back leg of the Aracnio, and it pitched forward. That same blade took out two shadow creatures behind it, too.

Quinn glanced around, noticing Hal was almost done with the second sedimentite. Geneva was hidden next to Malakai, nursing her side as Eric still lead the others on a merry goose chase, kiting the shadows around while Geneva and Mal picked them off.

And Jasper was almost done with the door.

Not many of the either of the shadow armies remained. They seemed perfectly adept at ripping each other apart.

Dru appeared to be okay. Several gashes down one of her sides left trickles of blood dribbling down. Quinn reinforced the healing regeneration shield, and the protection layer around her, feeding more power and energy into them.

Dro's eyes flashed back to Quinn, focusing on her and rendering her immobile for just a heartbeat. "You!"

Luckily, Dru took that moment to viciously attack her sister, breaking her sister's attention on Quinn in the nick of time. Only Quinn's calf was caught by a flailing remaining leg of the feebly bleeding-out Aracnio she faced. Another tendril of healing to her wound and Quinn was about done with this.

Her energy was starting to wane. Literally. While she still had substantial resources, she was dipping below fifty percent now. Protecting this many people with healing and regen was a drain.

A roar rang out behind Quinn, and she turned, coincidentally avoiding the attack of one of the shadow army behind her. Only to see

Dro partially transformed into what looked like a mini cosmicisodracus. About the size of two horses together.

Dro roared again, spewing fire directly in front of her, and Quinn reacted.

Motioning with her hands, she slammed a shield between the two dragons, instantly reflecting some of that flame back on the attacker. Dro screeched, rolling on the ground to put out the flames engulfing her own body. Flames of her own making.

But Quinn wasn't quite fast enough and neither was Dru.

Drukala screamed in pain as parts of her hair burned, still caught not quite fully transformed, and some of the skin on her face melted even through the scale barrier that sprouted up.

Suddenly, Hal was by Drukala's side, stopping the fire, placing himself between Dru and Dro.

For a second the crackle of fire as it petered out on Dro was the only sound in the entire cavern.

70

FIGHTING CHANCE

THE CRACKLING WAS ALMOST UNBEARABLE. QUINN WASN'T ENTIRELY sure what to do with it. She balked, even as she could hear the rest of them all around her coming back to themselves, remembering they needed to fight. Still needing to distract their attackers from where Jasper was busy creating the damned doorway they needed.

Hal shielded the partially melting form of Drukala. Although Quinn was relieved to see that the healing magic she'd tossed over appeared to be having some sort of impact, at least. She also knew that cosmicisodracus weren't exactly fragile, but their fire was also pretty powerful.

Dro rolled onto the ground. Ultimately, she'd received the lion's share of the backlash of her own spell. Her hide was crackled, still in the mini dragon form that she found herself.

Something tugged inside Quinn's chest, in her head, giving her that weird sort of déjà vu that always hung over her when her magic was about to do some of the solving for itself. Stretching out an arm, she envisioned the flames contained the charred hide of the dragon to snuff out the rest of the damage, and slowly begin to heal.

At the same time, her understanding of both fibers, their creation, and the permanency of thread ignited to create a magical binding around Dro . . . whose full name Quinn was dying to find out. She had to be trussed up. If she wasn't, she posed too much of a threat to them all. As it was, with Dru and Geneva down, Quinn herself injured and only marginally patched up . . . she wasn't liking the odds ahead of them.

Even Hal, now that she peered and looked closer with the flamed having died down, had scrapes and wounds littered across his body that were only slowly healing because of the regeneration she'd covered them in. Still, it didn't keep him from fending off more of the shadow soldiers and giving both him and Dru some distance from Dro.

A ripple echoed through the chamber. Though it was more of a feeling than a sound.

Jasper finally stepped away and back into the flickering light of the cave to reveal the doorway she'd created. Perspiration clung to her skin, lending her a sallow appearance. "Heavily warded areas are not meant for rituals, when it's not warded because of one." She flashed Quinn a wan smile, stumbling to rest against the wall.

"Retreat!" Quinn called out, although that wasn't really what this was. After all, they were just going home, thanks to Jasper, whom she tossed a grateful half-smile. She glanced at Dro for a second, wondering if they should take her with them.

Hal caught her eye and shook his head. The older cosmicisodracus was still immobile, thanks to Quinn's bindings, but was also gasping wheezing breaths, as if she was struggling to live at all. Quinn needed to study dragon fire in a wee bit more detail, but knew that restraining one would be nigh impossible.

She kept her concentration on the bindings as she moved across to the door.

Malakai moved fluidly, hauling Geneva gently onto his side as he kept aim with his bow at the remnants of the shadow army while Eric still took care of them. He stepped over their traps easily, his eyes never straying from his targets despite the fact that he didn't miss a step in the direction of the door.

Eric, in the meantime, continued to lead the shadows on a strange chase, despite the fact that there were plenty more of them to fight. They seemed entranced by something he'd done. Like they were charmed, as if they compulsively had to follow him.

Quinn was so preoccupied as she moved through the cavern that she let her guard down slightly. The Aracnio she'd presumed to be dead caught her boot, one of its last remaining legs cutting deeply into her calf. She stumbled, going down, losing her concentration. And then Hal was there, scooping her up underneath her arm and guiding her toward the door as he leveraged a ball of lava to finish off the Aracnio that sought to fell her.

"Move. As fast as you can."

Quinn didn't need to be told twice, and she pushed her magic through her body, healing herself instinctively.

Malakai arrived first, and she could hear him and Jasper talking.

"Hospital obviously. We can't pour out into the damned main section of the Library with potentially badly wounded members." He sounded irritated, as if he thought the information was commonplace and logical.

She couldn't blame him, and Jasper seemed suitably chastised. "Yeah. I'll recalibrate it for a second. Step out of the circle."

Malakai turned his attention back to picking the last shadow stragglers off.

"We should take . . ." Quinn began, but Hal silenced her with a pointed look.

"We have too many of us injured already. While Dru is friendly and we can help her, I cannot guarantee that Dro won't place the Library and all of us in imminent danger. I can't express how much of a bad decision it would be to take her. Not even *my* cells can hold your type."

"Should we kill her?" Malakai asked, his voice soft, forthright.

Hal glanced back at where the charred dragon body lay, barely breathing. He shook his head. "Couldn't manage that if you tried. There's a reason the Library shapeshifted like it did."

Drukala groaned next to him.

"She looks pretty out of it."

The King of Halschius shrugged. "Dragon fire is probably the worst thing they could use against each other. It does damage they can't immediately heal fully."

Eric began to make his way over and Jasper finally stepped back from the door.

She twisted the strange handle and pulled it toward them, revealing the corridor that led to the hospital wing of the Library just beyond.

Quinn couldn't help but heave a huge sigh of relief but then, as Malakai entered, carrying Geneva carefully, Quinn turned to Hal and asked, "Are we just going to leave her there or let her escape?"

He shook his head. "No. I'll come back and get her as soon as we have everyone else settled."

On his arm, Drukala seemed to wilt ever so slightly more, but Quinn was purely grateful she'd managed to stop some of the damage from spreading, at least.

Eric remained, as if standing on guard while Hal and Drukala ventured through next. Quinn's foot still smarted, but it wasn't a bad injury, nothing she couldn't heal on her own and spare the doctors in the hospital. She motioned for Jasper to walk through first, but her friend only offered a tight smile. "Nope. Caster has to go through last."

"In that case . . ." Eric winked at them and flitted through first.

The shadows left in his wake were few and slowed down into a sort of dark molasses as created by his lava attacks.

Quinn stepped through, looking back to make sure Jasper followed her.

But Jasper shook her head. "No. You won't be able to get back through the door if I close the ritual circle. I'll just wait."

Something flashed in Quinn's peripheral vision, brief and hot, but suddenly time felt like it slowed.

Quinn reacted faster than she thought possible. Reaching through and around, she grabbed Jasper's hand, tugging her forward as abruptly as she could. Still, the arrow of fire lanced through the doorway, clipping Jasper's side instead of impaling her fully, and they both stumbled through the door, spilling to the ground as it shut behind them.

Immediately alert, Quinn reached out to the Library, sounding the medical alarm.

"Jasper . . . Jasper," she said, sending as much healing energy as she could through her friend.

No. No. She wasn't sure if she was muttering it out loud. All she could do was pull everything she knew about healing, everything she knew about magic and try and repair the damage.

Red tendrils spread from the wound in her side, a whole chunk of flesh missing, of her body. The wound gaped like a maw, hungry and relentless.

Quinn had no idea about this anatomy, but she was fairly sure it looked like something mostly important was missing now.

And her healing magic did nothing.

Nothing at all.

Jasper's breathing came in short, staccato bursts as the wound spread . . . shallow and painful. Her eyes were unfocused and her hand gripped Quinn's with far too little strength for the Librarian's liking.

The edges of the skin began to blacken, and Quinn poured in everything she had. All the healing affinities she'd read about, all the anatomy she'd scanned. It poured from her in a halo of blue and purple power pooling around them both.

And still Jasper's grip grew weaker, even if her breath seemed somewhat steadier.

And still the blood leaked from her body, spreading out like a pool that would never end.

"Don't you dare . . . you stay with me. You owe me ritual circles for days," Quinn muttered, just wanting to give something for the injured woman to cling onto.

There was no recognition in her eyes at all. They were fading, clouding over.

Quinn didn't know how much time had passed, but she knew it couldn't have been that long could it? The Library could pull strings. It could help.

They'd save her. They had to.

Dr. Miles was there, suddenly, barking out orders that Quinn couldn't quite comprehend. She found him asking her questions and giving him answers in a monotone voice that didn't sound like her own.

Jasper was deftly but gently removed from her hands and leveraged, while Quinn remained on her knees, her hands in her lap, trying to process everything that'd happened. The blood pooled around her and she realized in a detached sort of way that Jasper bled a sort of purple hue of deep red.

It was so pretty.

Quinn replayed the moments in her mind and realized belatedly she'd lost control of the binding spell on Dro when she'd tripped. She hadn't even realized she'd been actively maintaining it.

Funny, that.

"Quinn?"

She blinked up to find Malakai and Milaro standing over her, looks of sincere concern on their faces, and she was fairly sure those were tear tracks down their cheeks, but it was hard to see through her own.

Mal crouched in front of her, a frown appearing. "I'm pretty sure at least some of that is your blood."

Quinn blinked at him and looked down. Flashes of the car accident passed through her head as the blue scales flickered in the light of the hospital. "Oh. I think I healed myself."

Milaro uttered a phrase she couldn't quite pick up, and then his lips pressed into a thin, exasperated line briefly before his magic washed over her. "Sometimes I think you have a death wish," he muttered, but he didn't sound angry. Instead, he sounded sad.

"I'm fine," she started to say. It was what she wanted to say until she realized she couldn't. "But I couldn't. It didn't . . . she's not . . ."

Nausea swelled in her gut, threatening to overwhelm her, followed by a wave of dizziness so extreme she finally registered just how wet her left side was.

"Oh. I think some of that blood might be mine." A giggle escaped her before she crashed to the floor.

A breeze drifted across her skin, pulling Quinn out of her doze. Even though she knew it couldn't possibly windy in here, in their little pocket of existence that kept trying to crash down on them, the sensation was still welcome.

"Glad to see you awake. You really worried my grandfather," Malakai said from next to her. He tried to smile, and almost succeeded, but Quinn could tell it didn't reach his eyes.

Quinn tried to remember the events that had led her here, into the infirmary. Or the hospital.

Jasper's crumpled body, Drukala's melting skin . . . and her own gaping wound.

"Ah, yeah." Quinn rolled the words on her dry tongue before opening eyes that felt way too crusty to look in Mal's direction. "Just worried Milaro, right?"

Jasper's gaping wound.

The crease in Malakai's brow deepened, and he shook her head, taking her pale hand in his as he spoke words that belied his actions. "Yeah. Just my grandfather."

Jasper's purple blood.

Quinn smiled and then grimaced. They would talk about this at another time, but for now, it was enough. "How long?"

"You've been out for two days."

Jasper's clouded, sightless eyes.

"Damn it." Quinn's throat was one huge croak. At least the damned book was safe. What a consolation prize. She didn't want to ask the question, but knew she had to. "Are they?"

But Malakai didn't get a chance to answer as Lynx popped into the room.

"You have to stop worrying me like that!" he said. The concern in his voice was loud and sad, and tinged all around with panic.

"Didn't set out to." Quinn felt weak.

She knew. But she didn't want to.

Lynx scowled at her. "Don't try to move. I'll make sure you get hydration. Taking glancing dragon's fire for a friend. What were you thinking? We can't replace you. You know that!"

Beneath his frantic words and actions, Quinn knew he was worried for her. And she knew he was grieving. Not just as the Librarian. She stole a breath, determined, even if she was unsure of the answer. "Dru?"

"She's fine. Hers was all superficial. Well . . . for a cosmicisodracus anyway. Yours was practically a laser rifle concentration. Much harder to heal than a general sheath of fire." Lynx was taking medical recordings and wouldn't meet her eyes. "She's in the core with the Library sorting things out. You need to give me the book so I can pass it on." Then he paused, giving her a closer inspection. "Whenever you're ready, though. They'll probably want you down there, anyway. So much has happened."

She didn't want to know. Not definitively.

"Do tell?" It wasn't the question she wanted to ask, but it was the one she had to ask right then.

"With Drev and Dro both working together, we have to sort through our original hypothesis. We'd expected one. He'd always been opposed to the Library and only grudgingly helped, but two of them?" Lynx shook his head as he gathered further readings on her.

Quinn didn't need him to spell it out for her. The Library might be an all-powerful depository of knowledge, but it was made from a singular cosmicisodracus sacrifice . . . technically. At least if she understood it right. Sure, there was a hell of a lot more involved. But if they now had two of the primordial dragons working against the Library, it made them that much more vulnerable. Just that much more susceptible to attack.

Quinn enabled her storage ring and directed the book out to Lynx's hands.

He gaped in surprise and then scowled. "Stop doing magic until I've cleared you."

She shrugged. "I figured having the book back would help."

Because she certainly hadn't helped her friend.

"What helps," Lynx said as he began imprinting something on the chart in the system at her bedside, "is that book never got into Drav's hands. Right now, that's one of our saving graces. Or at least we hope so."

The question wriggled under her skin like worms trying to break out.

They sat in silence for several seconds while Lynx finished his exam. All the while, Quinn had to work up the courage to ask her question. One she wasn't even sure she wanted the answer to.

The question broke.

"Jasper?" Quinn forced out, already fearing the worst.

Lynx wouldn't meet her eyes, but Malakai tugged on the hand he still held, drawing her focus once again. Quinn tried to breathe and waited.

"You tried," was all he said.

Past tense.

Quinn gasped, the action hurting her chest.

No future.

"Hey," Malakai said sharply. "It wasn't your fault. You couldn't have predicted there'd be a bloody dragon fight."

It was no excuse.

"Yeah." Quinn knew it wasn't her fault, but also knew it was.

Jasper was dead.

There was a part of Quinn that knew her training to be lacking, her skill to be wanting, and her power to be substandard. She swallowed the despair, and locked it away before locking eyes with Malakai.

"I need to get stronger."

And make the Sölem pay.

Read Book 5 on Patreon now!

ABOUT THE AUTHOR

Born in Australia, K.T. Hanna met her husband in a computer game, moved to the U.S.A. and went into culture shock. Bonus? Not as many creatures specifically designed to kill you.
KT creates science-fiction, fantasy, and LitRPG, with a dash of horror for fun! She is a member of the SFWA and NINC. Her hobbies include gaming, reading, and lake time!
No, she doesn't sleep. She is entirely powered by caffeine, Chipotle, and sarcasm.

Find her on her website: kthanna.com
Join her in all the places, including Discord!

ACKNOWLEDGMENTS

I have a lot of people to thank. Even those who don't contribute directly through the writing craft keep me going and help me write my best stories.

Love of my life, Trevor, and my little Bria. It's his fault I found the genre, and her fault I never give up on writing.

I wouldn't be here without the following friends (and I know I've probably forgotten to mention someone:

SSODA

Crown

Eric Ugland

Quinton Shyn

Andrea Parseneau

M Evan MacGregor

Daniel Schinhofen

Michael Chatfield

Luke Chmilenko

Tao

Jami

Geneva

Jez

Ririn

DE Sherman

Ino

Honor

J.M.

<u>And of course my family:</u>

Mumskin & Papilie, Tracey, Jett, & Robbie.
<u>The entire Coteh server</u>
<u>My Legion Family</u>

<u>And every one of my Patrons.</u>
Faelor
Ma & Pa
Foxies
Quinton
Matt
Warren
Kristen
Joshua
Corwin
Johann
Renn
Irene
ChaosOmega98
Erwin
Isaac
Ty
Bryan
Joe
Kagami
Onean
support!
daavko
Table Top
Kevin
Pyro4224
Doomsongs
Jorden
Silverfox#7631
Cybernetic Angel
JSC

Skye
JewBot9000
James Rutter
Emily
Colin
Oken
Naomi
Gnathrak
Persnicketykat
Ron
Ninjamode67
Monique
Bjbrewster
Naomi Bonnin
June
Brian
Samuel
Not to mention my FB Group/Page, and people in my discord.
Thank you
You all help me maintain a level of sanity.

ALSO BY K.T. HANNA

Somnia Online

System Apocalypse Australia

The Domino Project

Last Chance Trilogy

KT Hanna's Author Page

LITRPG

Do you love LitRPG?
Do you want to find more of it?

These are amazing places to do just that!
FaceBook:
LitRPG Books
LitRPG Legion
GamelitRPG Society

Reddit:
LitRPG

Adjacent genres like Progression Fantasy/Cultivation:
Reddit: Progression Fantasy
Facebook: Cultivation Novels

MORE LITRPG

Love LitRPG?

To learn more about LitRPG, talk to authors including myself, and just have an awesome time, please join the LitRPG Group!